THE
OWLSTONE
CROWN

X. J. Kennedy THE OWLSTONE CROWN

Illustrated by Michele Chessare

A Margaret K. McElderry Book

ATHENEUM   NEW YORK   1983

Library of Congress Cataloging in Publication Data

Kennedy, X. J.
  The Owlstone crown.

  "A Margaret K. McElderry book."
  Summary: Orphans Timothy and Verity are cruelly treated
by their foster parents before escaping to another world
where they are caught up in a struggle
against a despicable tyrant and his wicked ally.
  [1. Fantasy]   I. Title.
  PZ7.K3880w [Fic]   81-3513
  ISBN 0-689-50207-9 AACR2

Published simultaneously in Canada by McClelland & Stewart, Ltd.
Composition by Westchester Book Composition, Inc.
Yorktown Heights, New York
Printed and Bound by Fairfield Graphics
Fairfield, Pennsylvania
Designed by Felicia Bond
First Edition

For Kate, Dave, and Matt,
who kept asking,
"When are you going to write down
the story of the Moonflower?"
and for Dan and Josh as well

Contents

THE
OWLSTONE
CROWN

1. *A Detective Calls*

Ice. Ice everyplace. It made the branches of trees creak in the wind like hinges that hadn't been oiled. The snow wore a hard, bright crust. Every step you took mashed a spiderweb of cracks in it. That afternoon would have been great for skating, if we'd had skates, but instead we were out in the fields, my sister and I, trying to loosen some winter parsnips.

There was this one stubborn old vegetable. I dug around it, kicked it, but it wouldn't budge. I was jimmying my spade in under it, chipping at the frozen dirt, when—

TWAN-NN-NG-G-G!

A half-moon of iron snapped off and left me holding the handle of a spade that all of a sudden didn't have any point to it.

"Well, it isn't *your* fault, Timmy," said my sister.

"What do they expect? To make us dig parsnips in January!"

But I was scared to my bones. Paw Grimble was going to kill me for sure. A new spade would cost him seven dollars and ninety-eight cents. I knew it would, to the penny, because Paw was forever running on about the price of everything.

"Sis," I begged, "knock the dirt off those parsnips, will you? If we go home with an empty basket Paw will be TWICE as mad. And Maw won't give us any supper."

"Oh, who wants their old supper anyway? What do you bet it's parsnip stew again?"

Her forecast sounded likely. In the almost two hundred days we had been living with Maw and Paw Grimble—as they'd told us to call them—they must have fed us a hundred and fifty parsnip stews.

NOTE BY VERITY TIBB: *A hundred fifty-four. I kept count.*

You can see what a stickler for facts my sister is. All the while I'm telling this story, she'll probably keep putting in her fussy little two cents. Anyhow, the Grimbles weren't much on eating. Saving money was more in their line. They had fetched us out of the orphanage because they had needed two kids to work on their farm in Metal Horse, New Jersey, close to the Delaware Water Gap. They made medicine out of parsnips and sold it by mail. Maybe you've seen ads for it in

all the TV-star and soap-opera magazines—
GRIMBLE'S PARSNIP PUNCH FOR ABDOMINAL PRES-
SURE, THE SWEETHEART OF SEVENTY THOUSAND
SUFFERERS. Once I sneaked a gulp of the stuff.
Exploding dynamite would have tasted better.

NOTE BY VERITY TIBB: *Exaggerating. Always exaggerating. Making mountains out of mouseholes. That's
my brother, as usual. Watch out for him.*

Glumly, I picked up my shortened spade and
tried to loosen another parsnip. Verity, on her
hands and knees, felt around till she located the
last vegetable I had tossed her. She thumped it
on the frozen ground till its dirt fell off. That
was her part of the job. She couldn't see the parsnips well enough to dig them. All she could ever
see was the shapes of things.

We struggled on. All of a sudden a dirty parsnip whizzed past my left ear. Verity hadn't been
aiming for me, she was just letting go of her feelings.

"YEE-EE-E-K-K!" she screamed, "I can't stand
any more of this!" And she plunked down onto
a snowbank.

With a sigh, I collapsed next to her. The wind
whistled between its teeth. A passing crow jeered
down at us.

Verity was tucking her long brown hair back
up under her knitted cap, and with her handkerchief, she was scrubbing frost from her thick,
glass-doorknob glasses. "Timmy," she said in her

best wheedling voice, "let's go play in the bear cave, why don't we?"

She'd been born twelve minutes ahead of me. That's why she was always trying to tell me what to do.

NOTE BY VERITY TIBB: *Well, back then, Timmy was such a cowardly sap. He never would have figured out what to do if somebody hadn't told him.*

For once I resisted. "Only a few more parsnips, Sis. Let's finish. It's getting dark."

"Timothy Tibb, I hate you! You're a boring drudge and I'm going to beat you up!"

And sweeping me off my feet with a cross-ankle pickup, she dropped me to my back and pinned me in a half-nelson. She was girls' wrestling champ of Walter B. Pitkin Junior High.

With kneeled-on chest, I lay helpless in the snow, staring at the white peak of Mount Peewee-hockey on the skyline. It looked like a head facing left, with a big bump for a nose.

"It's dull!—dull!—dull! around here," said Verity, kneeing me in the stomach with every *dull*. "I'm sick and tired of weeding parsnips"—knee-bump—"and pulling up parsnips"—knee-bump—"and shaking dirt off 'em!" She glowered down at me with magnified eyes.

"Ugh," I grunted, "do you—have to—murder me?"

"YES! I am The Strangler! I kill little boys! I'm

going to grind you up and feed you to the parsnips!"

"Look out, Sis, don't scratch your nose. You'll crush it."

"Crush what? My nose?"

"No. That ladybug."

"Liar!" Another knee landed in my stomach. "There aren't any ladybugs in January."

I managed to work a hand loose and bring it up to her nose. A spotted ladybug lifted the covers from its wings and flew down onto my outstretched finger.

"Now it's on me," I told her.

"Oh sure," my sister said. In a taunting voice she recited the old nursery rhyme:

Ladybug, ladybug, fly away home!
Your house is on fire and your children will burn!

Now comes the part of this story that sounds crazy. Even now, I can hardly believe it myself.

"Skip the wisecracks, angel," rasped a tiny voice. "I don't keep house and I don't have kids. If you must know, I'm a bachelor."

NOTE BY VERITY TIBB: *My brother can be an awful exaggerator, only this time he's right. That's exactly what the voice said. I remember, because I was so surprised I fell over backwards in the snow.*

Slowly and carefully I picked myself up, the ladybug still clinging to my finger. My hand in its glove was trembling so hard you'd think I was

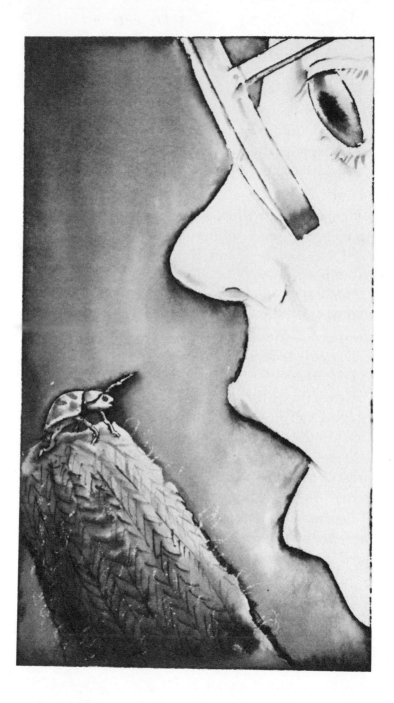

waving goodbye. The little beetle didn't look different from any other ladybug I'd known. Black and red, with seven spots. Now it was pacing around and around my finger, its head down, its rear end raised in the air.

"Did—did you say something?" I stammered.

"What's the matter?" came the same small voice with a buzz in it. "You have wax in your ears? Aren't you Timothy Tibb, age almost thirteen, and isn't this doll with the punk sense of humor your sister Verity?"

"How did you know our names?"

"Had 'em on file. You see, chum, I've been hired by your grandmother to check up on you."

"Don't joke," I pleaded. "Our grandmother is dead, and so is our grandfather. They drowned at sea off Cape May a year ago."

"No, they didn't," said the ladybug flatly. "They're alive and in pretty good shape for anybody locked in the slammer. I'm supposed to find you, see, and tell you so."

Gran and Gramp alive! How can I tell you what that news meant to us? We didn't have any mother or father, you understand. They had died when Verity and I were babies. I could barely remember my mother. A warm and fuzzy feeling when she had tucked a blanket around me on a cold night—that was all I had left of her. Anyhow, our grandparents were just the greatest people. Gramp built wonderful kites and hang-gliders, but mainly he was a philosopher. He'd written a book called *The Light to Live By* and he'd had it printed, but I don't believe anyone ever bought a copy. We would have gone hungry, I guess, if Gran hadn't taken to painting pictures and got good at it.

Gramp's last project had been a catamaran—a sailboat with two hulls joined side by side. When he had it all built, he had trucked it to the shore. I won't ever forget that day. The catamaran had lain along its pier, varnished and shining in the late afternoon sun. Gramp, wearing a captain's hat, had lifted a hand to Gran, and she, in a new sailor suit, had stepped into one swaying hull as proud as a queen. Then Gramp had hoisted the sails and the boat had skimmed out of the harbor and dwindled and dropped out of sight. Verity and I had stayed on the pier waiting for our promised ride while the sky had slowly reddened and grown dark and a full moon had risen. At last, after we told the police, a Coast Guard cutter with searchlights went looking for them. But they had just disappeared, as if they had dropped through a trapdoor, and the cutter hadn't found a trace of them.

"If," I said to the ladybug, "just IF our grandparents are still alive, where are they? What do you mean, they're in the slammer? Are they prisoners?"

"Rats!" said the ladybug harshly, "I can't stand here yapping. Us ladybugs can't stand cold climates. I've been on your freezing planet a long time—too long—checking every farm for miles around. OK, so I've found you. You've got your message. It's supposed to make you feel better and you're not to worry. Now so long—keep your noses clean!"

And he lifted his wing-cases to fly away.

"Hold on!" shrieked Verity at my elbow. "Who are you, anyway?"

"Ten above zero," groaned the bug, "and this doll has to have identification. OK, beautiful—look, here's my business card."

With a forefoot, he stuck out a white speck no bigger than a grain of sugar.

"I can't read it," said Verity.

"What's the matter?" snarled the bug. "Don't they teach you anything?" Then all of a sudden his voice softened. "Oh. Excuse me, kid. At first I didn't catch on to your eye problem. Maybe this palooka brother of yours will read the card for you."

"It's too little for me," I said.

Our visitor sounded annoyed. "Do I have to do everything for you? Lucky I come with a magnifying glass. Here, buster, take a squint through my left rear wingtip. Hurry up, this freezing cold makes me want to hibernate."

The wing was transparent, and as I stared through it, the white speck on my fingertip became a card with printed lettering. I read it aloud to Verity:

LEWIS O. LADYBUG

Private Investigator

Office: Moonflower (fourth blossom from the top)

Missing persons   Wandering child jobs

Low rates   Quick reports   Totally confidential

"Got me?" snapped the detective. "Now, boy, if you'll kindly move your ears out of the way, I'll be off. Hey! What are you doing? Let go of me!"

Lewis O. Ladybug was cornered. Just as he had begun to lift off from my little finger, I had lightly brought my thumb down on his back. I held him the way a jeweler studies a pearl.

"Maybe you had better go on talking," I told him, looking him straight in his compound eyes. "What's all this about our grandparents being prisoners?"

The little detective wriggled in my grip. "Buster," he snarled, "are you trying to get yourself a wooden overcoat?"

"Do you want a squeeze?" I bluffed.

"Go easy with that fat thumb of yours," he said threateningly. But reluctantly, he told us a little more. Our grandparents, catamaran and all, had dropped through a door into some other world. Now they were the prisoners of a dictator.

"Take us there," pleaded my sister, "so we can rescue them."

"Angel," said the bug with a sigh, "what chance would you kids have against a whole army of stone owls? Even if you *could* get to your grand-folks, you couldn't rescue them. Those owls are like rubber tires. They'd roll right over you."

"*We*'ll worry about that," I told him. "Either you help us find Gran and Gramp or I pinch you flat. Which?"

"Then I guess you pinch me, Fat Thumb. Your grandma gave me strict orders to keep you here on Earth and out of trouble. She's my client and I don't let a client down."

"Show us the door to this Other Earth," I said grimly.

"Nothing doing, buster. I'm not showing you any such door. Not today, not tomorrow, no time. Go ahead and pinch."

What a brave little guy! I really admired him. I lifted my thumb off his back and set him free.

"All right, Lewis O. Ladybug," I said. "Thanks for the message. You can go on back where you came from. And if you see our grandparents, please tell them—oh, I don't know. Tell them we miss them something fierce."

Still clinging to my fingertip, the bug fluttered

cramped wings. "OK. Only, come to think of it, I can't go back there yet. The nearest door won't open till the moon comes out. You kids wouldn't know where I could find me a couple of aphids, would you? Plant lice, you call 'em. That's my meat."

Verity wrinkled her brow. "Maybe you'd find some on Maw Grimble's cactus plant. Want to come inside with us and find out?"

The wind had sharpened its edge. The detective didn't need coaxing. Skimming along ahead of me, sometimes lighting on my coat-collar, he kept us company as we crunched across the snow back to the farmhouse, to the people I dreaded— me stumbling and bumping into trees because the light was dim, Verity sprinting and bounding because to her the darkness didn't much matter. I carried a new, wild hope and my broken spade and our half-empty parsnip basket.

2. *We Plot an Escape*

The farmhouse, like Maw and Paw Grimble themselves, looked worn-down and awful. Loose sideboards, their paint fallen away, stuck out all over it. That house always made me think of some bony old horse in need of combing.

I stood my pointless spade up against the cement block that served for a back doorstep. I wasn't about to mention my seven-dollar-and-ninety-eight-cent accident. All too soon, Maw or Paw would happen on the wreckage. Already I was twitching with cold dread.

NOTE BY VERITY: *See what I mean? About how my brother used to be a cowardly twerp?*

I'll admit it. Back in those days, I was scared of the Grimbles—and of everything else. I didn't climb trees for fear I would fall. To avoid meeting a strange dog I'd walk six blocks out of my way, and once, on hearing a bat twittering overhead,

I dived under a parked station wagon. I was a bundle of fears, all right. But I was working on them.

"Don't let the Grimbles see you, Lew," I whispered to the red dot on my coat collar.

"Right, kid—I'll lay low," came his rasp.

Nervously, I jiggled open the back door. Maw Grimble in her gray apron, her bent-wire masher in hand, was hunched over the stove, boiling something.

"What kept you two all this time?" she shrieked while Verity and I were stomping the snow off our boots and hooking up our coats and hats. She let out another, fiercer shriek when I set down our half-empty basket.

"Is that all the 'snips you got dug this afternoon? Didn't you finish them twelve rows like Paw told you to?"

"Finished all but eight, Maw," said my sister brightly.

"Daydreaming again!" Maw Grimble bellowed. Her bent-wire masher shot out and bopped Verity on one ear, then it shot out again and bopped me. "I declare," Maw went on, "you kids ain't worth the eats I keep wasting on you. Here I been standing on my sore feet fixing this nourishing parsnip stew, and poor Paw has been wearing his head to the bone figuring how to improve business. And all afternoon you kids have been having a fine time lallygagging around in the fresh air. Now you set down at that table and get them labels licked. Paw needs a load of bottles to take to the express office Monday morning."

Most of the kitchen table was taken up with bottles awaiting labels. Verity and I slumped into our chairs—mine had only three legs—while Maw hovered over us, fussing. I lifted a sheet of labels from a stack and ripped a label off and licked its back and stuck it on a bottle. Then I lowered the finished product into a pasteboard box.

Lew Ladybug took off from my collar and began touring the room. Verity and I kept working, not saying anything. My chair was trying to keel over onto its missing leg.

"Look out, boy!" Maw's masher pointed to the label I was sticking. "You've put a dirty fingerprint in the middle of it! Why didn't you wash your hands? Go do it. Then you clean off that label with the eraser."

As I was rinsing my hands in the kitchen sink, Lewis O. Ladybug sailed down, lit on a can of Ajax, and demanded, "What's the old turkey mad about?"

"Me," I muttered. "She always is."

"Talking behind my back, are you?" Maw thundered. A fresh blow of her masher clipped my ear—this time, my other one. That was the one nice thing about Maw. She always gave both ears equal time. The wind from her blow caught the ladybug by surprise. He went swirling into the air. After that, he cruised away and made himself scarce.

From her post at the gas stove, Maw kept jawing at us. Her tight gray hair bun wobbled as she punished the boiling parsnips with stabs of her masher. Despite the heat thrown by the stove, the kitchen was so cold you could see your breath. Once in a while the spiders, on their webs in the corners of the room, had to run around to keep from freezing solid.

On the wall I faced there was a battleship-gray cuckoo clock that said SOUVENIR OF OCEAN GROVE, N.J. Years ago the cuckoo had decided to give up and stay in hiding. Just over the clock, suspended by a tire-chain, was the potted cactus. I could see Lew crawling around on one of its dusty spikes, his red back the brightest thing in the household.

As we worked, Verity said in an undertone, "Timmy, are you thinking what I'm thinking?"

"How should I know?" I whispered. "Unless you're thinking we ought to trail the ladybug and find the door to this Other Earth. Are you thinking anything crazy like that?"

"You bet I am! The ladybug will stay here till the moon comes out. By that time, Maw and Paw will be sound asleep. We can escape! We can follow him!"

"But suppose we find that door? Wouldn't it be—uh—dangerous to go through it?"

"Timothy Tibb, if you aren't a chicken! Do you want to stay here with the Grimbles all your life? You want to come with me and rescue Gran and Gramp, don't you?"

An angry twittering on my shoulder made me jump.

"I heard you," rasped the detective. "Now get this straight. What's on the far side of that door is bad medicine. Worse than Parsnip Punch. You're staying right here. Oh, don't think for a minute that you guys can tail me. I'm an old pro at giving people the slip."

"Don't worry, Lew," I assured him. "*I* don't want to go to Other Earth. Honest, I don't."

But my voice had been louder than I had intended. Maw Grimble whirled around and raised her masher. I braced myself for a fresh bop on the ear, but she muttered something about me losing my mind, always talking to myself, and went back to beating up her parsnips. The ladybug flew back to his cactus.

Verity kicked me under the table and shot me a look that told me I was a caterpillar. She didn't care, it seemed—she still wanted to be a heroine.

"No more gabbing," Maw warned. "Keep lapping them labels while I take Rouser his supper."

Rouser was Paw Grimble's hunting dog—half hound, half timberwolf—and I lived in terror of him. His ribs stuck out, his back was covered with scabs. If you stepped up to his cage and tried to talk to him he'd snarl and bare his teeth and throw his body at you so hard he'd almost break the chicken wire of his cage. Maw was holding a dish of beef bones, cooked, with plenty of juicy meat on them. It looked so much better than the parsnip stew we were in for that I felt like racing the dog for it. Maw flung a scarf around her neck and barged outside. Now she would see the broken spade. I was a goner!

Sure enough. The second she returned from the dog's cage, she let out her best shriek ever. The back door bashed open again and in she

strode, holding the rusty spade like a terrier shaking a rat.

At the sight of her blazing eyes, I completely panicked. I lost my grip on the three-legged chair. The thing pitched over sideways, dumping me off, and I slid in under the kitchen table. There I lay, flat on my back, while loose labels snowed all around me. PARSNIP PUNCH, said the flakes. THE SWEETHEART OF 70,000 SUFFERERS.

"Paw! You, Paw!" Maw Grimble screamed. "You come in here this minute and see what this fool boy has done to your brand new spade!"

All afternoon while we had been working in the fields, Paw Grimble had been dozing in his rocking chair in the parlor. Maw's screams had wakened him, and soon his checkered slippers appeared out beyond the hanging edge of the plastic tablecloth. He stooped down and peered in on me. His bald skull was as gray as a burned-out light bulb.

He studied me from in back of his steel-rimmed glasses. "Boy, what are you doing in under there?"

"Just thinking how to improve business, Paw," I quavered.

One of his bony fists gathered my shirtfront into a knot and hauled me out and stood me on my feet.

"Now what's this about a spade?" he wanted to know.

"He broke it," Maw said, sniveling, shaking the pointless spade under Paw's nose.

"*WHAT?*" Paw's glasses sparkled angrily. "SEVEN DOLLARS AND NINETY-EIGHT CENTS PLUS TAX. Boy, can you understand how much MONEY that is?"

I just shook in my shoes.

"ANSWER ME!"

"Well," I said lamely, "it's two cents short of eight dollars."

My answer turned him purple in the face. "I could thrash you, boy. Thrash you within an inch of your life."

I didn't expect he would beat me. That would have meant work for him.

"You're going to pay," he bleated. "You're going to stick extra labels. Every ten extra labels you stick, you'll make a cent. That's seven thousand nine hundred and eighty labels you can stick, not counting the ones you have to stick anyway. You can get up every morning at three o'clock till you get 'em all stuck. And from now on you can go without breakfast."

Verity's wild plan to run away to Other Earth was looking better and better to me.

Supper, as you might expect, was pretty miserable. I managed to force down two or three bites of stew, all the time wishing I was a ladybug and could eat aphids. Verity sat at the table winding parsnip strings around her fork, which had lost all but two of its tines, and looking sick to her stomach. Paw, he kind of inhaled his stew the way a vacuum cleaner will suck up anything. Nobody talked except Maw. Between jawfuls of stew, she kept up a running complaint about me and that spade. You'd have thought I had murdered her cousin.

"Now, after supper," she went on, "you kids clean your shoes. Use your toothbrushes, only wash 'em out real good afterwards. Always walk with your feet flat on the ground so your shoes will wear out even. Verity, have you been saving them little gummed paper strips off of the postage stamps? Never can tell when they might come in handy. Timothy, pinch your nose so you don't sneeze. Sneezing wears out handkerchiefs. Verity, why ain't you eating your good supper?"

"Aw, Maw, I can't get it down tonight. I'm afraid I'll choke on it."

"Uppitty girl," Maw said with a sniff. "Never do appreciate anything. I suppose you wish you was back with your old grandfolks again, eating chicken and ice cream and rich junk like that. But your grandfolks is dead, child, deader than doornails. Why, you'd still be in the orphan house if Paw and me hadn't had the kindness to take you in. Ain't you grateful, girl, for the loving care and nourishing food and nice clothes we been giving you?"

"Well, no, Maw, now that you ask, I can't say

I'm grateful a bit. This parsnip pulp isn't worth eating. Couldn't you give us a carrot once in a while? And our clothes aren't nice. They're old holey hand-me-downs you fish out of other people's garbage."

You can imagine how *that* speech landed. Maw's jaw dropped. Her eyeballs bulged like a couple of soft-boiled eggs.

To my despair, Verity kept on talking. "Sure you feed us—sort of—and the State of New Jersey sends you a check for doing it. We don't get much to eat, so you must have a lot of money left over."

Whack!

Maw placed a slap across my sister's mouth that knocked her thick glasses flying.

"Don't you dare say that," Maw warned in a low, quivering voice. "Don't you ever say that when the lady from the State comes snooping around checking up on us, you hear?"

Verity looked determined not to cry. I retrieved her glasses for her. Maw carried on and on about why didn't the State send them some hard-working kids for a change instead of a blinky with too much mouth and a boy that couldn't dig parsnips without destroying property. I was growing so mad I was almost forgetting to be scared of her. And all this time Paw Grimble kept his steely eyes drilling at the ceiling, a mean smile tugging his lip corners.

We didn't get a minute's peace till the dishes had been put away and Verity and I were back to sticking labels. I nudged my sister under the table to let her know that now I was on her side. I'd run away with her. But every once in a while my common sense would return, and I'd start shuddering. Did our scheme really have any chance? The ladybug suspected us. How could we hope to follow him?

From their parlor the Grimbles could see out into the kitchen and could police us while we worked. In a stiff-backed chair, Maw was soaking her feet in a bucket of water and baking soda. Paw, in his creaky rocker, twisted the old black-and-white TV to his favorite program. It was a game show played in a supermarket. The idea of it was to heap a shopping cart with as many groceries as you could grab in so many minutes. The program repeated itself a lot, and Paw knew every show by heart. "Look, Maw," he cackled, "here's the one where the lady from Pasadena don't take nothing but them nine-dollar canned hams."

Verity, trying to cheer herself, was humming. "Stop that!" Maw called.

His TV show over, Paw snapped off the set and declared that tonight he felt considerable pressure on his abdomen. He came out into the kitchen and grabbed six bottles of punch that we hadn't labeled yet. Then he shuffled back into the parlor and just sipped and rocked, rocked and sipped. Now and again he'd burp.

Lewis O. Ladybug, looking rounder and heavier, skimmed down to the top of a bottle I was identifying. "Rubberiest old aphids I ever ate," he said wolfishly.

"Listen, Lew," I pleaded, "you've got to take us with you to Other Earth. You can't leave us here! Don't you see what the Grimbles are like?"

"They're a bum scene," admitted the detective. "But at least, living with them, you'll stay alive."

A skinny shadow fell across our table. I glanced up to see Paw, a bottle of punch in his hand, standing over us, swaying.

"Who are you kids talking to?" he wanted to know.

"This ladybug," said Verity matter-of-factly.

My heart just about froze. If only my sister could tell a little white lie once in a while! I don't know why she couldn't. She just hated to. And we were always getting into trouble as a result.

Paw lowered his nose to the bottlecap Lew was sitting on. "Ladybugs don't talk," he said thickly.

"Oh, don't they?" said the detective evenly. "I know your type, Grimble. All you are is a cheap two-bit slave-driver. I ought to replace your teeth, but I never pick on a drunk. Now get back to your rocking chair and suck your homemade poison before I twist that ugly beak of yours into a knot."

With a gasp, Paw drew back his nose. For a

moment I thought he was going to crush his hand down on the little detective. He looked as pale as if a vampire had just guzzled him.

Then, to my relief, he straightened up, staggered to the sink, and poured in what was left of his bottleful.

"Maw," he said in a hollow voice, "I believe I'll need to correct the strength of what's down cellar in the vat. This new batch is a mite too powerful."

If Verity and I could have laughed, we'd have had hysterics. We had to cram our knuckles into our mouths, and for a long time we didn't dare look at each other.

By and by, when I could risk a glance into the parlor, both Paw and Maw had their heads down on their chests and were breathing like a couple of leaky accordions.

Through the window over the sink, the moon was blazing, yellow and round as the center of a giant daisy.

"Time to take off, chums," said Lew Ladybug. "So long. Keep your chins in the air. Don't take any wooden nickels."

And he darted off through a crack under the back door.

"Quick, grab your coat!" I whispered to Verity.

But I must have whispered too loud. Maw Grimble woke up with a snort.

"You ain't going no place," she said.

3. *The Seventh Step*

Maw Grimble's words landed on my ears like blows from her terrible masher. Verity and I fell to labeling bottles again, like a couple of good robots, but on the inside, I was boiling with frenzy. Now the ladybug was gone. Flying away. Soon he'd be forever lost to us.

"See you don't use too much spit on them labels," Maw advised. "Your tongues will go dry and you'll want a drink, and water costs good money..."

Her voice mumbled away. And then—great snakes and little green hoptoads, didn't our luck improve, because the next sound out of her was a beautiful big fat snore.

We didn't waste any more time. We jumped from our chairs, flung on our coats and hats, and not bothering with overshoes, inched toward the back door. My heart was slamming my ribs. As we eased past the stove, moving slowly and carefully so the floorboards wouldn't creak, Maw gave a new snort. For an instant we stood there petrified, me with one foot in the air, but soon Maw fell back to the land of dreams, so I lowered my foot and worked open the door and held it wide for Verity. Without a sound, we stepped out into the January night.

Verity let out her breath. "All right, Eagle-eyes, where's the ladybug?"

The moon on the ice-covered snow made the back yard blaze. On the leafless trees, every twig stood out. But I couldn't see the detective. He was too small. Or had he—after our delay—already taken off for Other Earth?

And then, hardly a stone's toss from us, a bat dived for something in the air.

"Beat it," a voice rasped, "before I poke you one."

The bat gave a twitter and flew away, no doubt surprised at having a bite of food talk back to it.

"There he is!" I cried—too loudly. Rouser must have pricked up his ears. From his cage by the side of the barn, he gave a piercing whine.

Verity's green eyes, looking huge behind glass, threw me a hopeless stare. "That dog will wake Maw and Paw!"

A slam. A groan of boards. The mean mutt

had bombed himself against his chicken wire. A thud. He had dropped back to make a second charge.

From inside the house, Paw Grimble's voice rang out. "Whatsa matter, Rouser? Somebody out there, boy?"

I was desperately keeping my eyes fixed on the ladybug. He was flying along the path, with the moonlight glinting on his wings.

"He's heading for the woods!" I cried.

Verity and I broke into a run. She could run faster than I could, any day. She knew every tree and pebble on that farm. Skidding and sliding on the glass-topped snow, we charged down the path and rounded the barn, following the ladybug, while the wolf-dog bounded and howled.

But the detective could fly faster than we could run, and by the time we got to the edge of the woods, we had lost him in among the trees.

From the farmhouse came the noise of Paw stumbling around, cussing and bumping into things. No doubt looking for his shotgun. By this time, Rouser was howling like a stuck steam whistle.

"Into the woods!" I cried. "Come on, Sis, let's do the coat-tail!"

NOTE BY VERITY: *The coat-tail was our method of steering me whenever we had to travel fast through woods or through someplace I wasn't familiar with. I'd*

grab the back of Timmy's coat and we'd run. That's
how we traveled together.

We barged into a thicket. The ladybug, I figured, would keep to the main path, the shortest
way through the woods. We'd avoid the path, so
he wouldn't see us. The woods closed in around
us. Behind our backs, the Grimble farm dropped
away like a bad dream.

But soon, from the rim of the woods, came a
dog's baying, followed by the steady *crunch, crunch,*
crunch of bootsteps in the snow.

"After 'em, boy!" Paw Grimble was bawling.
"Don't let 'em get away!"

I tugged Verity down behind a thorn bush. The
baying and the crunching drew near. Now we
could hear the click of Rouser's toenails on the
crusty snow and Paw's mutter, "When I catch
them kids, they'll skip a month of suppers, they
will..." Butterflies were beating around in my
stomach. No, they were pterodactyls.

Luckily, the wind was aiming straight for us,
so that Rouser, running the other way, didn't pick
up our scent. We stayed down till Paw and the
dog had passed, then we got up and moved on
through the underbrush as quietly as possible.
Still, the creaking of snow under my feet sounded
louder to me than fire sirens.

For a long time we went around in circles, getting scratched by brambles and twigs. At last I

stopped, and Verity, clinging to my coat-tail, slammed into me.

"What's the matter? Why are we stopping?" she demanded.

"I don't see the ladybug," I admitted. "I don't know which way to go."

"Dumbhead! Bubble-brain!" she exploded, while I dodged her attempts to strangle me. "You've let the ladybug get away? What have we been running around in these scratchy bushes for, the last half-hour?"

"Sorry, Sis. Finding a ladybug in the woods at night isn't the easiest thing in the world, you know."

"So *you* say. Oooh, if only *I* could see better!"

Then, from out of the thicket near us, came the crashing and bashing of the dog. The wind had shifted. Rouser had picked up our trail!

"For heaven's sake, Timmy! Let's not stand here! Aren't we close to the river? I can hear it gurgling. Come on! If we cross to the other side, we'll lose that dog!"

The river *was* nearby. It was a deep stream that came racing down out of the hills fast enough to keep flowing and not freezing even in January. Stepping-stones led across it in a chain maybe twenty feet long.

"Come on!" my sister urged me, when we'd got to the river's shore. Hoisting her pants legs to keep them dry, she fastened a sneakered foot down on the first stepping-stone.

"Those stones are covered with ice. Won't we slip?"

She gave me a sniff of contempt. Sure-footed as a mountain goat, she was hopping from stone to stone across the rushing water.

"ARRR-OO-OO-OOO!"

That howl made me whirl. From the bushes along shore came a furious crackling and smashing, then Rouser's lowered head and bony forelegs broke through. He looked at me. He froze. The moonlight made his teeth and eyeballs glow. I felt like a cornered rabbit.

Maybe I'd follow Verity. I stepped down onto the first round stone—the second stone—the third. By the light of the moon, the ice on the stones looked silver. Once, I slipped and got a wet foot, but I kept going. When I came to stone number six, I met a gap in the chain where I'd have to jump—oh, for maybe a yard. Where the seventh stone ought to have been, the reflection of the full moon blazed on the speeding water.

But where was Verity? Had she already crossed? In the moonlight, everything looked sharp and exact, as if somebody had traced all around it with a pencil. I scanned the opposite shore, but I couldn't see a sign of Verity.

"Sis?" I called.

No answer.

"Sis! SIS!"

No answer at all. No sound but the wind and the river and a night bird—maybe an owl—sleepily crying.

It was as though my sister had disappeared from earth.

I was baffled. Verity wasn't in the water. I stared at the place where a stepping-stone was missing. At the reflection of the moon on the racing river, blazing, not being budged.

And then I knew. The reflection of the silver moon looked just like a moonlit stone coated with ice. With her dim eyesight, Verity had mistaken the moon on the water for a stepping-stone. She'd been charging along, not counting. Trustingly, she had set foot on the seventh stone—the moon—and now she was gone.

A furious snarling came from behind my back. Eager to get me, Rouser had tiptoed out as far as the second stone. Now he was crouching, a paw lifted, getting ready to spring on to stone number three.

I had to decide. Fast. Which would it be—the dog or the river?

To tell you the truth, I didn't much care for either. And yet I lifted my right foot and just as Verity had done, stepped down on the seventh stone. On the moon in that hurrying stream.

The water blurred. The reflected moon swayed under me. It loomed bigger than any moon I'd seen before.

I was falling. Falling into the moon.

The wolf-dog gave a disappointed howl.

4. *Our First Stone Owl*

I splashed down into deep water. I plunged in over my head, touched bottom, came up again. Warm water dwindled away from me as though a swimming pool I swam in was being drained. When my eyes opened, the river had shallowed down again. I was standing in water up over my ankles. Flowing water. The wet familiar stepping-stones gleamed under the moon.

I was on Other Earth, I knew suddenly, and yet nothing looked different. *Nothing?* I took a closer look. No ice on the river's stepping-stones, no snow along its shores. The air was as warm as an electric blanket. Overhead, a weak and hazy moon was fighting through a traffic-jam of clouds. It didn't seem right—the night sky in New Jersey had been *clear*.

Verity was sitting on the far bank of the river, hatless, coatless, her long hair stringing her face.

"Sis!" I cried, grateful to see her.

"Slowpoke. You took your time getting over here!"

"Well, at first I couldn't figure out where you'd gone."

"What do you mean? I didn't go anyplace. Except over the stepping-stones."

"Then how come you're all wet?"

"I slipped and fell in. What's happened to Rouser? Did he get lost?"

She didn't know where she was! Her weak eyes couldn't see that anything had changed. She hadn't yet registered the change in temperature. Setting foot on the last stone in the chain, I finally landed on the shore I had set out for in another world. My soaked coat weighted a ton, so I wiggled out of it. I slumped down next to Verity on the riverbank.

"Sis, don't you understand? We've done it. We've come through the door."

"Quit kidding, Timmy. For Pete's sake, I want to find the ladybug and go through the door just as much as you do. But it's nothing to kid me about."

On a nearby milkweed, a red-and-black speck had settled. It was shaking a drop of water from its wings.

"Think you're smart, do you?" the ladybug accused. "Well, you kids are in trouble. So am I, when your grandmother finds out you've followed me."

Verity looked as if a lightning bolt had fallen in her lap. "Lew, is that you? Then you mean we really DID—?"

"Why don't you kids go back where you came from?" the detective growled. "Hurry up, step back through that moon on the river before the door shuts. Before our moon and your moon slide out of line. I'm telling you—this will be your last chance for a month. Go on! That door will stay open for a few minutes more."

"We're never going back," Verity said firmly.

"If we did," I put in, "Rouser would mangle us."

"Lew, we're staying with you," said Verity as if *that* was *that*.

The detective groaned. "Just my luck. A couple of kids to look after. That's all I need."

A strange fact hit me. The ladybug was sitting on a milkweed. Since when did milkweeds grow in January? Only it wasn't January. There wasn't any snow. All around us, crickets and tree toads were making music. A warm, sweet-smelling wind rustled leaves and scurried through the knee-deep grass.

"Sis," I said in wonder, "do you know what? It's summer!"

"Of course, it is. Don't you think I can hear

crickets? But now I can hardly see *anything*."

I looked her in the face. Something was missing. "Sis, where are your glasses?"

"I don't know. They must have dropped off between Earth and Other Earth."

I turned to the milkweed. "Lew, is there any place around here that makes new glasses?"

"Naw," said the bug. "The kid needs glasses? Then why don't you both just walk out on those stepping-stones again and go back to that nice safe parsnip farm?"

"Glasses or no glasses, we're staying," Verity said. "Timmy can help me find my way around. We came here to rescue Gran and Gramp, you understand, so please take us to them."

"Hello, Lew, how's tricks?"

This greeting came from a ghostlike thing that had suddenly drifted toward us. It was a sort of moth the size of a kite. Two long feathery antennas wobbled on its brow, and as it flew, a pair of rainbow-colored wings revolved at its sides like a couple of paddlewheels. Lew greeted it in return—Dutch, he called it—and the beautiful moth flew on past us.

"That was a windmill moth," said the detective, starting to thaw a little. "Nice-looking, aren't they? There used to be millions of the things, but there aren't many any more. Not since that bum who calls himself Raoul Owlstone threw the dome over the Moonflower. Keeps the moths from drinking its juice. *Oh oh.* Here's trouble. DUTCH, LOOK OUT—!"

From out of the sky a batlike shape descended. It dived straight for the windmill moth and caught it in midair. The moth disappeared with a crunch like a bitten potato chip. Dark wings flapped as the hunter flew away with a terrible shriek that sounded like "*Meat! Eat meat!*"

Silence. A lonesome bird called sadly in the night.

"That was a muckhawk," Lew said at last. "One of Raoul's pets."

"Let's not meet any more of them," I said.

Suddenly the ladybug was staring through me, goggling his compound eyes. "Don't look now, kid," he said tonelessly, "but something a lot worse than a muckhawk is standing in back of you."

I turned around. I looked up and gasped.

The stone owl peered down at me with electric cells for eyes. They glowered, but didn't cast light. The owl looked like a statue made out of dark gray stone with a pattern like feathers all over it. It loomed above me, taller than a skyscraper.

NOTE BY VERITY: *Yeah—I'll bet!*

Stickler! That was how tall the owl looked to me at the moment, I mean. All right, it was about six feet six inches tall. It stood bolt upright on a ball of the same kind of gray, feathered stone. The ball was maybe fourteen inches across. The

owl traveled along on top of that rolling globe, just standing there while only the globe moved. Now it was flapping the lower half of its beak, and a flat machine-made voice came grating out— "State your names."

My mouth was dry. I couldn't say a word.

"Go on, answer it," the ladybug urged from my right shoulder.

"I—I'm Timothy Tibb," I stammered, "and this is my sister Verity. We're with Lewis O. Ladybug, Private Investigator."

"Reply unsatisfactory," droned the robot voice. "Ladybug is not a person. Delete."

"Delete who?" the detective snarled. "Where do you get that stuff? I'm a lot more of a person, buster, than you'll ever be. Why don't you go choke on an owlstone mouse?"

SNAP! The owl's beak made a swoop at my shoulder, but the detective had leaped to safety in the air.

"Names, Timothy Tibb and Verity Tibb," the owl went on. "State your places of residence."

"Oh, we don't live in this world," said Verity, "we live in Metal Horse."

"Residence, Metal Horse World. State your business."

"Please," I quavered, "we've come here to talk with Raoul Owlstone. He's keeping our grand-mother and grandfather in jail, and we're going to ask him to let them go."

The owl's eye-cells glared. "Reply unsatisfactory. Our master does not speak to children. Our master never releases prisoners. You are unsatisfactory. You are under arrest. Stand where you are."

The ladybug, from my collar, let out a whistle. "I don't like this."

The owl lowered its head, which appeared to work on a hinge, and rummaged around under one stone wing. When its head snapped back up again it wore a thing shaped like a cone that fitted like a muzzle over its beak.

"Wouldn't you know," said Lew glumly, "it's calling headquarters. Looks like you're bound for the cooler, kids."

"V Q Twenty-Nine reporting," the owl droned. "Send stone egg at once to sector Thirty-One W. Two unsatisfactory persons without business." We were going to jail! For keeps! Never to find Gran and Gramp! Something inside me went wild. If I'd had time to think what I was doing, I wouldn't have done it, of course. The owl stood facing me, its back to the river. With all my might, I bombed myself into its chest. Its body felt cold, like a shark's. I'd caught the owl just right. It flipped over backwards with its big ball-bearing up in the air and lay on its spine, teetering, balanced on the closest stepping-stone. I couldn't stop now. Wading up to the owl, I cupped my hands under its stone tail and jerked up hard. The owl, like a log going down a chute in a lumbermill, slid neatly into the reflected moon on the water just off shore. Slid into the moon and was gone. The river sloshed and tilted in its bed.

From my shoulder, Lew gave a gasp. "Kid, that was beautiful! Sweet! You're a chip off your grandfather's block!" Then he recovered himself and growled, "Only you've made things worse. Just wait till the other owls find out."

The splash of the owl in the river hadn't been lost on Verity. Now she gave me a squeeze and said, "Timmy, I'm proud of you. But Lew, what will happen to that owl?"

"It'll take a trip. It'll shoot through to *your* earth like a cannonball."

"Then Timmy has turned a monster loose on Northern New Jersey?"

"Naw. Not for long, anyway. That owl's batteries ought to run down in a day or two. But when it first hits Earth, I wouldn't want to be the first one it meets."

"That will be Paw Grimble," I said. Somehow the notion of Paw meeting the stone owl in the woods cheered me greatly. Verity and I started to laugh and laugh.

"Stick around, you kids," the detective snarled, "and you'll be laughing out of the other sides of your mouths. Don't you understand? That owl put a call straight to headquarters, and there's a stone egg coming. In fact, it should be here right now."

A fit of the galloping shakes came over me. "Lew! You're our friend! Tell us—what'll we do?"

"Hide," said the detective.

"But where? We don't know this country."

"Sure you do, kid, you know this neighborhood better than anybody. Where would you hide if this was your old Earth?"

I thought fast. "Ummm. There's a little cave we used to play in. You mean—there's a cave just like it on *this* earth?"

"Right," said the detective, "haven't you noticed? Other Earth is shaped exactly the same as yours. Same rivers, mountains, everything. I know the cave you mean. It's the only cave for fifty miles around. Can you get to it?"

I nodded. In the distance I could see a familiar landmark. Mount Peeweehockey, with its big bump for a nose.

"Then MOVE, why don't you?" Lew urged. "Duck into that cave and lay low till the heat dies down. So long—I've got to report to your grandmother. Wish me luck. I'd rather face a couple of stone owls. In the morning I'll come meet you at the cave."

He spiraled away from my shoulder and was gone.

"Hee-hee-hee!" came a tittering laugh from the

nearby darkness. "I heard you! I saw everything!"

Startled, I jumped. The voice was a mean little peeping one. I looked around to see where it was coming from. Under the dim moon I could barely make out a little grayish-green blob on the trunk of the nearest pine. It was a tree toad about two inches long, the color of pine tree bark.

The toad threw me a wink. "I saw you push that owl into the river. Oh, don't worry, I won't tell. Not if you'll make your payments regularly."

"What do you want?" I asked.

"For a start, you could round me up, say, two hundred June bugs. That will be plenty for to-night. Then you can bring me two hundred every day for the next six weeks."

"Whoever you are, get lost!" shrilled Verity. "We came here to rescue Gran and Gramp, not to go bug-collecting."

"Hee-hee-hee! I know where you'll be hiding. In the cave on the side of the hill!"

"No, no," I denied, "we're not going there."

"What are you talking about, Timmy?" countered my sister. "Of course we are!"

I grabbed for the toad, but he was too quick for me. He skittered around to the far side of his tree trunk and flung back, "You'll be sorry!"

"Sis, you goof," I groaned, "why did you have to admit we're going to the cave? That toad will tell the owls on us for certain. Now we have to find a better place to hide."

"Know any?"

She had me. The cave was the only hiding place I knew. Unless we went there, how could Lew find us again? I thought I heard a roar from overhead.

We didn't wait around for the stone egg to come down and grab us—whatever a stone egg was. In a hurry, we struck out through the woods, following a path that seemed new to me. Still, I didn't have any trouble keeping my bearings, because the mountain on the skyline stayed in front of us.

As we ran, doing the shirt-tail through the underbrush, we passed a horrible sight. There was this house in a field, a house with cheerful red shutters, painted lately. Only it had been crushed. Smack in the middle of its roof sat a ball of mud as big as an elephant. Loose shingles strewed the yard. Next to a gate swinging idly in the wind, a mailbox stood, its flag lifted, lettered with the people's name, WEEDBLOSSOM. I guessed they didn't live there anymore.

The sight picked me up and made me run on faster. At last we came to the bear cave—that was our made-up name for it. It was a slot big enough for six or eight kids to fit into, in the side of a knobby hill. We scrambled inside and threw ourselves down on its hard, cool floor and let our breaths catch up with us.

Verity wrinkled her nose. "Phew-w-w-w," she

said, "it certainly smells worse than our cave in Metal Horse."

We sprawled on our backs and talked, and I tried to cheer us up. But Verity, with her usual bluntness, said, "Timmy, let's face it, we don't have much reason to be glad. Here we are—alone in some screwy world. Our clothes are wetter than dishrags and I've lost my glasses and now all I can see is a little bit of light. You'll have to look out for us both, and as you know, you're kind of incompetent. An army of owls is looking for us, and that tree toad is going to tell them where we are."

It was a pretty convincing list.

"We'll be all right," I said, but my words, hitting the ceiling of the cave, boomed hollowly.

In my shirt pocket I had a chocolate bar I'd been saving. Now I divided half of it with Verity and returned the other half to my pocket for another day. We munched, and my sister wondered about the doorway we had fallen through. I had it all figured out. The full moon had shone on our river in New Jersey, and on Other Earth, in a river just like ours, a door had opened. Gran and Gramp, I reasoned, must have dropped through a different door, one out in the Atlantic. Both earths must be sprinkled with such watery doors that needed a full moon to open them.

I rattled on and on, warming to my theories.

"Sis?" I said.

No answer. She was snoring. I lay there on the cave floor, my mind going around. Now that my sister had lost her glasses I would have to lead her around and find my own way besides. In the past she had always told me what to do. Now, I would have to think for myself. And that house crushed by the mudball—that bothered me. I thought of Gran and Gramp. It wasn't going to be easy to rescue them. Oh, why did I have to be such a coward? I was worried and scared, but I was also tired, tired to the bone, and soon a breaker of sleep washed over me.

I had a beautiful dream. Rouser, whining in terror, was clinging to a tree for dear life. A seven-foot-tall stone owl, clicking its beak, was chasing Maw and Paw Grimble around and around the frozen parsnip patch.

5. *Cornered in a Cave*

When you wake up to find a huge shaggy head bending over you, snuffling loudly, and you feel a cold nose exploring your shirtfront and bristly hairs rubbing your chin—oh, you think you're having a loser of a dream.

But I was awake. I wanted to yell and didn't dare to. I shut my eyes again and kept lying on my back, playing dead. The cold nose prowled my chest till it came to the pocket with the chocolate bar. Teeth tugged out the candy, and I could hear its wrapper being swatted off, then the sound of slow, heavy chomping.

I opened my eyelids a slit. By the weak light of dawn I could see the bear, a thick brown giant of a guy, easily nine feet tall. Done with his snack, he licked his claws thoughtfully with a long violet-colored tongue. Then he returned to me and sniffed my pants pockets, looking for a second helping. At last, to my relief, he gave up the search and lay down on his side, looking annoyed. I studied him. He had deep-set eyes, a sloping brow, small, rounded ears, and a short stiff beard under his chin. He was so big he practically blocked the mouth of the cave.

Verity was still sleeping. I'd have to face this shaggy monster on my own. Of course, I was scared silly. Desperate for some weapon, I glanced about. On the cave floor inches from my right hand lay a piece of tree branch about a foot long. My hand stole to it and closed around it.

I'd take him by surprise! Whipping the hunk of wood out in front of me, I jumped to my feet— bonking my head, because the cave wasn't as tall as I was—and I shook my weapon under the brown bear's nose.

"All right, you big crook," I glowered, keeping my voice as steady as I could, "get out of here! Beat it! Scat!"

NOTE BY VERITY: *Wasn't Timmy brave? Already, Other Earth was starting to improve him. Of course, he was dumb to take on a strange bear like that. Really stupid, you might say.*

The bear just looked at me as though I was a bothersome flea. Then, with insulting laziness, one shaggy paw came out and removed the stick from my hand, the way you'd take a toy away from a two-year-old, and dashed it to the floor.

His deep voice found words slowly. "This is *my* cave. Sit down. Don't be afraid."

I sat. There was something gentle about this bear. His soft voice took the fear out of me.

The wood hitting the floor had roused Verity. Now she was rubbing her eyes, squinting at the bear's dark, shaggy form.

"It's a bear, Sis," I explained.

"A BEAR?"

The owner of the cave looked at her. "You scared of me?"

"YES!" she shrieked.

"How come?"

"Because you have teeth and claws. Because you're going to bite my head off."

The bear seemed to quake all over, silently. "Your head wouldn't taste good," he boomed at last. "You kids hungry?"

"Starving," I admitted.

"Then have a fish."

A string of wet brook trout glittered on the cave's floor. Next to it stood a pail overflowing with blackberries and a honeycomb, thick and white. The bear had been out all night collecting grub.

"Uh—about the fish, no thanks," I faltered. "But we could use some berries and honey."

"Picky eaters, huh?" muttered the bear, with a help-yourself wave of a paw. Ripping a trout from the string, he stuffed it between his jaws. Another trout followed, and then another. As he polished off each fish, he would toss its head onto a pile of garbage at the back of the cave.

The blackberries were cold, as if their pail had been sitting in an icy spring. The honey, gritty as salt, filled your mouth with flowers. Verity and I hadn't had a meal that good in almost two hundred days. After breakfast, the three of us propped our backs against a cave wall and felt comfortable. The brown bear was licking off his nails, one at a time. Yellowish-white and curved they were, like shelled Brazil nuts.

He sighed. "Honey gets harder to find every day. The bees had to stop drinking from the Moonflower."

"Does everything in this country talk?" Verity wanted to know. "All the animals and bugs, I mean?"

"Not all of them," said the brown bear after some thought. "I knew an earthworm once who was kind of a blob. You could hardly get two words out of him. Who are you kids anyway?"

Briefly, I told him our story. Just for fun, I introduced Verity by her school nickname, which she hates.

"Hello, Terrible Verity," said the bear, while my sister took her revenge by yanking hairs out of my scalp. "They call me Fardels. That's what I'm always carrying—burdens—bundles of wood—and that's what Fardels means. I'm in the business, see?"

I hadn't noticed till now, but most of the cave's

walls were piled high with split logs and bundles of sticks. On the floor lay an ax in a heap of wood chips. At the entrance to the cave hung a small hand-lettered sign, which, in our haste to get into the cave the night before, had passed me completely by:

FARDELS BEAR
Firewood

Don't chop. Buy yours here.
Why grunt and sweat?

"Mustard Weedblossom made me that sign," the bear said proudly. "He's the kid who used to live in that busted farmhouse. I've been swapping wood with people for something to eat. Now that there isn't a zoo to feed me any more."

"Ouch!" I cried, as Verity uprooted a whole clump of my hair. "You're a zoo bear?"

"Used to be. I'm a Kodiak brown."

"*Yow!* Do you miss the zoo?"

"Sometimes. Mine was the biggest cage. Had my own swimming pool. Always had plenty of fish. Didn't have a thing to do except make people laugh. But that was before Raoul Owlstone!"

As he said the name of the Dictator, Fardels Bear gave a terrible growl and flashed his teeth. For a minute I thought he was going to tear the world apart. Just then came a tiny commotion in the air, and a familiar voice rasped, "Aw, can it, bear, all this yap about the good old days. On your feet, you kids! You need to blow this dump! Fast!"

"Lew!" cried my sister joyfully. "You've come back to us! Did you see Gran?"

"No time to shoot the breeze, baby," barked the detective from his perch on the bear's nose. "You've got to get out of here. Now!"

"What's the rush, Lew?" the bear wanted to know.

"Stone owls. A flock of 'em. They're searching for these kids and they're heading straight this way. Will you *move*, Tim and Verity?"

The ladybug's warning hadn't come too soon. From outside the cave, high in the air, came a grating mechanical voice over a loudspeaker. Its echoes scampered up and down the hillside:

BEAR!	BEAR!	BEAR!
WHERE	WHERE	WHERE
ARE BOY	BOY	BOY
AND GIRL	GIRL	GIRL?

"This is Peepy Treetoad's work," said Lew bitterly. "He ratted on the kids. I overheard an owl talking. Fardels, step out front, will you, and tell 'em the kids aren't here."

With a heavy paw, the bear shoved Verity and me behind him. Then he crawled outside and stood up and, pretending to be grouchy, boomed, "What's all this noise? Can't a bear sleep in the morning? What boy? What girl?"

BA-LL-LL-OO-OO-OOOM!

A dark streak whistled down from the sky. It slammed Fardels in his midsection, knocking him over backwards into his cave. He sprawled on the floor with a round thing squatting on his belly — a glob of dripping muck the size of a bowling ball.

When Verity heard the bear hit the floor, she scrambled over to him. "Fardels! Fardels, are you all right?"

"Yeah," the bear grunted. "Just got the wind knocked out of me." He sat up, brushing off slop.

Having seen the bombardment clearly — as my sister hadn't — I wanted to crawl back into that cave like a scared mole. I didn't want to look out at the stone egg that hovered in the sky, talking down to us.

LIE!	**LIE!**	LIE!
COME OUT!	**OUT!**	OUT!
OR DIE!	**DIE!**	DIE!

"I don't like this," said Lew. "They aren't just whistling 'Dixie.' They've got a cannon. That first little muck-pill was only a warning. The next one is going to flatten this cave."

I remembered the ball of mud that had crushed the farmhouse. Where the family named Weedblossom didn't live any more.

"We'll go out and give ourselves up," said Verity briskly. "We don't want the owls to knock down Fardels's cave."

"All right," I quavered, after she'd twisted my arm a bit. "You go first."

"No, you don't," said the bear firmly. "Let 'em flatten the cave! You're staying here."

"I don't like this," said Lew Ladybug glumly. "They flatten this cave and they flatten the bunch of us, too."

All of a sudden a brilliant idea hit me. Hit me so hard I thought my head would burst.

"I've got it! I've got it! Listen! Why don't we all just take the back way out?"

The brown bear looked at me in honest puzzlement. "What back way?"

"Well, *our* bear cave on Earth has a back way," I insisted. "Why don't we take a look?"

The cave's rear wall was hidden by a mountain of fishheads and a load of dead leaves that the wind had driven in. My hopes toppled. I didn't think we could dig through it in less than a year.

Verity examined this garbage with her sniffer.

"Why, Fardels," she said in annoyance, "you have gone to the bathroom in here."

The bear shrugged. "It's a bear cave. What did you expect? Crocheted doilies?"

The owls' loudspeaker made a new demand.

ALL OF YOU!   YOU!   YOU!
COME OUT   OUT   OUT
BY THE COUNT OF THREE!   THREE!   THREE!

The detective was dancing excitedly in the air. "For Pete's sake, Fardels, can't you move this trash out of the way and get that back door open?"

"I'll try. Come on, help me dig, Tim and Terrible Verity."

ONE!   ONE!   ONE!

It was a smelly job, but the owls' warning made us hop to it. Fardels hoisted armloads of fish-heads and flung them aside. I dropped to my knees and swatted the dead leaves madly, while Verity, wrinkling her nose, somewhat gingerly helped.

TWO!   TWO!   TWO!

"Timmy," said my sister, "I just had an awful thought. What if this bear cave isn't built like our New Jersey one? What if there isn't any back way out?"

"Keep digging," I suggested, digging harder myself.

Then Fardels whooshed aside a final armload, and there it was—a beautiful up-and-down crack in the rear wall.

THREE!   THREE!   THREE!

Verity and I jostled into the crack. Grunting, the bear followed.

BA-LL-OO-OOM! The cannon had spoken. Then from behind us came a closer *THA-RR-RR-RR-OO-OO-OOMMM!* The roof of the cave had fallen. Like a bunch of fleas blown by a puff from a bellows, we were picked up and flung, carried through the air on a swirling cloud of dust and pebbles and fishheads and torn-apart bundles of wood.

6. *"The Very Air Has Ears"*

Coughing and sneezing, our eyes burning from the dust, we found ourselves heaped at the bottom end of a narrow, downhill passageway. Luckily the bear had landed first, and his soft bulk had cushioned the rest of us. I picked myself up, only a little scraped. Lew was twittering comments about the owls, so I figured he was all right. As for Verity, she was laughing so hard you'd think she had just had a ride on a roller coaster.

The dust thinned, and I found myself looking out through a hole in a rock wall, easily wide enough to crawl out through, just like our bear cave on Earth. Beyond the hole I could see a patch of daylight. Grass-covered ground and bushes with green leaves.

On hands and knees, I crept out through the hole and emerged under a bush. Fresh air! I opened my dusty mouth and guzzled it. From

over my head came a loud mechanical roar. I parted the leaves and cautiously peered through.

What I saw just about froze me solid. Right over my bush, there hung this giant egg. It was a helicopter made of the owls' gray stone. It hung so low that the wind from its whacking propeller rumpled my hair. Behind its one round window sat an owl—the pilot, no doubt. I gulped and let the leaves rustle shut over me.

Had the owls seen me? Slowly and noisily, the stone egg circled overhead, making sure it had finished us off, while I stayed crouched down under my bush like a chicken afraid of a hawk. Satisfied at last that we were done for, the egg withdrew. The noise of its motor grew faint as it buzzed away.

Fardels and Lew and Verity crawled out after me and together we went around to the front of the hill to see what was left of the cave. All there was was a jumble of rocks with one corner of the FIREWOOD sign sticking out. On top of the ruins sat a dripping wet ball of muck as big as a house.

Fardels sighed. "*Now* where am I going to live?"

"Be glad you've still got that problem," Lew rasped.

"Yes, but *how* will I live? What'll I do—go around from door to door, dancing and begging for handouts? I can't live on nothing but honeycombs, you know. I'm a civilized bear. I like chocolate bars."

Verity made noises of sympathy, stroking the bear's brown fur.

"That's enough of that," said the bear gruffly, although I could see he didn't mind her attentions in the least.

I had a fresh brainstorm. "Fardels, why don't you come with me and Verity? We're going to go see this Raoul Owlstone and ask him to let loose of our grandparents. Why don't you talk with him too? Maybe he'll build you another cave."

A furious twittering sat down on my collar. "Kid," Lew exploded, "are you stark raving nuts? Can't you see this stone owl gang is merciless? Raoul Owlstone wouldn't even listen to you. He's so low that, even if he got up on stilts, he could walk under a gartersnake's bellybutton. Forget it. You go see him, baby, and you'll end up in the muck mine working a pick and shovel till you keel over."

"The bug is right," the bear said with a sigh.

"Then what'll we do?" I wanted to know.

"You'll stay out of trouble," Lew said evenly. "From now on"—he punched the air with a forefoot to stress his point—"I'm the one who's giving orders around here."

"Now look here, Lewis O. Ladybug," broke in Verity, all mad, "since when do we have to take orders from you? All you are is a tough-talking little bug no bigger than my fingernail. So if you think you're going to boss Timmy and me around like a crumby Grimble, you have another think coming."

"What are you getting sore at?" the detective snarled. "You're playing ball with me, angel, on account of your grandmother wants you to."

"Gran told you to stay with us?"

"Right. I've been retained. If you must know, your grandmother was mad at me. She said it was all my fault you kids followed me through the door. So I had to promise her I'd keep an eye on you. What else could I do? I take a case, I stick with it."

"All right, then," said Verity, "take us to our grandmother."

"Beautiful, be reasonable." The bug sighed. "Can't you guess what you're up against? You set one foot on Moonflower Mountain and—"

"Isn't it Mount Peeweehockey?" I interrupted, looking at the mountain on the skyline.

"Kid, you're not in New Jersey anymore. Like I say, just set one foot on that mountain—"

"Why would we want to?"

"Because that's where your grandfolks are. Only you'd better not go looking for them. You do, and a couple of thousand owls will swarm all over you."

I stared in curiosity at the far-off mountain. Wasn't it Mount Peeweehockey? I could barely see it for the dark oily clouds that hung around it—then for a moment the clouds parted, and on the mountain's nose I could make out a kind of wart, sort of toadstool-shaped. Besides, the mountain wore a black thing like a skullcap on its head.

The detective guessed my questions. "That mushroom-thing sitting out on that ledge—that's Owlstone Hall, Raoul's house, where his factory is. And that black hat on top of the mountain is solid glass. It's a dome, and Raoul stuck it over the Moonflower. Your grandmother is a prisoner under that dome, too."

"Then what are we waiting for?" Verity cried. "Let's get her out! And let's find Gramp, while we're at it! That's why we came to this crazy country. Timmy, why are you kicking me?"

"Just trying to shut you up," I said.

"NOW CUT THAT OUT!" said Lew, in a pretty loud voice for so small a person. "There isn't going to be any rescue. Haven't you two got me into enough hot water? You're not going to fight a whole owl army. I won't let you. A month from now, the full moon will come back and the door to Earth will reopen, and you can both go back to New Jersey again. Get me?"

"We get you, Lew," I said, keeping my fingers crossed.

Wearily, the detective turned to Fardels. "Bear, do you see what I'm up against? Keeping these kids in line is going to be tough. Especially the girl. I'll need help. Interested?"

And so the brown bear, having nothing better to do now that he'd lost his firewood business, took a job as Lew's assistant, and to pay him, Lew promised to help him hunt for honey and fish and blackberries. The two of them decided we would all set out for a nice quiet pond they knew about, where there'd be trout for the bear to catch. The owls wouldn't bother us there.

NOTE BY VERITY: *Were they ever wrong! But I'll let Timmy go on with the story.*

Fardels led the way, on all fours, his head and his hind end swaying from side to side. For anyone so big and clumsy-looking, he moved fast. It was all I could do to keep his stubby tail in sight. Verity, clinging to my shirt-tail, kept tripping over things. Seeing her difficulties, Lew ordered the bear to give her a ride on his back, and after that, we moved along at a more comfortable pace, following a trail thick with weeds, keeping underneath trees as much as we could, so as not to be seen from the sky. Every twenty minutes or so, Fardels would halt, and Verity would dismount, and the bear would scratch his back against a tree.

Around noon—it was hard to tell, because the sun always stayed behind clouds—we came to another river, a wide, important one. The way across it was over a wooden bridge. Leading up to the bridge ran a road of crushed pink shells that didn't look tire-tracked or oily. Cars, I figured, hadn't been invented in this country yet.

Just the same, the road was having a rush hour. That really handed me a surprise. People—a whole thick crowd of them—were flowing along that highway of unspoiled pink and over the bridge. The first Other Earth people I'd laid eyes on!

As soon as Lew had made sure that there were no owls in sight, we blended in with the moving crowd. Six or eight deep, all were trudging in the direction of Moonflower Mountain. We were to mingle with them till we were safely over the bridge, then we would drop back into the woods on the other side.

While we flowed along with the people, Lew on my collar kept saying, "No owls yet!" and "So far, so good!" while Fardels threw worried glances up to the sky.

You never saw a crowd more sad and dejected-looking. Most of the people kept their gaze fixed to the bridge and they walked as if they hoped they would never get where they were going. Some of them were staggering under big boxes and sacks that held, I guessed, all they had in the world. I trudged beside them, talking with them, and some told me that the owls had ordered them to leave their homes and go work in the mines. One guy was a mailman—he still wore a hat like a mailman on Earth, only with a bright purple flower in it. He was out of a job, he said, because there wouldn't be any letters any more. Raoul had decided that people didn't need to read or write, so he had done away with the mails, and with books and newspapers. Shuffling along beside me came a popcorn man. He was trundling a cart with a glass case that had once been filled with hot white stuff. Now it held his sweaters and socks. There was a woman who told me she had once sold balloons to children in parks, only now all the parks were kept locked. She too was off to the mines.

An old fellow in patched work jeans bustled up to me, a wicker basket swinging by its handle from one of his arms. From his upper lip, yellow moustaches stuck out like a couple of brushes for putting melted butter on raw piecrust with. "Want a tomato?" he asked, dipping a hand into his basket and holding out a ripe red thing as big as a fist.

"You bet!" I said.

"Thunderation!" said the farmer, watching me chomp away, "you eat like somebody hungry. You're good to see. Ain't you full of that fake muck like everybody else?"

"Muck?"

"Guess you ain't from around here, son. No, I can see by your clothes you ain't. Let me tell you, everybody's full of muck these days except you foreigners. Muck pills—the stone owls give 'em out. People eat 'em and get filled up, and they forget what real food tastes like. Nobody wants tomatoes any more. I can hardly give 'em away."

His moustaches quivered when he talked.

"I'll take one, please," said Verity from Fardels's back, as the brown bear fell into step along with us.

"Welcome to it, young lady," the farmer said. "Likely to be the last I'll ever raise. Can't grow a thing without sunshine." He glared at the cloud-choked sky.

All of us tramped along over the wooden boards, and while Verity and I lightened his basket, the old guy unloaded his mind. Once, he told us, the Land of the Moonflower had been ruled by a handful of wise old men and women called the Elders. "Not that they ever did much," the farmer explained, "because nothing much ever needed doing. The people were happy just to breathe out and in, and the Moonflower kept blooming all night and most all morning, and the air wasn't nothing but perfume. Then Raoul Owlstone came along. He met with the Elders and the next thing we knew, they declared that Raoul was the Dictator. Then Raoul, he clapped that glass dome over the Moonflower. Nobody could see it any more. Well sir, that was the worst thing he done, I'll tell you."

"You really miss the Moonflower, don't you?" said Verity sympathetically.

"Miss it? Why, child, the Moonflower was the center of everything. All the bugs and bees and windmill moths depended on its juice, and they'd fly around helping the crops to grow. People, too, needed that flower. When they were tired from work or worry they'd just look up at it there on the mountain, and they'd drink in the air and say, 'Ah! that makes me feel better!' So when Raouly Owly put that deadly dome over it, he took the heart right out of us. That dome was a terrible thing to build, too. I know. They made my brother work as a glassblower, blowing it."

We walked on in silence. Then the farmer said, "That's Owlstone Hall up there," and he pointed to the wart on the mountain's nose. "There's a factory in back of it for making owlstone. You know what owlstone is? It's gray foggy-looking stuff. The owls are made of it, and the flying eggs, and Owlstone Hall. Anyhow, that factory has smoked up everything. Makes me so mad I could—hello, Missus, want a tomato? Take your choice!"

This last was addressed to a woman who'd caught up with us. She wore a flowery dress and an apron and a worried look. She had one green eye and one brown. Anxiously, she wanted to know, "Has anyone seen my son? He's eleven, a little younger than you kids. Wildmustard Weedblossom, his name is. Have you heard anything of him?"

"I've heard of him," put in the farmer sourly. "The pesky brat, him and his model rocket ship that used to buzz circles around my barn. Scared my best milk cow so bad she dried up on me. Mustard Weedblossom—I'd like to catch him!"

Fardels growled, "The kid was only having fun," and I remembered that this Mustard—if it was the same kid—had painted the brown bear's firewood sign.

"Didn't you live in that house with the red shutters?" I asked the woman. "The house that got crushed by a muck bomb?"

"Ours wasn't the only one," she said sadly. "The owls have been muck-bombing everybody. They want all the people to leave home and go work in Raoul's mine."

"What's become of your husband?" asked Lew. "He's Doc Weedblossom, the inventor, right?"

The woman's different-colored eyes grew moist. "If only I knew where he is! But I've lost him too. You see, as soon as Raoul became Dictator the owls arrested my husband and they flew away with him. I was practically out of my mind. Wildmustard wanted to rescue his father. I begged the boy not to try, but he headed for Owlstone Hall. That was weeks ago. I—I don't know what's happened to either of them."

Bombed out of her house, Mrs. Weedblossom, too, was headed for the mountain. She hoped Owlstone Hall could use a waitress. If she got such a job, she might hear news of her husband and her son. I liked her a lot, and I hoped she would have some luck, and then she hugged Verity and me and hurried on, pleading for news from the other people.

"Sometimes," the popcorn man said slowly, "I wonder if Raoul Owlstone is doing right."

"Doing right?" shrilled the farmer. "Why, un-gum your eyes and ears, you dad-burned butter-slinger! Doing right? Why, bless you, Raoul is doing as wrong as ever he can. Look up at that mountain with that ugly glass dome on it. Look at that old Owlstone Hall of Raoul's, like a toad-stool on the mountain's nose. Don't you remember when you could look up and see that mountain all covered with blossoms and shiny vines? Remember them windmill moths streaming up and down, like a river o' rainbows? It ain't Moon-flower Mountain no more. They ought to call it Blacktop Bump. What's the matter with the El-ders, anyhow? They must be fast asleep. Raoul Owlstone has turned this country all around, and the whole thing's a durned sight worse."

"Careful," the popcorn man said worriedly, "don't let the owls hear you. They've got listening devices, you know. The very air has ears."

"Plague take them and their devices!" bawled the farmer, growing madder all the time. "Who ever saw a stone owl in the daytime, anyway? Night's when they fly. They're like bats. Oh, I know, they go a-sneaking round the country in their flying eggs, listening in on folks, but what are you worrying for? There's nary an egg in the sky."

"LOOK OUT!" shouted Lew, whose compound eyes had been keeping watch. To Fardels he yelled, "Dive off, bear!"

Without a murmur the brown bear leaped to his hind feet, dumping off Verity, strode to the side of the bridge and straddled a railing. He took a deep breath and, feet first, let himself go.

He dropped like a furry brown bomb until he splashed into the water. It must have been seventy feet down to the river below.

Why had Lew given this order? All of a sudden a stone egg swooped down from the sky, its huge propeller whacking right over our heads. From under it a long thick tube came curling. As I watched in horror, the tomato farmer was snatched right up. He went whooshing into the tube like a mouse caught by a vacuum cleaner. A sucking noise—*shloof!*—and then another, and the popcorn man also disappeared.

For a couple of minutes the stone egg hung in the air above us, snarling as if to say, "Does anyone else want to speak?" And then, as suddenly as it came, it shot straight into the sky and churned away. The people on the bridge fixed their eyes on the planks under their feet and went back to trudging the road.

7. *The Rising of the Pond*

Slowly and soggily, his fur all pasted flat, Fardels hauled himself up onto the riverbank. The rest of us, having crossed the bridge, had dropped out of the mournful parade.

"Bear," said Lew, "you look like a drowned sofa. Hey, stop! Don't shake the whole river on us!"

"You got me into it, boss," the wet bear growled.

The detective glowered. "Well, you *had* to take that dive. What if the owls had seen you and these kids together? The owls are rock-heads, all right, but maybe they would have wised up. Now they'll still think their bomb finished us off. OK, let's move."

With Verity once more on top of the bear's back, we set off along a path through a thick pine forest. It was hot. All around my head, gnats kept doing dances. We kept heading in a zigzagging beeline toward Moonflower Mountain. The weak sun hung low in the sky when at last we reached our destination—a little bright pond in the shape of an oval, not twenty yards wide. A sign on one of its shores gave its name. CRESSIDA POND.

Right away Verity declared she was hot and dusty, and she was going for a swim.

"Now, Sis," I said uneasily, "you don't know how deep this pond is. What if it's crawling with snapping turtles?"

Wrinkling her nose at me, Verity kicked off her sneakers and strode into the pond, shirt and pants and all. I watched her swimming around having a fine time, and after a long debate with my fears, I jumped in too.

Cressida Pond was warm, its water clearer than glass. You could just barely touch your toes to the bottom. On my back, lazily floating, I watched a windmill moth go twirling by. A rainbow trout jumped for the moth, missed it, splashed down again. In the birch trees circling the shore I could see Lew Ladybug hunting for aphids and the brown bear searching for honey-trees. Suddenly all that had troubled me packed up and vanished—my worries about finding Gran and Gramp, about Mrs. Weedblossom and her lost husband and son, about the farmer and the popcorn man. For the moment, I was as happy as a little kid in a tub, and not in any hurry to get lathered.

After our cooling swim, Verity and I felt like doing something to thank the pond, so she took a stick and raked dead leaves away from the shore and I relieved the water of a rotten picnic basket.

Lew made a landing on my collar. "Not one single aphid," he said. "Nothing but runt-sized mealybugs."

Fardels joined us, cupping a group of blackberries in one paw. "All I could find," he said gruffly. "You kids have 'em." But Verity made him take a share of them, too.

Luckily, watercress grew at the edge of the pond, so I bundled up an armload of the crisp green stuff and the three of us mammals had supper, sort of a vegetable one. Then Lew tried working his magnifying-glass wings on some charcoal that a picnicker had forgotten. Perched on a charcoal pellet, he brought a few weak sunbeams to a point, and after a while he got a fire smoldering. Verity and I huddled next to it, and soon our clothes felt less soggy.

As we sprawled in the grass I asked, "Lew, what's it like to be a ladybug?"

"It's the cream, kid—that is, it used to be. Back before Owly threw a dome over the Moonflower. When I had my office on the Moonflower I used to spend my days picking big, sweet aphids off of that swell plant. Runny and warm they were, like your breakfast soft-boiled egg. After I'd had my fill, I'd pick out a blossom and crawl in between its petals, find me a warm spot, and just dream till the moon came out. Then I'd watch the Moonflower open. Kid, until you've watched the Moonflower open, you haven't seen anything. There isn't anything more beautiful in this world."

Birds were singing their last numbers for the day, and now the sky looked shadowy. Fardels Bear was sloshing around up to his belly in the pond. "Got you!" he shouted, making a catch. A plump trout wriggled between his paws.

Just as the bear was lifting the fish head-first to his jaws, it happened. Something strange and beautiful and—well, I can hardly believe it even now.

From the center of the pond rose a woman's head. She had flowing hair, and twined in it, she was wearing a huge white water lily. But she wasn't an ordinary person. Her hair was slightly green, and, the strangest thing of all, you could see right through her. Her eyes and nose and hair and everything were made of water. That's right. Water. It was as if she'd been carved out of ice and had melted, keeping her shape.

The water woman frowned. Her lips moved, and when words came out, they sounded tinkling and far away, as though they had bubbled up from several fathoms.

"Let go of her! Let go of Fiona!"

The rainbow trout spurted from between the brown bear's paws, creased the surface of the pond, and wriggled away. Thunderstruck, Fardels stumbled backwards out of the water.

"Excuse me, lady," he stammered, "I—I thought—"

"You thought you would sup on my fish," the liquid voice finished for him. "Well, you won't. You're welcome to drink from me and to pick my watercress, but the fish are under my protection. Is that clear?"

The bear nodded, shuffling from foot to foot like a kid caught stealing apples.

Then the transparent face turned to Verity and me and gave us a beautiful smile. "Thank you. That was kind of you to rake my shore and take that trash away."

"Who—who are you?" Verity wanted to know.

"I'm Cressida Pond, of course. Who did you think I was?"

"You're *alive?* And we went swimming in you?"

Cressida Pond tossed back her head and laughed a long, tinkling laugh that sounded like one hundred gallons of water falling down a flight of stairs. "People swim in me all the time. That is, they used to. Lately there haven't been many picnickers. In fact, until you came along, I was feeling neglected. Would you like to meet my fish? They're Finn and Fiona MacCool. If you like, they'll put on a show for you."

"Oh yes, please!" said Verity and I, almost together.

The two rainbow trout leaped into the air and made a kind of bow. For the next ten minutes we were treated to the most unusual water show ever. The fish kept doing back flips and jackknife dives, bursting up from below and spouting like fountains and letting the water woman juggle them in her hands. I kept up a running account of the show for Verity, and when it was done we clapped, and the bear clapped the loudest of anybody.

Cressida Pond wanted to know what was the matter with the country. A windmill moth seldom went by. Nothing seemed to multiply, except muckhawks. "And look at my white birch trees! Their bark is turning gray! What has gone wrong with the world?"

"What's wrong, ma'am," said Lew, "is Raoul Owlstone. He's built a dome over the Moonflower so that nobody can see it, and the moths can't drink its juice. All the trees and plants are croaking right and left because Raoul's factory smokes so bad it blots out the sun. You see, ma'am, Raoul loves muck and murk. For him they're a whole way of life."

The surface of the pond quivered with her rage. "The nerve of him! To hide the Moonflower from its country! What's to be done about this polluter, this outlaw, this—?"

The detective shrugged. "I wish I could tell you. What makes things tough is that he's got an army of owls."

"Maybe," Verity put in, "the answer is just to talk with him. To tell him he isn't treating the country right. Maybe Timmy and I will see him. We want to ask him to let go of Gran and Gramp."

The detective blew up. "Stow it, baby! For the last time, I'm telling you it would never work. It wouldn't do any good to talk to Raoul Owlstone. He wouldn't listen. You're not going to see Raoul Owlstone, you're not going anywhere near Raoul Owlstone. Now will you behave yourself and knock that goofy notion out of your head?"

"Sure, sure, Lew," I tried to calm him, "whatever you say."

Verity, disgusted with me, threw a punch at my ribs that missed. But Cressida Pond's clear face wore a knowing smile.

"Timothy Tibb," she said to me, "I can see through you as easily as you see through me. You're frightened, you don't trust yourself, but there's courage at the bottom of you. It's a good thing you have this ladybug to advise you. And Verity, you too need an adviser and a friend. I have a gift for you. Here, take this!"

A transparent hand had reached in under a lily pad and was offering something to Verity. The gift was little, round, and yellowed like ancient ivory.

"Always keep it with you," said the water woman. "It's name is Percy-Mary Bysshe-Wollstonecraft Shelley Snail."

In Verity's right palm, the snail opened a tiny mouth underneath it, and spoke in a high, shrill voice with a pause after each word:

"Call. Me. Shelley. For. Short."

"Oh, thank you, Cressida Pond," said my sister excitedly. "You're so lovely—if only I could see you! Be my good luck charm, Shelley Snail. All right if I carry you in my back pocket?"

"That. Ought. To. Be. A. Quiet. Place. I. Guess. —My. Favorite. Food. Is. Mildewed. Watercress."

Lew snorted. "Takes this joker a week just to get a sentence out."

"Patience, ladybug," said Cressida gently. "You'll find the snail well worth listening to. It is a poet and a prophet. It can tell you what tomorrow holds in store."

"Shelley, can you actually do that?" Verity wondered.

The snail's pinpoint eyes wobbled on little stalks. He spoke again, in verse:

I. Draw. Into. My. Shell. And. There. I. Hear.
The. Ocean. Of. The. Future. Rushing. Near.
I. See. Its. Breakers. Stumble. In. And. Bow.—
My. Shell. Is. Small. —I. Can't. See. Far. From.
  Now.

"OK, then, snail, how about a short-range prediction?" Lew demanded. "It's getting dark. Where are we going to spend the night?"

The snail's horned head drew back into its shell. After what seemed forever, it reappeared.

You'll. Climb. A. Hill. A. Stone's. Throw. From.
   This. Beach.
On. Whose. Crest. Grows. A. Celebrated. Peach.

Fardels wrinkled his brow, working at thinking. "Could the snail mean—? I know! Old Man Clingstone's place! Nobody's peaches are more famous. His orchard's right over there on top of that next hill."

"Yeah," Lew said grudgingly, "yeah, it makes sense. I was thinking of that very hill myself. We'd be on high ground. We could watch out for anything coming."

"Then be off with you before darkness falls," said Cressida. She waved a slender arm. Her smile took us all in, even the forgiven Fardels.

A path climbed upward. We tramped our way up the side of the hill, me with Lew on my collar. I glanced behind me to see Cressida's face and flowing hair slowly dissolve to a level surface of water.

I felt glad that she had given the snail to Verity, not to me. I would have felt sort of strange carrying a poet and prophet around in my back pocket.

8. *The Snail Foretells*

The full moon, bales of cloud in front of it, had a hard job trying to shine. Standing close to the first peach tree in the orchard, I could just barely make out a sign, hand-lettered by some terrible speller:

Gon 2 work
in the mine

FREE PEECHES

Help Yorself

Sure I would. Hungrily, I twisted a big peach loose from the nearest branch and bit into it. The fruit was so hard and green I almost fractured my teeth.

"Save your appetite, Tim," said the detective. "Those fuzz-balls used to be famous, but now they aren't getting ripe any more."

In spite of my disappointment with the peaches, I was happy to get to the orchard on top of the hill. Its trees clustered around us like good buddies. At least we'd be able to get our sleep tonight.

Or would we? Fardels was patrolling the hillside. All of a sudden he rose on his hind legs and sniffed the air. "Something's coming," he growled. "Hear it?"

I listened. A low rumbling sound crept uphill out of the pines—a steady boom, like faraway traffic.

"Stay here, bear," Lew told him. "Don't go down there—a big bozo like you is too noticeable. I'll fly down myself and take a look-see." He darted off.

Beneath us the tops of the pine trees stretched to the edge of the sky. From the hilltop it was like looking down on a campground pitched with a thousand dark green tents. Moonflower Mountain stood on the skyline, its nose hidden in clouds. Near the foot of our hill, Cressida Pond slept inside her circle of white birches, her waters calm under the faint moon, but dancing with pinpoints of light.

The rumbling drew closer. Now a river of shadow was flowing out of the woods, steadily creeping uphill. Shapes with round heads were bobbling along in it.

Lew was back on my collar. "Bad luck," he rasped. "It's owls. Hundreds of 'em. That noise is their ball-bearings rolling on the ground. I picked up some of their radio chatter. A muck-hawk saw you kids down by the pond."

A chill shot to my toes as if an ice cube had slithered down my back. "Lew, let's run! Come on—"

"Use your head, sweetpuss," the detective cut in, snarling. "They've got this hill surrounded. Anyhow, you can't outrun a rolling owl."

"Lew, what'll we do, Lew?"

"Shut up while I think."

Verity was drumming her fists against a tree trunk the way you'd beat on a bolted door. "Why?" she was wailing, "why did I have to lose my glasses? If only I could see, even a little bit—"

With an effort I gulped down my own fear. "Sis, you *can* help. Dig out that snail of yours, will you? Ask it how we're going to get out of here."

"Oh, skunk cabbage," said the bear. "By the time the snail answers, the owls will be all over us."

But my sister, remembering the water woman's gift, quit howling. She drew the little yellow shell out of her pocket and started talking to it.

Mixed with the far-off rumble was a new sound now, like that of a great weight jolting along. The ladybug had heard it. Perched on the back of my hand, he broke out his rear wings and placed one on top of the other.

"Look through me, kid," he barked at me. "Take a squint down there and tell me what you see."

NOTE BY VERITY: *That was one of Lew's features. He could make himself into either a magnifying glass or a telescope, depending on how he arranged his wings.*

Through the simple telescope of the detective, I studied the land below. At the bottom of the hill six owls were dragging a sort of log made out of owlstone, that rolled on two owlstone wheels. They got it where they wanted it and aimed it up the hill.

"It's a cannon," I said, keeping my voice steady. But my nerves were jingling like dimes in a jelly jar.

Lew flicked himself shut. "Rats," he commented.

"Don't worry, boss," said the bear. "I'll make trouble for them."

"Yeah," the detective grunted, "but for how long? Verity, for Pete's sake, hasn't your snail come out yet?"

BOOM!

A *whoosh* in the air over our heads and down sailed a mudpie as big as a bathtub. It crash-landed in the top branches of the tree we stood under. Twigs and blobs of muck showered on us.

Lew gave a whistle. "That one was high. Next time they'll aim for your ankles."

A column of owls, two abreast, had rolled half-way up our hillside. Now they kept on climbing, their electric eye-cells gleaming through the dark. Beside me, Verity talked worriedly into her cupped hand, trying to get the snail to answer her. I was starting to fall to pieces with the shakes.

Then an extra-tall owl out in front of the rest waved a wing and the column halted. The tall one was so close I could watch its beak flap as it talked. "Bear—Boy—Girl! You are up there in the orchard. Surrender!"

"Keep quiet," Lew shot to us. "Don't answer it. You'd only improve their aim."

"This is your last warning," the machine-voice droned. "Surrender. Surrender or we will come up after you."

"Just you try, you rotten rock-hunk," the brown bear said under his breath.

Another *BOOM!* and a second bathtub of mud dropped in front of us. This time, to my amazement, Fardels stepped forward and caught it in his arms. Staggering under its weight, he lifted it high and with a terrible roar flung it back down-hill into the column of owls.

And do you know what?—his aim was perfect. The owl commander caught the muck-bomb right in the beak, keeled over backwards, and lay under it.

Loud cheers rang out on our hilltop. They were coming out of *me*.

Their leader fallen, the rest of the stone owls turned around in confusion and rolled back down to the bottom of the hill. But their cannon hadn't quit.

BOOM!

BOOM-A-LOOM!

BA-LOOM!

Fresh tub-sized hunks of muck kept splattering down on us. Faithfully, the bear would catch every one and toss it back. He did fine for a while, but soon I could see he was tiring.

"Can't keep this up much longer, boss," he said between his teeth. "Must be some easier way to fight owls. Why don't I just go smash 'em?"

"Hold on," Lew said sharply, "you can't fight a whole army."

This excitement was too much for me. My legs collapsed and lowered me to the ground.

Verity was waving a hand with a poet-and-prophet in it. "Quiet, everybody! Shelley is going to utter!"

The snail's head had poked out of its shell, horns twitching. We listened as it piped:

Stone. Legions. Fall. Before. A. Raging. Beast—
Beware. The. Smells. Of. An. Engaging. Feast.

"Horsefeathers!" sputtered the bear. "Who's a raging beast?"

"Fardels, it means you," I told him. "Stone legions—that's the owls—will fall before you! Hooray!"

"But what's this stuff about a feast?" put in Lew. "Makes no sense to me."

Verity frowned in puzzlement. "Shelley, don't be so mysterious. Will you please explain yourself?"

"I. Just. Make. The. Prophecies," said the snail word by word. "I. Don't. Make. Sense. Of. Them."

I kept turning the prophecy over and over in my mind, picking at it the way you'd pick at a tough knot. *The smells of a feast.* But then I didn't have any more time to ponder, because the enemy had rallied. Now they were flowing back up the slope again in a column six owls wide, a new tall owl commander rolling in front of them.

The sight threw Fardels into a rage. He didn't wait for any orders from Lew. His huge head bent, his paws swatting left and right, he went charging downhill straight for the oncoming column. Owls fell, then bobbed back up again— their rounded bottoms made them hard to knock over for keeps—but the bear just kept on swatting. He was a whirlwind of fur. Sometimes he'd take two owls and slam their heads together and stun their mechanical brains. Then they'd roll back down the hillside looking absentminded. Sometimes he'd toss owls to either side of him. He kept on charging downhill through the middle of the column, dividing it the way a comb makes a part. Before long the whole hillside was strewn with gray stone, like the columns of some knocked-over temple.

At last, after they'd lost yet another commander, the owls retreated once more down into the shadows. All this time, I had been giving Verity a blow-by-blow account of the fight. When Fardels, panting and tired, rejoined us, Verity hugged him hard.

A merrier get-together you never did see. The brown bear pranced around on his hind legs, growling what he thought was a song. Verity danced around him in a circle. The snail had been right! A raging beast had beaten a legion of owls! I felt pretty cocky. With Fardels to fight, Lew to scout and direct us, and Shelley to foretell the future, how could we lose? What dictator could beat us now?

Lew had guessed my thoughts. "Don't be smug, kid. We were just lucky this time, that's all."

A cold gray dawn was breaking. At least, the oily sky was growing somewhat light. And then— had I gone crazy? Floating down out of the air came wonderful breakfast aromas.

Bacon...

Scrambled eggs...

Buckwheat pancakes with honey...

Oatmeal with brown sugar and plenty of cream...

Hot blueberry muffins with butter on them,

and the sharp tang of lemon marmalade...

It was too much for me. I was starving. With Verity right beside me, I bounded out from under the peach trees and followed my twitching nose.

Fardels was on his feet and moving. "What's that I smell? Fresh brook trout?"

"It's a trap, you ninnies!" the detective shrieked from my collar. "Don't you understand? The owls, they've lured you out of the orchard! The smells of a feast—that's just what the snail said to watch out for, right?"

Dumbfounded, we stood under open sky on the hillside. And then a stone egg—which had broadcast those artificial odors—swooped low and hung right over our heads. Its vacuum-cleaner tube came squirming downward, like the tube that had caught the tomato farmer and the popcorn man.

"Look out, bear!" cried Lew—too late.

A sickening *SHLUPPP!*—and Fardels, kicking all four legs, shot up into the nozzle and was gone.

Another *SHLUPP!* Up and away went Verity. I watched the soles of her sneakers wigwag and disappear.

I was rooted, too terrified to run. A rush of air hoisted me up off the ground. Now I was shooting straight up into the swallowing tube—

SHLUPPPP!

9. *Between the Worst Two Beaks*

Rouser was barking. The muck-cannon was booming. Bacon and pancakes and muffins came snowing down out of the air. Now I was sitting on a lily pad in the middle of Cressida Pond, cracking a soft-boiled egg. Bits of shell crumbled, and inside the egg was Peepy Treetoad. He snickered, "I saw you shove that owl into that river," and I hollered and flung him away. Now I was squatting on my three-legged chair in the kitchen of Grimbles' farmhouse. A label was sticking to my tongue. Maw Grimble was coming toward me, lifting her masher—no, all of a sudden it wasn't a masher, it was a miniature Moonflower.

I was having nightmares. When the nozzle had whooshed me up, I must have blacked out. Next thing I knew, I was coming to my senses inside the owlstone helicopter, lying face down on its vibrating deck, listening to its propeller's steady *whack—whack—whack—*

Slowly, my eyes got used to the gloomy light. I could make out an owl pilot sitting at a control panel. On the deck beside me, Verity was rubbing her eyes, and nearby, ringed by more owls, Fardels Bear lay on his back, growling quietly. But where was Lew? For a moment I thought I had lost him. Then a twitter under my left ear told me that he had only changed collar lapels.

"Well, kids," he said dryly, "it looks like you're going to get your wish. They're taking you to see him—Raoul Owlstone—the big cheese himself!"

At last! We would meet the mysterious Dictator! Once I had thought I wanted to. Now I wasn't so sure.

I stared out over the owl pilot's head through a round porthole. Beneath us, black treetops were racing by. The pit of my stomach was falling like an elevator. I'd never been up in any kind of aircraft before. High places always scared me. And then the mountain that looked like Peewee-hockey filled the whole porthole, its black glass skullcap giving off faint light. The giant dome, I remembered, held my grandmother a prisoner— and the Moonflower, whatever *that* was.

Circling the mountain now, our stone egg suddenly plunged into a dirty snowbank of cloud, while my stomach tried to climb me like a ladder. Fog swirled around us—thickened—thinned— and the nose of the mountain appeared, wearing its round, gray blob.

"Last stop," barked Lew, "Owlstone Hall!"

Scared though I was, I was fascinated. A co-lossal toadstool, that's just what the house looked like. It was completely made of gray owlstone—just a round, bulging roof on top of a thick stem. Instead of windows it had narrow slits for peering from. One lonesome smokestack rose from the toadstool's crown. Thick smoke poured out of it—from the factory that made the owls, no doubt. Two more stone eggs like ours went swooping by, circling the Hall, guarding it. On the edge of the roof sat a muckhawk gobbling a songbird. A bright green feather dropped.

Soon, with a jolt, our egg bumped down onto the rooftop. A slab of its wall fell out and became a gangplank, which the owls urged us to walk. Four owls took charge of Fardels. Verity and I rated only an owl apiece.

Inside the Hall, we were hurried down an owl-stone stairway and along an owlstone corridor, then we were prodded into a tremendous owl-stone room. It was the biggest room I'd ever seen, and so dim I could barely see to its opposite side. And *cold?* Like a North Pole cave. A cave the size of twenty-four basketball courts.

NOTE BY VERITY: *People*—reliable *people*—*tell me the room was no bigger than twenty basketball courts. If that many.*

By the light of guttering candles, I made out a woman and a man. They were sitting face to

face at the two ends of a table a hundred feet long. At first I thought the man was made out of owlstone like everything else. He was big and round. From across the room, one of his shoulders looked higher than the other, but as we hiked and hiked and finally neared him, I could see that a large brown-spotted bird—a muckhawk— was using him for a perch. The man had his nose sunk into a plate as big around as the lid of a trash can. He was tearing into a stack of pancakes. Buttery steam blew my way and reminded me that I hadn't had any breakfast, only the smell of it. Silent owls in gold-roped uniforms kept rolling up to the table, forking more pancakes onto the big man's plate.

The woman, too, was breakfasting, from a dish as small as a doll's. If she was on a diet she didn't need to be, because already she looked as skinny as a skeleton. Her face and her hands were chalk white. Her reddish hair was screwed tightly into a bun. Her nose was a sharp white beak with little red-berry warts on it, and she had on a long white dress with a cape the color of fresh blood. Clenched in her right eye was a rose-red monocle. Her teeth were ratty and sharp, and her face wore a sneer that seemed printed there. Together, that man and that woman were a couple of real mean birds, let me tell you. Like an overstuffed gray owl and a bony red-and-white buzzard.

"That dame," Lew whispered to me, "calls herself the Baroness Ratisha von Bad Radisch. She's poison, junior. Keep your lip buttoned."

When we arrived at his end of the table, the master of Owlstone Hall raised a beaklike nose and, glaring, looked us over. He could have passed for a stone owl himself. His eyes stared out from dark gray circles. His pointed ears seemed hairy, or feathery. He wore a gray, moth-eaten sweater that a bowl of oatmeal must have spilled on long ago. He scowled at us and chewed, not saying anything.

The Baroness Ratisha quit picking at her birdseed, or whatever it was, and fixed a beady eye on us through her rose-red monocle. "So here they are!" she sneered, "the ones who defeated the Army of Owlstonia! Two little kids and a bear! Raoul, your owls must be slipping!" She had to shout to her breakfast companion, the table being so long.

"As a rule," said the Dictator in a deep, hooting voice, "I don't see troublemakers. But I wanted a look at you. You knocked over forty-seven of my owls. There are only three of you?"

I quaked in my shoes, keeping my lip buttoned, but Verity spoke right up. "Five of us, Mister Dictator, counting Lew Ladybug and Shelley Snail. Turn on the lights, will you please? I can't see a thing in here."

Raoul gave a low, mocking laugh. "Oh, you won't be in the dark for long. What'll we do with them, Chuckles?"

This question went to the muckhawk on his shoulder. The bird opened its beak and let out a scream: "*Meat! Eat meat!*"

The Dictator peered at me with narrowed owl-eyes. "You, boy, are you the one that pushed the patrol owl into the river?"

"Tell him it was somebody else," Lew advised me.

"It—it couldn't have been *me*," I quavered.

"Certainly, it could have," butted in Verity, mad at my fib. "Timmy did it, and I'm proud of him."

The Dictator chuckled unpleasantly. "Let's call another witness. I happen to have one on me."

A hand fished into the pocket of his filthy sweater and pulled out something little and green and squirming. Peepy Treetoad, the spy who'd wanted Verity and me to collect June bugs for him.

"Look 'em over, Toad," Raoul commanded. "Ever see these kids before?"

Up from the palm of Raoul's pudgy hand, the toad blinked at us with glee. "That's them," he chirped.

Fardels growled and took a stride forward, but the owls closed in on him. From my collar, Lew burst out in angry twitters: "Cheap stinker! Judas toad! You'd sell your own mother for a June bug! Toad stool-pigeon!"

Raoul was watching me as if he was getting ready to swoop down on a mouse.

"Say," piped up the toad, "what about my reward, Your Excellency? A thousand June bugs you promised me, isn't that right?"

Raoul leered.

"Er—five hundred, maybe?" suggested the toad, coming down in price.

Raoul just chuckled.

"Well now," said the spy, looking worried, "fifty June bugs would be plenty. That would be very generous of Your Excellency."

"Worthless toad," said Raoul, "why should I pay you anything? Chuckles, baby! Here's a snack for you!"

The tree toad let out a squeak as Raoul's fat hand raised him to the muckhawk's beak. I hate to tell you this, but the bird, in finishing off Peepy, had to take four bites. At last Raoul lowered his empty hand and wiped it on the tablecloth. Then he smeared jam on a shingle of toast and pigged it down. Somehow, I didn't feel hungry any more.

My sister had heard the toad's last moments. "Raoul Owlstone," she said, almost in tears, "I think you're perfectly horrible."

Raoul was pointing at Fardels. "That bear. Isn't it the brown bear from the zoo, the one that escaped? Speak up, bear, is it you?"

"It's me," growled Fardels. "And I want to know what you've done with the other zoo animals. Where's my friend Boswell Boa Constrictor?"

Raoul hooted a laugh. "I—ho! ho!—threw 'em into the meat locker. Had a lot of 'em ground up for sausage. Why, this happens to be your buddy I'm eating now. I like a little snake meat with my pancakes."

And he forked up a sausage and waved it, steaming, under the brown bear's nose. "Want a bite?" the Dictator jeered. "You *used* to be fond of him, eh?"

The brown bear arched his back and bared his incisors. I expected he'd throw himself straight at Raoul. The muckhawk on the Dictator's shoulder fluttered nervously. But more owls quickly rolled in between their master and Fardels.

"Have a care, bear," Raoul taunted. "I could run you, too, through the grinder." He lifted the sausage to the muckhawk. The bird gaped its beak. The sausage vanished. The empty fork came down. The bird chomped hungrily.

Fardels looked ready to cry. "Boswell. You did that to Boswell. Boswell was the finest snake I know."

The Dictator scowled. "I've tasted better."

"Oh, la-de-da," said the baroness impatiently, drumming the tabletop with her sharp red nails. "Spare us the sermons, bear. Raoul, dear," she called down the long table, "haven't we had enough animals and children for one morning? They bore me dreadfully."

"Hold on, Ratisha," the Dictator shot back. "I want to question them. Speak up, boy, what are you doing here on Other Earth?"

I mustered all the bravery I had. "Mister Dictator," I began in a voice that shook, "we came here because you've got hold of our grandparents, Agamemnon and Agatha Duff of Morris Plains, New Jersey, and we want you to let them come home with us."

"And another thing," Verity put in hotly, "when are you going to lift that awful glass dome from over the Moonflower? It's hurting all the bees and the windmill moths. In fact, everything in this country is dying. Why don't you stop all the muck and smoke? Why don't you tell your owls to start being kind to animals? Bears, especially."

The Baroness Ratisha was staring through her eyepiece at my sister the way you'd look at your toothbrush if you had found a caterpillar on the end of it. "What sentimental parp," she said.

The Dictator scowled more darkly. "You think *your* grandparents are the only ones? Why, girl, I've got lots of people's grandparents down in the mine. As for the Moonflower, I'd like to burn it, chop it, root it out. So. You don't like the way I'm running this country? Do you think *you*, a blind kid like you, could do better?"

Verity thought. "I guess I could," she said slowly, "if someone showed me how."

"*Eat! Eat meat!*" the muckhawk screamed.

The baroness flashed white rat-teeth. "Raoul, these urchins are insulting you. Why waste your time on them? Can't we get on with breakfast?"

"How can I get on with it?" shot back Raoul. "Why, there isn't a pancake on my plate! Waiter, some food! Are you trying to starve me? OK, now, bear, tell me, how did you destroy all those owls? My valuable owls, made in my image? Talk fast, or it's the sausage grinder."

"Ahhhh," said Fardels in disgust, "your owls are pushovers."

Raoul's fork, with a new pancake on it, hung in midair. "Pushovers, did you say? My owls?"

"That's right," said the brown bear, "they're as easy as kicking over toadstools. Want me to show you what I did to them?"

Raoul nodded, interested.

Two owls stood between the bear and the Dictator. Quick as a shaggy lightning bolt, Fardels lashed out with his front paws, slamming the owls in their chests. Off balance, the pair crashed over, their ball-bearings spinning. They hit the floor. They lay still.

The Dictator's jaw sagged. The fork with its untasted pancake slowly settled to the table.

"My owls," Raoul said wonderingly. "I didn't

know anybody could do that to my owls."

At his command, two fresh owls rolled in and cleared away the wreckage of their companions. Four more owls surrounded Fardels, two on each side.

The baroness was trembling with fury. "You fool, Raoul, are you going to sit there stuffing your face while this hairy brute destroys your whole army?"

The Dictator flung her a snarl. "Hold your tongue, Ratty, or I'll have it held for you. All right, bear, that was a lucky trick. Got any more?"

"If you really want to know," said Fardels, "sometimes I did *this*—"

Turning to the owls on his left, he collected the pair in his arms and bashed their heads together. *THUNK!* The owls dropped to the floor, their transitors—or something—broken. An instant later the brown bear did the same to the pair on his right side, too. The air was choking with the thick black dust of cracked-open batteries.

For a long while Raoul and Ratisha sat there looking at each other. A thick blanket of dust had settled over Raoul's pancakes.

"Nincompoop!" the baroness shrieked at last, dabbing dust from her rose-red monocle. "Honestly, Raoul, at times I suspect you of stupidity. Ugh—this dust! I insist you put that bear through the sausage grinder!"

Her idea didn't set well with Fardels. A low

roar rumbled out of him. On his hind legs, paws extended, he made straight for the baroness.

But the skinny witch just froze. In her right eye, the pink eyepiece flashed, and she murmured, "Watch, bear, just watch. Look at the lovely red light."

The monocle started to spin. Around and around it went, faster and faster, brighter and brighter. I had to tear my eyes away from it, it was so fascinating.

"Now, bear," the baroness said oozily, "you will do as I say. Lie down!"

Like a good dog, the brown bear slumped at her feet. He had been hypnotized! The monocle stopped its spin, a gleam of triumph in it.

"Ratty," said the Dictator with a chuckle, "I'll have to hand it to you. Your eyeglass puts 'em under, every time."

He clapped his hands. In rolled a dozen more owls—this time, extra-tall ones. He was opening his mouth to give more orders and get rid of us when Lew chirped, "Wait! Hold on!"

And the loyal detective skimmed from my collar to the tablecloth and marched straight on up to Raoul like a knight in spotted armor. Drawing himself to his full height—an eighth of an inch— he threw down his words with studied carelessness.

"Listen, Raoul Owlstone, you don't have any say over these kids. They aren't even citizens of this country. Let them go in my custody—I'm a licensed private investigator—and I'll see that they leave Other Earth on the next full moon."

For answer, Raoul just puffed his cheeks and blew a gust of air that swirled Lew up off the table. The ladybug fell back down, underbelly up, feet waving. After a few tries, rocking back and forth, he got his third pair of legs to touch the tablecloth, and righted himself.

"Let those kids go?" jeered the Dictator. "Nothing doing, bug. They'll never leave Owlstone Hall. Do you think I want them running around telling people that my owls are breakable? Anyhow, this is MY country and I'll do what I like. I'm the Dictator here, and that puts me above the law. All you are is a puny ladybug."

Lew glared at Raoul with contempt. "Maybe so. But a little ladybug casts a long shadow."

The Dictator lifted a hand to swat Lew, but the baroness had been squinting at the detective through her monocle. "Wait, Raoul. A detective, is he? I have need of a sharp-eyed spy. What do you say, bug? Will you serve me?"

Lew kept quiet as if thinking. Finally—to my surprise and horror—he asked, "What's in it for me, lady?"

"How much are you making?" demanded the baroness.

"Thirty-five aphids a day, plus expenses."

"Very well, I'll pay you forty. Turn down my offer and"—she made a pinch in the air with thumb and forefinger—"you perish. Take it or leave it. Well?"

"I'll take it. When do I start?"

"Lew!" my sister wailed in agony. "Lew, you can't walk out on us! You can't quit us and go work for this—this witch—just for five more aphids! Why, whatever will Gran think of you?"

The baroness flashed her rat-teeth. "Every bug has his price. All right, detective, you're hired. Come sit on my shoulder."

And without another word, Lew sailed over to her. Oh, it was a bad hour. To see our small friend on the side of the enemy made me sick at heart. I couldn't believe he had abandoned us. As ever, his insect face wore no expression at all, but for a moment I could have sworn that, from his roost on Ratisha's shoulder, he had thrown me a wink. And yet—how could he? His eyes didn't have any lids.

The Dictator settled back in his chair, lit a gray cigarette, and spat out a vile-smelling cloud. "Remove these brats. Take 'em and throw 'em in the mine and let 'em shovel muck till their backs snap."

"Only the boy goes to the mine," the baroness corrected. "I'm keeping the girl. I know a use for her."

"All right," Raoul agreed carelessly, "and throw

the bear into the meat locker. He'll do for steak when he has been properly marinated. His skin can make Ratisha a stuffed animal to take to bed at night. Now bring me a pot of coffee with some beer in it."

10. *In the Mountain's Cellar*

The elevator wasn't much more than an owlstone box. It fell down—down—down—till at last it jerked to a stop.

"Out!" said the tall owl, so out I stepped, and sank up to my ankles in cold water.

The mine was no easier to see around in than Raoul's dining room. As I stood there trying to focus, a shape rolled up out of the dark. It was another tall owl, the one in charge. It carried a shovel in its beak, the way a dog will carry a stick, and when it got within six feet of me it flung the shovel at my head. By luck, I made the catch.

"Prisoner eighty-seven-two-o-eight," my escort announced me. "His Vileness wishes this prisoner to work here until his back snaps."

The other flashed its eye-cells, recording my number. "Prisoner," it droned to me, "you will notify me as soon as your back has snapped."

Then the boss owl raised a wing and swatted

me into my place in a long row of bent-over slaves.
By the flickering light, I could tell they were digging with shovels and slinging wet muck onto
carts. There were people of every kind—women
and girls, men and boys, and they came in all
ages. They were ragged and skinny and plastered
with muck, like a lot of shaggy, dripping, slowly
moving animals. Because the mine was chilling
cold, they were coughing and wheezing and snuffling. Their job was to keep filling carts. Tall owls
stood guard over them, and any worker who took
a moment off to rest soon felt the jab of a beak.
The carts, when filled, slid along a rail and hooked
onto a moving chain and climbed up out of sight,
lifting the muck, no doubt, to the factory that
made more stone owls. Like overgrown bats,
muckhawks kept thrashing by, just missing our
heads, shrieking and pooping and adding to the
general misery. All you could hear were cold-
symptoms and muckhawk wings, the drip of
water, the groan of loaded carts.

The only light came from buckets of oil suspended from iron spikes, that burned with un-
steady blue flames. It was enough to show the
tunnel's ceiling and walls, all twined with pale
white tubes like macaroni, only thicker than sewer-
pipes. These, I found out later, were the roots of
the gigantic Moonflower.

So there I stood, cold muck-juice soaking my
shoes, never again to see Verity or Gran or

Gramp! I was starting to feel a hopeless, squeezed-in feeling. And to think that Lew, faithful Lew, had sold out on us! Almost as bad was the thought of Fardels, his bushy skin stuffed with cotton, his kindly eyes traded for buttons, as a teddybear in the Baroness Ratisha's bed! Maybe I've had worse moments in my life than that one, but I don't remember any.

Once, I read this book by a Frenchman about these two twin brothers who could feel what each other felt. When one was being tortured, the other, a hundred miles away, woke up hollering. I shut my eyes and tried to tell if Verity, wherever she was, felt anything special. But all I could feel was the ice water trickling down my backbone, dripping from the ceiling of the mine.

Maybe I'd keep warm if I worked faster. I drove my shovel into the muck at my feet and hoisted a glob of the stuff, which came loose with a *SUCK-KK-K-K!* Savagely, I slung it into the nearest cart.

"What's your hurry?" asked a voice at my right elbow. "Slow down, or you'll wear yourself out."

The friendly voice had come from the shoveler next to me. He turned his face my way, and I took it in by the light of the oil-bucket overhead. He was just a kid, younger than me, with tumbledown hair and a grin that shone through his falseface of mud.

"Can you be Wildmustard Weedblossom?" I asked him.

"You're right. Mustard, to my friends. How come you know me?"

"You look like your mother. The same mustard-colored hair. And you both have one green eye and the other brown."

I told him how we'd met his mother on the highway, and he pressed me for news of her, and I gave him what little I could.

"Timothy Tibb!" he kept repeating. "That's a funny name. Hey, look, Timothy Tibb, here come our ten o'clock muckolates!"

An owl with a big stone jar was rolling along our line, pausing at every shoveler. Each person held out a hand for some little dark objects to rattle into. When the owl came to Mustard and me, we stuck out our hands, and the jar poured and the owl rolled on, and Mustard cried, "Chug-a-lug!" and gulped his ration.

"What are they?" I asked suspiciously, sniffing my handful of clay-colored jellybeans.

"Muck pills. They're really rotten, but they're all the breakfast, lunch, and dinner you're going to get."

I tried one. It tasted like a mudpie that, on a dare, I had once eaten in kindergarten. But I was starving. I opened wide and tossed down all the rest.

Right away my stomach began to play leapfrog. Soon I was throwing up.

"You'll be all right, Timothy Tibb," said Mustard gently. "Everybody gets sick the first time. You'll get used to them."

I decided I'd much rather starve.

From behind my back, now, came a sudden rumble. I spun, to see a frightening machine go wallowing by. It was owlstone-gray, the size of an army tank, and it moved on a rotating tread. On the end of its nose, a drill was whirling.

"That's an owlstone mole," Mustard told me. "Some new kind of weapon, I guess."

The mole slogged on through the muck till it came to a wall. But it didn't stop. It just drilled its way through that solid rock like a corkscrew put to a cheese. Then it rumbled on into the hole it had bored, and the darkness swallowed it.

Despite my new friend's reputation for making trouble—trouble for the tomato-farmer's cows, at least—I soon decided that Mustard Weedblossom was all right. If you had heard him kidding with the other slaves, cheering them up, you'd have thought so too. In our work gang there were some frail-looking old gentlemen. Once, when one of them keeled right over, worn out from shoveling, Mustard barged over to him and helped him to his feet again, and for a long while the kid not only did his own shoveling, he did the old gent's shoveling besides.

Mustard's good-humored gab improved that dismal mine. As we worked side by side, not very fast, I told him my story, and he told me his.

After the owls had arrested his father, Mustard had made a beeline for the Hall to try to rescue him, but had been promptly captured. I told him about me and Verity and Lew, and when the younger kid heard how Fardels had trashed six owls in front of the Dictator, he threw a laughing fit. Then and there, he and I made a vow to be brothers, and we shook on it, locking our little fingers. While we were sealing this pact, a suspicious owl rolled over and lightly pecked at us. We went back to our shovels again and worked hard until the owl, satisfied, rolled away.

"That old owl," said Mustard, "hardly can peck any more. Its gears must be wearing smooth. Guess it was the first owl Dad ever built."

"Huh? Your dad built it? I thought Raoul invented stone owls."

"Raoul couldn't invent a thumbtack. My dad was the one that discovered owlstone in the first place. He cooked up a batch of the stuff, and at first he didn't know what shape to put it into. Then one day Raoul came along, a stranger. He looked so much like an owl that Dad had him pose, and Dad modeled the stone owls after him."

"That figures. I thought Raoul and the owls looked a lot alike. But what did your dad want to invent those mean things for?"

"Dad meant the owls to help people. To catch mice in farmers' barns—gently, not hurting the mice, of course. But then Raoul changed everything. He stole the secret recipe for making owls, and he took Dad prisoner. If only I knew where Dad was!"

Three bent backs down the line from me, a middle-aged man let out a strangling gasp, pitched forward on his shovel, and lay still. Mustard made a jump over to help him, but the old owl, with a swat of one wing, knocked the kid aside. Two more owls picked up the collapsed miner by the feet and dragged him away into the dark. When they came back, they had a fresh miner in between them, to replace the one who'd worn out.

"Keep away, you statues," said the replacement. "I don't need to be forced."

And he took up the shovel of the fallen miner, and he gave it an expert thrust into the muck. When he bobbed up again, he stood straight as a flagpole. His hair was so white it sparkled, even under the feeble light.

I'd seen this man before.

My heart tried to leap into my throat.

"GRAMP!" I yelled. "Is it really *you?*"

Oh, it really was my grandfather, all right. Nobody had whiter hair or stood straighter or talked that way, making every word count. At my shout, Gramp whirled, and he saw me. He let out a beautiful grin.

"TIM!" he bellowed, loud enough to bring every owl in the mine.

I flung down my shovel and started toward

him. I wanted to throw myself at him and hug him half to death.

"I'm coming, Gramp!" I hollered.

But I wasn't going. A weight—it must have been an owlstone wing—slammed into the back of my head. I dropped to the floor of the muck mine like ten tons.

11. *A Poison Seethes*

NOTE BY TIM: *While I was having my troubles down in the mine, big things were happening up in the kitchen of Owlstone Hall. But I'll let Verity tell you about them. She was there.*

You understand, I'm not an experienced storyteller, like Timmy. I'm going to tell you the truth. After the owl went rolling away with my brother—I knew they were gone, because the floor shook and then it stopped shaking—the Baroness Ratisha von Bad Radisch said to me, "This way, girl! We'll see how much work you have in you! Step along, step along!"

She pinched hold of my ear and dragged me with her. Behind us, a door bumped shut. Then we were in the kitchen—as I guessed from all the sour old cooking smells. The baroness shoved me in the back of the neck and I stumbled forward into something that clicked against my belt buckle. It was a sink.

She said, "Now, my tender chicken, you shall stand there and scrub those pots until they shine like diamonds. DIAMONDS, I say!"

Tender chicken, huh? I could have strangled her. And how could I know when her dumb pots shone? With my glasses missing, I could hardly tell day from night.

I said, "You can't mean it. You aren't really going to throw Timmy in the muck mine till his back snaps, are you? You aren't going to soak Fardels Bear in vinegar and make steaks out of him."

"Oh, aren't we?" said the baroness, with a laugh I didn't like. "Muck is the very thing for boys, the noisy monsters. As for that filthy bear with his muzzle all sticky—ugh! Marination is too good for him. But Raoul has his heart set on a bear steak dinner. Now get busy—scrub!"

What could I do? I asked her for a scouring pad, but there wasn't any. She said, "Haven't you any fingernails? Use them to dig!"

That struck me as a mean thing to ask of anybody, so I said I wouldn't do it. The baroness didn't like that. She ordered me to look into her monocle. I guess she wanted to hypnotize me, the way she had done to Fardels, but I told her it wouldn't work. I was practically blind, didn't she know? I couldn't even see her old monocle. That made her just furious. She threw me a slap on the cheek that stung. I warned her, "Look out, don't make me mad, or you'll be sorry."

Oh, what a nasty, shrieking laugh she gave. "*I* should fear *you?* A puny little string bean who is blind?"

That did it. I'm not puny. After all, I was wrestling champ of our junior high. I shot out my arms to where her voice was coming from, took her around the neck, threw a half-nelson on her, flipped her up in the air, and slammed her down. It was easy. She didn't weigh very much at all.

For a long time the baroness lay there with her breath knocked out. At last I heard her scramble to her feet.

"For that, my fine chicken, the muckhawks shall tear you to tatters. No, no, that won't do—I want you to die by slow degrees. *You will scrub pots.*"

"You can't make me."

"Oh, can't I? Do you know, I'm holding your friend the ladybug between my thumb and my pointing finger. Shall I crush him, or will you do as I say?"

I thought about it. Lew was a traitor. He had let the baroness buy him away from us. I was ready to say, "Go ahead, crush him," when I remembered how good he had always used to be.

"All right." I gave in. "I'll scrub pots."

"That's better. Dip those pretty fingers into that kettle and scrape. Now as for you, ladybug—"

"At your service, ma'am," Lew said politely. "You wanted some detecting?"

The baroness lowered her voice. "Listen, bug. I have reason to believe that old Aspen Apple-yard, the eldest Elder, suspects me of plotting against his life. Of course, his fears are ridiculous. But I don't trust him. I think he is planning trouble for us. You will fly to his home—do you know it?"

"Yeah. He lives in a treehouse in the big orchard south of here."

"Exactly. I want you to hide there and eavesdrop on everything he says. You will report back to me."

"Right, Your Highness." A tiny flurry in the air told me that the detective had taken off. Oh, the turncoat! I could have pinched him to a pulp.

"Aha, very good, the poison is now bubbling," Ratisha was telling her chef. "You will stir it slowly with your wing for the next seven hours. Put in a few dried serpent tongues from this jar. Serpent tongues add zest."

"Execrable, Madam," said the owl.

While the poison-chef was getting its briefing, I kept trying to scrape the crust of some old soup from the bottom of an iron kettle. I could hear splashes inside the kettle. They must have been my tears.

Now, you understand, I didn't feel sorry for myself. That wasn't it. I was just so boiling mad—to be so helpless, at such a time! Then, all of a sudden, from out of my back pocket, a shrill little voice said, "Don't. Cry. Verity. —Couldn't. Things. Be. Worse?"

"Huh! A lot you know about it, Shelley Snail! Worse? How could things be? Timmy and Fardels are someplace being put to death. Lew is working for the baroness. She's boiling some terrible-smelling stuff to poison somebody. We're never going to rescue Gran and Gramp. My glasses are lost and I can't see a thing, and I'm never going to get the crust out of this scuzzy old soup kettle."

"I'm. Sorry."

"Oh, Shelley, forgive me, what a no-good friend I am. I'd forgotten you. Aren't you hungry?"

"Yes. Please. I. Am. Famished. —Please. Set. Me. Down. On. That. Cart. Full. Of. Mildewed. Cabbages."

My nose soon led me to the cart it meant. I felt around, found the biggest and soggiest cabbage, and without the baroness noticing, set Shelley down on it.

Just then, heavy footfalls came into the kitchen. A panting and wheezing, and the flapping of wings. The Dictator had arrived, no doubt with his pet muckhawk, as usual.

"Gaze!" he cried out in a deep, commanding voice. "Gaze upon me, Ratisha! Did you ever see such a magnificent thing in your life?"

The baroness gave a surprised gasp. "Why, Raoul, the crown—it looks perfectly dreadful! I mean that," she quickly added, "as a compliment.

And the snakeskin—yes, it glitters beautifully. But where are the jewels?"

"Oh, the crown isn't finished. It still needs its sparklers set into place. Weedblossom is working on it. But I just had to borrow it from the laboratory for a minute and give you a preview of me. Me—in my owlstone crown! The Emperor of Owlstonia!"

I couldn't see the crown Raoul was wearing, of course, but owlstone, snakeskin, and jewels—that sounded horrible.

After he had paraded around in front of the baroness for a while, Raoul told an owl to take the crown back to the laboratory. Weedblossom should get moving on it. Then the clanging and banging of pot lids told me that the Dictator was looking into kettles, to find out what was for lunch.

One kettle made him just about retch. He said, "Ratty, this stuff had better not be for ME to eat. Are you trying to poison somebody?"

"Yes, of course. We must prepare the refreshments for your coronation, must we not? We are brewing a tasteless little substance that will work with lightning speed. Soon you'll have no enemies."

"Good. I knew I could depend on you. Just don't put the wrong kind of flowers on the refreshment table. What if—ULP!"

His words stopped in a gurgle, as though the baroness had clamped a hand across his mouth.

"You idiot, Raoul," she said to him. "You nearly gave away the secret of Owlstone Hall in front of this big-eared little pot-scrubber!"

At that, I *was* all ears. What secret could she mean? And what did flowers have to do with it?

Well, they rattled on about this and that, and Raoul said, "Do you realize, Ratty, that our dream is about to come true? A land all to ourselves! A land of owls, with just me and you—the only two people alive!"

"Shelley, do you hear that?" I said to the snail on its cabbage. "How can we stop them in time?"

The baroness had heard me. "You, girl, what are you doing at the cabbage cart? Who is that you're talking to?"

"My snail Shelley," I said. "The poet and the prophet."

You see, I never deny anything that will only be found out.

At my words, Raoul sounded all interested. He must have picked up Shelley in his hand. "Snail," he said in a soft wheedling voice, "are you the kind that knows what is to come?"

"I. Can. Foresee. Most. Things," Shelley said.

"Aha! This is my lucky day! I've always wanted to meet a snail like you. All right, snail—Raoul Owlstone commands you. Look into my future. What do you see?"

"You. Are. A. Large. Order," said Shelley. "Your. Future. Will. Take. Me. A. While."

"Then start!"

A long silence fell in the kitchen, except for the Dictator, grumbling impatiently. After many minutes, Shelley's high voice piped:

Stone. Owls. Shall. Roll. Till. Owlstone. Walls.
Dissolve.
And. Raoul. Rule. Till. Moonflower. Mount.
Revolve!

"Hmmm," said Raoul, trying to think. "*Till Moonflower Mount Revolve,* eh? Who ever heard of such a thing? Mountains don't revolve. They're not on turntables. Bah! that couldn't happen in a million years. Ratty, do you understand? This wise snail says I'm going to rule forever!"

A clapping, whooping and stomping told me the Dictator was doing a dance all around the floor. *Awwkk-k-k!* cried his muckhawk in alarm.

"Fool," said the baroness. "Surely you don't believe a fortune-telling snail!"

"Why not? Everybody knows snails never lie. Come on, snail—tell us Ratty's fortune too!"

This time, Shelley's prediction was worth waiting for:

Before. Day's. End. A. Stranger. Shall. Let. Fly.
A. Punch To. Close. Ratisha's. Spinning. Eye.

"Why, you little slime," said the baroness.

The prediction didn't make a bit of sense to me. Raoul gave a hooting laugh. "Too bad for you, Ratty! Anyway, MY fortune is beautiful! Raoul shall rule till Moonflower Mount revolves! Long live Emperor Raoul! Long live me!"

And trying to skip with joy—and stumbling—he left the room.

No sooner was he gone than the baroness said to Shelley, in a cold, threatening voice, "So, snail. You foresee a splendid future for Raoul and an insulting one for me. I'll fix YOUR future for you!"

What was she going to do? I had to save Shelley! I flung myself in the direction of her voice. Squinting as hard as I could, I could make out a dim blur. The blur was reaching high, swinging—

I made a grab for it.

Too late.

A gust of wind blew into the room from an open window-slot.

Tears stung my cheeks. I wailed, "What did you do? Where's Shelley?"

The baroness gave a laugh that ran up and down all the scales. "So, little chicken, you're worried about your snail, are you? Well, you won't have to worry any more. I have thrown it out of the window. By now it's smashed to powder. From here to the rocks at the foot of the mountain, there's a drop of a quarter of a mile."

12. *I Fulfill a Prophecy*

It's me, Tim, again. After the owl slammed me over the head I must have taken a nap. When I woke up I was lying on my back on the mine floor listening to a faint, familiar twittering. A tiny breeze was blowing down on me, as if from a pea-sized electric fan. Slowly, everything focused. The twitter was Lew, hovering over me and fanning me with his wings.

"Kid, are you OK?" he rasped.

The back of my head felt like a mine cave-in. "I—I'll live," I answered. "Lew, what are YOU doing here? I thought you took a better-paying job with the baroness."

"Wrong," grunted the detective. "I didn't work for that witch. I only pretended to, till I could slip away. Your sister's OK. She's up in the kitchen scrubbing pots."

Then the whole past rushed back to me. I sat

up. "Gramp!" I cried. "Where's Gramp? I saw him, Lew, I really did!" My head hurt.

"Not so fast, kid," Lew said gently. "Yeah, yeah, you saw your grandfather, all right. Only he isn't around anymore—the owls moved him to a different tunnel. Guess they figured he was disturbing the peace."

With the help of an arm from Mustard, I struggled to my feet. Weak though I was, I was hopping mad and I wanted to fight. "They took Gramp away! I'll fix them!" But my head felt as though it had a steam drill pounding on it.

Lew barked from my collar, "Calm down, kid. In a minute the owls will notice you're awake, and they'll throw you and Mustard back on the shovels. But before they do, we're getting out of here. I know, see, where the exit is."

"Lew, I can't go. I've got to find Gramp again. Where did they take him to?"

"Listen, junior, get your head on straight. This is no time to play raiding party. You stick around here much longer and you'll dig muck till you rot. Which won't do your grandfather any good, especially."

"That's right, Timothy Tibb," Mustard said urgently, "you've got to come along."

Two wishes were battling inside of me. What should I do? Try to save Gramp all by myself? Or escape, then try to rescue Gramp and the other miners? It was too big a problem at the moment. Dizzy as a washed cat, I sat back down in the muck.

"On your feet, Tibb!" snarled the detective. "Don't pass out, for crying out loud! You've got to walk another thirty or forty yards."

My eyes blurred—cleared—blurred again.

"I won't go," I said as firmly as possible. "Can't run out on Gramp. Only just saw my Gramp again."

"We'll come back!" Mustard promised. "Right now you've got to come with Lew and me. Remember, Timothy Tibb, we have to stick together, you and me! We're brothers—don't you remember? You swore!"

Half-dragging, half-carrying me, he was moving me along the corridor, while I kept trying to pass out and slide back down in the muck. But at last we were standing before a wooden door in the tunnel wall—a door maybe two feet square. Mustard yanked it open. I stared into a square hole full of darkness.

"I won't go," I said.

Lew blew up at me. "Listen, Tibb, you stick your foot through that door before I haul off and beat the American Beauty roses out of you. Move!"

Once more, the mine was slipping out of focus. As I stood there swaying, a tall owl caught sight of us. Now it came speeding toward us, eye-cells flashing. *"You! Prisoners! Halt!"*

Somehow, that decided me. I lifted a leg into

the dark open doorway, and Mustard gave me a boost and he shoved me right on through. Lew darted in, and Mustard climbed in behind me, and only seconds before the owl reached us, the kid slammed the little wooden door.

We had squeezed ourselves into a pitch-dark compartment, so narrow that my elbows bumped its sides. I groped down and felt a platform under my feet.

I said, "Lew, where are we?"

"In a dumbwaiter, kid—Raoul's personal food elevator. Just make believe you're a tray of chicken sandwiches."

"Then you mean we can ride up on it?"

"You catch on quick, sweetheart. How's your head?"

It was better. In fact, it suddenly cleared altogether, with a *poof!* like a cap coming off a soda bottle. But still, we were in trouble. In the cavern outside, the owl was bawling, "Prisoners have escaped!"—while it kept up a steady thunder on the dumbwaiter door. That door would have crashed in on us, no doubt, if Mustard and I hadn't thrown our shoulders against it. Splinters were raining in on us, and soon a crack of light appeared in the door right where the owl's beak must have been bopping it.

Mustard sounded worried. "The owl is busting through!"

"Yank the rope," Lew urged from my collar.

Two ropes, in fact, hung in front of me. I could feel them in the dark, so I grabbed the closer one and yanked down on it. High over our heads, an invisible wheel creaked, and underneath us the platform lurched, and we climbed a few inches up a narrow shaft.

"That's the way, Timothy!" Mustard breathed, "you pull down, I'll pull up."

You had better believe we fell to tugging on those ropes like a couple of busy demons. Lew rasped encouragement—"Heave, heave, you mutts!" and "Will you PULL, you lazy palookas?"

Soon the dumbwaiter, which hung from a pulley, was climbing steadily. From under us came a huge CRASH as the door caved in, and then the owl was hooting up the shaft at us:

"*Stop! Do not escape! It is not ordered!*"

I was pulling as hard as I knew how, and yet for some reason, we had stopped climbing.

"We're stuck," I quavered. My old fears of dark closed-in places were swooping back to me.

"Rats," said Lew with feeling. "What do you bet that that owl has caught hold of the ropes?"

"Let me try something," said Mustard. It was so dark I didn't know what he tried, but in a few seconds there came a loud CRUNCH from the shaft directly below.

"Pull some more now, Timothy," Mustard told me, and I pulled and he pulled, and sure enough, up we went.

"What did you do to that owl?" I wanted to know.

The kid guffawed. "Dropped my shovel on it."

As we kept on tugging and hauling and the platform kept on rising with us, I wondered out loud what a dumbwaiter was doing down in a mine. "Raoul," explained Mustard, "likes to visit the mine and watch the slavery. Naturally, he has food sent down to him. One time I saw him strutting around our tunnel munching a whole ham like it was an apple."

We had risen into a beam of dim gray light. It fell from a horizontal slot at the top of the shaft overhead. My hands were sore from the rope, but I kept on pulling until at last, puffing and gasping, we had worked our platform up to the level of the slot. When we got there, we saw that a downward-sliding door had been left open a crack, giving us a slot just wide enough to peer out through.

To my big surprise, I found myself looking out into the kitchen of Owlstone Hall. At a deep sink, Verity was scrubbing a frying pan with her fingernails. Smack in front of me stood Raoul Owlstone and the skully-looking baroness and four stone owls.

"It's Verity!" I whispered. "We've got to save her!"

But how? We had no weapons. I searched my

pockets, but all I could find was an old unstuck label for parsnip punch.

"Will you look at that," said the detective. "Something funny's happening."

Raoul and Ratisha and the owls were standing around a table that had a muckhawk lying on it. "Chuckles, baby," the Dictator cooed, "Chuckles, chick. Does Daddy's lovely muckhawk have a tummyache?"

Well, it gave ME a tummyache to hear such a fuss made over that dirty bird. Chuckles Baby weakly lifted his head, croaked horribly, and bleated, "Gut hurt! Chuckles gut hurt!" then he fell back flat again.

"Scruffy thing looks ready for the dump," said the baroness with a sniff.

"No, no!" Raoul said quickly. "This must be just something he ate. Owls, turn him upside down and shake him out."

Two owls grabbed the muckhawk by the feet and hung him up in the air, head dangling. Mechanically, they swung him to and fro while Raoul kept slapping his back like a doctor trying to get a newborn baby to start working. After a little of this treatment, the muckhawk let out a burp. A round yellowish thing dropped from his open beak and rattled down onto the table.

Shelley!

The snail poked its head out of its shell and

made a face. "Ugggghh! I've. A. Terrible. Taste.
In. My. Mouth—Would. Someone. Put. Me. Back.
On. That. Mildewed. Cabbage?"

Verity was jumping for joy.

"Cabbage, indeed!" shrieked the baroness. "You
slimy leaf-licker, I thought I had got rid of you!"

At that, Raoul pricked up his pointed ears.
"What's that? Tell me, snail, what did the baroness do to you?"

"She. Threw. Me. Out. Of. The. Window-slot.
But. Chuckles. Caught. Me. In. Midair. Thinking.
I. Was. Some. Tasty. Morsel."

"Liar!" said the baroness, twitching nervously.

"So, Ratty," said the Dictator, glowering, "you
tried to do away with this snail. This prophet who
sees a fine future for me. My poor Chuckles almost died of indigestion. This time, Ratty, you've
gone too far."

The baroness turned whiter than usual. "Now,
Raoul, remember, I'm your Empress-to-be—"

The Dictator took a menacing step toward her,
but the baroness blazed her rose-red monocle.
The eyepiece spun, and Raoul stared into it. In
a moment he quieted down.

"I—I forget," he said, "what I was angry about."

"That's all right, my dear," the baroness said
oilily. "You were excited about saving Chuckles,
that's all. Why don't you go take a nap?"

"Good idea," said the Dictator vacantly. Picking
up his pet, he placed the muckhawk back on his

shoulder and left the kitchen without another word. I had to hand it to that monocle. It made even Raoul behave like a good dog.

Verity had groped around on the table and found Shelley. Tenderly, she wiped the snail's shell dry with her handkerchief and returned the little mollusk to her pocket.

"Owls!" shrieked the baroness. "Grab that girl and her snail! Throw them BOTH out the window!"

Naturally, none of us inside the dumbwaiter wanted *that* to happen. "*Let's go!*" I yelled.

Mustard flung up the sliding door, and he and I exploded into the kitchen. We hit the floor in front of the baroness. She took one look at us and screamed. No doubt we were an awful sight, being slathered with mine-muck from head to toe.

The owls just stood there blinking their eye-cells, awaiting orders. The baroness reacted in a flash.

"Gaze!" she commanded, glaring hard at me and Mustard. "Gaze into my monocle!"

In her right eye socket, the rose-red glass began to spin. Despite myself, I couldn't tear my eyes from it. Lew was beating the air in front of my face, crying, "Tim! Tim! Shut your eyes!"

I shut my eyes and reopened them. That snapped me to my senses. But Mustard looked asleep on his feet.

"Do as I say," the red-and-white witch crooned to him.

What could I do? My fingers tightened around the only weapon I had—the GRIMBLE'S PARSNIP PUNCH label still in my pocket. I'd try anything! I whipped it out and gave it a speedy lick. I stepped right up to the baroness. With a thrust, I pasted the sticky label on top of her spinning monocle.

Mustard woke, as if he'd been sloshed with a bucketful of icewater.

NOTE BY VERITY: *Remember what Shelley predicted? A stranger—that was Timmy—had let fly a punch to close Ratisha's eye, all right, all right.*

The baroness let out a gurgle. "You fool, you've broken the spell! You—you—you—you CHILD!"

Out of her good eye, then, she spied Lew on my collar. "Two-timing gumshoe," she flung at him. "Have you betrayed me?"

"Don't break my heart, sister," grunted Lew. "Remind me to laugh at you on my day off."

Three stone owls rumbled toward us. I didn't like the gleam in their electric eyes.

"Follow me, kids!" the detective barked.

"Sis, grab my shirt-tail!" I cried.

We ran for our lives. We kicked open the nearest door and went barging out into a shadowy, unknown corridor.

13. *Ominous Inventions*

BRR-RR-RRANNG-G-G!

Somewhere in the corridor an alarm bell jangled. A loudspeaker started to hoot in Raoul's hollow voice:

Intruders! Intruders in the Hall! All owls report to the kitchen! NOW!"

Mustard, my sister, and I were legging down that corridor like crazy, while my heart kept trying to break out through my chest. Lew, scouting the corridor ahead of us, made a U-turn in the air and cried, "Owls coming! Run the other way!"

A rumble was heading toward us. We whirled around, but now a second rumble was coming from the corridor behind us, too. The owls had us in a squeeze. They were closing in on us from both directions.

All I could see was a sign on a door:

LABORATORY
KEEP OUT

Well, I wouldn't keep out. I grabbed a handle and tugged, and the heavy door swung outward. Then we were inside the laboratory, a high-ceilinged room all glitter and glass, hearing the door thud shut after us, hearing our pulses beat like drums, hearing—outside in the corridor—two thunders of owls roll by.

A man in a long white coat strode toward us— a lean, pale, youngish man with a chin that hadn't been shaved lately. From behind horn-rimmed glasses he blinked at us intently, as if we were specimens fallen from Mars.

"Who are you?" he demanded briskly.

"We—we're the intruders," said Verity, panting. "The owls—they're after us. Can you let us hide?"

The all-in-white man—I guessed he was some kind of scientist—removed a forgotten pipe from his jaw. I expected him to holler for the guards. Just as I was screwing up my courage to jump him and try to beat him up, his face broke into a beautiful big wide grin. He was looking straight past Verity and me. At Mustard.

Then, didn't he and Mustard fling themselves at each other and pound each other's backs.

"Dad! Dad!" Mustard was yelling.

"Son, where've you been lately?"

Well, you're right. The man in the white coat was Mustard's father, Oak Weedblossom, the inventor of owlstone and stone owls. He couldn't believe it was really his son standing there, and it wasn't any wonder he couldn't, because Mustard was covered with mine-muck from head to foot. Now the pair of them were jabbering, laughing, trading news. They were so wrapped up in each other I began to feel out of place. Mustard had a dad and I didn't. Down in the mine, I had found my grandfather. But for only a minute, no more.

Then Mustard introduced us all around, not leaving out Shelley, and he told his father how he and I had sworn to be brothers. Dr. Weedblossom pumped my hand in the warmest way, and he let me know I was welcome in his laboratory, and Lew and the snail and Verity besides.

"In fact," he said cheerfully, "you picked the right place to hide. The owls won't look for you here. They're under orders from Raoul not to bother me. You see, I'm supposed to be thinking."

"About what?" Verity wanted to know.

"About inventions. I'm supposed to think up a new one every day." He groaned. "As if I hadn't invented enough terrible things already."

"Like stone owls?" my sister asked brightly.

"Don't rub it in." The inventer sighed, and looked sorrowful.

Even though stone owls were the pits, in my opinion, I wanted to ask for his autograph. I hadn't ever met a real live inventor before. Only because Mustard begged, Dr. Weedblossom showed us around his laboratory. Not that he acted the least bit proud of what he was working on. There was a noise machine that, at the flick of a switch, gave out a clatter like slammed-down trash cans. Raoul planned to use it to drown out some waterfall. There was a machine for making smoke out of morning mist and another for giving roses a rotten egg smell. But the strangest and most terrible object of all sat on a workbench. Just to look at it gave me the shakes.

"That," said Dr. Weedblossom when I asked him, "is the owlstone crown. The baroness designed the awful thing. When I've finished, Raoul will crown himself Emperor. That will be a grim day, for then he'll destroy the last of his enemies."

"And who are they?"

"Oh, the Elders, of course. Months ago, the baroness hypnotized them into naming Raoul the Dictator, but lately they've been growing rebellious. No doubt Ratisha is cooking up a way to put them to death."

"She certainly is," Verity put in. "She's cooking poison. I got a whiff of it."

A fresh chill went racing to my shoes. I stared at the owlstone crown. Round and gray and icy-looking, it squatted on the workbench like some giant horned toad that had slithered out of a freezer. From all around its rim, sharp spikes, each a foot tall and pointed like an icicle, stabbed the air. A dome of glittery silver snakeskin bulged up from inside its headband to cover the wearer's scalp. On the forehead, two jewels were fixed, green-and-yellow stones like the eyes of a snarling cat. More of the same lay loose on the workbench, waiting to join the rest. All in all, the crown glowed with cold, evil power. I shivered again and turned my back on it.

But we had another bad scene in store for us. Dr. Weedblossom fingered a button and the whole rear wall of his laboratory slid aside, and there it was, taking up the back half of Owlstone Hall— the stone owl factory. Assuring us that the workers wouldn't pay us any notice, Mustard's father led us out onto a balcony to watch the action below. No people worked in that factory, just hundreds of tireless owls. Around and around the owlstone floor they rolled with a steady boom, like a rink full of roller skaters. Carts of muck kept arriving from the mine on an endless chain, and the owls kept dumping them into the hoppers of machines to turn out pills and grenades and bombs. Half-finished owls, riding along on a moving belt, were being sandblasted smooth and having bills stuck to their heads and ball-bearings fixed to their bottoms. Stone eggs were being assembled, too, and stone moles with drills, like the one I had seen chew through a wall in the mine.

In the middle of the tremendous room stood a furnace as tall as Owlstone Hall itself. Worker owls were dumping fuel into it. This fuel, I was told, consisted of toys, books, magazines, paintings, boxes of candy, letters that hadn't been delivered—anything that would have made somebody glad. The furnace cooked all the owlstone used in the country. And what was owlstone made of? Fog, ice, muck, and polluted water. The furnace gurgled. You couldn't see its fires.

At last, our eyes smarting from the dust and our ears beaten down with the din, we returned to the quiet laboratory, and the rear wall slid back into place. Dr. Weedblossom looked glum. "To think I had to invent owlstone," he moaned. "To think I had to build stone owls. All I ever meant to do was make a better mousetrap. Now look at all the misery I've caused."

"It isn't your fault, Dad," said Mustard loyally. "Owls were a good invention. Raoul just used it wrong."

Verity flared up. "Excuse me, but I think it IS your fault, Dr. Weedblossom! At least *some* of it. Why do you keep working for Raoul Owlstone? Why do you have to invent *more* of these terrible things? You could stop inventing terrible things, you know."

Looking cornered, Dr. Weedblossom tugged his chin stubble and chewed on his empty pipe. His answer came slowly, as if he didn't much want to let go of it. "All right. I guess I *am* to blame. You see, Raoul told me that unless I kept inventing things, harm would come to Wildmustard and to my wife. Don't you understand? I wanted to protect my loved ones. And so I did what Raoul and Ratisha told me to. I built stone eggs for the owls to ride in. I made muck-bombs for them to throw."

"Yes, and they threw one at *our* house," said Mustard sadly. "Dad, you shouldn't have helped Raoul. You shouldn't have worried just about Mom and me. You should have worried about the whole world."

"That's very hard for a human person to do, Mustard," said Verity.

Dr. Weedblossom looked so sorry that Mustard sat down next to him and put his arms around him. The inventor kept murmuring, "Why? Why didn't I see through Raoul's lies? If I had known he had bombed you and your mother, boy; if I had known he had sent you to the mine—! Your poor mother—oh, Heaven only knows what's become of her!"

"I know," put in Verity. "We met her on the highway yesterday. She's on her way here—to Owlstone Hall."

At this news, the scientist brightened. He stuck his pipe determinedly back into his jaw. "Then I'll find her. As for Raoul, I'm done with him! He'll never get another idea out of me!"

"Terrific, Dad," said Mustard. "By the way, is there anything to eat around here?"

Right away Dr. Weedblossom barked into a squawk-box and called for lunch. He ordered six times his usual amount of milk and sandwiches. "Oh, yes, and some aphids. I must have aphids! I'm starving!"

All of us intruders hid, and pretty soon in rolled the owl chef pushing a cart stacked high with sandwiches, peanut butter ones, and the tallest pitcher of chocolate milk you ever did see. For Lew, there was a red rose on a plate, its stem swarming with tiny white aphids. I could hear the detective on my collar smacking his lips.

NOTE BY VERITY: *Or whatever he could smack, Timmy ought to say.*

On its way out, the owl chef droned, "Doctor

Weedblossom, you will let no intruders into your laboratory. Raoul is searching for intruders. You will report at once if you should see any."

When the owl had gone, the inventor cried, "Dig in!" and the milk and sandwiches disappeared faster than a magician's rabbit. Lew, like a hungry dog gnawing a sparerib, skimmed up and down the stem of his rose till he had picked it clean.

After that good feed, and after Mustard and I had rinsed off our mine-muck in his father's showerbath, I felt greatly improved. But Verity looked crosser than ever.

"What now?" she demanded. "Here we are— stuck, trapped in this laboratory. And, oh, do you know what? Shelley made the worst prediction. Say it again, will you, Shelley?"

From her cupped hand the prophet intoned:
Stone. Owls. Shall. Roll. Till. Owlstone. Walls. Dissolve.

And. Raoul. Rule. Till. Moonflower. Mount. Revolve.

I stood stunned. What a scary forecast! Dr. Weedblossom puzzled his brows and said, "Hmmm, I don't see how a mountain can ever revolve. But owlstone, now—it can perish, you know."

"It can?" I yipped. "How do we make it perish?"

Just as the inventor of owlstone was opening

his mouth to answer, the loudspeaker over his workbench let out a squawk: "*Weedblossom!*" It was Raoul.

"Don't shout, I can hear you," said the inventor, frowning.

"Weedblossom, haven't you finished my crown yet?"

"Not yet."

"Back to work, Weedblossom! Get the thing done before I put you on a muck-pill diet. Wouldn't hurt you if I did, you gobbling swine. Oh, the chef owl told me what you ordered for lunch today. How can a grown man eat half a dozen peanut butter sandwiches? That's kid food. And how can you eat a roseful of aphids? That's bug food. By the way, Weedblossom, if you ever see three kids and a ladybug running around, let me know. They're escaped prisoners. One of the kids is named PARSNIP PUNCH. He pasted the Baroness von Bad Radisch with one of his calling cards. Tomorrow! I want my crown done by tomorrow! Tomorrow night's my coronation ball!"

14. *Prisoners at Large*

"If I know Raoul," Dr. Weedblossom said gloomily, "he'll be barging in here every five minutes to see that I finish his crown. This lab won't be a safe place for you to hide."

"Don't worry, Doc," Lew rasped. "We won't hang around here much longer. The heat's on, a whole army of owls is looking for us, and I know a place where these kids can lay low for a while. But first, I've got to get them out of this Hall."

"How? Every door is guarded."

"If we only had Fardels," Verity said wistfully. "He's the world's best owl-smasher."

Lew's compound eyes took on a crafty gleam. "Baby," he said to my sister, "you just hit on it. We're springing the bear."

"I know where Raoul keeps the zoo animals," said Dr. Weedblossom, eager to help. "They're all in cages in the meat locker, right next door."

"And how," I wondered, "do we unlock Fardels?"

"No problem," the inventor said. "Who do you think built every lock in Owlstone Hall? Me. Now, here"—he took down a key ring from a nail—"are the keys that open all the cages. Come on, let's release your friend right now."

"Hold on, Doc," the ladybug cut in gently. "We'd like to have you come with us, but you can't. You've got to stay here and work on Raoul's crown, or else he will miss you in a hurry. Take your sweet time finishing that bad hunk of ice, why don't you? I don't care, myself, if you never get it done."

"Then you're leaving?"

"Yeah. Soon as we jail-break the bear. I'm going to take these kids to a safer hiding place. A place where Raoul wouldn't look in a hundred years."

Now, Dr. Weedblossom was a brain, of course, and he saw that Lew was right. Just the same, he looked sad to have us go off without him. He hugged Mustard a whole lot and the rest of us to some extent, and he saluted Lew respectfully. He promised he'd try to stall Raoul and hold off finishing the owlstone crown for as long as possible. Our goodbyes said, the rest of us opened the laboratory door a crack and peered out into the corridor.

After a stone owl rumbled by, the coast was clear. We hurried to a door that said MEAT

LOCKER. In we went, into a racket of howls, chitters, growls, tweets, screams, gibbers and roars. In cages stacked to the ceiling, there were zebras and monkeys and wildebeests and—oh, about anything else you'd want to find in a zoo.

Off in a corner, hunched inside a cage four sizes too small, sat Fardels Bear. The minute we came in his kindly eyes glistened with joy.

"What took you guys so long to get here?" he said gruffly.

"We were waiting," Lew said dryly, "for you to be properly marinated."

I twisted key after key in the lock of his cage until one worked, and then the brown bear lumbered out happily. Verity flung her arms around his neck and tried squeezing the life out of him.

"Ooof!" grunted the bear. "Take it easy! Let me stretch, will you? My back has a kink in it."

Someone else had come slithering out of the cage, too—a bright green snake as thick as a fire hose. At the sight of it I wanted to turn and run, but the bear said, "Hey, meet my pal, Boswell. Boswell Boa Constrictor. That lying Raoul didn't grind him up for sausage after all."

"Pleas-ss-ss-ssed to meet you, I'm ss-ss-sure," the boa constrictor hissed.

My fear of the snake evaporated. I'd have been glad to shake hands with him, even, but that didn't seem possible.

"Say, you kids," called a gorilla from another

cage, "why don't you let us ALL out of here?"

"Why don't we?" I agreed. Lew thought it a good idea too. Maybe the zoo animals, running around loose, would keep the owls busy while we escaped from the Hall.

I turned every key on the key ring. Cages sprang open and the animals, loony with joy, came barging out. A mountain goat told me he'd never forget me. A chimpanzee gave me a kiss that tasted terrible. A river of fur and fangs overflowed the meat locker, bubbled on out the door, and soon filled the corridors of Owlstone Hall with bellows and roars and fearful trumpetings.

"OK, bear," Lew rasped, "we didn't spring you just because we like your looks. Think you can help us break out of this overgrown toadstool?"

The brown bear grinned. "Which way is the door?"

He and Mustard and Verity and I lit out down the nearest corridor, wading through a mob of happy animals. Four tall owls passed us, but didn't even pay us a glance. They were too busy trying to recapture a kangaroo.

All went well until we got to the Hall's big pair of front doors. A couple of sentinels stood guard. Extra-tall ones. They heard us coming. Their eye-cells flashing like angry traffic lights, they rumbled straight for us with their owlstone spears all ready to run us through.

Well, you know me. Naturally I started to tremble. But the brown bear, with a wonderful growl, just reared up on his two hind feet and collected the pair of owls in his arms and bonked their

heads together. Only one of the sentinels dropped. The other poked its spear into Fardels's belly. Luckily, the bear had thick skin. He just snarled, wrenched the spear away, and threw it clattering to the floor. Then he caught the owl in one shaggy arm and flung it down—KER-SMASH!—on top of its partner. It twitched and gave a faint hoot and lay still. A cloud of black dust rose from the owls' cracked batteries.

"You did it, Fardels!" yelped Mustard.

One swat of a heavy paw and the front doors flew wide open.

"Follow me, you mugs!" the detective cried. "I know a place a whole lot better than this!"

15. *Under the Dome*

"Drink," urged my grandmother, "drink, it's good for you. Slowly, now—not too fast. There isn't much to share with you today."

Gran was standing at the foot of the colossal Moonflower, pouring water out of an old paint bucket. She was soaking the soil right where the thick, twisting vines came out. She had on her painter's smock, leather boots, and the gold-and-green slacks she'd designed and dyed and woven all by herself. Now she was tucking a lock of salt-and-pepper hair up under her headband. As ever, her face was bright, with a ferocious, big-eyed look. The look I loved. A tan-colored bird, a mourning dove, perched on a vine, cooing and keeping her company.

She was facing my way, but she didn't see me. With Verity and Mustard and the brown bear, I was crouched down behind a boulder. We had

wriggled in under the thick glass dome, squeezing through a gap Lew knew about. We'd sneaked up on Gran, and we were going to give her the surprise of her life.

"It's so withered," Gran said aloud to herself. "Poor thing! I declare, it droops lower every day. Oh, if only I had more water! A couple of pitchers a day can't keep it alive..."

Sadly, she gazed up into the Moonflower's branching vines. You absolutely *had* to gaze at the Moonflower. The more I gazed, the more it dumbfounded me.

NOTE BY VERITY: *For once, doesn't Timmy sound tongue-tied? But the Moonflower WAS a dumbfounding thing, of course. All I could see at the time, though, was a shimmer of silver light. Lew had told me that the Moonflower was a climber, a member of the morning glory family, only gigantic. It had grown there since anyone could remember. It had wrapped its vines around the peak of the mountain and had sunk its roots clear down to the mountain's floor.*

Imagine. On the very top of the mountain, there was this towerlike formation of rock. And the Moonflower had twined all around it, every vine as thick as the trunk of an oak. Dark leaves like heart-shaped platters grew on it, and thousands of blossoms like huge silver bells. The blossoms were closed now, their heads hanging, but still they gave off a clear silver light. They made the whole room under the dome as bright as noon.

When they opened, I guessed, each blossom would be as big around as a marching-band's tuba and probably dazzling. But their smell! Most perfume makes me gag, but not the Moonflower's. It made me want to sing, even though I can't.

Huge as that round dome was, it wasn't big enough. The blossoms were pressing against its black glass ceiling, getting crushed. The great vines seemed to be writhing around, while the blossoms rustled and whispered, *No room to bloom...under the dome!* And then again, softly, more yearningly—*Room to bloom! Oh, for room...room to bloom!*

"Makes you almost cry just to listen to 'em," said my grandmother with a sigh. The dove made a low moan of sympathy. "It's that Raoul," muttered Gran. She dashed her empty watering bucket to the ground and kicked it with the toe of her boot. I guessed she wished the old bucket was the Dictator's rear section.

"He's trying to kill it," she said grimly, seating herself on a full paint gallon. "He'd have killed it long ago, no doubt, but he doesn't dare come near it. Nor his owls, either."

A giggle got away from me. Gran whirled, her eyes popping even wider. She peered all around, but couldn't see anything. Finally, she sighed and went back to thinking out loud.

"And why," she asked the dove, "is Raoul afraid of the Moonflower? Can't he stand anything beautiful? Works of art. Birds. Animals. People, beautiful people. If only I could see my twins again! And Agamemnon Duff—is he still down in that dreadful mine? Oh, what's the use? I'll be trapped here under this dome forever. I'll never see a one of them again!"

Well, I couldn't stand to hear her go on like that. It seemed high time to unhide. Quiet as a mouse, I tiptoed up to her, till I could have reached out and touched her, and said, "What do you mean you aren't going to see us again?"

With a shriek, Gran leaped to her feet. "Who said that? Who's there?"

"It's me, Gran!" I shouted. "Don't you know me? I'm Timothy, and Verity's here too!" Unable to hold myself back any longer, I grabbed her and gave her a huge hug.

But the effect on my grandmother wasn't what I'd expected. She screeched and staggered backwards, fighting me off. Now she was booting at me, missing me, booting at the air.

"You're a ghost!" she cried. "I'm hearing things! Feeling things! I'm off my rocker! They've kept me under this dismal dome too long!"

"No, Gran, no!" yelped my sister, right beside me, "it's really us, Timmy and me! Look, look at us!"

"No!" said my grandmother firmly, clapping a hand across her eyes. "I won't look. My lonesome old head is playing tricks on me!"

I felt sorry, now, that we had been so sneaky. Gran wouldn't be reassured. She had hold of her paint bucket by its handle and she was swinging the thing like a bomb she was going to hurl.

"One step closer, you ghosts," she threatened, her eyes clamped shut, "and I'm braining you!"

She would have done it, too, if Verity hadn't kept talking to her, calming her down, until at last Gran opened her eyes and said, "Timothy? Verity? Is it you?"

Soon the three of us were trading hugs, and Gran was half crying and half laughing all together. She really had believed that Verity and I were ghosts. The lying baroness, just to torment her, had told her we had both caught our deaths of cold down in the mine.

"My twins!" said Gran, her eyes shining. You ARE my twins! I can't believe it! Why, Timothy, Verity—children, how you've grown!"

"Yeah, that's right, Mrs. Duff," put in Lew from my collar, "they've grown—in lots of ways. The boy kid, especially. He's a little braver than he used to be."

"Wonderful!" Gran cried, on hearing how we'd made our way to Other Earth. "To step through a river! To fight stone owls! Why, what has become of my dear old timid Timothy? Oh, but— my stars! You could have been hurt!"

Suddenly she was staring behind me. "EEEEK! What ever is *that*?" On all fours, the brown bear had come shambling to us, and now he had reared up on his hind feet.

"Don't be scared, Gran," I said quickly. And when I told her how Fardels had defended us, Gran folded him into another of her famous hugs. When we introduced Mustard to her, Gran looked at him sharply and said, "Young man, there's something familiar about you. Haven't we met before?"

The mustard-haired kid shot her a grin. "No, Ma'am, not that I know of. But I wish I had met you long ago."

All seated on the ground in a circle around Gran's paint-bucket chair, we divided a box of soda crackers—Gran's food rations. Lew, the lucky stiff, took off for the vines of the Moonflower and soon he was gorging on aphids. Shelley, with a boost from Verity, fixed himself on a gigantic Moonflower leaf, where he soaked up a supper of juice.

Forced to live under that grim black dome and eat just soda crackers and sleep on a moldy old rug, Gran had managed, in her clever way, to make the place fit for a queen. She had collected small beautiful items: a lump of quartz, a few bright feathers. Floating in a paint bucket were some silver petals dropped from the Moonflower. Gran even had a water-soaked copy of Gramp's book, *The Light to Live By,* brought along inside her pocket from our Earth. During her stay under the dome she had painted a lot of new pictures, using brushes twisted together from fur and twine that the windmill moths had gathered for her. She had done portraits—from memory—of Verity and me and Gramp. All were painted in black, the only color she had available.

Most of the painting she did, we soon saw, was of a different kind. All of a sudden, from a loud-speaker, a mechanical voice roared: "Prisoner Four-seven-three-four!"

"Oh-oh," Gran said to us. "More work for me."

"You are resting, prisoner," accused the voice of an owl. "Moonflower light is escaping from section nine-thirteen of the dome. Correct this at once. Moonflower light must not escape. Reply!"

"Yes, yes, I'll see to it," Gran called wearily, reaching for her paint bucket and a house-painter's brush. Parking a ladder against a wall of the dome that said 913, she climbed to a section of glass where the paint looked worn, and she hit it a swipe with her brush. That must have stopped the escaping light, because the loudspeaker quit barking at her.

"That's my job," said Gran, rejoining us. "To keep on painting all the time. You see, the Moonflower's light is powerful. It keeps wearing the color off the dome, and Raoul doesn't want that happening."

"But Gran," said Verity, "aren't you better at landscapes?"

"That's what I told Raoul Owlstone, but do you think he cared? No—I was *some* kind of painter, that's all that mattered, he had work for me. Now, Raoul doesn't know it, but I help out the Moonflower. Every night I scrape away some of the paint and let a patch of moonlight shine in on the flower. That feeds it. Then in the morning, I cover up the scrape with paint again."

All the while we talked, the restless Moonflower kept stirring. One of its thick green vines cruised down and stroked me on the cheek, gently, like the trunk of some shy, inquisitive elephant. Then it drew back.

"It approves you, Timothy," Gran said with a smile. "You see, right now is when the blossoms try to come out for the night. They know when evening is near, even with this dreadful bowl on top of them. The plant wakes up and stirs and twists, looking for room to bloom. It keeps searching for more moonlight and not finding any. And so nowadays it just sleeps day and night. This dome! Oh, I wish I could smash it to smithereens!"

Just then a feeble scratching made me turn. A weak-looking windmill moth came squeezing in through the gap under the edge of the dome, its wings going around, but just barely.

"Any—juice?" it begged in a frail voice.

Gran helped the moth over to a blossom and pried open the petals for it. The starved moth uncurled a long tongue, like one of those paper favors you blow out at a birthday party. Soon it gave a grateful *Aaaahh-hh-hh!* and, much revived, went churning away, its wings working like speedy paddlewheels. By now, if it hadn't been for Gran, the last of the moths—and the Moonflower— would have been goners.

By the time we ran out of talk, the night was half through. Soon it would be Raoul's coronation day. We laid plans. With Fardels to fight and Lew to scout, the three of us kids would creep up on Raoul and the baroness and somehow overpower them. Slim as our chances might be, we had to try. But right now, feeling pretty tired, we stretched out for a nap on the warm ground, while Gran and the mourning dove and the Moonflower watched over us.

When we were ready to leave the dome, Gran took a necklace from around her own neck and she hung it around Verity's. She kissed Verity and said, "Child, wear this for me. It's only a simple thing I made. I want to give you something."

Even though the necklace was nothing fancy— it was only a piece of string painted black—its pendant was something special. It was a Moonflower seed, an oblong thing like an almond that gave off a clear silver glow.

Then Gran kissed me, too, and she told me to take care of myself and Verity. We promised her that as soon as we had captured Raoul and Ratisha we'd be back for her.

Fardels was the first to depart. The brown bear had a hard time wriggling his bulk out through the gap. Mustard followed, then Verity, with the snail in her back pocket. Then, with Lew on my collar, I crawled out last.

As I inched my way through the space under the thick glass wall—a distance of maybe a yard— I was humming with hopes. Seeing Gran and the Moonflower had cheered me mightily. Today was a whole new day. We were going to show Raoul Owlstone a thing or two!

But when I emerged into the glum dawn of the mountainside, I was in for a shock.

A gang of tall owls had been waiting for us. They'd already surrounded the bear and Mustard and Verity, and now they closed in on me and Lew.

From out of the fog a large round bubble swam. It drew closer, and I saw it was a man.

"Well, well, well," said Raoul Owlstone. "It was worth getting up early this morning to win a few prizes like YOU. The dome is alive with hidden microphones. My owls heard everything you said."

On the Dictator's shoulder, a batlike shape stood up and fluffed itself. Its shrill cry rang down the mountainside:

"Eat them! Eat! Eat meat!"

16. *Who Cracked the Lock?*

Was the dungeon of Owlstone Hall ever *cold!* You could just about hear the tinkling of your breath. The owls had flung us into a cell and slammed the bars, and they'd snapped a padlock to keep us there. Our luck, it now seemed, had hit bottom. And my sister was throwing a temper fit.

"Dimwits! That's us!" she yelled, stamping on the owlstone floor. "Now tonight, Raoul will crown himself Emperor and kill everybody! While we sit here like a bundle of dopes!"

Nobody was in a mood to argue with her. Fardels, quietly growling to himself, was slumped in one corner of our jail cell, uselessly cleaning his claws. Lew clung like a button to my collar, saying nothing. Even Mustard had run out of his usual cheer.

That cell wasn't long on furniture. All it held was a bench too short to stretch out on and, for drinking water, a bucket of sea-green slime. To warm up, I paced the cell, reading comments that prisoners before us had scratched into the walls — things like RATISHA IS A MUCK PILL and STAMP OUT STONE OWLS. When I had run out of reading matter, I went over to the one window-slot we had. From out of it, you could stare down a quarter-mile to the floor of the valley. Below me sat the abandoned zoo, with its vacant cages and its forgotten popcorn stand. Already, the tops of the trees were turning a muck-colored brown. Summer ought to last longer, but the fall now hurried on. No doubt the season was changing early because Raoul's factory smoke had shut off the warmth of the sun. Muckhawks, shrieking taunts, glided past me.

"So what now, Lew?" I asked the red dot on my collar. No answer. Worried, I hollered his name.

"Huh? What?" said the ladybug, waking. "Oh. Sorry, kid — cold weather makes me sleepy. If it gets any colder than this, I'll have to go look up my cousins on the mountaintop. Our whole family gets together every winter for a slumber party." He yawned.

"NO!" howled my sister. "Lew, you can't leave us now! This is the day of Raoul's coronation! He has to be stopped!"

"Raoul?" the detective said blankly. "Raoul who? Oh, yeah — I remember him. You'll have to excuse me, beautiful, I'm a little bit thick in the bean. Can I come sit on your Moonflower seed a minute? It looks warm."

And shaking himself, the detective went wobbling through the air and landed on Verity's pendant. Where it hung from its string, the seed gave a silvery glow. Lew sat on it and rubbed his forefeet together like someone warming himself in front of a fire.

Fardels gave a yawn like the roar of a lion. "Sleepy—that's how I feel. When there's frost in the air, I look for a nice warm cave." He yawned again. "Maybe I'll just go to sleep right here. Wake me up when it's April, all right?"

Grabbing the bear around the shoulders, I tried hard to give him a shake. His dreamy eyes were starting to cross.

"Come on, Fardels," said Mustard, doing some fancy footwork in front of him, "put up your paws and let's go a few rounds."

Fardels struggled to his hind feet. The kid was throwing punches at him. "Yeah," said the bear, "let's spar. Help me keep my eyes open. Come on. Mix it up." He and Mustard went through the motions of a clumsy boxing match, with nobody landing any blows.

The warmth of the seed had brought Lew back to life. "Wouldn't you know," he rasped, "that's just what the doctor ordered. Think I'll take a spin around the Hall and see what's up." And he skimmed out between our cell-door bars and vanished down the corridor like a dart.

All morning long, as I stared out into the gloomy passageway, stone owls kept rumbling by. None of them gave us a glance. "Hey, jailer!" I yelled. "Don't we get fed today?"

An owl with a chip out of its head came tooling over. No, Raoul had not ordered any food for us, so we would not be given any.

That was one thing I liked about owls. They would answer all questions put to them.

"Why," I asked through the bars, "are you owls so busy this morning?"

"Dictator Owlstone will be crowned Emperor this evening," the machine-voice droned. "We prepare the celebration."

"Well, I don't see how Raoul can be coronated. Dr. Weedblossom can't have finished the owlstone crown."

"The owlstone crown is finished. Dictator Owlstone could not wait. He had Dr. Weedblossom sent to the mine. He finished the crown himself."

Then the inventor hadn't been able to stall! Mustard, at this news, groaned hard and clenched his fists.

This owl was full of answers. Just for fun, I asked, "Listen, owl, what's the secret of Owlstone Hall?"

A whirring and clicking came from the owl's stone head as it searched its memory. Finally it droned, "That information is not in my supply."

Oh well. No harm asking.

"Who bopped you on the head?" I wanted to know. "How come there's a chunk of you missing?"

"A woman named Maw Grimble. She hit me with a metallic object called a potato masher."

For Pete's sake! I was flabbergasted! From the back of the cell my sister called, "Really, owl? Then you must be the same owl Timmy shoved into the river, am I right?"

The dumb dodo! Now why did she have to go and remind a dangerous owl of that? But the owl just flashed its eye-cells and droned, "Assumption is correct."

"Then tell me, owl," I persisted, "when Maw Grimble bopped you, what did you do?"

"I deposited her and her mate into a pen with their dog called Rouser. I then returned to Other Ear-rr-rr-r—*awwwk-kk!*—*squawwk-k-k!*"

The owl made a noise like a garbage truck with a bottle stuck in its lifter. This was because another owl, a tall boss, had rolled up behind it and ordered, "Stop talking to prisoners. You will remove your violin from storage and report to the Grand Ballroom."

Our informer had to turn and roll away.

"Now why," said Mustard after the owls had gone, "why do you suppose Raoul wants an owl to play the violin?"

"I can tell you," said the detective, sitting back down on my collar. "Raoul and the baroness are throwing a party tonight. It's going to be a swell affair—so they claim. They've invited all the Elders from all over the country. They're going to have music and dancing and sandwiches."

"What? Raoul and Ratisha giving a party?" Fardels looked surprised. "Since when did those two stingy birds ever *give* anybody anything?"

"Oh, they're giving away plenty tonight," said the detective sourly. "They're going to give away doses of poison. Verity got a whiff of the stuff when the baroness was boiling it. Those Elders' lives aren't worth a plugged nickel."

"Lew," I said, "Lew, how can we warn them?"

"Too late, junior—the invites went out days ago. Any minute now, all the Elders should be starting to arrive."

I was miserable. But just then, a fresh worry came along. From deep in the core of the mountain, there was a long, low muttering. Suddenly the floor of the cell shuddered under our feet. Our bucket of slime tipped over. For a minute I hoped the walls would split open and set us free. But the muttering stopped as quickly as it had begun.

"What was that?" growled the bear.

"Only a little earthquake," said Lew. "Probably just a few timbers falling, down in the mine."

"A mine cave-in? Oh, no!" shrilled my sister.

"Gramp and all those miners are still down there!"

"Sorry, beautiful," said the ladybug. "I didn't mean to throw you any scare. But there's something funny going on inside this mountain. Just what, I only wish I knew."

The mysterious tremor had left us edgy and nervous. And Fardels kept looking sleepier all the time.

Day wore on, and the light—what could squeeze through our window-slot—inched slowly around to the west. Soon it would be Coronation Night.

From high above us, from the Hall's Grand Ballroom, faint music drifted. Well, something like music. We could hear the woody squawk of clarinets, the scrape of fiddles, a tuba's deep syrupy burp. The orchestra of owls was tuning up.

"Sis, what'll we do?" I pleaded with Verity. In the past, she had always told me.

"Timmy," she said, shaking her head, "we can't do anything. Raoul and Ratisha are going to poison all the Elders. Raoul is going to rule forevermore. It'll happen. Shelley predicted it would."

All this while, the snail had been napping in her back pocket. Now, hearing its name, it poked its tiny horns out over the pocket's rim. "I. Am. Sorry. To. Foresee. Such. A. Future," it apologized.

I sighed. "Aw, Shelley, the future's not your fault. What about *our* future? Have we got any?"

In Verity's cupped hand, the snail retreated into its chambers. We waited and watched. What was it doing in there? What movie of things to come was being projected on its walls? What did it hear from the slosh of invisible tides?

At last, its horns came back out, quivering. A high small faraway voice said:

Stone. Owls. Do. Not. A. Prison. Make.

Nor. Owlstone. Bars. A. Cage.

"Huh?" said Lew. "What does that prove? Isn't there anything more?"

But the prophet had spoken. Verity thanked it and put it back into her pocket. Now she was leaning against the floor-to-ceiling bars of our cell door, her dim eyes staring hopelessly down the corridor.

Mustard decided he'd test the prophecy, slamming himself against the thick stone bars of the door, dropping back. He just bopped his head uselessly. "These bars sure make a cage, if you ask me."

"It's no use," I said glumly, "we won't get out of here in a million y—"

My words quit, because my jaw had fallen. To my amazement, the round stone padlock on the bars was springing a leak.

I bounded to Verity's side and blinked at it. Out of its keyhole a fast stream of dirty water was trickling. In front of my eyes, the whole lock was dwindling like a snowball in July. A second later it turned to slush and it dropped with a *ploop!* to the floor.

"Well I'll be a monkey's uncle," said Lew Ladybug.

"The lock's been cracked!" Mustard trumpeted. "Who did it? Who cracked the lock?"

"It wasn't me," said Verity in puzzlement.

"What do we care who cracked it?" bellowed Fardels, suddenly wide awake. "The bars are melting too! Let's get out of here!"

The bear was right. As we watched, the floor-to-ceiling bars of the door grew thinner and thinner. Fardels shoved a paw against them and they tinkled to the floor, leaving a hole—which we quickly stepped out through.

But our jailer, the tall owl, had heard us. Speeding down the corridor it came, its beak darting underneath a wing, searching for its cone-shaped radio to sound an alarm.

Not able to see where she was going, Verity had stepped right into the jailer's path. The tall owl rumbled down on her and she bumped into it. Thrown off balance, the owl leaned forward on its ball-bearing, almost touching her.

"Sis, get away from that owl!" I yelled.

But then, in the gray stone chest of our jailer, a black hole opened. A hole as big around as a basketball. Just like the bars and the padlock, the owl was melting. I watched its body twist around on top of its rolling ball. Then its head collapsed, and the rest of its body trickled down into a puddle of slush. A mess of ice, fog, muck, and polluted water. The owl had gone back to its elements.

"Timmy, what's happening?" my sister wanted to know.

I started to tell her—and then it hit me. Hit me like a meteor.

The secret of Owlstone Hall.

I said, "Listen, everybody. I've got a plan..."

I talked fast, and when I'd finished, Lew looked at me with glee in his compound eyes. "Right as rain, kid," he said, "that's the secret, all right. Your plan is about as likely to succeed as a pig is likely to sing opera. But it may be our only chance."

My plan split us up into two bunches. Bunch One—Verity and the snail, Lew and I—would try to enter the ballroom. Mustard gave me the clasped little-finger handshake. Then we set off, Mustard commanding Bunch Two, the powerful brown bear loping at his side.

17. *The Crown Descends*

A night with no moon. Gray fog, filmy as tissue paper, surrounded Owlstone Hall, making the giant toadstool look like a gift that had been wrapped carelessly. In the stem of the Hall, the big front doors had been flung open, letting the hoots and squawks of the orchestra drift outside.

We had all made our way out of the dungeon. As mysteriously as the lock had melted, and the jailer owl, a hole had gaped in a wall for us to step out through. Now Bunch One—Verity and Shelley, Lew and I—were outside, crouched behind a screen of bushes, where we could watch the Hall's front doors.

Raoul and Ratisha stood in the doorway greeting the Elders. The baroness had on a long black dress that made her look as if she'd been dipped in ink. Raoul, in a purple tuxedo, looked shiny and round as an eggplant that's all set to rot. On his right shoulder, Chuckles, his pet muckhawk, littered the night with screams.

In a parking lot in front of the Hall, the Elders were pulling up in their horse-drawn buggies. The Elders were a white-haired lot—some women, some men—and they walked with dignity. Suddenly Lew, on my collar, gave a whistle. "Here comes the biggest shot of all."

Clipping and clopping along the driveway came the buggy of someone important. He had *two* white horses pulling him, with a driver for each. Right away, Lew knew him: Alder Appleyard, the eldest Elder.

"Are we close enough?" one of the horses inquired, turning his head to his driver. The buggy halted in front of us.

Twittering, Lew darted into the air. "Elder Appleyard!" he shrilled.

Out of the buggy's window poked a head without hair. A wrinkled, leathery face inspected us, and a kind voice said, "Why, Lew Ladybug. What can I do for you?"

"Plenty," said the detective, touching down on the buggy's windowsill. "You're risking your life to come here, do you know that?"

"Just as I thought," said the eldest Elder with a sigh. "And suppose I'd refused to come? No doubt an owl would have dragged me. Well, Lew, have you investigated? What does Raoul plan for us?"

"Sudden death. So don't eat anything. Don't drink anything. Just close your trap."

Then Lew introduced Verity and me to Appleyard, and he said I had a plan. He asked the Elder if he knew any way to smuggle us into the ballroom.

Appleyard pondered. Then his face lit into a grin. "They'll be my gift-bearers," he said, and he skimmed the hats from the heads of his two drivers—three-cornered hats, like what George Washington's soldiers wore—and he clapped them on me and Verity. The hats were too big. Mine slumped to my nose.

"You see," Appleyard went on, "every guest was told to bring Raoul a gift tonight. We weren't told why. Now, me, I've brought a crate of eating apples. You two children look good and strong— you can carry it. Keep your hats pulled down, and maybe Raoul won't notice you."

Oh-oh. This would be a pretty thin disguise! I felt a sudden chill, not just from the night. Lew took off to go scout the ballroom, saying he'd meet us inside. With the help of Appleyard's drivers, Verity and I boosted the crate up onto our shoulders. It must have weighed half a ton.

NOTE BY VERITY: *Exaggerating. Always exaggerating. The crate didn't weigh more than thirty pounds, if that much.*

Keeping our heads lowered, marching side by side in back of Appleyard, we approached the front steps of the Hall. Dry leaves crackled under our feet.

"Go slow, Timmy!" my sister whispered. "I can't see, you know!"

"Well I can't, either," I told the inside of my hat.

At the foot of the steps, an owl crossed Appleyard's name off a list. It droned, "Ascend and be greeted by their Vilenesses."

Up the steps we went. Panting under the weight of our cargo, we marched—with me quaking in my shoes—straight up to Raoul and the baroness.

"I'm here," I heard Appleyard say grimly.

"So you are," said the Dictator. "And what's this present you've brought?"

He was looking at our burden! I quaked harder. What if he recognized us? But luckily, Raoul had eyes only for the present. He didn't bother to check the faces under it.

"It's apples," said the Elder. "The best I can grow these days. Hard and green and riddled with worms. Rotten spots in 'em."

"Never mind," Raoul hooted. "I can bite around those. All right, old man, don't stand here blocking the doorway all night. Into the Hall with you!"

Verity shot at me under her breath, "Oh, the big lunk! I'd like to give him a karate chop!"

"Wait!" broke in the thin sharp voice of the baroness. "You—you bearer who just whispered! I know your voice. Have we not met?"

Holy smoke! I suddenly longed for a canyon to open up under me. I expected my sister to answer, "Sure, you know me—I'm the girl who used to scrub your pots."

But Verity just kept her head bent. "Met?" she murmured. "Oh, yes, we must have met *somewhere*. Let's go, brother!"

From behind us, another Elder, a gabby one, bounced forward and grabbed the baroness by the hand and said how much he'd been wanting to meet her. Before Ratisha could think twice, the two of us and our apple crate swept past her into the Hall.

"Well done," Appleyard said admiringly. "But—whew! That one was close!"

The Grand Ballroom, as it turned out, was the same big room where we'd first seen Raoul and Ratisha breakfasting. A few extra candles had been added, but the place was still dim as the inside of a tomb. The table, a hundred feet long, now overflowed with presents, and we added our rotten apples to its pile. An owlstone vase held a couple of table flowers—the kind that trapped and digested flies.

Tall owls, in gold-roped uniforms, lined every wall. There was music, but no one was dancing. The owl fiddlers—I recognized our friend with the dented head—were sawing mechanically. That orchestra could barely carry a tune, although I managed to make out "The Funeral

March" and "The Worms Crawl In, the Worms
Crawl Out." Somehow, in that dismal cold gray
ballroom, that music sounded absolutely right.
My tumbledown hat kept me looking at the
floor, and there I got a sudden shock. At my
feet—in the middle of the room—lay the familiar oval form of a small pond.
"*Cressida!*" I wailed. "What's happened to you?"
I flung myself down beside her. The water
woman didn't sparkle any longer. Her waters now
looked thick and green and full of soggy cigarette
butts. As I stared, a rainbow trout—Fiona, I
guessed—made a tired leap out of the pond and
sank back again.
Now Verity, too, was kneeling on the floor beside me, and Shelley, who had once lived in the
pond, poked its horns out of Verity's pocket and
said, "Oh. No. —Don't. Die. Beautiful. Mistress."
Dimly, the water woman tried to shape her face.
It looked vague and blurry and wavering. Cressida tried to thrust out a hand to us, but she
couldn't quite form her fingers.
"Is that—you—Timothy Tibb—Verity?" she
whispered.
"Cressida," I said urgently, "we'll get you out
of here."
Her faint lips made slow ripples. "Don't let
them—catch you—as they—caught me!"
"How did they catch you, Cressida?"
"The owls heard—that I—befriended you.

They—brought me here—in an egg."

By my side, Verity was weeping bitterly.

"Be careful," the liquid voice trickled. "Raoul—
is planning—something terrible . . ."

Then her eyes clouded over. Her face seemed
to sink and withdraw from us.

"Sis, this is awful!" I said. "Cressida is in a bad
way. She looks as if Raoul has been using her for
an ashtray, or something."

"Watch out, Timmy—I hear high heels coming!"

It was the baroness. She had been circling the
room, making talk to people, and now, still suspicious of Verity and me, she came over to our
side of the pond, clicking her ballroom shoes.

"Admiring the birdbath, are you?" she purred.
"Raoul's muckhawk often takes dips in it."

Verity kept her hat lowered, but she answered,
"Yes—it's the only thing of yours that we admire."

I could just imagine Ratisha squinting through
her monocle. "I beg your pardon?" she said as if
annoyed.

"She means," I quickly piped through my hat,
"it's what we MOST admire."

"So glad you do," said the baroness absently.
No doubt her eyes were roaming the room, looking for somebody more interesting to talk to than
a couple of apple-luggers. Soon, to my relief, she
murmured and was gone.

Raoul Owlstone, too, was touring the crowd. When he came to us, he snarled, "You cheap flunkies, those apples you brought me taste terrible. Don't swill too much of my lemonade."

Cringing deeper into my hat, I made him a bow.

Lew landed on my collar. "Just like you'd expect," he rasped. "It's to be a wholesale poisoning. I can't figure, though, how they plan to give out the poison. Nobody's keeled over yet, so it can't be in the lemonade. But something bad is supposed to happen at nine o'clock."

Out of the crowd swam another face we knew— Mustard's mother, Mrs. Weedblossom. Just as she'd hoped, she had found work as a waitress in the Hall. Wearing a short black dress and a wrinkly white starched cap, she had been going around the ballroom, a pitcher in her hand, refilling glasses with lemonade—the cheap kind made with powder and water. When she laid her green-and-brown eyes on us, she came right over and tossed me a smile that warmed me all over. "Aren't you the boy I met on the bridge?" she asked.

"Hello," I said.

"And who is your friend under the other hat?"

"Shhh-hh!" I warned, "don't give us away, please. That's only my sister. We're spying."

"How can I help?"

Lew raised a rasp from my collar. "Keep your ears unlatched, Mrs. Weedblossom, will you? Find

out how they're going to slip the poison to everybody."

"Poison? Don't tell me!" The friendly woman's
two-colored eyes looked ready to pop. But just
then came a new disturbance from down inside
the mountain. Under our feet a rumbling grew,
like a giant clearing his throat. A chandelier over
our heads started to sway. Next to where I stood
by the gifts table, a shudder ran down a wall.
People were screaming and yelling, "Oh! Oh!"

"It's an earthquake!"

"We're doomed!"

"Quiet!" bellowed the Dictator. "Maybe you're
doomed, all right, but not by a quake. It's nothing
but a little rumble down in the mine. This mountain is honeycombed with tunnels. They're all the
time caving in on somebody. Don't give it a
thought—we've plenty of miners to spare! Drink
your lemonade! Play, owls, play!"

The fiddlers grabbed their bows in their beaks
and began to assassinate a waltz. With a glance
that promised to help us, Mrs. Weedblossom went
on with her rounds.

My sister was growing anxious. "Timmy, is
Raoul really going to be Emperor? Well, is he?"

"How should I know?" I said with a groan. "Oh,
what in heck is keeping Mustard and Fardels?"

A grandfather clock in one corner of the ballroom kept on ticking—ticking faster than I liked.

Now all of a sudden it spoke with a slow, solemn chime—

CLUNNGG-GG-G-G-G!

Raoul, in the middle of the room, gave a hoot of glee. "One minute to nine!" With a sweep of one fat hand he shut off the orchestra.

"Now listen, all of you," he said commandingly. "I suppose you wonder why I've asked you here tonight. Well, it isn't because I like you. I'm sick and tired of you yapping Elders, always complaining about the way I run things. So I've asked you here to watch a little ceremony. I'm not going to be just your Dictator any more. When the clock strikes nine I'll crown myself Emperor. Emperor of Owlstonia!" The muckhawk on his shoulder screamed happily.

A giant gasp went rippling through the crowd. Someone cried, "Emperor? Owlstonia? Never!"

"Why should you be Emperor?" cried somebody else. "This is the Land of the Moonflower. Why change the name to Owlstonia?"

"Because I want to be Emperor," said Raoul. "Because soon there won't be a Moonflower anymore." He stood there rocking on his heels, a satisfied smirk on his face.

CLUNNGG-G-G! went the clock, for the second time.

Aspen Appleyard was striding forward, shaking a fist at the Dictator. "Raoul Owlstone, we've had enough of you! I don't know why we ever made you Dictator. Your baroness must have bewitched us. But you won't become Emperor! We won't stand for it!"

Raoul's little owl-eyes shrank to pinpoints. "Appleyard, you're a troublemaker. I'll soon settle you."

CLUNGG-G-G-G-G!

The hollow sound vibrated through the ballroom, shaking the owlstone walls. Four tall owls rolled into the room, each holding the corner of a cushion in its beak. In the middle of the cushion, a huge gray object squatted. It was studded with tall spears and cat's eye jewels. The owlstone crown.

At the sight of this menacing thing, Raoul was oozing happiness. "Clean out your ears, all of you! When the clock strikes the hour, I'll be Emperor—and all you Elders will be nobodies!"

CLUNG!—CLUNG!—CLUNG-G-G!—

"For crying out loud!" Lew rasped from my collar, "where in the Sam Hill are Mustard and the bear?"

CLUNG-G-G-G!

Now the Elders were going wild. Yelling and bawling, they made desperate grabs at the Dictator—but tall owls wheeled out from the walls and slung them away.

CLUNG-G-G!—

"Oh, I've got butterflies inside me," said Raoul

nervously. "I don't get to be Emperor every day!"

The ninth note of the clock echoed through the gloom, a long wobbling CLUNG-GG-GG-GG! that died in a hideous CLUNK.

Nine o'clock in Owlstonia.

We had lost.

"What are you waiting for, Raoul, you ninny?" the baroness jeered. "Take that crown and set it on your head!"

"All right. Don't rush me—I want to enjoy myself. Owls, give me the crown!"

Inside me, I felt as if a hard, cold sleet was falling. To think that I knew Raoul's secret—the secret of Owlstone Hall! And it didn't do the slightest bit of good!

Raoul was holding the crown in both hands, looking at it the way a hungry man studies a T-bone steak. With a grunt and a heave, he hoisted the great weight of stone and set it down squarely on his head.

A groan as tall as a tidal wave rolled through the room. The muckhawk, which had been fluttering in the air, settled down on the shoulder of the new Emperor.

"Has he done it?" asked my sister, ready to cry. "Has he crowned himself?"

I put my arm around her. I gulped down my own tears.

18. *The Flight of the Hawk*

The crown jabbed the air with its owlstone spears. Its snakeskin cap was glittering. Its jewels shone green-and-yellow, like cats' eyes.

From under it, Emperor Raoul the First gave a booming laugh. "We're going to celebrate! Elders, you'll all get some freshly made sandwiches. This waitress"—he pointed to Mrs. Weedblossom—"will pass among you with a tray of them. Make sure you each take one and chew it good, or you'll insult my hospitality."

"What?" cried Aspen Appleyard. "Only one tray of sandwiches for this crowd?"

"Don't worry, Your Eldership," said the baroness coldly. "There'll be enough to take care of you."

"So that's their plan!" shrilled Lew. "The poison's in the sandwiches! Let's warn everybody. I'll tell Mrs. Weedblossom. You kids help spread the word!"

"Eat! Eat!" shrieked the muckhawk on Raoul's shoulder, and the Emperor hooted, "That's right, eat, eat, everybody! Lobster salad! Lettuce and tomato! Enjoy!"

Verity and I scurried around the ballroom together, hissing to everybody, "The sandwiches— don't eat the sandwiches!" And you can imagine how flabbergasted those Elders were, to have a ladybug suddenly twitter into their ears, "One bite of that sandwich, kiddo, and it's your last."

Raoul kept urging the crowd to dig in, and yet Mrs. Weedblossom's tray, I was happy to see, stayed piled high. But when the waitress came to one crusty old fellow—Elder Elm Elderberry— she met trouble. While she was warning him, the Elder's face went red as a beet.

"See here, Owlstone," he stormed, "what's the meaning of this? Your waitress offers me a sandwich, and she tells me that if I taste it I'll die."

"Guards!" snarled the Emperor, "arrest her!" Two tall owls rolled out and fenced in Mrs. Weedblossom. With a flourish, the baroness swept the tray from the woman's hands and offered it to Elm Elderberry.

"Go ahead, Your Eldership," she purred. "Try the lobster salad."

"Don't mind if I do," said the Elder haughtily.

Just as the old fellow was going to bite into a mouthwatering poison-on-rye, a commotion broke out. Chuckles the muckhawk had leaped from the Emperor's shoulder. With a squawk and a thrash, the greedy bird swooped down and ripped the sandwich right out of Elderberry's hand.

"Crook!" shouted the Elder in a rage.

Under his crown, Raoul's smile fell apart like a melting popsicle. "Chuckles, baby! Don't swallow that! Spit out that sandwich, quick, before it's too late!"

"Do you mean to say," thundered Elderberry, "that a sandwich fit for an Elder isn't fit for a muckhawk?"

The baroness quickly rustled to his side. "No, no, Your Eldership, calm yourself. Of course there's nothing wrong with the sandwich. It is simply that lobster and muckhawks do not agree."

Perched on the chandelier, Chuckles Baby uttered a sickening burp. His snake-eyes crossed, and he began to croak horribly. Then he took off. Like a runaway comet, he started to roar around and around the ballroom, while everybody dived to the floor.

"Shoot him down!" hooted the Emperor. A guard with a pistol in its beak shot off a splatter of muck. It missed the whooshing bird, but it muddied a few of the guests.

What happened next was pretty awful. As Chuckles was making another circle around the ballroom, he let out one ear-splitting scream. From beak to tail, the muckhawk stiffened—right there

in the middle of the air. Swooping down, down, down in a lazy glide, his dead body went skimming out through one of the room's look-out slots and dived for the swallowing valley.

"Good riddance," grunted Lew.

"Eh!" cried Elderberry in amazement. "If that's what the lobster sandwiches do, I'll try the salami."

"No, don't, Your Eldership," sang out Mrs. Weedblossom from between her guards, "the salami can kill you, too!"

"Elderberry," said the Emperor, "you're a slow eater."

"And what if I had gobbled down that sandwich?" the Elder retorted. "Would I—just like that dirty bird—have gone whizzing around the room and out the window?"

"Owlstone," roared Appleyard, "I accuse you! You are trying to poison us all!"

"So you know," the Emperor said bitterly. "All right, it's true. I invited you stuffed shirts here only to wipe you out."

A gasp of horror came from the crowd.

"Monster!" shrieked a woman Elder. "Call my horse and buggy—I am leaving immediately!"

"Oh no, you're not," the Emperor glowered. "Nobody's leaving. One move out of any of you and I'll blast you to a blot."

In Raoul's hand, something black and stubby glittered. It wasn't anything made of owlstone.

Lew whistled from my collar. "He's got a .45!"

Now where in Other Earth could Raoul have found such a weapon? The pistol was deadlier, I knew, than any gun that splattered muck.

"You're first, Appleyard," Raoul said evenly. "Then I'll see about the rest of you. This will be just like shooting fish in a barrel."

His pistol came up and took careful aim at the eldest Elder's head. On the owlstone crown, the green-and-yellow jewels glittered like the eyes of dangerous cats.

I stood next to the table where our crate of apples lay. I didn't really think—there wasn't time—I just grabbed apples and I flung them with all my might at Emperor Raoul.

I never was much of a pitcher. Three or four of my fast balls went wild. But the last one scored. The apple—a really rotten item—struck the muzzle of Raoul's pistol with a plop. The Emperor stood there, his mouth open, looking stunned, while the business end of his gun kept dripping applesauce.

I couldn't help laughing like crazy—but then my laugh kind of gurgled to a stop. A tall owl was standing to the left of me. Another stood to Verity's right. From behind us, the baroness stepped up and knocked off our hats.

"Ha! It's *them!* I might have known!" she shrilled.

"You kids again!" Raoul grated, his face turning blue with rage. Slowly and deliberately he wiped off his pistol with a dirty handkerchief. Now the mean little hole in the gun's muzzle was looking me straight in the eye.

From my collar, Lew talked rapidly. "Listen, Owlstone, are you itching for a wooden overcoat? I'm telling you, you hurt one hair of these kids and—"

"So long, bug," Raoul said coldly. "You can take these pestering kids along with you."

Paralyzed, I watched the trigger squeeze. Close by my side, my sister cried my name.

A blast of fire came out of the pistol's throat. Only it didn't touch us—it hit the ceiling. A slim arm of water had flashed out at Raoul's hand. With an effort, Cressida Pond had lifted an arm and swatted the pistol. Now her waterfall voice spoke: "Leave those children alone!"

She flipped the gun into the air and her waters caught it. It splashed in, gurgled, and disappeared.

Behind us, the baroness Ratisha was screeching quietly.

And then it happened.

From outside the Hall came an ear-splitting CRACK-KK-KK!—like something breaking. A sound that must have reached to the mountain's floor. A wave of silver light surged in through the window-slots, flattening the shadows back against the walls.

"Timmy, I can see something!" Verity shouted. "Bright light. REALLY bright. Are they here?"

"They're here, Sis! They've done it!" I capered around and warbled in my joy.

I raced to the nearest window-slot. A beautiful scene was unfolding before my eyes. Up on the mountain, hundreds of miners had circled the base of the Moonflower's huge dome. They were smashing away with picks and shovels, and the hated glass bubble was crumbling in to smithereens. As they worked, they were roaring their happiness. Slabs of glass coasted down the mountainside, and some of them whanged onto the roof of Owlstone Hall. I could see, right in the thick of the fun, Fardels and Mustard and Dr. Weedblossom. The brown bear was smashing away at the dome with a fierce pick. A trim lady— it must have been Gran—was swinging away with a shovel by his side.

In the roof of the giant bubble a jagged crack had opened, and out of it shone a blinding stream of light. As I watched, dazzled, the crack widened, and with a tremendous groan the dome split into halves and those halves rolled slowly aside.

And now, like some immense bird hatching, the Moonflower itself was unfolding, untwisting its cramped vines, climbing the sky. All over the mountaintop, silver blossoms were popping open like a thousand colossal firecrackers on a string. Every time one opened, it gave out a beam brighter than any searchlight's, and it made a chiming sound. The blossoms were alive. They were whispering, *Room to bloom! At last! Some room to bloom!* With a sound like the gong that must have begun Creation, still another blossom was opening—the highest blossom, the biggest one of all. There on the mountain's peak it unfolded its petals, glowing like a kindly bonfire consuming the world.

19. *The Secret of Owlstone Hall*

As the Moonflower opened its blossoms, the Elders were gazing up out of the window-slots of the ballroom, sniffing the rich perfume. They were marveling:

"It's magnificent!"

"Spectacular!"

"Well, I'll be jingoed, I will!"

Being a wrestling champ had helped Verity capture one of the better window-slots. Her upturned face was silvered with Moonflower light. Even *her* eyes could take in that brilliant glow. I waited to hear what she'd say—

"Timmy, something cold is going drip, drip, drip on the back of my neck!"

The drops were slush. They were falling in a steady downpour from the ceiling overhead. I glanced around the room. Wherever the light of the Moonflower was striking, owlstone was starting to melt and drip.

"Ho-ho!" Appleyard chortled, "just look at that stone egg!"

Outside in the air, one of the owlstone copters that circled the Hall was in trouble. It was dissolving like a snowball in the sun. A zigzag crack shot down it, then the whole egg split in two, dumping out several owls who fell, bottom-heavy like raindrops, straight down for a quarter of a mile. Then the halves of the shell spun after them. Seconds later, the other egg cracked open, too, and followed its companion down into the mixing-bowl of the valley.

Just in time, I yanked Verity back from the window-slot before a ton of melted ceiling fell, missing us by inches. Now the whole of the Grand Ballroom was blazing with silvery light. Walls were turning into waterfalls. The ceiling was trickling a steady rain. Cressida Pond had slushy icebergs.

And me, I was hopping with happiness. Things were turning out just the way I'd hoped. The collapse of the dome over the Moonflower had shattered Raoul's greedy dreams. In the middle of the room, the Emperor stood petrified. His crown was dribbling a stream of gray slush down over his brow, and its spikes were bending like wet grass.

"This was your secret, Emperor!" I taunted him. "Moonflower light melts owlstone. Turns it back to what it's made out of—polluted water, ice, fog, muck. You were afraid of a flower, all right—the Moonflower."

Raoul puffed out his chest. "You think I'm finished, do you? Think you won't have Raoul Owlstone to kick around any more? Think again! Didn't the snail make me a prophecy? I'm to rule till the last day of time!"

From Verity's back pocket, Shelley had pricked up its horns. Now, in its shrill, piping voice, it repeated:

Raoul. Shall. Rule. Till. Owlstone. Walls. Dissolve—

"Yeah," Lew said gleefully, "and now they're dissolving, all right."

"But go on, snail," the Dictator begged in a whining voice. "That wasn't ALL you said!"

And. Raoul. Rule. Till. Moonflower. Mount. Revolve, the snail finished.

"How about that!" Raoul chortled. "I'm still the boss of this country. And I'm to rule, the snail says, till the mountain turns around. But it isn't ever going to!"

With a look as if she had bitten into a lemon, the baroness was squinting out through a lopsided window-slot. "Raoul," she said worriedly, "I hate to tell you this, but didn't Owlstone Hall always face *west*?"

"Whaa-aa—?" The self-crowned Emperor leaped to the slot, gasped, and staggered backwards as if hit by a football team. "We're facing EAST! I can see the zoo! This is impossible! A mountain can't do an about-face!"

"Sure it can, chubby," the detective grated. "Especially *this* mountain. The Moonflower's roots go deep. Ever since you clapped a dome over it the big plant has been turning every which way looking for room. It must have twisted the mountain around by a hundred and eighty degrees. I'd bet that, because you mined so much muck out of it, you hollowed out the mountain and made it easy to twist."

Verity clapped her hands. "Then that's what all those earthquakes meant! The mountain was starting to revolve!"

The Baroness von Bad Radisch was seething with rage. "How stupid!" she snarled. "Can mere *children*"—she ground out the word with hatred—"stop an army? Destroy an empire? *Children*, one of them blind, and a bear and a snail and a bug?"

"Sure they can." Lew chuckled, enjoying himself. "Now just hand over your pink eyepiece, baby, and tell that fatso next to you to give up, too."

"Surrender?" cried the baroness. "To an insect? Never! Raoul is an Emperor and I—I am a baroness of royal blood!"

Lew took a long time laughing a laugh that wasn't nice to hear. "You can drop that phony

baroness stuff with me, Sadie Spittlespoon." He
grinned wolfishly. "Yeah, that's right—I know
your given name. Oh, I've read the New Jersey
State Police blotter on you and your partner. Hugo
Pugh, isn't he really called?"

"Great snakes!" exclaimed Elm Elderberry.
"Then Ratisha is no more a baroness than my
Aunt Tillie's goat?"

"The goat," said the detective coolly, "probably
has a lot more class. These two are just a couple
of small-time hoods who once ran a crooked massage parlor in Union City. While Sadie here was
giving the customers a rubdown, Hugo was rubbing out their wallets and watches. One day the
cops gave 'em the chase, and the pair of 'em
jumped down a sewer and flowed out to sea. It
was our tough luck that there was a full moon,
and they fell through a door in the ocean, and
landed in this world."

"Don't think I'm a worry-wart," said Verity,
"but look down. Isn't the floor dissolving under
our feet?"

She was right. Besides, the walls of the ballroom
were bulging alarmingly. With a terrible SPLOP!
the chandelier let go of the ceiling and shattered
all over the floor.

"TIMOTHY! VERITY! ARE YOU ALL
RIGHT?"

This shout had come from my grandfather. He

and Gran were battling their way in through the slushy water. The mourning dove from under the dome sat on Gran's arm. Mustard, too, came wading in, and Dr. Weedblossom in a muck-streaked coat of white.

"Gramp!" cried my sister as he swept her into his arms.

Dr. Weedblossom was skidding around the melting floor, studying the damage with interest. "Always thought houses shouldn't be made out of owlstone," he remarked.

"Hi, brother," I greeted Mustard, giving him our secret handshake. "Have any trouble getting the people out of the mine?"

"Naw. That Moonflower seed of your sister's worked like a charm. All we had to do was shine it like a flashlight, and it melted every owl we met. Just the way it melted the lock on our cell, and the bars. Boy, were those miners ever glad to be rescued! So was my dad."

"And so was I." Gramp beamed, putting one arm around me and one around Mustard.

The younger kid grinned. "Tim and Verity and Shelley and Lew did the risky part."

"But where's Fardels?" I wanted to know. "And what's happened to that Moonflower seed, by the way?"

"Fardels is rescuing the zoo animals. Raoul had 'em all slung back into the meat locker. As for that seed, just look—your grandmother is putting it to use!"

It was a joy to watch Gran, with the glowing seed in her fist, marching along the ballroom's walls, dissolving owls. She'd go up to a tall one, shine the seed in its face and cry, "Oh, go be a puddle, you corny thing, you!" The owl's head would nod and its whole body would slump, and it would flush down out of its uniform into a puddle.

Working her way down the line of owls, Gran arrived face to face with Mrs. Weedblossom. Gran stopped. She stared.

"Why, Ottoline!" she yelled.

"*Mother!*" Mrs. Weedblossom yelled back.

What went on? We gaped in amazement as the two women swooped into each other's arms. When Gran was able to talk again, she turned to Verity and me, her eyes wet with gladness, and she said, "Twins, don't you know who this it? It's your very own mother!"

I was so stunned I could have fallen through the floor. In fact, I almost did, because a great hole had opened up next to me. I gazed in wonder at Mrs. Weedblossom, who was doing the same to me. I'd always liked her a lot. But, so help me, this was too much to understand at the moment. I didn't know whether to laugh or cry.

As for Mustard, the kid was ogling me as if I

was something out of a flying saucer. "Timothy—
then you and I really *are* brothers?"

"We really are, I guess," I said dumbfoundedly.
Now I knew why, when Gran had first laid eyes
on Mustard, the younger kid had looked familiar
to her. He had mustard-colored hair and two-
colored eyes just like his mother. Just like *our*
mother, I mean.

NOTE BY VERITY: *In case you're wondering—years
ago when Timmy and I were babies, our father, Mr.
Tibb, had died. Then Mother had accidentally fallen
off the Cape May ferryboat and disappeared. But Gran
and Gramp hadn't ever given up hope of finding her.
They'd kept on looking. That was why Gramp had built
the catamaran. They had wanted to sail in the neighborhood of the ocean where Mother had last been seen.
Mother, of course, had fallen through a door at sea,
and she had been washed up in the Land of the Moonflower. There, she had soon met and married Dr. Weedblossom. So you see, Mustard was only our half-brother.
But he was as good as a whole one, any day.*

"For Pete's sake!" Lew Ladybug exploded, "save
the family reunion, will you? This whole joint is
falling down around our ears!"

"Let's blow, Ratty!" bellowed Raoul, grabbing
the fake baroness by the arm and splashing toward the door.

"Never mind them!" Dr. Weedblossom shouted.
"Outside, everyone! This house will collapse in a
minute and a half!"

But the Elders just milled in confusion. To add to the uproar, Fardels came busting in through a soggy wall, with the whole pack of romping, liberated animals at his heels. Ostriches, zebras and monkeys were slopping around in the slush, having a fine time, filling the room with bleating and honking and trumpeting.

But now the Grand Ballroom's floor was tilting down at a sharp angle. A river of slush was racing downhill toward the door. A few Elders struggled away in the door's direction, but waves crashed, knocking them off their feet. The floor was pitching like the deck of a boat getting ready to turn turtle. A wave slapped me across the shoulder and flicked off Lew. Now the detective was adrift on the surface of the water. Crooking a finger, I scooped him to safety and shook him off and set him back on my collar to dry.

But this was bad. I'd expected Lew to take command of us—to lead us out of the Hall. For the moment, the detective was too groggy. What to do? We were lost—unless somebody showed us the way.

Somebody?

Anybody. Even me!

Desperately, I shot a glance around the room. The only furniture that hadn't melted—it was wood and not owlstone—was the table a hundred feet long. Overturned, it lay on its back, legs up, floating like an island in the flood.

"THE TABLE!" I bawled. "Climb aboard the table, everybody!"

It took a lot of bawling to make myself heard. Dr. Weedblossom urged Mrs. Weedblossom—was she really my mother?—onto the table, and he sloshed through the hip-deep water and saw to Gran and Gramp. Mustard helped Verity. The two dozen Elders clambered aboard, and the brown bear rounded up the last of the struggling animals.

"We're leaving, Cressida!" I yelled to the water woman. "Can you flow along with us?"

"Right behind you, Timothy!" she chimed.

Then we took off. The ballroom floor propelled us. With a lurch, it pitched downward at a fierce slant, and the table started moving down a steep hill, like a loaded sled, bumping and jolting and gathering speed as it went. I was sitting up front like a captain, between the two front legs, but of course there was no way to steer. All I could do was shout, "Hang on, everybody!"— and hang on for dear life myself. At my back some of the Elders were screeching louder than the rhinos, cheetahs, and baboons.

As the table picked up momentum, carving a fast path through the water—which was bobbing with owl heads—cold slush sprayed past us left and right. Whooshing along like a comet, we shot out of the ballroom and down a corridor, making for the big front doors. They were bolted, but that didn't stop us. We shot right on through those two slabs of slush like a cannonball passing through a couple of bricks of butter. Down over the front steps we sped. Cressida Pond flowed onward, by our side. Like a canoe shooting rapids, we went bounding along a dirt road that led down the mountainside. Rivers of melted owlstone thundered around us, helping to sweep our vessel on. We skimmed halfway down the mountain before the mud slowed us to a stop.

Fascinated, I gazed back up the mountainside. The stem of the Hall was twisted like a corkscrew. The roof drooped like a toadstool in the sun.

From under us, the ground gave a rumble. As if trying to shrug off something it could no longer stand, Moonflower Mountain was giving itself a final, heartfelt shake.

With a rubbery shudder, Owlstone Hall slithered clean off its foundations and went waddling out to the tip of the mountain's nose, dragging its ponderous factory. There, for a second, the huge house balanced, teetering back and forth. Then, like a ton of soft snow dropping off a rooftop in spring, it plunged on over the edge.

Silence.

Then a shivering BAA-AL-LL-LL-OOOO-MM-M-M!

I stared down into the valley. A mess of small

gray icebergs covered its floor. The giant toadstool had burst to a thousand bits.

At the side of the road, a fragment of the owlstone crown was melting. From the bottom of its puddle, something shone—one bright green cat's-eye jewel. All that remained of the Empire of Owlstonia. Somehow, even though I collect souvenirs, I didn't feel like stooping to pick it up.

20. *A Different Light*

Sprawled on my back in the warm grass, I watched the windmill moths paddling up and down the mountainside. Moonflower Mountain wasn't the only thing that had turned around. Just days ago, back in New Jersey, Verity and I had felt completely alone. But now we had family and friends galore.

Our picnic cloth had been spread on the shore of Cressida Pond. In her new home at the foot of the mountain, Cressida was once again so clear that you could see Finn and Fiona cruising around in her.

"No need," said my grandfather, thinking out loud, "no need to live under clouds or in shadow. Now, you young ones—all of us—can live by the sun and by the moon and by the Moonflower. By a light with a tinge of wonder to it. By a steady, clear, forgiving kind of light."

"Agamemnon," Gran said gently, reaching an arm around him, "sometimes I believe you love to hear yourself talk."

"Places, everyone!" cried Mother. "It's time for Fardels's cake!"

The birthday cake had wild honey frosting. On its top layer stood a miniature brown bear leading a column of animals. Last in line was a ribbon of green frosting. Boswell Boa Constrictor.

"That's the ss-ss-ss-spitting image of me," hissed the snake.

Verity's eyes were dancing behind the new glasses Dr. Weedblossom had made for her. "Listen up, will you? Shelley Snail has a fortune for Fardels!"

From the palm of my sister's hand came the poet and prophet's clear, small voice:

For. Fardels. Bear. And. All. Who. Hold. Him. Dear.
This. Day. Begins. One. Honey. Of. A. Year.

"Why," said my mother, "that includes everyone in the Land. And the animals. Fardels, you're doing a great job at the zoo. All the animals say they've never been so happy."

"They'd better say so, the bums," growled the bear, doffing a hat that said CHIEF KEEPER on it.

"And what about Lew?" my sister put in. "Isn't he doing a great job, too?"

Perched on a blade of grass, the Land of the Moonflower's Official Detective blushed redder under his spots. "Forget that stuff, angel," he rasped. "I do my job. Not that there's much crime around here these days."

It was true—the worst criminals had been banished. Raoul and Ratisha—somehow, I couldn't think of them by their real names—had been sent back to Earth to the Grimbles' parsnip farm. That had been the punishment the Elders had handed them. They had had to replace Verity and me at digging parsnips and licking labels and shipping the famous punch to its seventy thousand faithful sufferers. And I figured that Raoul and Ratisha and the Grimbles and Rouser ought to get along fine. Somehow, they all deserved each other.

Later that day, after the Elders had got together and elected Gramp one of them, he and I were collecting chestnuts on the mountainside. We stopped to look down over the trees, all golden and orange and red. High places still gave me a few cold shakes. But I was working on them.

All of a sudden a great rustling stole out of the air, and the sky glowed with a thousand wands of light. Gramp and I looked up to see the Moonflower unfolding its blossoms to the early-rising moon. It was as if a bunch of silver bonfires were burning on the mountainside. As if they'd been burning there since the opening day of time.

"Tell me something, Tim," said my grandfather. "You and Verity don't ever get homesick for Earth, do you?"

"No sir," I said truthfully. As far as I knew, we

hadn't even thought of that.

"Then you won't mind staying in this country"—he spoke his next word carefully—"*for-ever?*"

I picked up a chestnut and skimmed it down over the treetops and watched it disappear.

"I guess that will be long enough," I said.

NEW AGERS
& Other
Cosmic Types

VGM Careers for You Series

NEW AGERS
& Other
Cosmic Types

Blythe Camenson

VGM Career Books

Chicago   New York   San Francisco   Lisbon   London   Madrid   Mexico City
Milan   New Delhi   San Juan   Seoul   Singapore   Sydney   Toronto

Library of Congress Cataloging-in-Publication Data

Camenson, Blythe.
    Careers for new agers & other cosmic types / Blythe Camenson.
        p.   cm.
    ISBN 0-658-00189-2 (hardcover) — ISBN 0-658-00190-6 (paperback)
    1. Vocational guidance—Unted States. 2. New Age persons—
Vocational guidance—United States.   I. Title: Careers for new agers and
other cosmic types. II. Title. III. Series.

HF5382.5.U5 C25187 2001
331.7'02—dc21   00-66815
                                                                      CIP

VGM Career Books

A Division of The McGraw·Hill Companies

1 2 3 4 5 6 7 8 9 0   LBM/LBM   0 9 8 7 6 5 4 3 2 1

ISBN 0-658-00189-2 (hardcover)
      0-658-00190-6 (paperback)

This book was set in Goudy Old Style by ImPrint Services
Printed and bound by Lake Book

McGraw-Hill books are available at special quantity discounts to use as
premiums and sales promotions, or for use in corporate training programs.
For more information, please write to the Director of Special Sales, Professional
Publishing, McGraw-Hill, Two Penn Plaza, New York, NY 10121-2298. Or contact
your local bookstore.

This book is printed on acid-free paper.

To Richard Ryal, who has just
the right amount of New Age
mixed with the solid, old-
fashioned, traditional age, a
hearty thank-you for getting
me started on this project.

Contents

Acknowledgments

The author would like to thank the following professionals for providing insight into their careers in the alternative world of the New Age:

Maggie Anderson, Astrologer

Rev. Jennifer Baltz, Minister, Spiritual Teacher, and Counselor

Cheryl-Lani Branson, Therapist/Career Counselor

Theresa Bulmer, Health Food Store Manager

Robert T. Carroll, Professor of Philosophy, Writer

SuZane Cole, Dream Interpreter

Rev. Paula Cooper, Spiritual Counselor

Elizabeth English, Feng Shui Consultant

Joseph Hayes, Freelance Writer

Joyce Kennett, Bookstore Owner

Charles Lewis, Horticultural Therapist

"Mara," Psychic

Richard Mattson, Horticultural Therapy Professor

James Miller, Yoga Therapist

Joe Nickell, Paranormal Investigator

Victoria Pospisil, Eastern Healing Arts Practitioner/
Licensed Massage Therapist

Lynne White Robbins, Psychic

Nancy Stevenson, Horticultural Therapist

Abigail Trafford, Writer for the *Washington Post*

Mary Tribble, Event Planner

Roy Upton, Herbalist

Rita Valenti, Tarot Reader

NEW AGERS
& Other
Cosmic Types

CHAPTER ONE

Inspirational Careers in an Expanding Field

"*T*his is the dawning of the Age of Aquarius, Age of Aquarius," or so the song lyrics from the musical *Hair* proclaim. Fact is, no one really knows when the so-called New Age—the Age of Aquarius—dawned, or when it will end.

The composers of *Hair* thought it began "when the moon is in the seventh house and Jupiter aligns with Mars." British astrologer Nicholas Campion gives his own opinion in his book *The Great Year: Astrology, Millenarianism, and History in the Western Tradition*: "It is the shift of the constellations that forms the astronomical basis for the twentieth-century 'New Age' belief in the coming Age of Aquarius, expected to begin when the Sun rises in the constellation Aquarius at the vernal equinox."

When's that? This same astrologer conducted extensive of research trying to answer that question. He found fifty-nine different opinions on when the beginning of the New Age is— from the year 1457 all the way up to the year 3550.

So, maybe the real New Age didn't start in the late sixties or early seventies, as so many of us thought. Maybe it hasn't even started yet and we're still in the Age of Pisces. But something started about three decades ago and is persisting now.

Most "New Agers" are hard pressed to provide a definition for the term *New Age*. Some believe the New Age movement began as an offshoot of the hippie days; others think that it could be a by-product of that time but that it developed on its own, independently.

Some feel the New Age will be a period of greater self-knowledge with a focus on the improvement of the world for all who dwell here. (But, as one astrologer dryly said, "On the other hand . . . knowing Aquarians, I would think there will be millions of started and unfinished projects by the time we are ready to roll into the Age of Capricorn."

Some cynics feel that the term New Age is synonymous with radical thinking; others brand New Agers as far-out flakes. For the purpose of this book, we'll consider New Age to be anything slightly alternative to the well-established mainstream. This covers communications—with and without the benefit of electronic means—alternative medicine and health, merchandising, teaching, spirituality, and the paranormal.

What Makes a New Ager?

To answer this, we must first understand that the whole isn't always equal to the sum of its parts. An interest—whether passing or fervent—in New Age subjects doesn't necessarily mean a person is a New Ager and only that. Just because you check your horoscope every morning doesn't mean you'd visit a Chinese herbalist to cure your stomach ulcer. And though you might have arranged the furniture in your home based on Feng Shui principles, you have no intention of calling a psychic to help you invest your recent inheritance.

Having said that, there probably are some people who embrace every aspect of New Age, who reject mainstream ideas and practices entirely for the nontraditional every time.

How far into the realm of New Age you've stepped doesn't really matter, though. If you're reading this book, chances are you like the idea of turning your avocation into a vocation. Even a foothold in one interest area could be translated to a viable career—a light but lucrative livelihood. These careers appeal to

spiritual students who want more adventure in their lives. Such livelihoods are often profitable and gratifying, generating and sustaining a positive, uplifting attitude in both practitioners and clients. We all have to earn a living. So why not do it in a field we love?

The Employment Outlook

In a capitalistic society, one where profit and the bottom line reign supreme, New Age is not just a funky approach to life that old folks patiently tolerate in the young. Early hippies might have eschewed the never-ending quest for the almighty dollar, but today's New Agers aren't as impractical. Business folks and entrepreneurs have long known that where there is an interest, there is a dollar sign, too.

Astrology columns and books, psychic hot lines, metaphysical bookstores, health food stores, and a variety of New Age services and service providers, such as Feng Shui and alternative medicine consultants, abound. Any average American town today is likely to have someone offering psychic reading and astrology classes, past-life regression workshops, and healing lectures. Someone's offering something that is wanted—and making money from it. That's nothing to be ashamed of.

It's the tried-and-true principle of supply and demand. There are needs out there and people willing to provide for those needs. If enough people want little doohickeys in the shape of pyramids or need pouches of crystals for whatever metaphysical purpose, there is no reason someone shouldn't be on the other end, manufacturing and selling this merchandise—and for a profit.

Similarly, it's the people seeking psychic readings or answers from the stars who keep psychic readers in business. It's a relationship grounded in history and not restricted only to New Age. It's how society has sustained itself over time.

The conclusion? The employment outlook will continue to be good—way into the next age—the Age of Capricorn.

Heaven-Sent Jobs for New Agers

A glance through the table of contents will give you an overview of some of the possibilities. The options don't end here, though, and a dedicated career investigator will undoubtedly cover additional job alternatives. Here are just a few to get you started.

Psychic Reader

This covers everything from astrologer and tarot card reader to a "for entertainment purposes only" psychic on a phone hot line.

Mind and Body

This is a huge field, covering nontraditional approaches for the most part, such as acupuncture, armomatherapy, reflexology, Rolfing, Reiki, herbology, hypnotherapy, past life regression, and much more.

Communications

Although the methods of communicating covered in this section are along the lines of the traditional—print, Internet, and so forth—the topics covered are not necessarily so. Closely related to the self-help field, metaphysics has spawned many how-to volumes. These are written by writers, edited by editors, and published by publishers. In addition, there are New Age magazines, newsletters, and other sorts of publications, all needing experienced writers and editors who are in the know.

Throughout this book, in addition to career specifics, you'll find firsthand accounts from real people working in the actual professions. What better way to learn about a calling than straight from the medium's mouth (so to speak).

Do You Have the Necessary Qualifications?

New Age careers range from those that require licensing to those that cannot be legally defined. Each field has its own requirements, and these are covered in the chapters ahead.

It is most important that the New Age enthusiast carry that enthusiasm into his or her work. New Age is almost synonymous with upbeat, positive attitudes. Needless to say, an open mind and a caring attitude will add to your qualifications for most New Age endeavors.

Salaries

Salaries can range from the modest to the glamorous. Some publications, for example, don't pay their freelance writers very much. But psychic hot lines, on the other hand, can charge hefty hourly fees; so do acupuncturists and other alternative medicine providers.

New Agers do not need to undervalue their products and services. Just as in any field, business savvy—knowing how to make money—is important here. With many of the professions covered in this book, the New Age entrepreneur is free to set his or her own fee schedule.

The Job Hunt

For those of you not wanting to start out in your own businesses, let your fingers do the walking—through the Yellow Pages and across your keyboard—as you conduct your on-line searches. Search words such as *jobs* and the name of the field that interests you, such as *New Age publishing,* will bring hundreds and thousands of website listings to your screen.

For More Information

At the end of most chapters and in the Appendix, you will find resources for further information: professional associations you can contact, reference books to consult, and training programs in which you can enroll.

CHAPTER TWO

Insight and Second Sight
Careers for Psychic Readers

W ho doesn't want to know what the future holds or what life is like on the other side? Those with the power (or creativity) to see "beyond" have a huge and eager audience waiting for them.

Psychic Reader is a general term that covers a range of activities. Let's first look at some definitions.

Psychic Phenomena

When referred to in relation to the human mind, psychic phenomena usually fall into two categories: extrasensory perception and psychokinesis.

Extrasensory Perception (ESP)

ESP is the ability to obtain information without the benefit of the five senses. It is usually split into two subcategories: telepathy and clairvoyance. (But you probably already divined that.)

Telepathy is the ability to perceive someone else's thoughts. *Clairvoyance* is the ability to sense an object or event outside the range of the five senses. In general, someone who can do either or both of the two is considered to be psychic.

Zener cards were specially designed to test ESP ability. A deck consists of a series of five cards, each having one of five symbols—star, square, circle, plus sign, or three wavy lines.

Psychokinesis (PK)

PK is the ability of the mind to influence animate or inanimate matter without the use of any known physical or sensory means. In other words, it is the ability to move or alter matter by thought alone. Psychokinesis includes:

- *Telekinesis*—the ability to move objects

- *Levitation*—the ability to overcome gravity and rise or float in the air

- *Materialization*—causing a spirit or the like to take a bodily form

- *Poltergeist activity*—mysterious events such as rappings, overturned furniture, and flying objects

- *Paranormal healing*—the ability to cure disease or affliction by no known scientific means

Spiritualism

Spiritualism is a system of beliefs focused on efforts to communicate with the dead or with spirits. *Channelers* facilitate communications between the earthly and spirit worlds. Some channelers also attempt contact with extraterrestrials or spirits from ancient mythical societies, as well as with the recently deceased. Channelers are also sometimes referred to as mediums.

Automatic writing is a way for spirits to communicate with earth. A channeler, or medium, will hold a pen and pad of paper, then enter a trance. This allows the spirit to express his or her thoughts, using the medium's hand.

Other Psychic Readings

Other psychic readers might involve themselves in the following activities:

- Astrology

- Tarot cards

- Auras

- Dreams

- Palmistry

- Numerology

Astrology

Astrology is a system that claims the positions and aspects of celestial bodies, such as the moon and planets, have a direct influence on human and other earthly affairs.

Most people are familiar with the twelve signs of the zodiac and, in particular, with the sign that corresponds to the date of their own birth. In the late sixties and early seventies, "What's your sign?" was a common, let's-get-acquainted question. Those who asked it usually knew what the responses meant. "Oh, wow, you're a Virgo? I'm a Taurus. A match made under the stars!"

Astrologers plotting horoscopes based on the exact time and place of birth feel they can produce a very personal reading about the character, strengths, weaknesses, and potentials of an individual and can also predict how all sorts of relationships will work out, including lovers, husbands and wives, friends, and business partners.

Although astrology might have been around as far back as Mesopotamian civilization in 3000 B.C., western astrology did

not reach its peak until the influence of the ancient Greeks during 330 to 323 B.C. From there it was adopted into Islamic culture, which later influenced western astrology during the Middle Ages.

Even the rise of the Christian church, which tried to prohibit the interest in and practice of astrology, could not prevent astrology from being used and developed by the populace and important academics. The universities at Florence and Paris, among others, all had chairs of astrology in the late Middle Ages.

The view of creation that resulted from the discoveries of the astronomer Copernicus (1473–1543) led to the decline of astrology and its discrediting as a scientific discipline. Even though most scientists today reject astrology as groundless superstition, interest in this form of understanding human nature remains strong.

And to the astrologer wanting to make a living at this craft, that's good news. Some astrology books routinely become bestsellers. Astrology columns abound in newspapers, magazines, and at on-line websites and on-line services such as America Online.

Almost everyone at one time or another has looked up his or her own horoscope, even if just for a laugh. And then there are the serious believers, who consult the stars on a regular basis before planning day-to-day activities or major life changes.

Astrologers often work privately with these people, doing charts and readings, either through on-line websites, on the telephone, or face to face in home offices or rented office space.

If you have studied the nuances of astrology, have become an expert in the field, and can write, then you can land yourself a column or two or come up with a new angle for a book. Add some private readings to the mix and you can create for yourself a fulfilling part- or full-time career. (Read Maggie Anderson's firsthand account later in this chapter.)

There are several subspecialties of astrology:

- *Event or electional astrology* considers possible dates and times for an upcoming event and chooses the most beneficial

one according to aspects of the sun, moon, and planets to the natal horoscope of the person involved.

- *Horary astrology* is an ancient method of divination in which the astrologer constructs a horoscope chart for the time a question is asked and finds the answer in the chart. It's good for all kinds of specific questions that are not answerable via a natal horoscope. For example, the natal horoscope can identify the general area for a career, but only horary can answer a question such as "Will I get the job with XYZ company?" It is also used to find lost objects, animals, and people.

- *Mundane astrology* is concerned with interpreting and predicting public events, such as political and economic developments at national and local levels; natural disasters, such as earthquakes; or man-made disasters, such as the Oklahoma bombing.

- *Natal astrology* interprets the horoscope of an individual based on the date, time, and place of birth. It also compares horoscopes of two or more people for compatibility.

Tarot Cards

The actual origin of tarot cards is not certain. Some believe they first appeared in medieval Europe; others have uncovered legends that suggest they migrated with Gypsies from India. Others believe they are left over from the ancient Egyptian Book of Thoth.

Tarot cards are used by some to get a glimpse of the future; some seek advice in working out problems and weighing decisions. Whether the cards work or not is up to the individual. Any tool that helps an individual seek self-awareness can't be easily dismissed.

Tarot readers work similarly to astrologers, providing their readings electronically or in person. Often astrologers or tarot

card readers combine talents and offer services in several different areas, including the following.

Auras
Some people feel that each individual has a visible aura outlining his or her body, an aura that by its color and strength expresses health or sickness, life or death, and so on.

Dreams
Professional psychologists and psychiatrists and laypeople alike are fascinated with dreams. Freud was the first to write about dream interpretation. Those in the traditional helping professions work with clients' dreams; some work intuitively without the need of formal training.

Palmistry
Palmists feel that the lines in the palms of our hands reveal information about length of life, love potential, and other aspects of living.

Numerology
Numerology is a system using numbers to understand human characteristics and perhaps to predict future events.

Firsthand Accounts

"Mara," Psychic
"Mara" worked for three years for the now-defunct Psychic Friends Hotline.

"I prefer to use my stage name because I had problems with clients who bordered on being stalkers. Unfortunately, it's the nature of the business that some people become too attached to their psychics.

"All psychic phone lines use a disclaimer that says they are for entertainment purposes only—to avoid lawsuits—but I consider myself a legitimate psychic. I also gave private readings by phone and in person. Now, I do it for free for friends and family.

"At the time, when I worked for that company, you were screened. You had to give cold readings to interviewers and obtain a recommendation from another psychic. I don't think most companies are that vigilant these days. The Psychic Friends Hotline had pretty strict rules and standards. For instance, you were supposed to discourage callers from staying on longer than twenty minutes, whereas today, the psychics are pressured to keep them on as long as possible! (By the way, I never met Dionne Warwick.)"

Getting Started

"I've always been psychic, or at least I've been as far back as I can recall. When I was about ten years old, I woke up and knew my sister had just had her baby. Minutes later, the phone rang and we were given the news that she had indeed just had her baby. It wasn't something I consciously tried to do or enhance. For several years, I simply ignored it. Then I had other similar experiences, and I realized the ability wasn't going to disappear.

"In college I helped raise money for the arts by giving readings to strangers at a street fair. I realized then that my abilities had strengthened and focused. I found myself giving very specific details, such as where someone's father lived, why they were estranged, what the person's hobbies were, and so on.

"I never even asked their names; the information just flowed. But lots of times, I only picked up vague impressions, and there were times when nothing came to me at all. I found it odd, and

occasionally disturbing, but mostly I tried only to read people when asked.

"I'm extremely careful about respecting privacy. And, of course, like most people, I can rarely read for myself. I only pick up on certain things, and no, I've never picked the Lotto numbers (sadly).

"Due to an illness, I was forced to work from home, and a friend suggested I start giving private readings. I was bored and lonely, and it sounded like something positive I could do. During my research into the private-reading sector, I met a very talented psychic who directed me toward the Psychic Friends Network."

What the Work Was Like

"As a psychic, my duties involved answering specific questions as well as giving information that I picked up that didn't have to do with questions asked; I also had a long list of resource numbers that I gave out when a caller had certain crises, such as domestic abuse, substance abuse, depression, and so on.

"We made it clear that we were not the end-all, be-all answer to all problems. We were very conscientious about directing people to the nonprofit organizations that could help them. Along with spiritual guidance, we all believed that real-world solutions were very crucial. We had to be very responsible about not instilling blind faith in our abilities. Instead, we tried to help our clients help themselves.

"We psychics were there to help, not to play God. I saw myself as someone who tried to shine a little light and show people the different pathways they could take. I firmly believed (and still do believe) in free will. I told people I was not 100 percent accurate and that, at most, I could claim 75 percent to 80 percent.

"If I couldn't read them (which rarely happened), I'd immediately let them know, so that they could move on and call another psychic. If they were unhappy with their experiences, they were issued a refund.

"I worked from home and kept a separate phone line. I'd log on for at least four hours a day, and sometimes as many as eight. Sometimes, calls would flood in, and other times it would be quiet and boring. Late nights were usually very busy. I kept logs of all of my calls, recording names, birth dates, the nature and length of the calls. Full names and addresses were only used if the callers wanted to get the free psychic newsletter; otherwise I'd simply write down a first name. Confidentiality was very important, and no one but the caller and I knew what the calls were about. Since I had repeat callers, I'd make sure I'd record when they planned on calling next, so that I'd be on duty at that time. Otherwise, they'd be disappointed. Repeat callers were important, but we were instructed not to let them call us more than once a week. It wasn't just the cost of the calls, but the possible dependency issue. Clients could become addicted to the psychic lines. We were supposed to prevent that and notify the company if anyone became a problem. They could be blocked if this happened.

"Working from home sounds idyllic, but in truth, I was a 'slave' to the phone. I absolutely had to pick up by the third ring, and I always had to be 'on,' meaning I had to be open, empathetic, and positive, no matter what domestic crisis I was right in the middle of. If friends called on the other line, they'd know I often had to hang up on them with little more than a good-bye. The same went for visitors and household chores. Family members, especially, had to be compliant or it wouldn't work.

"My hours were flexible but odd. My schedule would vary from week to week, and it was all up to me to choose the times I was logged on."

Upsides and Downsides

"I really enjoyed talking to so many intriguing, complex people; no two people were the same, though most of their questions revolved around three subjects: health, love, and money. So

many of the people were sincere and truly seeking guidance. I was touched by the courage so many displayed despite their often heartbreakingly difficult lives. I heard more tales of sorrow and desperation than I'd ever dreamed of. I also heard tales of great love, sacrifice, and selflessness. The job opened my eyes and heart to the wide spectrum of the human experience. The greatest joy I felt was when I reached someone or helped someone in some small way.

"I remember when I told a woman that I felt concerned about her husband's health. (I never predicted diseases, death, or anything so extreme, but I felt a sense of pressure in the chest area.) I urged her to talk him into seeing a medical professional, which I clearly told her I was not.

"She called me back a week later and thanked me. She took her husband in that day, and they were able to stop a heart attack that might have killed him.

"I also enjoyed the moment when I told a young woman that she'd be getting a job offer any moment; just then, she was beeped by Call Waiting. It was the job offer she was waiting for! Naturally, I was thrilled for her.

"Then there were those less concrete moments when a client would tell me that they felt better—lighter after my readings, even though nothing had really changed in their lives. I felt humbly pleased that I could help if only in a small way.

"My repeat customers were also joys. I could never give them private readings or step over the professional boundaries, but I felt a real bond with them. I often wished we could be friends, though I knew it wasn't possible. I think of them often.

"The downside was when no calls would come in and I'd be waiting. Nothing is lonelier than a silent phone. I also agonized over my obsessive callers, those who were locked in torment over unrequited love. Nothing I said ever got through to them. One woman had put her whole life on hold for ten years for a radio personality she'd met once or twice. She hadn't spoken to him or

seen him since, but she was convinced he'd someday realize that he loved her and would come and sweep her off her feet.

"I also talked regularly with a wealthy man who was destroying himself over a woman who'd married another; he was consumed by his need to get her back. Nothing I said ever reached him. He was also seeing therapists, whom he ignored as well. None of the obsessives could let go. It was absolutely tragic.

"I also grieved when I spoke to a caller whose life was so deeply unhappy and who'd suffered so unfairly that I wanted to force the Fates to make things better for her. I am still haunted by the saddest cases.

"Once in a while, I'd receive prank calls, but they were rare. I'd promptly report them to the company. I also on occasion received hostile calls. People would actually take the time and money to try to confound the psychic. They were calling to disprove psychic phenomena and were often angry if you actually saw through them.

"Occasionally, I answered calls from individuals who could only be described as dark. One sweet-voiced young woman told me of how in her past she'd committed a heinous crime and how she'd only been sentenced to a few years of prison time for it. She giggled a little as she confessed that she knew she'd really gotten off easy. Luckily, those chilling calls were very rare. Thankfully, I never had someone confess to a crime they hadn't paid for."

Salaries

"This may surprise many, but we psychics made little money. As independent contractors (which meant we had to pay our own income and Social Security taxes), we grossed about twenty dollars per hour. I've heard that the rate is much lower these days. Sounds like a lot, but you realize the psychic had to have been giving readings for that entire hour. You were not paid for simply being logged on, only for actual talk time.

"The most I ever grossed was a thousand dollars one month. I usually averaged about three to four hundred dollars gross per month.

"Some people logged on more and made more, but they also burned out faster because readings take a lot out of you."

Advice from Mara

"Make sure you are doing this because you feel you have the gift and have the genuine desire to give to others. You won't get rich, as a rule, doing this job.

"To start out, attend New Age festivals and talk to professionals. Reading books can help, but I feel you learn the most from other psychics.

"Let a few psychics read for you and listen to what makes you feel 'right' and what doesn't.

"Never give gloom and doom readings or dark readings. Most psychics concentrate on the positive, even if they see something that could be negative. Nothing is engraved in stone, and psychics can always be wrong. You can try to open some doors for people, to show them the possibilities, but you can never play God. I believe all people have some degree of psychic ability, and you can develop your own."

Lynne White Robbins, Psychic

Lynne White Robbins has worked as a professional psychic, most recently through the Crystal Ball Forum on America Online (AOL).

How It Works

"The Crystal Ball Forum is one of the channels of AOL and features 'rooms' for live, on-line psychic readings, including tarot, clairvoyance, clairaudience, astrology, clairsentience, and even dowsing and pendulums.

"One of the divisions of the Crystal Ball Forum places professional psychics under contract, manages reading requests, and
offers a choice of a 900-line service, a live on-line service, or
E-mail readings. Prices are reasonable, and clients are given completely private readings."

Getting Started

"For this kind of work, experience has been the best teacher.
Although I have a master's degree in education and a bachelor's
degree in psychology, learning to read psychically has been a very
personal journey. It has meant taking courses—in astrology and
holistic theories—and studying theories about tarot and various
kinds of spreads and throws. It has meant learning the signifi-
cance of different decks and understanding what deck might be
best for which kind of reading or situation.

"In addition, there have been hours and hours of practice,
with clients throughout the country, both in person and over the
Internet. I have had to gauge the accuracy of readings based on
client comment and reaction, and I try to gauge what I might
need to work on or focus on to become more accurate or insight-
ful or helpful.

"I've taken most of my courses and workshops through a foundation in my area that offers many different types of workshops
in holistic and New Age foundations.

"I think I began this work when I was a child and was able to
'see' people that other people did not. One such person was a
Native American woman wearing formal costume (fringed
sleeves, a hair band) and sitting with a bowed head reading or
looking at something in the living room of our home! Many years
later, I read that a Native American tribe had once occupied the
land that the house was built on.

"For many years, I did not know what to make of this talent. I
did readings whenever the opportunity presented itself because I
was as curious about it as the people I read for!

"For several months, I corresponded through E-mail with one of the readers at the Crystal Ball Forum who had done a reading for me. I ended up reading for them, and they were satisfied with the reading.

"To get the job for the Crystal Ball Forum, I had to agree to do off-line readings as a volunteer. Off-line readings were E-mail readings that AOL clients mailed to a central post office at the Crystal Ball, with various questions for the readers. As time went on, I took training through classes offered by Crystal Ball staff in how to be a room host, how to handle offensive or disruptive clients, and so on. I was mentored before I actually went on-line as a room reader. I remember the day that I was to go on I got a huge splinter in my thumb, which made it very difficult for me to shuffle the tarot cards!"

What the Work Is Like

"I began working formally for the Crystal Ball on America Online about 1994 or 1995. I happened upon the room while looking for information on the tarot, visited, and had a reading done. Then I set about finding out how I could become a reader as well.

"I am psychic and was looking for ways to use this ability on-line. During some of my first readings I was stunned at how much information could come over on-line—the fact that I could conduct readings on-line, over the telephone/modem wires, or even just through E-mailed questions, without even meeting the people, knowing what they looked like, or where they were from. Often very strong impressions come through based on words, sentences, or even conversations—the more focused the question, the stronger the impressions.

"One of the first readings I did was for someone whose husband was waiting to hear about receiving clearance from a medical review board thousands of miles away in Hawaii. I saw that

he would receive the clearance as well as news of impending employment—and events proved it to be true.

"Another incident was with members of a psychic lost-and-found team for the Crystal Ball's psychic investigations unit. Not only was the team able to zero in on the person's surroundings and her kitchen, including what was cooking in it, but they were able to zero in on that person's situation in years past, in another environment, and in specific detail. No one on the team was given any information that would have informed them of specifics in any way."

Maggie Anderson, Astrologer

Maggie Anderson makes her living as an astrologer, astrology teacher, and astrological writer. She learned her craft through beginning and intermediate astrology classes in the Community Education Department at Kirkwood Community College in Cedar Rapids, Iowa.

She's had additional astrological training at professional conferences, and she belongs to the International Society for Astrological Research (ISAR), the Association for Astrological Networking (AFAN), and the Astrology Association of Great Britain (AAGB). She founded the Ascella Mundane Astrology Club.

In addition, she has an associate's degree in addictions counseling, a bachelor's in sociology, and a master's in marital and family therapy. She's been working in the astrology field for more than thirty years.

"I work from my Mount Vernon home in Iowa. I give astrology readings in person, by telephone, or I place them on a tape that I mail to the client. Occasionally, I will go to a client's home or office if circumstances require it, but then I charge for travel time.

"Writing as AstroMaggi, I write columns for Astronet on America Online (Keyword: Astronet), Women.com, and Yahoo!

I write several columns, including 'BirthdayScopes,' 'Humor-Scope,' 'Stars on Stars' celebrity profiles, and a weekly 'Your Unique Horoscope,' which is available by subscription through Astronet's weekly newsletter. 'HumorScope' is now in print syndication through United Media Syndication. I also write for another site, StarIQ, and a New Age magazine, *Sowell Review*.

"I now give readings each month at a New Age bookstore, Journeys In, in Marion, Iowa. I hold astrology classes in my home and other locations convenient to the students. If a student is willing to organize a group of friends or coworkers interested in studying astrology together, I will go to their homes or offices to teach classes.

"Approximately every three months I hold a special-topic, all-day workshop in my home. I lecture on astrology in a variety of settings, usually within a fifty-mile radius of my home."

Getting Started

"My interest in astrology began as a result of my becoming aware of the correlation between birth dates and occupations. I worked the night shift in a personnel department of a large aircraft factory in the sixties. I had access to hundreds of personnel files and security clearances and had several hours each night with little to do but explore the files. As a budding sociologist, I tallied everything in those files, from number of marriages and divorces to the variety of health problems.

"Finally, I began to tally birth dates and noticed a distinct correlation between occupation and sun sign. For instance, 100 percent of administrative staff in the department I worked in were Virgos, and 78 percent of the electricians were Aquarians, a sign ruled by Uranus and associated with electricity. The mechanic's birth dates were divided almost equally between Aries and Scorpio, which I later learned are both ruled by Mars and connected with mechanics.

"I was quite impressed with those findings and began to study astrology on my own. I took classes later.

"My original plan was to go into career counseling and use astrology as a diagnostic tool. I felt it could provide valuable insight for individuals looking for direction in their work, so I began my studies with this in mind. I began doing charts for friends and neighbors, and then, several years after I first started studying astrology, I received requests for charts from the public through word-of-mouth advertising only.

"I had several false starts, though, at full-time practice. My need for steady income and benefits led me to work in other areas and work in astrology only part-time. My own career path did include career counseling and work in various social service areas. No matter where I've worked for 'real money,' however, I've continued to practice astrology part-time and use it as a diagnostic tool with clients in my other work.

"Now I'm a full-time astrologer who also provides career consultations as a subspecialty. My private practice comes primarily through referrals and advertisements in the Yellow Pages. I have also placed business cards and flyers for classes and workshops in area bookstores, and I send E-mails to interested parties. To generate repeat business, I keep a running record of previous clients' birth dates and send them a reminder when it's time for an updated progressed and solar return chart reading.

"New clients receive a current fee schedule, a list of services, and several order forms for additional services. At the beginning of each year, I mail clients, students, and others who may be interested the next year's calendar, with Mercury retrograde periods highlighted.

"Twice a year I send mailings to students and potential students with a list of upcoming classes and workshops. As time allows, I generate mailings to organizations that might be interested in having me as a guest speaker, and sometimes I follow up with a phone call.

"I began holding classes at the request of some clients, and that work has grown considerably. The job with Astronet came as a result of a referral from a friend, another astrologer who was working in one of their chat rooms. He discovered they were looking for a writer and suggested I submit sample columns. I did and was hired."

What the Work Is Like

"There's a great deal of variety in being self-employed as an astrologer. No two days are ever the same, so I'm never bored. I set aside about a day and a half for writing at the beginning of the week because there are deadlines to meet. Appointments for readings and classes are scheduled around the deadlines. I take evening appointments several nights a week as well as Saturday, and occasionally I give a reading in a client's office or home.

"I offer a series of eight-session beginning, intermediate, and advanced classes twice a year and usually have students taking private lessons as well. Promoting astrology to the general public is important, so I've developed six lectures I give in a variety of settings. I also founded and coordinate an area astrology club, Ascella Astrologers. Last month I spoke at the local nature center on moon madness, the seventh and eighth grade classes at a Catholic school on moon lore, and at Barnes & Noble on children of the zodiac.

"I try to keep reasonably busy without becoming overextended, and I aim for a forty- to forty-five-hour week. There have been weeks when I've put in eighty hours with astrology work and others when I've had family and other obligations where I've only worked ten. Winters in Iowa can be ferocious, so I never schedule classes or workshops from December through mid-March, and I tend to do more phone consultations and planning during these months.

"To do an astrological reading, I first make a horoscope chart, which is the map of the heavens at the time and date the person

was born, as seen from the location of their birth. I have a computer program that will produce a chart in several minutes. Hand calculating and drawing the chart takes about twenty minutes, so having a computer is a real help.

"I interpret the chart and make notes on important patterns, majors themes, and future trends. I either make a tape for the client and mail it or do the reading over the telephone at a pre-arranged time. If I find something new in a chart, I'll go to the books and do some research.

"I'm a traditional astrologer and have a nice collection of older astrological texts. My primary resource is the work of William Lilly, *Christian Astrology*, written in 1647, and the writings of some of his contemporaries.

"If I'm seeing a client who is experiencing difficult problems, I'll make a point of updating my list of potential referral sources. I maintain a relationship with a former employer in the mental health field and consult with her whenever I have a client who is especially problematic, so I can direct that person to the right place to get help.

"I'm a morning person and so am often at work by 7 A.M. in my study. I'm really very fortunate to be able to work at something I enjoy from my home."

Upsides and Downsides

"The thing I appreciate most about being an astrologer is that all of my clients are voluntary clients! This is in stark contrast to work in the human services field, where approximately 80 percent of clients are mandated to counseling by the court, school system, or employers. I'm able to provide a desired service that the person I'm dealing with directly really wants.

"There is a great deal of flexibility in my schedule. If I want to take a day off and work in the garden, I'm able to do it. If I'm needed to care for a sick grandchild, I can be helpful to my family and still manage the work flow.

"The downside of working alone is the isolation. Since some of my work is done on the telephone or taped, there are days when I don't see anyone but my three dogs and two cats!

"Astrologers have a reputation for being very independent, so whether in the city or country, most work alone. The Internet has promoted networking among astrologers. I've met several others in the state through an on-line service. We exchange E-mails, talk on the phone, and get together in person several times a month. I keep in touch with what's going on in the astrological community through various professional publications, Internet mailing lists, and newsletters. I do volunteer work and meet friends for lunch and so am not exactly housebound or lacking for human contact."

Salaries

"My income is generated from several sources and is variable. Writing brings in about $600 a month. Classes and workshops bring in anywhere from $4,000 to $5,800 per year. Sales of computerized reports generate about $2,000 annually. Most income is from readings. I charge $80 for a natal chart and $50 for an updated progressed and solar return reading. Low for a week would be two readings at $160, and the most I'd do is ten, bringing in $800. Some astrologers can and will do many more than that per week. Five to six readings is average for me.

"Beginning astrologers should find out what the going rate for a reading is in their areas. In rural areas fees are very low compared to the city. Between $200 and $300 for a ninety-minute reading is a fairly standard fee for an astrology reading in a large metropolitan area. Of course, someone with a 'big name' in the field can command even more. Several astrologers in the Chicago area charge $500. It's a matter of supply and demand like anything else."

Advice from Maggie Anderson

"Most astrologers begin by interpreting charts for family and friends, then branching out with some free or low-cost services to friends of friends. After enough training and experience, you can develop a part-time practice that could grow to provide enough income to live on.

"I believe astrologers should have training through the advanced astrology level, either through local classes or correspondence courses, plus several more years of study and experience doing many charts before working with the general public. A year or more of college-level counseling classes would also be helpful. Many people approach astrologers for a reading at a critical times in their lives when they are experiencing some very serious problems. If you open your doors to the public, a few who enter will be mentally ill, alcoholic, or drug addicted.

"Some will be overly dependent, 'perpetual clients' with very poor boundaries. It's important to have strategies to deal with these types of people or your practice of astrology will become secondary to managing problematic clients. A primary reason given by hobby astrologers for giving up working professionally in the field after a few months is that they had difficulty dealing with these particular members of the public.

"As in any other independent business, you need to become proficient at self-promotion. You can do this by giving free public lectures, teaching classes, and writing articles about astrology for local publications. Advertising may or may not be necessary, depending on how large a practice you wish to have. If astrology work is going to be your primary source of income, advertising widely is probably a necessity.

"Location is important, too. Larger cities have a greater number of potential clients to draw from, and you can charge higher fees. You need to operate from a location that is accessible to clients or learn to love working over the phone and the Internet."

Rita Valenti, Tarot Reader

Rita Valenti works from her home on a part-time basis, giving readings on-line and over the phone. Currently, she is involved with an on-line forum called Crystal Visions.

She has bachelor's degrees in English and industrial psychology and has completed the necessary classroom hours for certification as a counselor.

Getting Started

"My work was never really 'started'—it always was. Some people define work and an exchange of services for dollars; this work is more like a calling. The idea of this work was, in fact, very unattractive to me at the start. As a child I always played with cards. I named the court cards, built houses, and developed stories about who they were and what adventures they were on.

"When I was about four, the phone rang, and I said, 'Pop died.' Pop was a very old man who was a friend of the family. The call was, indeed, a message about Pop's passing. There were one or two more incidents like this over the next year or two.

"When I was in first grade, the teacher accused me of cheating when we played games because I knew the answers to questions before they were asked.

"We also played a game in which one team member had to secretly select someone from the classroom floor to play in his or her place. It was with this game that I first tried 'willing' something to happen. I would select one of the players and mentally will them to select me. It happened more often than not, and, by the way, that teacher was also sure I somehow cheated.

"This got to be more of a problem than a gift. I not only had to defend myself to my teacher but to my parents as well. I knew better than to speak of voices, willing, or visions, lest I spend some time locked away.

"I set aside the ability to see, but as I grew older (with the flower children of the sixties), I developed an interest in astrol-

ogy, numerology, and general areas of divination without the mind-altering stimulation that often went along with such discoveries during that period of time.

"In my late teens, I found that when I had a pen in my hand and was not thinking, I would doodle some pictures, but I would also write out 'August 8th' or '8/8.' This date had no meaning to me. Soon afterward, I began waking up on Saturday mornings with tears in my eyes. There was no dream or upset to set my tears in motion.

"Years later, early one morning the telephone rang. As my husband reached to answer it I told him, 'My brother is dead.' It was Saturday morning, August 8. That was the message we received. My brother, a healthy eighteen-year-old, was killed in an auto accident. They were driven off the road by a drunken driver.

"There was no doubt that there was something different about me, but I did not want that to be seeing death. In my prayers and meditations I asked not to be able to see death, unless there was something I could do to change it, such as offer a warning or send someone to see a medical professional.

"For many years, I would pick up the cards just once in a while and read for a friend. I met a reader in Salem who said it was time for me to come back—without knowing I read. I began working in this field again.

"In 1994, I discovered America Online. I never imagined so many people would be looking for readings (free ones, of course). I found the only forum on-line that was doing readings and soon became a member of that group. I stayed for a while but eventually stopped reading there. I, of course, have read off-line, and I continue that practice. I also read on the telephone—but never for any 900 numbers. I also read in front of groups of people who want to provide entertainment to their guests (Halloween seems to be the busiest time).

"Currently I help out with a community of on-line readers called Crystal Visions. I read when a staff member is unable to

make a shift, and I share in some of the administrative work. I have now developed a following. Those people for whom I read come back year after year. As with any profession, you have to spend lots of time developing a client base."

What the Work Is Like

"I am a psychic tarot reader. I sit with clients and look into the past, present, and future, offering insights into the options they have for decision making. I also teach the intuitive method of tarot reading and give lectures and workshops to small groups on- and off-line.

"The job can be intense. I feel responsible for the information I relay to people. A good reader never offers advice—only options. The final decision is always up to the seeker.

"I am a channel. I am an empath. I see, hear, feel, smell, and taste the messages my guides receive for the seeker. I use the tarot cards as a map to direct me to where in the seeker's life the message I receive falls.

"Doing a channel-type reading is draining. It takes concentration and focus and at the same time, you cannot cross to a point where your thoughts are dominant.

"My day is structured and at the same time quite flexible. I can schedule appointments that fit in so that I do a certain number of readings per day and per week.

"I usually work at night on-line. I sign on and check that there is someone in the chat room to read or greet those who visit. If not, I fill that spot. The room is usually busy, and maintaining some type of order is often difficult. Most people are considerate of those fortunate enough to make the list for that evening.

"For my work at home, I have to prepare and make sure I will not be interrupted. Usually I try to clear my mind beforehand and try to relax. I focus on my feelings for a while before the appointed time. It will often take me an hour or so after hanging up to clear my mind of thoughts from this reading.

"The hours are sometimes difficult because of time zones. I have had situations where a friend (usually my clients become my friends) calls me in the wee hours of the morning—perhaps because of a family problem or because they are upset about an issue. I never say I am too busy, and this is never treated as a business arrangement."

Upsides and Downsides

"There are many joys to the profession, including sharing happy events and offering encouragement to those who just have to hear from someone else that they could do it!

"I do not give medical or legal advice; I leave that to the professionals. But I have suggested to people that they see their doctors when I feel there is some danger or need for medical attention.

"One person heeded my advice and was scheduled for a bypass almost immediately. I have told people they were pregnant when they did not know. And I have even, more than once, specified date of birth and gender before the parents knew they were expecting.

"I do not like being associated with scam artists—those who claim they can read and only do it for the money, those who play on what I call the three Gs: greed, guilt, and grief, and convince people they need high-priced spell-removing nonsense.

"Some people begin to depend on readings to make decisions in their everyday lives. I try not to deal with 'reading addicts,' and my policy of not reading for the same person more than once every three months usually keeps them away."

Salaries

"Because you are in your own business, the sky is the limit. Most readers when starting out read just to confirm they have the ability. Readers for 900 numbers do not earn what the seeker is

charged; some earn a by-the-minute charge—usually twenty to thirty-five cents.

"Some readers charge a flat fee for a service; that can vary depending on what the service costs. Some well-known psychics charge $500 or more per hour, and I have heard of a channel who speaks to those who cross over who charges $2,000 a session.

"I never charge for the reading—only for the time I spend. And even then I can sit for two hours talking but will only ask for compensation for the actual reading time.

"My rates vary between new clients and older clients, and for that reason I usually do not publish them. The going rate for the time spent on a reading seems to fall between $25 and $100 per hour, depending on the location, the method of reading, and the reader.

"When and if someone needs a consult and cannot pay for it, then I will provide them with a reading free of charge.

"New readers have to build up a clientele that feels confident in the reader's abilities. That might require doing some freebies or working with a group of readers. The work I do on AOL is mostly for advertisement. I get paid referrals from there."

Advice from Rita Valenti

"Any reader who reads because he or she felt pushed to do so by some unknown force is actually answering a spiritual calling; it is compelling, and you will do it regardless of other callings in life.

"If you are a people person, you can meet wonderful people on-line. Learn about people. Learn about different belief systems and cultures. Be willing to accept that there is no right and wrong; it is not up to you to judge—only to relay information. You have to realize you are a tool in the greater scheme of things.

"Although you can earn a good living doing this, be prepared to give of yourself. Reading is not just knowing the face meanings of a tarot deck."

SuZane Cole, Dream Interpreter

SuZane Cole works from her home and does her dream work with clients on-line and through E-mail. She has been working professionally since 1999.

Getting Started

"I have been intuitive all my life. As I grew older it became stronger. After my youngest son, age twenty, passed over in 1994, my abilities grew nonstop, and I began to seek ways of putting these abilities to work for the good of all. I began to listen and follow the direction of my spirit guides, trusting them more and more as the days went on. I was attracted to the fact that I could do this; it just came easily to me, and dreams have always fascinated me. People would speak of their dreams, and as I listened, I just *knew* things.

"An on-line friend of mine knew of my abilities and began to refer people to me who wanted help with their dreams. As time progressed, this friend and I chatted more and more. She then asked me if I would do a dream reading session on-line for a company called Crystal Visions. I agreed and followed the flow in that direction."

What the Work Is Like

"I spend approximately three hours a week—an hour and a half, two evenings a week—in a monitored on-line chat room on America Online where I do dream interpretations for people. But the amount of time can vary if I get dreams sent to me via E-mail, asking for an interpretation.

"I have a very talented hostess who sets up a list of the people in the room who want a dream reading done. When it is the next person's turn, he or she has fifteen minutes to tell me about the dream. I then interpret the dream, using information that comes

from a combination of universal dream symbols and my spirit guides.

"There are nights when I stay on to chat with people in the room; fifteen minutes is not a very long time. At times, there are some who need more information than I can honestly give them in that time, so I spend additional time in the chat room after my shift is over. If they feel the need for more information or have more questions, they can contact me by E-mail, but there is a charge for this."

Upsides and Downsides

"I enjoy the work; I enjoy helping people understand that dreams are about ourselves, about issues we are dealing with—either past, present, or future.

"Most times, the people I speak with understand what I am telling them and, after I explain it to them, are able to relate the dream to some area of their lives. I like knowing that many people leave me with a better understanding of what is going on in their lives. I feel good when I can clear up the messages that have come to my clients in a dream state.

"For example, many people have visits from loved ones in their dreams—I always enjoy telling them about this. It is always a pleasure to put a mind to rest after explaining to someone that, yes, this visit was real; your friend or loved one is fine.

"I have found that most people really want to understand themselves. They want to deal with things, not hide them away in a closet. But, there are those who, for whatever reason, simply do not understand. They keep asking the same questions over and over. It's as if they don't like the answer I give them and they think if they ask again maybe it will change.

"And then there are the times when absolutely nothing comes through. It is either because it isn't time for them to have the information yet, it isn't my place to tell them, or they are making up the dream—and, yes, this does happen."

Salaries

"The on-line work is volunteer. I charge $30 per dream through mail. The client mails me the check, and once it clears, I do the interpretation. But, I am not in this for the money. I do this because I was led to do it. It is my way of giving back to the universe, a way of saying thank you for all my blessings."

Advice from SuZane Cole

"Be honest. If you choose to use your gift, always use it in the highest regard. Don't let it come from your ego—ego has no place here. Always give thanks—thanks to your guides and to the universe—and trust your guides; they will lead you."

For More Information

Association for Astrological Networking (AFAN)
8306 Wilshire Boulevard, Suite 537
Beverly Hills, CA 90211
www.afan.org

AFAN is a network linking and informing the international astrological community. AFAN publishes a newsletter and organizes conferences.

Astrological Association of Great Britain (AAGB)
Unit 168, Lee Valley Technopark
Fottenham Hale
London N17 9LN
Great Britain
www.astrologer.com/aanet/welco.html

The AAGB has approximately sixteen hundred members around the world and produces four publications—the *Journal*,

published six times a year; *Correlation*, an academic biannual journal on astrological research; a newsletter containing information, debate, and opinion; and the *Medical Astrology Newsletter*, the only journal in the world devoted to medical astrology. The AAGB also organizes occasional seminars on all aspects of astrology, as well as an annual conference.

International Society for Astrological Research (ISAR)
P.O. Box 38613
Los Angeles, CA 90038
www.isarastrology.com

ISAR provides members with its journal, the *International Astrologer*, mailed quarterly. Other benefits of membership include reduced admission to conferences; a subscription to *UAC*, a weekly E-mail newsletter; and a free biennial membership directory.

CHAPTER THREE

The Mind
Careers in Spiritual Health

A lthough "Star Trek" proclaimed that space was the final frontier, scientists firmly believe the mind is. Some liken it to a muscle that, if not used, will atrophy. Others are convinced we possess psychic powers not yet fully explored (see Chapter 2); and still others feel that attending to the mind as well as the body (see Chapter 4) is the only way to complete spiritual, emotional, psychological, and physical health.

Those who choose professions devoted to the mind and our spiritual life fill traditional as well as nontraditional (New Age) careers. But some cannot really be separated into two distinct mind and body categories. For example, psychiatrists attend to emotional problems but often prescribe drugs to create an effect on the body to accomplish their goals. The hypnotherapist helping someone to recover from an addiction approaches the physical problem through mental processes. The yoga therapist, while concerned with attitude and mood, works predominately with muscles and physical exercise. For most of these professions, the practitioner takes a holistic approach, treating the mind as well as the body.

For the purposes of this book, those professions that focus on the mind or approach the body through the mind are covered in this chapter; those that focus mainly on the body are covered in Chapter 4.

But first, let me offer a disclaimer. The job titles mentioned in this chapter, for the most part, fall into the realm of traditional. There are a slew of therapies and the therapists who provide them that fall into what is known as New Age. But to many peo-

ple, these New Age therapies are considered bogus, the practitioners who work with them nothing more than quacks, the clients who participate nothing short of victims.

As in any profession, there are schemers and charlatans and people who do not have the best interests of their clients in mind. This seems a concept so foreign to what New Age stands for, but it is still true.

In no other areas than those dealing with the mind and body are traditional and New Age practitioners more at odds with each other. There are scientists and traditional therapists who believe that New Age therapies don't really work, that the therapist presses his or her belief system onto the client, and that the client, motivated to feel better, unconsciously adopts the therapist's belief system.

Therapy in the hands of the wrong people can be a dangerous tool. Traditional psychologists, counselors, and the like must go through years of training and internships and must meet governing body requirements to be licensed to practice. Anyone can hang out a shingle and pin on a job title. No one is there to police them; no one is there to warn patients that the so-called therapist has no actual training.

Know Thyself

Because most future therapists undertake therapy themselves—to know themselves—there are those reading this book who might pursue certain therapeutic avenues without knowing whether or not they are in good hands.

Although the title *Crazy Therapies: What Are They? Do They Work?* sounds more disparaging than the content, this is a must-read for any open-minded future therapist to see both sides of the coin. The book was coauthored by Margaret Thaler Singer and Janja Lalich and published by Jossey-Bass in 1996 in San Francisco. Margaret Thaler Singer has been a clinical psycholo-

gist, researcher, and teacher for more than fifty years. She is currently an emeritus adjunct professor of psychology at the University of California, Berkeley. For the past twenty years, she has also done work on cults and is considered an expert in the field of cult menaces. Janja Lalich is an educator, author, and consultant in the field of cults and psychological persuasion.

According to a thorough and entertaining book review by Dr. Robert Carroll, a professor of philosophy at Sacramento City College, the "crazy" therapies examined all claim to be miracle cures and to work like magic. All except facilitated communication claim that their one approach will work for just about everybody, no matter what the problem or situation. "It is unlikely that all these cookie-cutter theories—one size fits all—are correct," says Carroll, "but none of their practitioners seem interested in any scientific studies that might prove once and for all which theory, if any, is correct. . . .

"Singer and Lalich discuss the origins and dangers of each of these 'crazy' therapies. One thing they all have in common is that they have not been proven effective by any independent scientific studies, nor are they generally accepted as effective in the scientific community. Their support comes mainly from the 'insight' and observations of their founders, and patient feedback which is analyzed and evaluated by the therapists themselves. Most of the innovative therapists reviewed by Singer and Lalich seem uninterested in scientifically testing their theories, though most seem attached to technical jargon."

The full review of this book was originally published on the Web at www.skepdic.com/refuge/crazy.html. *Crazy Therapies* can be ordered through any traditional or on-line bookstore.

Possible Job Titles

The realms of counseling and therapy and attending to our spiritual lives are looked at in this chapter. Possible job titles include:

- Counselor

- Minister

- Pastor

- Psychologist

- Hypnotherapist

- Therapist

Under each main title can fall many specializations or subcategories. For example, under *counselor*, we could find *career counselor, marriage counselor, guidance counselor*, and so on. Psychologists have specializations such as school psychology, child psychology, counseling, social work, clinical psychology, and more.

Here we look at two main paths: therapists, as an umbrella term for counselors and psychologists, and the ministry.

Therapists

Now it's time for another disclaimer. Perhaps there are a lot of "crazy" therapies out there, but there is a lot of middle ground, too, with nontraditional therapy that is nurturing and that helps the client toward self-awareness and personal growth.

With all that in mind, let's take a closer look at three different therapies: hypnotherapy, traditional psychotherapy as performed by trained and licensed psychologists, and counseling.

Hypnotherapy

Even though Carroll's article states that there are no governing bodies for hypnotists/hypnotherapists, several professional asso-

ciations do exist. The American Council of Hypnotist Examiners (ACHE) is the primary hypnotherapy certification agency in the United States, with nearly ten thousand members. It was not the first hypnotist organization, but it was the first to initiate registration, certification, and significant educational requirements for its members. It is the only major hypnotherapist certifying organization in the United States that requires its approved schools are state licensed as required by law. Its address is provided at the end of this chapter.

Many other organizations with impressive-sounding names have in recent years claimed to offer certification. The ACHE feels that the vast majority have damaged the profession by approving illegal programs and schools, thus seeming to give them legitimacy.

If you're interested in pursuing training in hypnotherapy, the ACHE advises that you especially avoid any illegal (not state-licensed) schools and schools that claim any form of certification for less than 150 hours of classroom instruction.

What Is Hypnotherapy?

Hypnosis is a state of focused awareness. Hypnotherapy is a technique that uses hypnosis to access the subconscious mind. Hypnotherapists can learn safe and effective ways to induce hypnosis and utilize many forms of hypnotherapy to help clients stop smoking, lose weight, deal with pain, and achieve overall wellness.

Training in hypnotherapy can be for a career on its own or as an adjunct to another therapeutic specialty. One example of using hypnotherapy as a career on its own would be a certified hypnotherapist trained to work in harmony with local health care professionals to aid individuals in dealing with specific medical challenges and procedures. The goal is to reduce the stress the individual is experiencing as a hospital patient and/or surgical or dental patient.

Psychotherapy

Psychologists in applied fields counsel and provide mental health services in hospitals, clinics, or private settings. They can also work in other unrelated areas to the therapeutic setting and, for example, conduct training programs or market research.

Because psychology deals with human behavior, psychologists apply their knowledge and techniques to a wide range of endeavors, including human services, management, education, law, and sports.

In addition to the variety of work settings, psychologists specialize in many different areas.

Clinical psychologists, who constitute the largest specialty, generally work in independent or group practice or in hospitals or clinics. They may help the mentally or emotionally disturbed adjust to life and are increasingly helping all kinds of medical and surgical patients deal with their illnesses or injuries. They may work in physical medicine and rehabilitation settings, treating patients with spinal cord injuries, chronic pain or illness, stroke, arthritis, and neurologic conditions, such as multiple sclerosis. Others help people cope with life stresses such as divorce or aging.

Clinical psychologists interview patients; give diagnostic tests; provide individual, family, and group psychotherapy; and design and implement behavior modification programs. They may collaborate with physicians and other specialists in developing treatment programs and help patients understand and comply with the prescribed treatment.

Some clinical psychologists work in universities, where they train graduate students in the delivery of mental health and behavioral medicine services. Others administer community mental health programs.

Counseling psychologists perform many of the same functions as clinical psychologists. They use several techniques, including interviewing and testing, to advise people on how to cope with

problems of everyday living, whether personal, social, educational, or vocational.

Health psychologists promote good health through health maintenance counseling programs that are designed, for example, to help people stop smoking or lose weight.

Training

A doctoral degree is usually required for employment as a licensed clinical or counseling psychologist. Psychologists with a Ph.D. qualify for a wide range of teaching, research, clinical, and counseling positions in universities, elementary and secondary schools, private industry, and government. Psychologists with a Doctor of Psychology (Psy.D.) degree usually work in clinical positions. An Educational Specialist (Ed.S.) degree will qualify an individual to work as a school psychologist. People with a master's degree in psychology may work as industrial-organizational psychologists. Others work as psychological assistants, under the supervision of doctoral-level psychologists, and provide therapy to clients or conduct research or psychological evaluations.

A bachelor's degree in psychology qualifies a person to assist psychologists and other professionals in community mental health centers, vocational rehabilitation offices, and correctional programs. Without additional academic training, opportunities in psychology at the bachelor's level are severely limited.

The American Psychological Association (APA) presently accredits doctoral training programs in clinical, counseling, and school psychology. Psychologists in independent practice or those who offer any type of patient care, including clinical, counseling, and school psychologists, must meet certification or licensing requirements in all states and the District of Columbia. Licensing laws vary by state and by type of position.

Aspiring psychologists who are interested in direct patient care must be emotionally stable, mature, and able to work

effectively with people. Sensitivity, compassion, and the ability to lead and inspire others are particularly important qualities for clinical work and counseling.

Salaries

Last year the Bureau of Labor Statistics reported that the median annual earnings of salaried psychologists were $48,050. The middle 50 percent earned between $36,570 and $70,870 a year. The lowest 10 percent earned less than $27,960 and the highest 10 percent earned more than $88,280 a year.

Median annual earnings in the industries employing the largest number of psychologists are as follows:

Offices of other health care practitioners	$54,000
Hospitals	$49,300
Elementary and secondary schools	$47,400
State government, except education and hospitals	$41,600
Other health and allied services	$38,900

The federal government recognizes education and experience in certifying applicants for entry-level positions. In general, the starting salary for psychologists having a bachelor's degree was about $20,600 in 1999; those with superior academic records could begin at $25,500. Psychologists with a master's degree and one year of experience could start at $31,200.

Psychologists with a Ph.D. or Psy.D. degree and one year of internship could start at $37,800, and some individuals with experience could start at $45,200. Beginning salaries were slightly higher in selected areas of the country where the prevailing local pay level was higher. The average annual salary for all psychologists in the federal government was $66,800 in 1999.

Counseling

Counselors assist people with personal, family, educational, mental health, and career decisions and problems. Their duties depend on the individuals they serve and the settings in which they work.

School and college counselors—in elementary, secondary, and postsecondary schools—help students evaluate their abilities, interests, talents, and personality characteristics to develop realistic academic and career goals.

They operate career information centers and career education programs. High school counselors advise on college majors, admission requirements, entrance exams, and financial aid and on trade, technical school, and apprenticeship programs. They help students develop job search skills such as resume writing and interviewing techniques. College career planning and placement counselors assist alumni or students with career development and job hunting techniques.

Elementary school counselors observe younger children during classroom and play activities and confer with their teachers and parents to evaluate their strengths, problems, or special needs. They also help students develop good study habits. They do less vocational and academic counseling than secondary school counselors.

School counselors at all levels help students understand and correct their social, behavioral, and personal problems. They emphasize preventive and developmental counseling to provide students with the life skills needed to prevent problems before they occur and to enhance personal, social, and academic growth.

School counselors provide special services, including alcohol- and drug-abuse prevention programs and classes that teach students to handle conflicts without resorting to violence. Counselors also try to identify cases involving domestic abuse and other family problems that can affect a student's development.

Counselors work with students individually, in small groups, or with entire classes. They consult and work with parents, teachers, school administrators, school psychologists, school nurses, and social workers.

Rehabilitation counselors help people with the personal, social, and vocational effects of disabilities.

Employment or vocational counselors help individuals make career decisions.

Mental health counselors emphasize prevention and work with individuals and groups to promote optimum mental health. They help individuals overcome addictions and substance abuse, suicide, stress management, problems with self-esteem, issues associated with aging, job and career concerns, educational decisions, and issues of mental and emotional health as well as family, parenting, and marital problems.

Mental health counselors work closely with other mental health specialists, including psychiatrists, psychologists, clinical social workers, psychiatric nurses, and school counselors.

Other counseling specialties include marriage and family, multicultural, or gerontological counseling. A *gerontological counselor* provides services to elderly persons who face changing lifestyles because of health problems and helps families cope with these changes. A *multicultural counselor* helps employers adjust to an increasingly diverse workforce.

Training

Formal education is necessary to gain employment as a counselor. About six out of ten counselors have master's degrees. Fields of study include college student affairs, elementary or secondary school counseling, education, gerontological counseling, marriage and family counseling, substance abuse counseling, rehabilitation counseling, agency or community counseling, clinical mental health counseling, counseling psychology, career counseling, and related fields.

Graduate-level counselor education programs in colleges and universities usually are in departments of education or psychology. In 1999, 133 institutions offered programs in counselor education—including career, community, gerontological, mental health, school, student affairs, and marriage and family counseling—that were accredited by the Council for Accreditation of Counseling and Related Educational Programs (CACREP).

Another organization, the Council on Rehabilitation Education (CORE), accredits graduate programs in rehabilitation counseling. Accredited master's degree programs include a minimum of two years of full-time study, including six hundred hours of supervised clinical internship experience.

In 1999, forty-five states and the District of Columbia had some form of counselor credentialing, licensure, certification, or registry legislation governing practice outside schools. Requirements vary from state to state. In some states, credentialing is mandatory; in others, it is voluntary.

Clinical mental health counselors usually have master's degrees in mental health counseling, another area of counseling, or in psychology or social work. Voluntary certification is available through the National Board for Certified Counselors, Inc. Generally, to receive certification as a clinical mental health counselor, a counselor must have a master's degree in counseling, two years of post-master's experience, a period of supervised clinical experience, a taped sample of clinical work, and a passing grade on a written examination.

Salaries

Self-employed counselors who have well-established practices, as well as counselors employed in group practices, usually have the highest earnings, as do some counselors working for private firms, such as insurance companies and private rehabilitation companies.

Median annual earnings of vocational and educational counselors in 1998 were $38,650. The middle 50 percent earned between $28,400 and $49,960. The lowest 10 percent earned less than $21,230, and the highest 10 percent earned more than $73,920. Median annual earnings in the industries employing the largest numbers of vocational and educational counselors are shown below:

Elementary and secondary schools	$42,100
State government, except education and hospitals	$35,800
Colleges and universities	$34,700
Job training and related services	$24,100
Individual and family services	$22,300

The Ministry

In an age—a New Age—in which people are questioning and seeking all kinds of information, some people are no longer willing to accept the dogma of the masses. They have turned away from traditional churches and have embraced the beliefs of metaphysical or New Age churches.

According to Rev. Jennifer Baltz (read her firsthand account later in this chapter), the difference between metaphysical or New Age churches and traditional Christian ones is this: "For the most part, metaphysical churches are more open-minded, believe in reincarnation, and also believe that we have the ability to do some of the things Jesus did. In other words, that we are not saved by Jesus' death and rebirth but rather that we are able to follow in his footsteps and do as he taught and practiced. 'And greater works than these shall ye also do.' "

Those who choose to become ministers can either work as freelancers or be employed through the auspices of an organized church. Freelancers can specialize in one particular area, such as spiritual healing, or can generalize, offering a range of services, from conducting rites of passage to leading drum circles.

Ministers affiliated with a church usually must be generalists, working with parishioners in a variety of capacities—as a spiritual counselor or healer or even officiating at weddings. To become a minister, your search will take you to a church whose practices and beliefs match your own. Each church has its own requirements, and many even have their own divinity schools.

Firsthand Accounts

Cheryl-Lani Branson, Therapist/ Career Counselor

Cheryl-Lani Branson has worked as a therapist, career counselor, social worker, and client advocate. She earned her bachelor of arts in English literature with honors in 1975 from the University of Hartford. She also earned two master's degrees. The first is a master of science degree in counselor education, and the second is a master of social work, with a concentration in group work.

She has also participated in numerous workshops and training sessions including:

Science and Consciousness Conference

Bodywise—Newton Learning Systems

Life Balancing—healing system

Temenos (Accessing the Spirit Workshop)

Women's Mysteries Workshop

Voice Dialogue Training (personality subtype)

Pathways to the Psyche (which included ten days in the desert, four in silence and fasting, learning dream interpretation, tarot, symbols, and utilizing different healing methodologies)

Getting Started

"In 1978, I had an ovarian cyst. I went to a physician who suggested that if I ate differently, such as eliminating meat and caffeine and the like from my diet, that I might be able to get the cyst to drain out instead of surgery. Although I ended up having surgery, that was the time that began my awareness of nontraditional ways of healing.

"When I began to take awareness workshops, I realized that there were energies that we couldn't see or feel but existed around us. It's like going into a room and immediately having a reaction to someone, not based on their looks or the other senses, but based on a vibration or energy that comes off of them. And it is not transference or projection I am talking about; it's an energy field.

"When I finished graduate school the first time, I didn't want to be a guidance counselor, which was the traditional path for people getting a master's in counselor education. I wanted to work in corporate training, which I was able to do. I also noticed that I had an excellent facility for counseling individuals about their careers, and so I began a career-counseling practice at the same time. It was during this private practice that I began to utilize New Age practices.

"To me, New Age is work that is on the cusp, with much of the work based on energy systems. I think the majority of the population has a hard time comprehending what New Age is at first, but with the right exposure, they can slowly come to under-

stand it. Much of the work that is considered New Age is simply an alternate form of healing.

"A lot of my work with clients is not something I learned at workshops but rather through a lot of reading and experiencing. I think the best way to learn New Age methods is to experience them and to surround yourself with people who are open to energy work.

"I have been counseling in one form or another for the past twenty years. As a therapist, I use whatever tools will help the client. My job is to utilize my intuition as well as practical tools for supporting people.

"When I worked as a career counselor, it was in private practice, working with both individuals and groups. I would see the individual clients in an office, but the groups could take place anywhere—in a classroom, in an office, and even outside beside a lake."

What the Work Is Like

"I think it is a blessing for anyone to be able to use New Age techniques in a job or career. In my case, the work I've done has generally been counseling, but I've even been able to use some New Age practices in work I've done as an administrator of training programs. When I've had to deal with negative energy as part of a management team, I've directed rays of light and love through my heart to whomever was being negative. I've sometimes also used that healing light to assist a client in finding closure on some part of his or her life.

"New Age techniques have been especially helpful in my career-counseling practice. Nearly every individual client I ever had was 'stuck', and my prescription was to get in water, near water, get water in them. Water creates flow.

"At my last large consulting job I was able to utilize a variety of techniques, including meditation, visualization, manifesting (through treasure maps), and many other healing methods.

"My counseling these days is done with my heart sending love and staying open while we work. Sometimes it's hard to keep my heart open, and I need to remind myself.

"It's very important with this work to revitalize oneself, so I have a number of practices that support me, including yoga, hiking in the mountains (to be awed by the beauty on this earth and reminded of a greater spirit than what is physical), and every once in a while, meditating.

"I often use New Age tools to support myself—I have seven kinds of tarot decks that I use to divine information about a situation. Lately, I pulled runes every night for five days to assist me in determining if it was time for me to leave a work situation. The runes told me to sever, allow myself to change, and then to be still and trust while awaiting the next job opportunity. (Runes are Viking symbols, thousands of years old, used as divination tools.)"

Upsides and Downsides

"There are no downsides to this work—every challenge is just a lesson, either a new one or an old one that one needs reminding of. I feel blessed to be living at this time, when this work is being more accepted. I can use New Age techniques whether I'm working as a counselor, an administrator, or a business consultant. And I am paid to have my heart be open and to learn!"

Salaries

"I've been consulting for a long time, so my fees have a wide range—anywhere from $20 to $75 an hour. It very much depends on what the tasks are.

"A person just starting out, if grounded in some practical physical work aside from the New Age work, could probably charge about $35 an hour. It's all about listening to the voice inside—

intuition—and getting guidance from that in relation to the kind of work to do and the fees to charge."

Advice from Cheryl-Lani Branson

"Do the work! Utilize New Age techniques in healing yourself, and after a while, if you're spirited to do so, you will begin to want to share this work with others.

"If you're a person who is set in your ways, pessimistic, or close minded, New Age work is not for you. On the other hand, if you are open to the nonphysical realms and energy work, you may just be a healer waiting to emerge.

"Follow your path. Listen to your intuition. Don't dismiss anything New Age. Experience everything you can. Know that spending your money taking workshops and having sessions with people will return to you multiplied. Trust that you are where you're supposed to be. Be open to the education you are receiving as you do your own healing. If you don't read any books, take any workshops, or see any New Age counselors, just keep an open heart."

Rev. Jennifer Baltz, Minister, Spiritual Teacher, and Counselor

Rev. Jennifer Baltz lives and works in Northern California in the Sonoma County wine country. She is affiliated with the Church of Aesclepion Healing in Marin, California, and works out of her home, offering spiritual counseling and classes, officiating at weddings and other ceremonies, and managing her website, www.creativespirit.com, "a sanctuary for spirit on the Web."

Her education and training include: a B.S. in business from Santa Clara University; clairvoyant, minister's, and teacher's training programs at the Church of Divine Man Seminary, Berkeley (Berkeley Psychic Institute); and healing, spiritual

midwifery, and trancemediumship training at the Church of Aesclepion Healing in Marin.

Getting Started

"I've been attracted to religion and spirituality since I was a little girl. I always had ideas different from many Christians—I never believed in hell, for instance, and I remembered past life experiences before I ever knew of the concept of past lives.

"I began taking psychic classes with a visiting British medium in San Jose. She told me I needed to work on judgment and neutrality (which was very true) and that I would eventually find the right teacher and do this kind of work myself one day.

"Of course I didn't believe her. But a few years later, I was working at United Way in fund-raising, when I discovered that the marketing director had an interesting history—he was also a minister and a psychic teacher. Intrigued, I started taking classes at his church, graduated as a minister myself, and eventually ended up working there as assistant to the bishop.

"The clairvoyant, minister's training, and teacher's programs are all now required to become licensed—that's about three years or so. When I went through, it was only the clairvoyant program that was required, but I did the rest anyway. In the teacher's program, you learn how to teach meditation, intuition, and spiritual healing, and how to set the crown chakra, respond to questions and energy from students, and set the energy for a class. As I gained more confidence and graduated from the teacher's program, I began teaching meditation and intuition classes and offering spiritual counseling."

What the Work Is Like

"As a minister, I offer spiritual counseling and teach classes according to the tenets of my church. We humans are both physical body and immortal spirit. Too often we validate and recog-

nize the physical achievements and looks of a person rather than who he or she is inside as an immortal soul, on a spiritual path of growth and evolution this lifetime. So what I do, in individual counseling, classes, and in my writing, is to say hello to the spirit part—the divine within all of us—and help people reconnect with that part of themselves.

"Intuition is really just being in good communication with your soul, with God, and that is what I try to help people do. When you are in touch with your soul essence, you have much greater certainty about who you are, why you are here, and what you really want (as opposed to what everyone else wants for you). So it's both about having a happier life this time around and also about creating real growth and evolution as spirit.

"I think New Age is a very well-used term, but in essence, it is about bringing an understanding and awareness of spirit and spirituality into everyday life.

"At present, I teach classes by phone to people from all over the country. I also offer intuitive spiritual counseling to people in life transitions.

"I work mostly from home. It's very quiet and peaceful, and I usually spend my day doing spiritual counseling, writing class curricula and messages, and updating my website, where everything is posted.

"I have time to garden. Sometimes I attend local spiritual functions, and some evenings, I teach classes. I teach many classes by telephone, since many of my students live in other states. I'm working on some on-line classes, too."

Upsides and Downsides
"The upside is that I can create my day as I choose and I am not working in a corporate environment. I also have time for writing, which I like to do in my spare time. The downside is that I am home a lot and that I must stay focused to get everything done.

"I am always working—usually seven days a week, part-time each day—and it is very difficult to get away for vacations. Also, sometimes people call in crisis at dinnertime!"

Salaries

"I charge different fees and honoraria, depending on what I'm doing. For classes, it is usually about $15 for a one-hour class or $60 for four weeks. For spiritual counseling, it is generally between $50 to $90 per session, and for weddings, usually around $250.

"If you are just starting out as a spiritual teacher, you can expect to charge similar rates for classes—or more if you are teaching longer sessions. Local evening classes can be $25 per person, and weekend seminars can be $50 to $80 per day. I like to keep things reasonable for most people. Weddings depend on the area and the going rate among local clergy."

Advice from Rev. Jennifer Baltz

"As a spiritual teacher, you must maintain your boundaries and your center. To do this kind of work, it is important to have spiritual tools that you can use to stay grounded, to keep your certainty. In a sense, you have to keep one foot in the 'real world' and one foot in the spiritual realm—crossing over from one to the other as an intermediary.

"Your students need for you to be a Rock of Gibraltar, and it is important to have self-care practices that allow this. It is important to take care of yourself, otherwise you can start taking on the problems of other people. So, you must have some form of exercise, some kind of physical work to keep you grounded, and you must know how to separate your energy from the people you work with.

"I think to do this kind of work without taking on negative energies, it is important to have a generally positive attitude

about life and a willingness to see things from an innocent perspective. You must be willing to allow other people to succeed and grow in ways that perhaps you have not achieved yourself, and you must try to be as neutral as you can when handling charged situations.

"You must be committed to your own spiritual growth and evolution and try to live your life and conduct yourself in a way that promotes your evolution and sets a good example for your students. This doesn't mean that you have to be perfect—but be honest and real with people.

"You also need to have good business sense to work on your own. Most people I know who do this kind of work, teaching and counseling, are just scraping by. Why? They are not business savvy, and they don't know how to negotiate for things and ensure that their activities generate income.

"Income varies tremendously, depending on how real you are with people, whether or not you 'walk your talk,' and on your ability with money. It is income minus expenses, so you have to keep a rein on the expenses. A lot of spiritual people don't know how to do that. If you don't have this ability naturally, you need to go back to school. Your local junior college is a great inexpensive place to pick up some business classes.

"It takes two to three years to build up a reputation and clientele enough to do this independently and make a living with it. It is a lot of hard work, but it is also incredibly rewarding."

Rev. Paula Cooper, Spiritual Counselor

Rev. Paula Cooper works from a home office in upstate New York as a spiritual counselor. She earned a doctor of divinity from the Institute of Holistic Theology in Youngstown, Ohio.

She is an ordained minister and also has an extensive background as director of patient services for a four-facility radiation oncology center.

Getting Started

"When I was seventeen, my favorite aunt died of a cerebral hemorrhage right in front of me. She had been deteriorating for two weeks, and I had been praying for two weeks that she would live, that she wouldn't leave me. As she worsened, she fell into a coma. Her breathing was labored and sporadic; she was losing weight rapidly. One day, as I stood beside her hospital bed, I realized she wouldn't want to keep on living like that, and I was able to let go of my selfish desire of wanting to keep her with me and instead turn her fate to God. I went into the hall, and I prayed to God to help her stop suffering. Within moments, I heard her breathing change to what some people call the death rattle. Her body was making desperate attempts to draw air into her fluid-filled lungs. I stepped back into the room and stood with her while she died. For a long time afterward, I was angry with God for not answering my prayers to save my aunt, until I realized that God does answer all prayers, but sometimes the answer is no.

"As I grew older and learned more about God and prayer, I began to long to help others understand that even if God says no, God still exists and still loves them.

"I also want to help others understand how God's love and miracles manifest in many small, subtle ways every day and that sometimes 'healing' does not mean 'cure' but instead means acceptance and adaptation. But most of all, I wanted to help others return to their own divinity and to know that—no matter what—God is there, waiting to love them.

"Due to my strong belief that one's spiritual progression cannot and should not be mandated by any institution (governmental, religious, or educational), I pursued my training via nontraditional methods. I have devoted the past twenty-five years to the study of comparative religion, philosophy, Eastern thought, psychology, metaphysics, and the physical sciences (just to name a few!) through self-study, directed study with various

independent teachers and spiritual guides, auditing of college classes, as well as through my own independently directed research.

"I got my first job in a people-services field with a cancer treatment group for whom I had already been working. When the physicians wanted to improve their group's standing among the competition with other treatment centers, I suggested and was hired to develop and direct the Patient Support Services Center, which offers emotional support, coordinates volunteers to provide rides to and from therapy, and works with social service agencies in the area to find the patients whatever assistance they might require."

What the Work Is Like

"Currently, I am self-employed as a spiritual counselor and educator. There is so much need in our world, and I feel I can serve my clients' spiritual needs best by serving them from a nonaffiliated, interfaith perspective.

"I provide counseling and educational services to help others learn about the power of choice and how to make the right choices for themselves.

"Many people confuse spiritual counseling with pastoral and psychological counseling, but they are all very different. As a spiritual counselor, I work to help people more effectively use faith and religious beliefs in their everyday lives.

"Some spiritual counselors attempt to bring their clients into a state of 'divine perfection,' but I prefer to help my clients do two things—one: accept the unchangeable realities of life and learn to use their divinity to have happy, good lives in spite of them; and two: learn to recognize the aspects of their lives that can be changed and how to utilize their divinity to guide them in the right directions and to give them strength when things get rocky. I teach methods of effective prayer and choice making to accomplish these goals.

"Being self-employed, I do everything from ordering office supplies to providing counseling to fixing the computer when it glitches. Typically, my days are spent researching and preparing the materials I use in my ministry and counseling. This can mean anything from researching how a client's medical illness can affect his or her emotional stability and/or intellectual abilities to designing, writing, and creating a page for my website. I can honestly say I have yet to be bored with my work!

"I work an average of sixty to seventy hours a week. The majority of my work is done through written or electronic media, so I don't spend a lot of time in face-to-face counseling. Most of my time is spent alone with my computer and books and phone. You really need to be a self-starter and somewhat of a loner to enjoy this job. You must like the tedious (and very often frustrating) tasks of research, writing, and software development. At the same time, you must like working with and helping people, and you must possess the ability to be articulate and personable so that you're ready for those face-to-face clients and seminars.

"In face-to-face encounters, you must maintain your distance in the relationship, while balancing that with loving compassion. As in pastoral or psychological counseling, it is unhealthy for both you and the client to develop a personal relationship. Boundaries must be established and protected. Sometimes that's really hard to do because there will be people you will care about on a deeper, personal level, people you will just plain like and wish you could be friends with. You have to keep in mind that if this person were able to talk to a friend and get help from a friend, he or she wouldn't be seeking a spiritual counselor. Once you cross that line from counselor to friend, you've jeopardized the professional relationship."

Upsides and Downsides

"What I like the most is having the opportunity to help others reconnect with their spiritual selves and learn that they truly do

have the power to change their lives. It isn't necessarily—or often—easy, but it is truly possible. So few people believe that. They simply don't understand that they possess the power of choice and that choice is all that is really needed to change a life. It's such a great feeling to help others not only open but walk through that door.

"What I like least is that more people give up when things get hard than those who keep going. A lot of people prefer to place blame on others, or on God, rather than accept responsibility for themselves. It can be very discouraging. Sometimes it can feel very lonely, and sometimes you may experience so many failures you feel like not trying anymore. It takes great effort and determination—and faith—not to give up in those moments."

Advice from Rev. Paula Cooper

"Be sure of the religious/spiritual path you want to follow and what you want to do with your ministry. Those of you who want a physical church and who want to perform marriages, baptisms, and so on, should pursue your training through a church-run seminary. If you want to be a Lutheran minister, for example, you can't approach your training as I did, from a nontraditional perspective. You should attend a Lutheran seminary and be educated within their beliefs and teachings. If you want a church, you must learn about church management, which the seminary will teach you. It's not simply about preaching; it's also running a business, and like any business, it requires good management to prosper.

"If you're interested in providing spiritual counseling and/or teaching (such as in seminars or through educational materials) via the 'working for yourself' route, the paths you can choose to follow are endless. You can still pursue a traditional education, but you should take care not to limit your learning, unless that's what you want to do. If you attend a Baptist school, you're going to learn Baptist beliefs, which is great if you're going to be a

Baptist counselor, but not so great if you want to work with people of all faiths or no faith at all.

"In that case, I would heartily recommend a nontraditional education with a strong foundation of independent exploration into all religions and philosophies. Be open-minded. You'd be surprised how many similarities exist among all the world's major religions. Jesus and Buddha would have been great friends! Be willing to admit that your own beliefs and theologies may be inadequate or just plain wrong.

"Also be prepared for failure and be ready to confront rejection. This is going to be one of the toughest fields to break into and earn a living from. Don't give up when it gets tough. You may have to work a full-time job while building your practice or ministry, but you can build it.

"You may even have to work another job after you are established. Even some ministers who are full-time pastors at long-established churches still have to hold down other jobs to support themselves and their families. This profession is truly a labor of love, but the intangible rewards make it all absolutely worthwhile.

"It's very important to take care of yourself emotionally and spiritually. Ministers and spiritual counselors are exposed to many sad, horrific facts of life. It's easy to begin to doubt that God even exists. You will witness not only successes and joys but also pain and tragedies. Actually, you're going to see the pain and tragedy far more often because it's quite rare for a happy person to seek spiritual advice. Be prepared for that. It's heartbreaking and can be soul-shatteringly sad. You will feel depressed and hopeless at times. You will feel angry at times: angry at your clients, angry at yourself for not being able to help them, angry at God. Those are all normal reactions. Build a support system for yourself so that in those times you have someplace or someone to turn to."

For More Information

Counseling
American Counseling Association
5999 Stevenson Avenue
Alexandria, VA 22304
www.counseling.org

American Dance Therapy Association
www.adta.org

American Music Therapy Association
8455 Colesville Road, Suite 1000
Silver Spring, MD 20910
www.musictherapy.org

National Board for Certified Counselors
3 Terrace Way, Suite D
Greensboro, NC 27403
www.nbcc.org

Hypnotherapy American Council of Hypnotists Examiners
700 South Central Avenue
Glendale, CA 91204
www.sonic.net/hypno/ache.html

American Association of Professional Hypnotherapists
AAPH Headquarters
4149-A El Camino Way
Palo Alto, CA 94306
www.aaph.org

American Psychotherapy and Medical Hypnosis Association
www.apmha.com

International Medical and Dental Hypnotherapy Association
International Headquarters
4110 Edgeland, Suite 800
Royal Oak, MI 48073
www.infinityinst.com/index.html

National Board for Certified Clinical Hypnotherapists
1110 Fidler Lane, Suite L1
Silver Spring, MD 20910
www.natboard.com

Ministries

The religion- and spiritual-based professional associations and ministries are too numerous to list here. An Internet search will yield subcategories such as these, with the approximate number of individual websites in parentheses:

- Apologetics (2)

- Canada (20)

- Catholic (141)

- Churches of Christ (1)

- Evangelical (45)

- Evangelistic (13)

- Family (5)

- Humanitarian (72)

- International (25)

- Lutheran (34)

- Ministries (169)

- Missions (252)

- Orthodox (15)

- Prayer (4)

- Professional (8)

- Regional (12)

- Rescue (5)

- Seventh-Day Adventists (11)

- Society of Friends—Quakers (31)

- Student Christian Organizations (302)

- Unique Organizations (19)

- United Church of Christ (6)

- Youth (45)

Psychology
American Psychological Association
Education in Psychology and Accreditation Offices
Education Directorate
750 First Street NE
Washington, DC 20002
www.apa.org

American Association for Marriage and Family Therapy
1133 Fifteenth Street NW, Suite 300
Washington, DC 20005
www.aamft.org

American Association of Psychotherapists, Inc.
Board of Examiners
P.O. Box 140182
Dallas, TX 75214
www.angelfire.com/tx/Membership/index.html

Canadian Psychological Association
151 Slater Street, Suite 205
Ottawa, ON K1P 5H3
Canada
www.cpa.ca

Social Work

National Association of Social Workers
750 First Street NE, Suite 700
Washington, DC 20002

National Network For Social Work Managers, Inc.
6501 North Federal Highway, Suite 5
Boca Raton, FL 33487

Council on Social Work Education
1600 Duke Street
Alexandria, VA 22314

The Body

Alternative Healing Arts Careers

Many New Agers have embraced alternative medicine and alternative healing arts over traditional ways. Although fairly new to this country, much of alternative healing methods date back to Eastern arts that have been in practice for thousands of years. And though some have been slow to catch on here, others are fast becoming commonplace.

Health and natural food stores are no longer a rare sight; even small towns have these popular specialty stores with herbs, vitamins, and organically grown food products. (See Chapter 6 for this career option.) Today dieters, smokers, and others struggling with substance abuse might more readily seek out the help of a hypnotherapist, acupuncturist, or acupressurist than in the past.

Pains in your back and shoulders? A neck that stays permanently stiff? Massage therapists abound, with booths set up at conferences or even in the corridors of your neighborhood mall.

In the past thirty years or so, yoga and meditation have become so familiar to us they're now considered more mainstream than alternative. Then there's aromatherapy, an essence for every ailment; reflexology, a point on your foot that affects corresponding body organs; healing with crystals or magnets; herbalism; and more.

Some Possible Job Titles

Below are just a few of the possible job titles for this wide-open New Age career area. Your own search will undoubtedly uncover

a variety of subspecializations as well as completely separate job titles.

Acupuncturist

Acupressurist

Aromatherapist

Doctor of Naturopathic Medicine

Herbalist

Horticultural Therapist

Massage Therapist

Reflexologist

Yoga Instructor

In this chapter we examine the following job options and/or provide firsthand accounts from a:

Massage Therapist

Doctor of Naturopathic Medicine

Herbalist

Horticultural Therapist

Yoga Instructor

Massage Therapy

The healing power of massage has been recognized since ancient times. In as early as the fifth century B.C., the Greek physician Hippocrates wrote that doctors should be experienced "in rubbing... for rubbing can bind a joint that is too loose, and loosen a joint that is too rigid."

Various forms of massage were also used by ancient Chinese, Egyptians, and Romans. The technique we know today came into being in the late nineteenth century when Swedish gymnast Per Henrik Ling developed the principles of Swedish massage.

Massage is a systematic manual application of pressure to the soft tissue of the body. It encourages healing by promoting the flow of blood, relieving tension, stimulating nerves, and loosening muscles and connective tissue to keep them limber.

There are dozens of specialized massage techniques in use today, including Reiki, reflexology, Rolfing, and shiatsu. However, the most widespread variation builds upon the original basic strokes of Swedish massage.

Other specialized techniques employed for specific purposes include:

- *Neuromuscular massage*, also known as *trigger point therapy*

- *Deep-tissue massage* on areas of the body suffering from chronic muscle tension, especially effective with tense areas such as stiff necks or sore shoulders

- *Sports massage*, a rapidly expanding field popular among both professional athletes and fitness enthusiasts

Training

It's important to make sure you receive proper training and credentials. Membership in the American Massage Therapy Association (AMTA) means you have graduated from a training program approved by the Commission on Massage Training Accreditation/Approval; hold a state license that meets AMTA certification standards; have passed an AMTA membership examination; or have passed the National Certification Examination for Therapeutic Massage and Bodywork.

Licensing of massage therapists is now required in twenty-five states, and an increasing number of states are adopting the

National Certification Exam. A list of accredited training pro-grams is available from the AMTA. (The organization's address is provided at the end of this chapter.) You can also look in the Yellow Pages for a listing of local schools of massage.

Naturopathy

Naturopathy offers a wealth of mostly harmless and possibly helpful approaches to a healthier diet and lifestyle. Many of its tenets, such as a diet high in fruits, vegetables, and whole grains, are now standard recommendations for those hoping to reduce the risk of cancer, heart disease, and obesity. Its noninvasive physical therapy techniques offer significant relief from a variety of muscle and joint complaints.

Be cautious, though, when considering methods to try yourself or to learn to pass on to others. Some recommendations, such as heat treatments and hydrotherapy, for example, may not neces-sarily be the most effective way to treat an infection. The vari-ous detoxifying measures advocated in naturopathy are even more suspect. There is little proof that a toxic buildup can exist to be dealt with, nor proof that even if one did exist, these par-ticular methods would eliminate it.

Naturopathic practitioners include physicians, chiropractors, nutritionists, holistic nurses, massage therapists, and nonmedical personnel. Their approaches to diagnosis and treatment can vary accordingly. Evaluation of diet and lifestyle is considered the most important. Some naturopathic practitioners could also uti-lize laboratory analysis, allergy testing—a lot of people seem to be allergic to wheat—and x-rays, as well as a physical exam.

Depending upon your illness and the practitioner's ideology, treatment could include any of the following:

- Herbal medicines—herbs or extracts, prescribed as natural alternatives to synthetic medications

- Dietary supplements and restrictions—vitamins, minerals, enzymes, and other foods, recommended as a natural boost to health and resistance; elimination of certain food categories (such as dairy or red meat)

- Physical manipulation—massage, hydrotherapy, application of heat or cold, and exercise

- Stress management—hypnotherapy, biofeedback, counseling, massage, and other means to reduce or eliminate stress and to cope with any damage from that stress

- Detoxifying methods—fasting or enemas

We must now look at how effective naturopathic methods are—and how potentially dangerous. "First, do no harm." This is of the utmost importance. Second, don't rip off your clients. Selling high-priced protein drinks, for example, that have not been proven scientifically to do anything other than add to a person's daily caloric intake should be a practice to avoid.

Most naturopathic practitioners enter into the field with nothing but good intentions. How well naturopathy works depends on the aspect in question. It's no secret that traditional medicine, having ignored nutrition for decades, now preaches low-fat, high-fiber diets to prevent a range of diseases. Traditional physicians are also now giving credence to certain vitamins and herbs such as St. John's Wort for depression or valerian as a sleep aid.

Having said that, other practices have no proven scientific credibility. Traditional medicine pooh-poohs the notion of toxins building up in the body and discredits fasting or excessive consumption of water as particularly helpful. Megadoses of vitamins have shown to be ineffective in most cases and in some cases harmful. If your body ingests more than it needs of an element, it will either eliminate the excess through normal channels—or there could be a toxic reaction. So the treatment purporting to take care of toxins could actually be the cause.

And eliminating food groups can be dangerous, possibly leading to deficiencies that could cause anemia or other conditions.

We must approach with caution any practice outside the norm that has not undergone extensive clinical trials and research.

Training

Doctors of Naturopathic Medicine (N.D.s) have completed four years of graduate-level training at a naturopathic medical college. There are currently three accredited colleges in the United States: Bastyr College in Seattle; National College in Portland, Oregon; and Southwestern College in Tempe, Arizona.

There are only eleven states that license naturopathic physicians. These physicians must pass either a national- or state-level board examination.

There are now only about 1,500 N.D.s practicing in the United States, as compared to the 577,000 M.D.s and D.O.s practicing. However, judging by current enrollment figures in naturopathic medical schools, the number of N.D.s is expected to double within the next few years.

N.D.s often call themselves general practice family physicians (GPs) or primary-care physicians.

For specific details on admission and curriculum, contact the three accredited training programs already mentioned.

Healing with Plants

For thousands of years, people have recognized the healing properties of plants. Before the creation of synthetic medicines, ancient cultures were knowledgeable about each plant's function and how to tap into its strengths.

In modern times in the United States, this discipline has become almost a lost art. But not quite. Those interested in alternative healing arts still recognize the value of plants for healing.

In addition to their aesthetic value and life-sustaining importance as food, plants have always been the basis for curing common and not-so-common ailments. Products derived from plants and the act of working with plants in general provide us with therapeutic and curative powers.

Horticultural Therapy

Any New Age enthusiast who loves plants can tell you that being close to the soil, working with plants or just sitting in a fragrant and colorful spot, has therapeutic value. Horticultural activity has been long known to relieve tension, improve our physical condition, and promote a sense of accomplishment, pride, and well-being.

The earliest physicians in ancient Egypt prescribed walks in the garden for their mentally ill patients. A signer of the Declaration of Independence, physician Benjamin Rush encouraged his psychiatric patients to tend the gardens. In 1879, Pennsylvania's Friends Asylum for the Insane (today renamed Friends Hospital) built the first known greenhouse for use with mentally ill patients. And after World War II, veterans hospitals—with the help of scores of garden-club volunteers—also promoted similar activity for their physically and emotionally disabled patients.

Today, horticultural therapy is an emerging science based on this time-tested art. In 1955, Michigan State University awarded the first undergraduate degree in horticultural therapy, and in 1971, Kansas State University established the first graduate program in the field.

What Is Horticultural Therapy?

Horticultural therapists use activities involving plants and other natural materials to rehabilitate and/or improve a person's social, educational, psychological, and physical adjustment. This particular field could also be considered a form of spiritual therapy.

Therapists work with people who are physically or developmentally disabled, the elderly, drug and alcohol abusers, prisoners, and those who are socially or economically disadvantaged.

Charles A. Lewis of the Morton Arboretum says, "Plants possess life-enhancing qualities that encourage people to respond to them. In a judgmental world, plants are nonthreatening and nondiscriminating. They are living entities that respond directly to the care that is given them, not to the intellectual or physical capacities of the gardener. In short, they provide a benevolent setting in which a person can take the first steps toward confidence."

Horticultural therapists, in addition to utilizing standard gardening routines, also introduce alternative methods that are sensitive to the special needs of patients. This involves building wide paths and gently graded entrances accessible to wheelchairs and constructing raised beds. Tools are also adapted; short handles, for example, work best with wheelchair-bound individuals, long handles for those with weak backs.

Job Outlook

Because of the continued growth of horticultural therapy, the demand for trained therapists has continued to rise. Horticultural therapists find work in rehabilitation hospitals, nursing homes, substance-abuse treatment centers, prisons, botanical gardens, and through inner-city programs.

Finding That Job

Kansas State University in Manhattan, Kansas, maintains a job bank, and the American Horticultural Therapy Association (AHTA) lists any openings they are made aware of. (The AHTA address is provided at the end of this chapter.)

Some positions find their way into the classified ad section of local newspapers, but most horticultural therapists learn about positions through word of mouth—or they create their own.

Often, rehabilitation centers and hospitals and other appropriate settings aren't aware of the benefits of a horticultural therapy program. Enterprising therapists with public relations skills have learned how to convince administrators that their services are needed. Many begin by volunteering their time, working with patients or clients at the hospitals or through a local botanical garden.

Training

Because horticultural therapy is such a young discipline, finding training is not an easy process. Currently, Kansas State University's department of horticulture, forestry, and recreation resources is the only bachelor's and master's degree program offered in horticultural therapy in the United States. Three universities—Herbert H. Lehman College, Texas A&M University, and University of Rhode Island—offer bachelor's degrees in horticulture with options in horticultural therapy. Edmonds Community College awards a two-year associate's degree in horticultural therapy, and various other institutes, such as Massachusetts Bay Community College and Temple University, offer horticultural therapy electives.

There are several routes an aspiring horticultural therapist can take to become qualified. Dr. Richard Mattson, a professor at Kansas State University's program, recommends a four-year course of study that covers several disciplines.

"Originally, our program was narrowly defined in that we were training students to work primarily in psychiatric hospitals with mentally ill patients. We have a much broader definition today of horticultural therapy. It's more universal. We feel that the human benefits of gardening include mental improvement in areas such as self-esteem and stress reduction and generally improving the quality of life. Horticultural therapy is any kind of interaction of people and plants for mutual benefit. So, we work in community gardens or community farmer's markets. Students work in botan-

ical gardens or arboreta, in the public school systems, or within zoo horticulture. They work in vocational training centers or do international placements with the Peace Corps or in horticultural industry.

"Our concept at Kansas State is that the individual must be trained in a multidisciplinary approach," Dr. Mattson explains. "That means you have to cross over some of the traditional barriers that exist between discipline areas. For example, horticulture is one of the disciplines. Horticulture involves the art and science of growing and culturing plant material in intensive or adapted environments. But then, to work effectively with people, the student must be well trained in areas of psychology and sociology and in education. We think all of those are important. There are also supporting areas such as human ecology, which used to be called home economics. But it's a very important field because it deals with the growth and development of family and relationships. Architecture is also important for creating accessible landscapes. Students can also pursue a number of other areas such as speech pathology, communications, computer science, robotics, human anatomy, and muscle movement."

Also through the auspices of Kansas State's program, students spend a six-month internship gaining practical on-the-job training. Students are supervised by registered horticultural therapists in established programs and are placed coast to coast, from Friends Hospital in Philadelphia to the Chicago Botanical Gardens.

But although desirable, a four-year degree is not necessary to find work as a horticultural therapist. "There are different levels of entry into the field," says Dr. Mattson. "In this country, there are a lot of volunteers who belong to garden clubs and master gardener groups taught by the Cooperative Extension Service. There are some programs that train at the associate arts level, for people who don't have the extra time to devote to their training. But I do think that the bachelor's or master's is important. At some

time in the future, the entry for many areas of employment in horticultural therapy will be at the graduate level. Horticultural therapy is not just making flower arrangements or planting gardens. We feel that a multidiscipline training will help individuals apply what's best known in all the related fields. A good example is the importance of business and marketing skills. Many horticultural therapy programs today are cost effective; that is, they are self-sufficient. But in order to utilize the valuable products being produced—whether sacks of potatoes from a vegetable garden or flowers or a landscaping service being provided—an individual needs some kind of skills in how to market the product."

The Registration Process

Although not every employer of horticultural therapists requires registration, being a registered therapist greatly increases your chances of landing a good job. Registration provides the individual with recognition as an accomplished therapist and helps to keep the profession's standards high.

There are three levels of registration: the HTT designation is for the technician who has generally gone through a two-year program; the HTR designation is for someone with a bachelor's; and the HTM is for the person with multiple years of experience and a graduate degree.

Becoming a registered horticultural therapist does not require a degree in horticultural therapy. A degree in a related field or a combination of work experience and education can all lead to professional registration. Decisions about registration are reviewed by a committee from the American Horticultural Therapy Association. They follow a point system, awarding points for the number of years of experience, for publications, for attending seminars, for the number of degrees earned, and other related activities.

Herbalism

An old Webster's dictionary from the 1800s defined an herbalist as one involved with the commerce of plants; an herb doctor or root doctor. Today, most people refer to herbalists as those who use or pick herbs for medicine.

Herbalists fall into several different categories.

- Wildcrafters pick herbs that are going to be used for medicinal purposes.

- Farmers who specifically grow herbs for medicine are considered to be herbalists.

- Herbologists, as the suffix implies, are people who study herbs and identify them but don't necessarily use them.

Training

For those seeking training as an herbalist, there are a number of residency programs in the United States. There are also correspondence courses and various lectures, seminars, and workshops held across the country. The American Herbalist Guild publishes an inexpensive directory that lists all the different programs. It is available by writing to them at their address listed at the end of this chapter.

Although herbalism has been practiced pretty much in the same manner for thousands of years, finding recognition through established channels in this country could take another millennium or two, U.S. herbalists believe.

Herbalist Roy Upton (see his firsthand account later in this chapter) says, "There is a monopolistic control of health care in this country. Specialties such as midwifery, which is accepted worldwide, and herbalism, which is also accepted worldwide by other cultures, are not warmly embraced in this country. But that's changing.

"Presently, there are only two mechanisms by which someone can be licensed to practice medicine and utilize herbs in his or her practice. The first is to become licensed as a naturopathic physician. The other way to become licensed to use herbs is as an acupuncturist. Acupuncture is a foundation of Chinese medicine, and herbalism plays a large role in that discipline. But it has to be through a program that teaches herbal medicine. Not all acupuncture programs do."

Jobs with Herbal Product Manufacturers

There are several kinds of jobs available within the herbal product manufacturing industry:

- Research and development of products involves developing formulas and processing techniques.

- Quality control workers ensure that the plants being used are the right plants, that they are not contaminated, and that they have the potency they should have.

- Writers are needed to develop literature describing the products. (See Chapter 5 for careers in writing.)

- Teaching classes increases consumer awareness about the different products. (See Chapter 7 for careers in teaching.)

Pharmacognosy

Pharmacology is the study of medicinal actions of substances in general. Pharmacognosy is the study of medicinal actions of plants and other natural products.

It doesn't cover, as herbalism does, the practice of herbal medicine or the picking of medicinal plants. It is the job of pharmacognosy professionals to pick the product apart and study its constituents.

Roy Upton explains: "Native American herbalists, for example, might not know that a plant contains volatile oils, alkaloids, and polysaccharides. They don't care about that. They know how to use it, how it works, and that's what's important.

"A pharmacognosist would study those elements, though they wouldn't necessarily know how to use them. The end result of their study is to try to develop synthetic drugs from the natural substances.

"Like herbalism, pharmacognosy was sort of an endangered species. At one time, physicians were trained in botany because they needed to know where their medicines came from. But then there was the separation between pharmacy and medicine, and other subspecialties were created, such as pharmacology and pharmacognosy, which kept on studying medicinal plants. As the chemical revolution took place in the 1800s, there was a big push to develop medicines as patentable substances to create a pharmaceutical industry.

"The craft of the herbalist and the pharmacognosist was less valued. Doctors no longer studied botany, and the thrust was to synthesize medicinal plants so they could be standardized to a certain level of activity. The professions almost died. It's only been in the last twenty years that there's been a resurgence."

Firsthand Accounts

James Miller, Yoga Therapist

James Miller is currently twenty-nine years old and has been a practicing yoga therapist and fitness consultant for ten years. He is self-employed and leases space from Synergy Health Center, a holistic health/massage therapy business in downtown Cedar Rapids, Iowa.

James Miller was in the United States Marine Corps, attended Northern Illinois University for three years, and is certified as a

personal trainer and in hatha yoga. He is also a STOTT Pilates conditioning mat/reformer instructor.

Getting Started

"Fitness had always been important to me, and even as early as grade school, I can remember spending my money on vitamins and trying to lift weights. I attended a boarding high school, and the luxury of a weight room and plenty of free time started my commitment to working out. Although I wanted a career in writing, I decided to support myself first by taking a position as a sales manager at a local health club.

"When the time came for the trainers in the club to be certified, the owner asked if I would be interested in testing along with them. I scored the highest, even among trainers who had owned personal training companies for years, and was soon ranked the top trainer in the club. Since this didn't make me very popular and my ambitions were still to attend college and launch a writing career, I decided to enlist in the Marine Corps to reap the benefits of the tuition reimbursement programs. Still interested in fitness, I continued working out and training other marines, eventually organizing a small team to compete in the armed forces bodybuilding competition.

"During all of this, I remained a voracious reader, interested in reading mostly philosophical and spiritual books. This inevitably led me to read of yoga and the Eastern methods of fitness, and I was amazed at the depth of wisdom I found. This was philosophical fitness, a search for the complete expression of a human being's potential and a system so complete in itself that it could be adapted to fit even the most deconditioned clients and lead them to perfect health.

"My tour of duty in the marines complete, I opened my own personal training studio and began working with clients. Slowly, I began to use yoga more and more with each new client as I began to understand how powerful a tool it was to evoke change.

"Still interested in writing, I began to publish fitness articles in international magazines. I am currently working on a manuscript titled *Living Powerfully*. This book will attempt to redefine the reasons we exercise in the West, by showing the beauty and meaning behind the Eastern techniques."

What the Work Is Like

"In working with clients, I employ a host of Eastern techniques, from tai chi and hatha yoga to more esoteric forms of bodywork such as kundalini yoga and Thai massage.

"I am also an ACE certified personal trainer. ACE is the American Council on Exercise, and of the many certifying organizations, it is one of the most respected.

"I am also a STOTT Pilates conditioning mat/reformer instructor. Pilates is an exercise discipline founded by Joseph Pilates around the 1930s. It is yoga based, because of his experience in yoga, but would appear to be almost a preventative form of physical therapy for the mind/body connection. It is the current pinnacle of fitness in the Western world and is the trend both in the media and in the gym.

"STOTT conditioning is one take on the body of work written by Joseph Pilates as understood by Moira Stott, a former dancer and now a heavy hitter in the Pilates world. It is by far the most respected approach toward Pilates, for it combines the essence of Pilates with the most up-to-date information in the physical-therapy world.

"Mat certification is the first level; an instructor learns to facilitate classes without any particular machinery. Reformer certification is machine specific—being certified to facilitate exercise on a rather archaic looking machine with a wide variety of possible exercises. (Joseph developed these pieces of equipment while imprisoned in England during World War II; he used only the equipment available in the camp, such as hospital beds— hence the strange-looking equipment.)

"Overall, Pilates certification is more respected among the medical community than personal training or even yoga.

"The freedom of being self-employed allows me to adapt my work schedule to best fit my life. During a typical day, I begin working one-on-one with clients at 7 A.M. and book hourly through 2 P.M. I find that working back-to-back with clients allows me to keep my energy and attention focused on my work and is a more efficient way to earn money.

"After taking a break in the afternoon, I may work on a host of other projects designed to move my career away from working entirely with clients one-on-one and toward one-on-many, such as my upcoming book and my interactive website.

"The beauty of working for yourself is the endless opportunity and the amazing number of ways to expand your business. In the evenings, I usually teach yoga or Pilates classes at local yoga studios and health clubs. This may seem like a busy work schedule, but the things I do to earn a living are the things I am really interested in, so I rarely feel overworked. On the contrary, I usually feel energized. Working with people so intimately provides for almost a social atmosphere, and sometimes it's easy to forget I am doing my job. Clients become friends, and I look forward daily to seeing them develop and progress."

Upsides and Downsides

"The best part of my job is simple. Each and every time I work with clients, I see them at their best, making positive changes in their lives, becoming stronger, more confident and content with their lives. People are happy when they see me, and I rarely deal with the negativity and stress others experience daily in their jobs. Being a positive part of people's lives brings meaning to my own life, and nothing could be more fulfilling.

"I now realize that the reason I enjoy my job so much is because I am simply sharing the knowledge and skills I have

learned over the years with other people. No other job could be easier—or a more perfect reflection of me.

"It is difficult, though, to be a fitness consultant/yoga therapist because it is more than a job; it is a life you, too, must lead. That can be challenging. You must practice what you preach, and each day I continue to discipline myself as I travel the path to perfect health. The further you advance in yoga and in fitness, the further you can bring others, and so I am responsible daily for renewing my commitment to the things I believe in."

Salaries

"I charge $45 per hour of yoga therapy/fitness consulting, and I average between thirty and forty hours weekly.

"In addition to this are the classes I teach through local health clubs. They pay between $60 and $80 per class. Beyond this I have income through phone coaching, writing, and occasionally giving motivational talks on fitness and yoga."

Advice from James Miller

"Explore what you really believe about the human body and our individual paths toward self-perfection. You cannot convince other people to evoke positive change in their lives without believing it yourself first. Most likely the things you believe are represented by the way you are living right now, and this will help you decide if you are ready to help others.

"Read constantly. If you have a thirst for knowledge, this will continue to propel your career to new levels year after year. Become qualified by searching out the best available degrees and/or certifications, but continue to learn from yourself.

"The path you take to perfect health is the same path your clients will travel, and you are there to guide them through the same trouble spots that challenged you. And realize that in the end, if your intent is to help others, you will inevitably succeed. Everything else will take care of itself."

Victoria Pospisil, Eastern Healing Arts Practitioner/Licensed Massage Therapist

Victoria Pospisil is co-owner of Embody Health, a group practice in Mt. Vernon, Iowa, that includes several bodyworkers, counselors, a chiropractor, and an acupuncturist.

She has a bachelor's degree in business and English from Cornell College, Iowa, and she received her P.E.H.A. (Practitioner of Eastern Healing Arts) from Windemere School of Eastern Healing Arts in Decorah, Iowa, in 1999. She has also studied Reiki and received her master/teacher level in 1998.

Getting Started

"I began my spiritual journey in 1993 and discovered Reiki, which is a hands-on form of healing. From there my love for working with life-force energy became a passion. This naturally led to studying the Eastern philosophy of energy and traditional Chinese medicine.

"I kept asking in prayer 'How can I serve?' And the more I asked, the more doors opened for me along this path. As I delved further into Reiki and Qigong, I felt as if I were coming home. Friends and family began to seek out my healing sessions, and I knew I needed to be ethical and knowledgeable about my work. I sought out a school that would give me the information I needed."

What the Work Is Like

"Eastern healing arts incorporate the concept of energy in the form of a subtle life force that moves throughout the human body. This life force energy comes in many forms and can be transferred from one person to another.

"My job is to find imbalances within the energy field of a client and, by using various methods, facilitate balance and health. The various methods I use include Tuina, which is

Chinese medical massage, acupressure, shiatsu, or neuromuscular therapy. I always incorporate energy work, such as Reiki or Qigong, in my sessions. This way, I know I am addressing the physical body, but I am also seeking to help the client understand why this imbalance happened in the first place.

"Embody Health is in a small college town with larger cities within close driving range. Our clients are professional people with extra income and an interest in their health.

"My duties include setting up a quiet, comfortable healing environment. This sounds easy, but it is difficult to find all of these in one place. The next task is one of the most challenging parts of my job—staying centered all of the time. I am a mom with two busy teens and a farm. But, I find that when I arrive to work, I can easily move into a place of calm just by using my breath and allowing my mind to empty to receive the 'flow,' which is always available.

"In a typical day, I see about four clients. I allow ninety minutes per person, including time to greet them, talk about what their needs are for the session, give them time to undress and then dress afterwards, and then leave time for post-session communication. The time is barely sufficient, and it's one of my challenges.

"As for the hour they are actually on my mat, or my massage table, it is wonderful! It is just us and quiet music or silence and the intention of our mutual agreement concerning their needs. When you invite the divine into your work, wonderful things happen!"

Upsides and Downsides

"I love my work when I am in the session. I do not like the paperwork that is involved in the massage process as far as insurance companies are concerned. And, unfortunately, the paperwork is required more and more frequently."

Salaries

"I charge $50 per session. I usually work on four clients per day and work five days per week. This is all pretty loose, however, because some people cannot afford the fee, insurance won't cover them, and I am their source of comfort. I do ask for some energy exchange, but it may not always come in the form of money, and sometimes it is my form of tithing to God."

Advice from Victoria Pospisil

"Be prepared to handle the following: inconsistent income, paperwork, clients with their own agendas and timelines, the need to find creative ways to add on extra income, that is, other products to sell with your services.

"Also count on miracles—they are around every corner in the business of service with God.

"In my opinion, the field of energy medicine is virtually in its infancy. We have the benefit of thousands of years of practice from the East, but we have had little ways of measuring how it works or even why it works. This is an exciting field to work in, if this is your passion. This is also a field that has such a high level of gratification to it. To have someone come to you, totally stressed out or suffering from lack of sleep because of physical pain and to have them walk out feeling so much better, that is a great job!

"My advice would be to find a school with an excellent reputation for delivering competent, qualified therapists and then begin, knowing you will probably be studying and learning the rest of your life.

"You must be in good physical shape to approach this career, and you must be in excellent mental health, because you need to be well balanced to work with people at this level. There is also a level of organization needed in this field, and there is some paperwork, so these skills are useful. And before you dive in, talk with another massage therapist."

Nancy Stevenson, Horticultural Therapist

Nancy Stevenson has worked as a horticultural therapist for more than twenty years. She earned a bachelor's degree in political science, then later went on for a master's in human services and became registered by the American Horticultural Therapy Association (AHTA).

Getting Started

"I became interested in horticultural therapy in the early seventies when it was still just a fledgling profession. The national organization, AHTA, was founded in 1973. At first I was a volunteer at a boys' detention center, working with someone who had started an indoor gardening program there. My colleague, Libby Reavis, who I've been working with ever since, volunteered with me. We became more and more interested and realized there was a real need in Cleveland to develop some training for this field. We worked through the Garden Center of Greater Cleveland (now known as the Cleveland Botanical Garden) to start some workshops. We stayed as volunteers until 1981. Then Libby and I joined the staff sharing a full-time job between us. We went to them and explained that the job had become too big for us to handle as volunteers. We were spending twenty hours a week apiece on this. If they wanted to get into horticultural therapy in a big way, they needed a paid position. We helped them design the job and set the salary."

What the Work Is Like

"Over the years, we've had quite a varied program through the garden center. We contract with different agencies for outreach programs. Typical programs have been at children's hospitals or nursing homes. We'd go every other week and design a yearlong curriculum that included indoor and outdoor gardening. We have activities that involve repotting or propagation from seeds

and cuttings. We work with plants and dried materials for crafts—pressed flowers, flower arranging, and that sort of thing.

"A good 60 percent of our time is spent out in the community. We recently developed a three-year program of intergenerational gardening in a neighborhood center in the inner city. The program brings seniors and elementary school students together.

"We do a lot of public speaking to garden clubs and civic organizations to help educate people about horticultural therapy and its benefits.

"I have also been involved with training future horticultural therapists through the Cleveland Botanical Garden, which offers a six-month internship program."

Salaries

"The American Horticultural Therapy Association conducts an annual survey to determine salary levels for nonregistered therapists, HTTs, HTRs, and HTMs. The average salary of therapists with one year or less of employment experience is around $25,000 per year. Averages go up with the number of years of work experience, but not much. Therapists can expect to earn around $27,000 with one to five years experience, $28,000 with five to ten years experience, and $34,000 with ten or more years. Salaries increase by $1,500 to approximately $2,500 or so per year for those who have obtained professional registration.

"There are a lot of rewards to this profession, but money certainly isn't one of them. I think the reward for me is being able to combine horticulture and gardening, which have always been very strong interests of mine, with working directly with people—helping people learn about the therapeutic benefits of gardening and how working with plants can help them, no matter what their disabilities or limitations are.

"I think the relationship between therapist and client is very important. You set up a nonthreatening situation where positive change can occur for someone. You have to build trust."

Advice from Nancy Stevenson

"The ideal personality for a horticultural therapist is usually someone who's fairly outgoing and comfortable with people and able to express him- or herself well. You should have a natural bent for teaching and be able to communicate with people to instruct them on basic gardening techniques. It's kind of an elusive quality, but you should have whatever that something is that makes people feel comfortable with you, to be able to talk freely with you. It's similar to the qualities most kinds of therapists should possess.

"I think you also have to be able to stay fairly detached and not become too emotionally involved with the people you're trying to help, otherwise it can be hard on you."

Roy Upton, Herbalist

Roy Upton is president of the American Herbalist Guild and an herbalist who, through his writing and lecturing, is involved with teaching people the medicinal value of plants. He writes books and magazine articles and teaches classes across the country. He also works full-time for a manufacturer of medicinal products, where he is responsible for quality control and answering customers' questions.

Getting Started

"I came across my knowledge in an interesting manner. I lived for three and half years on different Native American reservations in Washington, Nevada, and New Mexico, learning about herbs and their uses. I learned about herbs as a process of living. People got sick; the medicine people picked herbs and made teas or poultices. I absorbed what I was seeing and started learning.

"I then spent four years in St. Thomas, Virgin Islands, and studied the Caribbean's ethnobotany—how cultures use plants for medicine.

"There are different herb doctors in the Caribbean; people go to them just like they go to regular doctors here. One of my teachers was too old to gather the plants, so I would do it for her, and then she would tell me what they were used for. I would then comb through all the literature in the libraries, and eventually, while working on a project for the local college in St. Thomas, cataloging the different medicinal plants and setting up medicinal herb gardens, I learned even more.

"From there I traveled to California, where I am currently based, and I entered into a three-year program studying traditional Chinese medicine."

What the Work Is Like

"I consult with people about their health needs and which types of herbs they can use to deal with different types of ailments. However, unless you are licensed, you cannot hang out a shingle and practice medicine in this country, even if in that practice all you are doing is recommending herbal teas.

"Under the FDA, the Federal Food and Drug Administration, you cannot legally dispense a substance for medicinal use unless that substance has been approved by the FDA. If you give garlic to someone, for example, and tell him or her that it can help lower cholesterol levels, you can be arrested for dispensing illicit drugs. Garlic. But we are pushing the system to change.

"If you walk into any nutrition and health store, you'll see rows of bottles and vials holding all the different herbs in their various forms. How do manufacturers and retailers buck the system? In essence, they are selling non-FDA-approved substances, which are therefore considered illegal.

"But the answer is simple. The products are not packaged as medicines; they are called 'foods.' Trained herbalists know what to do with these 'foods.' They are aware of how the popular medications used in this country—aspirins and sedatives, for example—can be substituted safely with common plants.

"Aspirin was originally derived from a plant called meadow-sweet, for example. The Latin name is *spirea*, which is where the word *aspirin* came from. So, if someone has a headache, we would use a natural source, a tea made with meadowsweet.

"With sedatives, there are more than a million prescriptions written for Valium every year, which involves an expensive doctor visit and an expensive prescription, not to mention all the harmful implications. Instead, we would start with something as simple as chamomile tea, which is what Peter Rabbit's mother gave him. Chamomile is a flower that has essential oils. These oils have calming and sedative properties. There are a whole range of calming herbs that get progressively stronger—from chamomile to skullcap to valerian root.

"Herbalists get the message across without resorting to breaking the law. We teach and write books and articles, we lecture and offer apprentice programs, or we work for herbal product manufacturers."

For More Information

American Council on Exercise
P.O. Box 910449
San Diego, CA 92191

Alternative Medicine Association
7909 Southeast Stark Street
Portland, OR 97215

American Association of Naturopathic Physicians
8201 Greensboro Drive, Suite 300
McLean, VA 22102
www.naturopathic.org

American Association of Colleges of Osteopathic Medicine
6110 Executive Boulevard, Suite 405
Rockville, MD 20852

American College of Sports Medicine (ACSM)
P.O. Box 1440
Indianapolis, IN 46206

American Herbalist Guild
Box 1683
Soquel, CA 95073

American Horticultural Therapy Association (AHTA)
362A Christopher Avenue
Gaithersburg, MD 20879

American Massage Therapy Association (AMTA)
820 Davis Street, Suite 100
Evanston, IL 60201

The American Medical Association (AMA)
515 North State Street
Chicago, IL 60610

American Osteopathic Association
142 East Ontario Street
Chicago, IL 60611

Flower Essence Society
P.O. Box 459
Nevada City, CA 95959

Friends of Horticultural Therapy
362A Christopher Avenue
Gaithersburg, MD 20879

Herb Research Foundation
1007 Pearl Street #200
Boulder, CO 80302

International Physical Fitness Association
415 West Court Street
Flint, MI 48503

The Lady Bird Johnson Wildflower Center
4801 LaCrosse Avenue
Austin, TX 78739

Touch Research Institute (TRI)
University of Miami School of Medicine
Coral Gables, FL 33124

Horticultural Therapy Training Programs

Cleveland Botanical Garden
11030 East Boulevard
Cleveland, OH 44106
(Six-month internship program)

Edmonds Community College
20000 Sixty-eighth Avenue West
Lynnwood, WA 98036
(Two-year program in horticultural therapy)

Kansas State University
Department of Horticulture, Forestry and Recreation Resources
Throckmorton Hall
Manhattan, KS 66506
(B.S. and M.S. program in horticultural therapy)

Kansas State University
Division of Continuing Education
226 College Court Building
Manhattan, KS 66506
(Short-term correspondence course)

Herbert H. Lehman College
The City University of New York
250 Bedford Park Boulevard
West Bronx, NY 10468
(B.S. in horticulture with options in horticultural therapy in
    cooperation with the New York Botanical Garden)

Massachusetts Bay Community College
Wellesley, MA 02181
(Horticultural therapy electives)

The New York Botanical Garden
200th Street and Southern Boulevard
Bronx, NY 10458
(Certificate program)

Rockland Community College
Suffern, NY 10901
(Horticultural therapy electives)

Temple University
Department of Landscape Architecture and Horticulture
Ambler, PA 19002
(Horticultural therapy electives)

Tennessee Technological University
School of Agriculture
Box 5034
Cookerville, TN 38505
(Horticultural therapy electives)

Texas A&M University
Department of Horticulture
College Station, TX 77843
(B.S. in horticulture with options in horticultural therapy)

Tulsa Junior College Northeast Campus
Department of Science and Engineering
3727 East Apache
Tulsa, OK 74115
(Horticultural therapy electives)

University of Massachusetts
Department of Plant & Soil Science
Durfee Conservatory, French Hall
Amherst, MA 01002
(Horticultural therapy electives)

University of Rhode Island
Department of Plant Science
Kingston, RI 02881
(B.S. in horticulture with options in horticultural therapy)

Virginia Polytechnic Institute and State University
Department of Horticulture
Blacksburg, VA 24061
(Horticultural therapy electives)

CHAPTER FIVE

New Age Writers
Careers in Print and Cyberspace

F or every area of interest, there is a body of knowledge committed to paper—books and articles for magazines, newspapers, journals, and newsletters. There is also the electronic media with megabytes to fill all over the Internet.

New Age writers have a wealth of subject matter to cover—everything from daily and weekly astrology columns to paranormal reporting, self-help, spirituality, and more.

Here is just a small, general sampling of possible book or article topics:

Acupuncture

Aromatherapy

Astrology

Channeling

Crystals

ESP

Feng Shui

Ghosts

Herbology

Horticultural therapy

Hypnotherapy

Massage

Metaphysics

Naturopathic medicine

Numerology

Paranormal healing

Psychic phenomenon

Pyramids

Reflexology

Reiki

Rolfing

Tarot reading

UFOs

Zener Cards

Each of the above topics lends itself to a specific focus or angle. For example, you could write a general article on hypnotherapy, explaining what it is; or you could describe one particular use, such as helping a client to quit smoking; or you could profile a hypnotherapist; or you could take the approach that hypnotherapy doesn't work and why. One topic, several articles. Similarly, when proposing a book project, you can narrow or broaden a topic as needed.

Markets for Articles

There are two major outlets through which you can locate markets for your New Age article—the current *Writer's Market* (Writer's Digest Books), which includes astrology, metaphysical,

and New Age among its many categories, and the Internet. Performing a search on the Internet using key words such as *New Age publications* or *New Age magazines* will deliver thousands of sites. The list that follows is not an endorsement but a sampling of what one such search can uncover.

- *Alchemy*—an E-zine reviewing websites covering a wide range of alternative beliefs and systems of thought.
  www.alchemy2go.com

- *American Spirit Newspaper*—includes articles on spirituality, meditation, psychic awareness, health, prosperity, and relationships.
  www.celestia.com/SRP

- *Atlantis Rising Online*—provides access to articles from back issues: *Free Energy, Atlantis, Hall of Records, Emerging Archeology, Astrology, Edgar Cayce, Spirituality, New Age, The Millennium.*
  www.atlantisrising.com

- *Awareness Magazine*—a bimonthly publication that reaches individuals concerned with many issues that involve the environment, holistic health, natural health products, fitness, and personal growth.
  www.awarenessmag.com

- *Bliss*—a monthly magazine that publishes articles, interviews, inspiring stories, news, vegetarian recipes, and book, music, and movie reviews.
  www.bliss2000.com

- *Circles of Light*—published weekly, with original articles and columns concerning astrology and metaphysics.
  www.circlesoflight.com

- *Conscious Creation Journal*—a bimonthly publication on all aspects of reality creation, metaphysics and consciousness.
  www.consciouscreation.com/journal

- *Four Directions Web-Zine*—an on-line discussion/zine, patterned after the four directions of the Native American medicine wheel, that includes poetry, reflections, and an interactive forum.
  www.momo2000.com

- *Galactic News*—a visionary site of current projects underway by the Mystic Broadcast Network.
  www.mysticbroadcast.org/g-news

- *Global Visionary Newsletter*—published by the Earth Rainbow Network.
  www.spacesbetweenthings.com/jean/hudon.html

- *In Light Times*—on-line and print newspaper dealing with metaphysical subjects, spirituality, astrology, UFOs, alternative health, relationships, and the paranormal.
  www.inlightimes.com

- *Innerchange Magazine*—North Carolina's leading resource for personal, spiritual, and planetary transformation, this bimonthly publication focuses on the New Age, spirituality, holistic health, and alternative healing.
  http://innerchangemag.com

- *INSPIRE, SICA: Online Cultural Quarterly*—explores an intensely personal and spiritual creativity across a broad spectrum of cultural endeavor with SICA Virtual Gallery.
  www.subud-sica.org

- *Lightworks*—the *Monthly Aspectarian* New Age zine, astrology, daily astro-weather forecast, visionary art gallery, daily comics, daily affirmations.
  www.lightworks.com

- *Living Traditions Online*—an on-line magazine covering spirituality and academia.
  www.livingtraditions-magazine.com

- *Magical Blend Magazine*—alternative spirituality magazine.
  www.magicalblend.com

- *Mount Shasta Magazine*—quarterly magazine featuring
  teachers in the New Age and alternative health communities.
  www.mountshastamagazine.com

- *New Earth News*—information about the people, places,
  events, and resources that are transforming our world.
  www.newearthnews.com

- *New Frontier*—an on-line magazine with the theme of
  transformation.
  www.newfrontier.com

- *New Millennium Being*—an astrological-based E-zine
  written with novice and non-astrologers in mind.
  www.yogatech.com/nmb

- Oasis TV—a comprehensive New Age portal featuring
  articles on holistic healing, spirituality, metaphysics, the
  environment, and world peace.
  www.oasistv.com

- *Pathways to Enlightenment*—on-line spiritual journal for
  meditation club.
  www.meditationclub.com/index.htm

- *phenomeNEWS*—an on-line New Age magazine.
  www.phenomenews.com

- *Planet Lightworker*—offers a cross-section of New Age
  material.
  www.Planetlightworker.com

- *Rebel Planet*—articles on mysticism, ancient religions,
  goddesses, gods, alchemy, hieroglyphics, magic, astrology,
  tarot, divination, and book reviews.
  www.lunarace.com

- *Romanticside*—articles on how to improve your health, live life more naturally, daily divination in both tarot and astrology, and candle magick.
  www.romanticside.com

- *Seeds of Unfolding*—ideas for spiritual growth and the development of consciousness, including meditation, spiritual exercises, inspirational biographies, and practical applications for daily living.
  www.seedsofunfolding.org

- *Soulful Living*—interactive on-line guide where topics of interest are explored each month with highly regarded experts and authors.
  www.soulfulliving.com

- *Spiritually Fit Webzine*—stories about spiritual experiences in nature and through music.
  www.spirituallyfit.com

- *The Delphi Oracle*—monthly on-line journal for the Omega Foundation, a New Age awareness community to help people improve their lives in positive and exciting ways through channeling, coaching, psychic development, hypnosis programs, and counseling.
  www.users.uswest.net/~omegafdn/delphi.html

- Whole Again Resource Guide—extensive database of New Age on-line publications and resources.
  www.wholeagain.com/welcome.html

You can look through each of the above sites to determine if they accept freelance work and, if they do, what their terms and conditions are. You can also request writers' guidelines via E-mail or by sending a self-addressed, stamped envelope (SASE) through the post office.

The Elements of an Article

Once you've located markets and determined what type of articles the editors prefer, it's time to sit down and write. Although the subject matter can be very different, most articles include many of the same elements.

All the best articles start with an interesting "hook," that first paragraph that grabs the reader's (and the editor's) attention. They use quotes from real people or experts, cite important facts, give examples, and sometimes include amusing anecdotes or experiences.

Some articles have sidebars, additional information that doesn't fit in the body of the article but would be important for readers to know. Examples of sidebars are a list of the signs of the zodiac and the dates they cover; a recipe to accompany a cooking article; or a list of stores where a particular product can be purchased.

The style or tone of the article will vary according to the publication. Some editors prefer chatty pieces that speak directly to the reader; others prefer a more formal voice.

The content, of course, would be specific to that particular publication. Spiritual growth magazines, for example, might include personal experience pieces, interviews with counselors or healers, and self-help pieces.

Some spiritual growth magazines might use only first-person personal experience pieces; others prefer third-person pieces. Some cover only a U.S. readership; others extend to Europe and beyond.

By studying a publication and sending for its writers' guidelines (a simple request with an SASE will quickly have information in the mail to you), you can see the style, word count, focus, and approach the editors prefer.

Getting That First Article Published

Study the Publications

Read as many publications as you can and, in particular, those you would like to write for. Send for sample copies, spend time at the library, or browse through the racks of newsstands. It's never a good idea to send an article to a publication you have never seen before. If you miss the tone or send two thousand words when they can use only one thousand, you might kill your chances for future acceptances.

Send Your Submission: Two Approaches

Once you have decided what you want to write about, there are two ways you can proceed. You can write the entire article on speculation, send it off to appropriate editors, and hope they like your topic. "On spec" writing is akin to a shotgun approach—fire out a lot of articles and see which ones hit the target. It can be time-consuming and will not necessarily pay off, but new writers usually have no choice—they have to write on spec before they establish themselves. Editors are often unwilling to make assignments to unpublished writers. They want to be sure you can deliver a professional, polished manuscript on time.

The second approach is to write a query letter, a miniproposal, to see if there is any interest in your idea first. Query letters will save you the time of writing articles you might have difficulty selling. Only once you're given a definite assignment do you then proceed.

The Elements of a Query Letter

The best queries are one page in length (single-spaced) and start with a hook—perhaps the first paragraph of your article—to

grab the editor's attention. The hook is the focus of your piece, the slant that makes it different from all the other articles out there. In the body of your query letter, you explain your rationale for the piece and your approach—whether you'll be using expert quotes or not, for example. The bio section of your query letter provides your related credits and explains how you are qualified to write this particular piece. You close by asking simply, "May I have the assignment?"

Once your query is done, you can send it to editors in the traditional way, via U.S. mail with an SASE enclosed for the reply. Or, if their guidelines allow it, you may send that query pasted directly into an E-mail. The latter method might get you a quicker reply—but it's oh so easy for that quick reply to be a negative. In addition, if an editor wanted to send you guidelines, or any kind of printed material or sample copy, an E-mail wouldn't always allow for that. So take that into consideration when approaching your markets. Markets that are strictly on-line will most likely be the ones to prefer E-mail transmissions.

Marketing Your Work

Do You Need an Agent?

Here freelancers go it alone. Most agents will not handle articles, unless you are one of their famous clients who also writes books. There is a lot of work involved in selling an article. A commission of 15 percent of $150 to $2,000 or so doesn't make it worthwhile for an agent to enter this arena.

Successful freelancers are aggressive marketers. The more query letters or articles you have circulating, the better your chances of landing assignments. Send out query letters on a regular basis—full-time freelancers reveal they send out forty to fifty query letters a week. That's a lot of work, but no one said it was

easy! Not all query letters, though, are for brand-new article ideas.

Resales

Successful freelancers have learned that writing an article, selling it to a publication, then writing another article to sell to the same or another publication is a slow way of going about earning a living. They count on being able to sell the same article to more than one publication.

When they come up with an article idea, they plan ahead: how many different markets can this article target?

Unless a publication has bought all rights (and you don't want to sell all the rights to your articles), you are free to resell your article as often as you can. However, the rule is that you must approach only noncompeting markets. For example, your travel piece on the "Ten Most Popular Vitamins" could appear in the health sections of both the *Washington Post* and the *San Francisco Chronicle*. These two newspapers do not share the same readership. But your piece on "Pyramid Power—Fact or Fantasy" could not appear in both *New Realities Ezine* and *ZenSpin*; chances are these two do share the same audience.

Reslant and Resell

The previous section cautions against selling the same article to competing publications. But there is a way to resell your pieces to similar markets—with just a little extra work. You've written a piece called "Macrobiotic Recipes for a Healthy Cat," for example, and have sent it off to either *Cat Fancy* or *Cats* magazine. Now it's time to sit back and take a second look at the article. It probably wouldn't take much work to reslant and come up with "Macrobiotic Recipes for a Healthy Dog" or to go even further for your horse, pet ferret, or your aquarium, even. A few new quotes from the appropriate experts, examples tailor-made for

the publication, and you're on your way to selling the reslanted piece as many times as there are interested markets.

Religious publications are abundant and are also very good markets for reslanted articles. *Spiritual Life*, a magazine targeted mostly to a Catholic readership, might use an article on contemporary spirituality. So might the noncompeting *SCP Journal*, geared toward nonbelievers.

Writing Nonfiction Books

Articles tell a short tale. If you have more to say and have something to say you think will sell, then a nonfiction book would be the way to go.

Of approximately one hundred thousand books published each year, 85 percent to 90 percent are nonfiction. That means that nonfiction writers have many more markets to approach than fiction writers, and their chances of breaking in with that first book are much higher.

Selling, Then Writing, Your Nonfiction Book

Often nonfiction writers can sell a book based on a detailed proposal, before they sit down to write the book. If your proposal is well crafted, has all the important information, and convinces the editor you can deliver a professional manuscript, and on time, you might just find a contract coming back in your SASE.

Some editors, though, might be reluctant to offer a contract to a writer with no track record or no real expertise in the subject matter. In this case, you would have to decide if it's worth the risk to write the book on spec. If you've done your research, know that there's a place for your project on bookstore shelves, and are a competent writer, it might be worth forging ahead.

What isn't a good idea is to write a nonfiction book first, then start looking for possible publishers for it. Just as with articles, you have to write to the market—know that there's a niche out there within which your book can fit.

The following eight steps to getting your nonfiction book published will show you the ideal procedure to follow.

Eight Steps to Getting Published

Step One: Develop an Idea

Sounds simple enough, but you must make sure your idea is viable and tightly focused. The next two steps help you accomplish this.

Step Two: Do Your Research

How many other books are out there covering your subject matter? A simple search on the Internet or at the library (*Books in Print*) can answer that question right away. If there are dozens and dozens of books on the subject, it could mean your idea isn't new and original and it's been done to death.

Don't despair, though. If your book has an original slant, a fresh focus, a perspective that hasn't been covered, you might be able to keep that project alive yet. For example, there might be hundreds of books out there that cover traveling through Europe. But if your book is narrowed down and is, for example, a guide to bike tours on the continent, or walking trails, then perhaps there is room for your title, too. The narrower your focus on a well-published topic, the better your chances.

But not too narrow. What if there are very few or even no books on your topic in print? Does that mean you're a shoo-in? Possibly. It could also mean there is no interest in the topic and

publishers don't want to take a chance. Say, for example, your bike tour book focuses on only one small city in an area that isn't attractive or accessible to tourists. The audience for this book would be too narrow—and that's why you didn't find other books on the subject.

Researching competing titles is only half of it. You also need to have a good idea who would buy your book and how this market would be reached. Are you considering a book on pet care? Then have a rough number of how many pet owners there are in the United States (and Canada, too, possibly) and how many pet shows are held each year where your book could possibly be sold.

Step Three: Target the Markets

After you've done your initial research and see there might be an audience for your book, you need to find the publishers you could approach with the project. *Literary Marketplace* (available in your library), *Writer's Market* (available in bookstores or on the Web), and *The International Directory of Little Magazines and Small Presses* (the address for purchasing this book is provided at the end of this chapter) are the best places to start.

Contact likely candidates and ask them to send you their catalogs. Then you can see exactly what they've already published and where your book may or may not fit in. Also ask for their writers' guidelines, so if you do decide to approach them, you can offer them exactly what they want. For example, the guidelines will tell you their word count requirements and if they expect authors to provide illustrations or not.

Step Four: Compose Your Query Letter

Just as with article writing, your query letter for a nonfiction book must be professionally crafted. Include a summary of the book's focus, a rationale for that book—why it should be published—and why you're the one qualified to write the book—all

in one page. At the end of your query, offer to send a detailed proposal.

Step Five: Send Your Query Letter

Once you have your list of potential publishers, mail your query letter with an SASE to just a few at a time. If you do get feedback on your idea, you might discover a need to revise your query. You want to make sure you haven't blitzed all the markets and have no publishers left to query.

Step Six: Craft Your Book Proposal

While you're waiting for those SASEs to come back to your mailbox, get your proposal ready. An excellent guide to help with this is Michael Larsen's *How to Write a Book Proposal* (Writer's Digest Books). In brief, your proposal should include the following sections.

A. Proposal Table of Contents

This is to show what sections you have included in your proposal and on what page of the proposal each can be found. (It is not the table of contents for your proposed book.) You would include the following topic headings (items B through J) in the proposal table of contents.

B. Introduction/Overview

This section is where you try to hook the publisher's interest. It should explain your book and make it sound compelling enough that the publisher will want to read the rest of your proposal.

C. The Competition

Here you want to show that there's a gap in the marketplace for your book. You should list all the competing titles out there and

discuss why your book is both different and better, what need your book fills that the others do not.

D. The Market

In general, it's the publisher's job to know the market—they are already well aware of school and public libraries, for example. But, if you know about special outlets for selling your proposed book, mention them here. Also, be sure to discuss the demographic and general profile of the reader of your book.

E. Format

In this section, explain how your book will be laid out—how many parts, how many chapters, whether illustrations are required. If you're proposing a cookbook, for example, give the publisher an idea of how many recipes will be in each chapter and what kind and how much additional information will be included with each recipe.

F. Author Bio

Focus your bio on the areas that show you are qualified to write this book. If your proposed book is a history of a particular region and you happen to be a Ph.D. historian, an expert in the field, then highlight that. Are you proposing a self-help manual for those living "alternative lifestyles"? Make sure you're a qualified professional who has counseled hundreds, if not thousands, of people on these issues.

What if you're not an expert in any particular field, and you just have your own experiences from which to draw? Then you've got a tough sell on your hands. Give your proposal extra credibility by pointing out that you'll be providing quotes and interviews with experts (both here and in the format section) and also consider finding an expert in the field who will coauthor the book with you or provide a foreword.

G. Sample Table of Contents

Provide in your proposal a sample table of contents, naming each chapter. You can mention a few of the chapter topics—but no need to go into great detail here. You'll do that in the next step. The sample table of contents is to provide the person considering your proposal with a quick look at what your book will cover.

H. Chapter Summary

Provide a brief, tightly written paragraph or two, summarizing the focus of each chapter. Avoid a common mistake—don't begin each chapter summary with "Chapter 1 includes . . . Chapter 2 includes . . ." Jump right into the meat of each chapter.

I. Delivery

Some proposals include a section letting the publisher know when you think you can finish and deliver the manuscript. However, this might show ignorance of the publisher's schedule. If you estimate you might need eighteen months and the publisher wants to go to press in a year, your declaration might put you out of the running.

If the book is already completed, then this section would say something to the effect that the manuscript can be delivered upon request. However, it's not a good idea to let the publisher know that the manuscript is finished. The point of the proposal is to get a contract before you actually write the book. What if you've written a two-hundred-thousand-word tome and the publisher is interested only in sixty thousand words? Certainly, you'll be willing to edit it down—but it's better to wait until you receive a response from your proposal before explaining you might have a monster on your hands. A publisher might be interested in your book and want to work with you, producing the finished product. Announcing a fait accompli might make the

publisher feel pushed out of the loop. The delivery section of your proposal is optional and often best omitted.

J. Sample Chapters

Some proposals include one or two sample chapters, to give the publisher an idea of your book's focus and the style of writing. However, if you're hoping to land a contract based on the proposal, this is a lot of work to do on spec. If you've already written the book, then by all means, include samples. If not, then omit this section and wait to be asked.

Step Seven: Send Your Cover Letter

If you've sent off a one-page query letter first and received requests for the detailed proposal you offered, make sure to include a cover letter that performs the following three functions:

- Reminds the publisher that your material is solicited
- Reminds the publisher in a sentence or two what your proposed book is about
- Reminds the publisher who you are and what qualifies you to be proposing this book

Keep the cover letter to less than a page. Make sure you have all your contact information, including your E-mail address. And don't forget to include an SASE for either the return of your proposal or a response.

Step Eight: Write the Book

If all has gone well—you did your research, sent out your queries, and followed through with requests for your proposal—you might just find yourself with a contract and a due date. Now it's

time to write that book. Don't be afraid of discussing the focus or approach with your editor. But, as with any writing project, you must apply bottom to chair—sit there and do it.

Do You Need an Agent for Nonfiction Books?

You've just read the Eight Steps to Getting Published, and now you're wondering why contacting agents was not mentioned. While fiction writers more often than not fare better with an agent representing them, nonfiction writers can often approach publishers alone. (Article writers have no choice—agents won't handle articles.)

There are many more publishers who handle nonfiction than their fiction counterparts, and often these publishers are open to accepting submissions directly from the writer. In fact, many of the smaller presses rarely are approached by an agent and are not used to working with them. This in part is because most agents prefer to work with the big publishing houses, where advances and subsequent print runs and sales are usually higher.

If your project is of global interest, you could approach agents first—following the same steps mentioned earlier. But if your project fits more into a niche market, don't be hesitant to go it alone.

Earnings

Articles

Most writers are thrilled to see their bylines—that is, their names in print—giving them credit for an article. And to writers, noth-

ing is more exciting than the finished product, getting to see their stories in print. But even more important to the full-time writer is the paycheck that makes this writing life possible. In the 1700s, Samuel Johnson summed it up by saying that no one but a blockhead writes except for money.

It is a well-established fact that writers for the most part are underpaid. Salary surveys conducted by the Author's Guild, National Writers Union, and others suggest that only 15 percent of freelancers earn more than $30,000 a year.

Publications usually pay by the word—anywhere from one cent to $1 or $2. This doesn't mean you can earn more money by writing longer articles or padding your piece with extra words. In their guidelines, publications state their minimum and maximum word count requirements—and the editors are certainly professional enough to recognize padding when they see it.

Other publications pay a flat fee—$5 to $1,000 or more for an article, with the national magazines at the top of the scale. (And that's why it's much harder to break into these markets—the competition is fierce, and many of them work only with staff writers.)

Some smaller publications pay only with complimentary copies and a byline. When you query an idea and are given the assignment, discussing payment is usually the next step—and negotiating for more money at this point is not inappropriate. In fact, editors often say they are quite willing to negotiate—and are surprised more writers don't come out and ask for higher fees.

Let's face it. Writers often go into this business not fully understanding that it is a business. A writer's expertise is with the written word—not with dollar signs and decimal points. But to be a successful freelancer, you have to overcome that mind-set, develop a strong business sense, and remember you are selling a valuable product. Yes, there's a lot of competition—other writers selling equally valuable products. And editors can pick and choose who to work with. But, if you approach the subject with tact and confidence, you won't turn off an editor and send them

looking elsewhere. Your article is something they have decided they want—they might have even given you input into what they'd like to see in it—and there is no reason you shouldn't be paid fairly for it.

Having said that, some of the smaller publications just don't have the budget to pay you what your piece is worth. If a byline and a credit are important to you, go ahead with the sale. But be sure to negotiate one-time rights so you can sell the piece elsewhere for additional income.

Some publications will accept photographs or other illustrations with your article—and pay you for each one. Sometimes you'll earn more for your photos than the actual article! One travel writer, who was also an accomplished photographer, realized this early on—and stopped writing articles to focus on creating a stock library of color slides to supply to magazines and newspapers.

As mentioned earlier, resales are the bread and butter for freelance writers. When investigating ideas for articles, keep resale and reslant possibilities in mind. You'll make more money in a cost-efficient manner selling one article to ten different publications than writing ten different pieces and trying to market each of them only once.

It is important to keep in mind that publishers are notoriously slow to pay for your material. Articles are usually paid for in one of two ways: upon acceptance or upon publication. "Upon acceptance" could mean the check will be cut right away—or it could mean four to six weeks before the accountant gets around to it. "Upon publication" means that your check will not be issued until the article appears in print. That could be six months to a year from the time you received your acceptance letter. Often your check will be mailed to you with the sample copy of the issue in which your material appears. With this long lag, you can see how important it is to have as many articles as you can circulating to the different publications.

Occasionally a publication might purchase your article and promise to run it—then for a variety of reasons, decide not to use it after all. Maybe an on-spec article they like better on the same topic just arrived, or they changed the focus of the publication or decided a topic was too controversial or is now passé. When this happens, some publications pay a kill fee—perhaps 15 percent to 25 percent of the agreed-upon fee for the article. This should be paid willingly and amicably—if they state in their market listings or guidelines that they offer a kill fee. But at least one editor has been quoted as saying, "Yes, we pay kill fees, but then we wouldn't work with that writer again." It's not fair, that's true, but again, there's not much you can do about it. Over time, you will learn to pick and choose the editors you submit to and continue to work with. Establishing good relationships with editors is in part how successful writers keep those assignments and checks coming in.

Books

Some contracts for nonfiction books provide an advance against royalties. Others offer a work-for-hire or flat-fee arrangement. This means that whatever you're paid up front for the book will be all you'll see. If the book goes on to be a bestseller, your bank balance will have no cause to celebrate.

Sometimes you have no choice, and if you think sales might be minimal—it's a small press with short press runs and limited distribution—a flat fee is not a bad idea.

If the publisher is confident and plans a fairly large initial press run of say ten thousand or more, and offers an advance against royalties, you can hope to see some checks down the road, once the advance is earned back and your royalty payments kick in.

Statements are usually issued twice a year, and it could be a year or so before sales have earned back the advance.

Dollar amounts are hard to pinpoint. Some of the small presses offer no advance at all, just a royalty percentage. With

this scenario, you have no money coming in while you're writing the book, but at least you won't have to wait too long to earn back a nonexistent advance. In theory, you should receive your first check when the next royalty period is due, probably six months from the time your book is on the market.

Other small presses offer advances that range from $500 to $3,000 or so. A large publisher might advance a new writer as high as $10,000 to $25,000 or sometimes more, if it's a hot topic and the sales team predicts healthy sales.

Keeping Track of Your Submissions

Accurate record keeping is an important aspect of your writing business. You don't want to submit the same article or book proposal twice to the same editor. Develop a system for yourself that allows you to keep track of possible markets, submission dates, responses, publication dates, payment, and rights information.

Some writers use an index card system; others use computer software specifically designed for this purpose. The more organized you are, the more successful you'll be.

Writing in Cyberspace

As mentioned earlier, there are many Internet publications out there—magazines, newsletters, and more—that never see a piece of paper. Some pay, some don't. Some E-book publishers will actually charge writers to post material in hopes someone will want to buy it. (This is nothing short of a vanity press and should be avoided. Legitimate publishers pay writers, not the other way around.)

There are also many websites needing content. Write a regular column for an astrology site, explain New Age terms to a

metaphysical site. Just fire up your favorite search engine, key in your search words, then make contacts with sites that seem appropriate. (For more information, see Maggie Anderson's first-hand account in Chapter 2. She writes for many on-line areas.)

Editing and Publishing

As with any publication, New Age publications utilize the services of a wide range of publishing professionals—from top executive to senior and associate editors to graphic artists, Web designers, and proofreaders.

Publishers usually expect their personnel to be experienced and well trained in a variety of platforms. Although a college education isn't a requirement, with all the competition out there from graduates with bachelor's degrees in English, communications, and journalism, the degree would keep you in the running.

Conduct an Internet search for publishers and jobs in publishing and see what you come up with. The Internet has become the best thing since the Yellow Pages—with such a broad range of listings, both by topic and geographic region. The world is there for you to approach!

Bookselling

A book idea starts with a writer, who nurtures it until it's a viable project, nudged across the computer screen until enough pages print out to form a manuscript.

Agents try to sell the idea to editors, and editors and other publishing company staff work together to transform the idea into print form.

But it's booksellers who get the idea out to the public. Read more about a career in New Age bookselling in Chapter 6.

Firsthand Account

Joseph Hayes, Freelance Writer

Joseph Hayes writes features for a variety of magazines and newspapers. His articles cover people, food, computers and technology, travel, music, and writing about writing. His work has appeared in the following publications: *Fiction Writers Guideline, Gila Queen's Guide to Markets, Inklings/Inkspot, iUniverse.com Nonfiction Industry Newsletter, January Magazine, Jerusalem Report, MaximumPC, Moments Aboard Spirit Airlines, MyMatcher.com, Orlando Magazine, Orlando Sentinel, Poets & Writers, savvyHEALTH, Venture Woman,* and *Writer's Journal.* His first article was published in January 1997.

Getting Started

"It began as an outgrowth of my other profession: I was a corporate sales trainer for many years, and as such, I developed a skill at taking complicated technical terms and processes and putting them down on paper so they were understandable to ordinary people. My first love will always be fiction writing, but I've been able to take those talents and use them to create what is called creative nonfiction.

"I got started by calling up the local newspaper and speaking to a regional editor. I suggested several concrete story ideas about the community I live in. She liked one, told me to write it, and I've been writing steadily ever since."

What the Work Is Like

"My first duty involves personal accountability—weighing the necessities of landing paying assignments with social responsibility gets high marks. Will I take any assignment, as long as it pays? So far the answer is no.

"Then the duties of the professional writer come in—meeting deadlines, being obligated to deliver the best work you are capable of, regardless of the subject matter, and being in contact with editors once they give you assignments so they know what you're up to.

"I love my job. Not only do I get to (and *have* to) set my own schedule, but I have the opportunity to meet incredible people, people whom I wouldn't ordinarily get to know. The hours are long, and there can sometimes be long gaps between paydays, but I'm paid for doing something I've always wanted to do.

"Mostly I write about people—about life. I like to tell stories about ordinary people who do extraordinary things: the guy who sells UFO abduction insurance, the woman who takes photographs of people's auras, the ex-police officer who teaches the bagpipes. My travel articles are about places a tourist wouldn't normally go; my technology pieces are based on helping people understand what on earth modern technology means to them. Bottom line, I'm a storyteller, whether I'm doing it in a piece of fiction or a newspaper.

"Ninety-five percent of my work is generated by ideas I send out. This is called the query process. If it's an editor I know or have worked with before, I will pick up the phone and give my idea a quick pitch. If it's a new editor or a new publication, I send a letter with a detailed but brief summary of the idea, along with copies of similar articles that I've published before—my 'clips.'

"In either case, it means that you have to have a very clear and specific idea of what story you want to do. Saying 'I'd really like to do an interview with a band' isn't an idea; it's a daydream. 'I've met the drummer for Back Street Boys, and he'll talk to me about the band' is a legitimate article pitch.

"How one decides who to approach depends on what you write. By looking at guidebooks such as the *Writer's Market* and visiting your local newsstands, you get to see which magazines print articles on topics you can write about, which magazines pay, and which ones accept pieces from freelancers.

"A freelancer's life goes through cycles: periods of waiting for work, followed by frantic episodes of meeting deadlines. A query can go unanswered for months, but when an editor finally decides he wants the work, he wants it yesterday. This year I had enough time to go on a two-week vacation, and when I got back home, there were six contracts waiting for me, all due in a month!

"I truly believe the job is what you make it. You can be as busy (and successful) as you want to be. Even at this stage, I'm still learning to pace myself when it comes to getting work, and I think I could be doing twice as much writing as I'm doing now if I wanted to but at the risk of doing less quality work than I demand from myself. As it is, I will often put in a twelve-hour day, between writing, researching, and interviewing."

Upsides and Downsides

"The best part is the freedom, working for myself. Of course, I don't work for myself, I work for magazines and newspapers and editors, but each job has a different boss, and I know if I have a bad experience with one boss, I need not work for him or her again.

"The thrill of stepping up to a magazine rack and seeing your name on the stands is one that I hope will never wear off.

"The bad side is waiting—waiting for an assignment, then waiting for a check. Keeping track of your submissions, your billing, even your expenses, can be tiring and overwhelming, but it's part of the job. A writer only writes part of the time. The rest of the time is spent with details and selling yourself.

"It can also be lonely—most of the time you are in your office, facing a screen, talking to yourself. And there are times when you have to convince your friends and family that you are actually working even though you are home, and they must respect that."

Earnings

"Someone just starting out can expect to earn very little, if any-thing. Most freelance writers do it as a part-time thing and very often get no pay at all for their work. It's part of establishing yourself in the business and getting experience.

"Once your reputation and skill warrant it, a freelance feature writer can expect to find widely varying pay rates—everything from five cents to a dollar a word is typical (and some lower than that), while the big, national magazines will pay thousands of dollars an article, but that's a tough group to join."

Advice from Joseph Hayes

"First of all, love language. Love to write. Some writers say they love having written, but hate writing. Such a waste of time! Enjoy every part of the process, of sitting in front of the computer or typewriter or notepad, and you'll never suffer from what is called writer's block.

"The article writer should be, first and foremost, an article reader—be aware of styles of writing, of how things are said. Be a reader, be voracious. Devour facts. Some people keep journals or diaries and jot down observations of people and places. Learn how to put those observations on paper; it's called finding your voice. Writer and teacher Larry Bloom says that voice, the per-sonal voice of the writer, is the most important part of any story—that is, what you yourself add to the article. Remember that only you can tell the story you are telling.

"To start out, find a discussion group at your library, local bookstore, or on-line and talk about your daily encounters. Learn to listen. Call your local newspaper or church, check the clubs you belong to, ask at local businesses and see if they have newsletters you can write for. The more words you put in print, the better your words get. And most importantly, never give up!

I've been very lucky, being as successful as I've been in such a short time. Some writers put in several years of hard work before they see real success. It can be very discouraging, but it's also very rewarding."

For More Information

American Society of Journalists and Authors
1501 Broadway
New York, NY 10036

The Dow Jones Newspaper Fund
P.O. Box 300
Princeton, NJ 08543

The Dow Jones Newspaper Fund offers summer reporting and editing internships.

Fiction Writer's Connection
P.O. Box 72300
Albuquerque, NM 87195
www.fictionwriters.com

The Gila Queen's Guide to Markets
  (monthly marketing magazine)
Box 97
Newton, NJ 07860

National Newspaper Association
1627 K Street NW, Suite 400
Washington, DC 20006

A pamphlet titled "A Career in Newspapers" can be obtained from National Newspaper Association.

National Writers Club
1450 South Havana, Suite 424
Aurora, CO 80012

For New Age publishing resources—directories, sites, magazines, teachings, articles—visit the website: www.newageinfo .com/res/newage_data.htm

CHAPTER SIX

Profit for Prophets
Careers in New Age Merchandising

Who knew when pet rocks and the yellow and black smile buttons went on sale years ago they'd be such big successes? (Well, maybe some of our psychics in Chapter 2 knew.)

After that came pyramids, crystals, magnets, special jewelry, special water, and more. In fact, there's a whole range of New Age products that are enjoying modest to glorious sales. You can start a new fad yourself or cash in on an existing trend.

At a loss for what product to sell or what service to offer? Try firing up Yahoo! or America Online and do a search using the keywords *New Age merchandise*. Here is just a sampling of what you'll get. The list is bound to spark some ideas of your own.

- Adirondack Artworks—an artist cooperative offering Native American sterling silver jewelry (authenticity guaranteed), Iroquois Nation stone carvings, wildlife wood carvings, crystals, New Age pen-and-ink prints and originals, Indian-made beadwork, fetishes and artifacts, and gifts from Mother Earth.

- Alchemistra Ltd.—New Age spiritual products, including jewelry, healing tools, and super-ionized water.

- Atmanbooks.com Inc.—books, music, gifts, and videos about the New Age, new thought, metaphysics, alternative health, and healing and spirituality.

- The Aumara Light & Healing Circle—a place for healing and inspiration for increased health, well-being, and spiritual awareness.

- Awakening Eye, Journeys for the Soul—customized workshops for group leaders, therapists, spiritual counselors and healers who are mind, body, and spirit practitioners.

- Beyond the Rainbow: Resources for Well-being/Gifts with Spirit—free, practical information about crystals, flower essences, aromatherapy, emotional/ spiritual growth.

- Dancing Frog Jewelry—handcrafted metaphysical jewelry in sterling silver and fused glass.

- Dancing Moon Metaphysical—bookstore and gift shop for spiritual and personal growth.

- Golden Light—an intriguing strategy of mystical experiences from a woman who had two near-death experiences.

- Just Wingin' It—spiritual products from 'Angel to Zen.'

- Lytha Studios—Celtic and spiritual jewelry, clothing, and accessories, including incense and burners, hand-mixed oils, tarot cards and rune sets, candles, crystals, and ritual soaps.

- The Magical Blend—on-line catalog offering a complete selection of esoteric & metaphysical supplies, including books, tarot, oils, herbs, candles, ritual tools, symbolic jewelry, runes, and incense.

- Peaceful Paths—enlightening books, visionary artwork, spiritually nourishing music, and gifts and gift baskets in themes of spirit and wholeness.

- Planet Earth Music—fresh, evocative, magical music from all over the world.

- Psychic Choice—on-line psychic readings; classes in tarot, metaphysics, and psychic development.

- Spheres To You—more than three thousand mineral spheres used for metaphysical purposes, healing, and collecting of beautiful natural earth materials.

- Unlimited Thought Bookstore—New Age bookstore and learning center.

- Wicca Supplies Shop—quality magical jewelry, ritual tools, books, music, essential oil blends, and tools for self-transformation.

Storefronts on the Web

In addition to sparking ideas, this list of New Age product websites tells you one other thing: with the advent of the World Wide Web, there is no longer a need for a merchandiser to open a costly storefront. Dispense with all that overhead by designing a website for yourself—or hiring someone else to do it for you. You'll pay a modest monthly server fee and a few hundred dollars for a few pages. Acquire a merchant account or contact any of the cyber cash outlets (find them using an Internet search engine), submit your site to the search engines, and then you'll be up and running—in business for yourself.

Expand Your Services

As your own search will reveal, there's a lot of competition out there. So, choose your product or service carefully. Make sure you have an audience you know how to reach, if not on the Web,

then through seminars or classes you offer or through some other means. Entrepreneurs think big. To make a living, you may need to offer as many related products or services as you can.

If you're a spiritual advisor with an office that clients visit, you can always display crystals or jewelry or soothing candles to sell to them. Tarot readers can try selling decks of tarot cards with fancy cases to their customers. (Don't worry. They'll still come back to you for interpretations.) Massage therapists can sell essential oils for clients to use at home. Counselors can sell books and tapes. The list is limited only by your imagination.

Storefronts with a Physical Address

Yes, it costs a lot more than a website, but opening your own store can be rewarding, both financially and spiritually.

There are three main factors you need to consider when going this route: location, location, location.

All right. You've heard that before. But it's true. You need to set yourself up in an area that is easily accessible to foot traffic, whether renting space in a mall or in a downtown shopping district.

There are two other things to consider as well—the product you'll offer and how you'll finance yourself.

First, a look at two popular enterprises—bookselling and health food stores.

Bookstores

You can have a hodgepodge of books and other products or specialize just in books. New Age bookstore sections in the chain and independent bookstores are growing like teenagers on vitamins. Enthusiasts read broadly about ancient and cutting-edge topics, keeping titles in print for many years. Closely related to

the self-help field, metaphysics has spawned many how-to volumes. Print magazines also abound.

A bookstore devoted to New Age volumes could do well, depending, of course, on the area of the country you're in. Santa Fe, New Mexico? Great. Deerfield Beach, Florida? Probably not so great.

Health Food and Natural Food Stores

Natural food stores, also known as health food stores, are specialty shops that cater to a wide range of people—not just New Agers. The wider your audience, the better your business.

These stores sell a full range of healthful foods and related items such as vitamins and food supplements. Employees in natural food stores must be knowledgeable about the different foods and products and be able to answer customer questions.

Disclaimer

Once again, New Agers who are in a position to affect the emotional or physical lives of their clients have a huge responsibility. Health food stores, for one, stock a variety of products that claim all sorts of properties—from the magical to the mundane. And health food employees dispense advice as readily as trained pharmacists. But they are not trained pharmacists, and that's where the cautions come in, for the consumer and for new health food store employees.

Many health food store clerks are trained on the job. Most have not had any formal training about the products, how they work together—or how they might adversely interact with other medications.

Abigail Trafford covers this topic in her article, "Second Opinion," which appeared in the *Washington Post*, Tuesday, July 25, 2000. She says, "There is much to gain in alternative remedies. Many products hold the promise of enhancing health and

mitigating symptoms of disease. And some health food stores have very knowledgeable salesclerks to guide consumers. But it's time for science to separate the wheat from the chaff in alternative remedies. Time for the FDA or some independent agency to evaluate products."

Until then, we're on our own.

The remainder of this chapter will introduce you to someone involved in bookselling and someone active in a health food store. What better way to get a feel for the business than from those already in the business.

Financing Your New Age Enterprise

Do you need to be rich to start your own business? It certainly helps. But while many enterprises require substantial backing, others, especially Internet-based concerns, could be started on a shoestring.

It's nice to have a fat bank account—or a rich uncle—but it's more important to have a good credit history. That's what lenders look at when you apply for a loan. And most of the time, starting a business requires financing. Good credit shows reliability, that you can and will pay back the loan in a timely manner. Collateral helps cement the deal.

Check in with your bank. Bank employees are familiar with a host of loan programs, especially those sponsored by the Small Business Administration. The SBA is a government-sponsored agency that helps small business, particularly those run by women or minorities. They have a lot of restrictions and qualifications—and in some instances won't fund writers or booksellers for fear of appearing to interfere with the right of free speech.

Read the firsthand account given us by former bookstore owner Joyce Kennett. She'll give you an idea of the finances involved.

Firsthand Accounts

Joyce Kennett, Bookstore Owner

From 1985 to 1990, Joyce Kennett was co-owner with her husband of the Psychic Institute, a metaphysical bookstore in Las Vegas, Nevada. Through the bookstore, they offered classes in the psychic arts and yoga.

Getting Started

"My husband and I were first employed by the store back in 1982—he as the hypnotist, and myself as a psychic. We purchased the store in 1985, but I sold it in 1990, after the death of my husband.

"I've always wanted to run a bookstore, and when this one came up for sale because of feuding partners, we snapped up the opportunity."

What the Work Was Like

"We had a double storefront loaded with books on a variety of religions, but the main focus was the metaphysical. We carried meditation music tapes and videos and stock of all sorts— incense and burners, candles, tarot cards, regular cards, joss sticks, crystals, crystal balls, runes—if you can think of a metaphysical tool, we carried it.

"We taught classes in tarot reading, psychometry, hypnosis, yoga, tai chi, and various psychic arts. We had free lectures on the psychic arts Sunday afternoons. We also had psychic affairs, offering mini-readings to the public on weekends, as well as private readings in the many psychic arts.

"We employed several psychics and two astrologers. At one point, we had three astrologers. The psychics were paid 60 percent of the reading fees, which were then $25 for a half hour, $40

for an hour. The mini-readings were $15 for fifteen minutes. Classes were usually $10 a night. The classes were taught by other psychics as well as my husband and me.

Upsides and Downsides

"My husband and I were doing what we loved, so were pretty happy, but as the business grew, we found we had to do more administration, advertising, TV and radio appearances, ordering, etc., leaving us with little time to do what we really loved—his hypnosis and my reading and teaching.

"We had to pay strict attention to stocking our shelves, maintaining jewelry, crystal, and other items, such as office supplies, bathroom tissue—everything you can think of a home needing, a business needs on a much larger scale.

"Sadly, one has to watch out for staff theft and customer theft. Antitheft mechanisms are necessary nowadays, which is a sorry state of affairs for an otherwise positive type of business."

Salaries

"As a store owner, one needs a minimum of $50,000 to start out with—to cover all the expenses. At least back in the seventies and eighties that was the amount. Now, it would be much more. Rents are very high; utilities are outlandish; property care, such as landscaping, business licenses, zoning laws and so on, adds up. The store owner is kept hopping. Any show of profit doesn't come until perhaps you are five years into the business."

Advice from Joyce Kennett

"The most important qualities a metaphysical-bookstore owner should possess are integrity and ethics. Business training is a must. Having trustworthy people to whom you can delegate some duties or authority is also a necessity.

"The best way to get started is to find a bookstore that is struggling. You might be able to get a good purchase price break, but have an accountant check their books carefully, and check out the stock very carefully as well."

Theresa Bulmer, Health Food Store Manager

Theresa Bulmer was the manager of Cabbages Health Emporium, a health food store in South Florida. It opened its doors in 1991 as a market stocking health-oriented products. They offer a line of organic produce, organic foods, and nonorganic frozen foods and groceries. They avoid food with preservatives, refined sugars, or additives. They will not sell any food that has been irradiated to prolong its shelf life.

Getting Started

"I've been into a more healthy lifestyle for many years, but I had no idea I'd end up in a health food store and really like it. I was unemployed back in 1990, and knowing very little about health food stores or the health food industry itself, I walked into a place that was being built. I got the job that same day. Ever since then, I've been led in this direction.

"I had a sales background and some skills but very little train-ing, so I learned on the job. You'll find that a lot of people learn on the job in the health food industry. Unless you're going to school to learn about health and nutrition, you end up being self-taught.

"To me, this is a way of life. The more people who know about organic food and health, the healthier we will be as a society. The more farmers who grow organic and the more people who buy organic, the sooner prices will go down and products will be more readily available. Then more people can be turned on to this way of life.

"I know people who have gone from doctors and pills and medication and have changed their lifestyles and now no longer need the doctors and pills and medication. I'm not downgrading traditional medicine; there are many people who have been helped that way. But there are alternatives, and if we begin to look at them, and if the holistic professionals and the doctors begin to work with each other as opposed to against each other, we can change lives."

What the Work Is Like

"Cabbages Health Emporium customers are people with special diet or health needs and those who just live a natural, healthy lifestyle, including vegans and vegetarians. We have a cafe and a vegan deli, and we also cater to sports enthusiasts and body-builders, stocking several lines of sports drinks and powders and different types of vitamins and formulas. In addition, we carry a line of environmentally safe cleaning products that are biodegradable with no harsh chemicals.

"The duties of a manager vary from store to store. I do a little of everything—I order goods, take out garbage, clean bathrooms, ring up sales, work on store operating policies, and talk to brokers, sales reps, and distributors—six days a week from 7:30 in the morning to 6:00 at night. I also supervise ten employees.

"And I talk to customers and try to keep them happy. The customers are wonderful, really. They can learn from us, and we can learn from them. Someone will come in with a product I've never seen before. I'll ask what you take it for, and they'll rattle off everything the product can do, and I get really excited because I'm learning something new.

"Some of our customers are very knowledgeable, sometimes even more knowledgeable than we are, and then we have those who are clueless. They tell us it's their first time in a health food store and they don't know what they should be buying. We're all customer-service oriented here, and if anyone is unable to help a customer, we refer him or her to someone else.

"I really like this store, and I enjoy what I do. But being a store manager, even in a health food store, can lend itself to stress. You have employees underneath you, an owner above you, customers, all kinds of salespeople, and you're being pulled in a lot of different directions. You need a lot of patience, a lot of love."

Salaries

"Entry-level salaries usually are quite low, from $5 to $6 an hour, depending on your knowledge and skills and the area of the country in which you work. As you climb up the ladder, the pay scale doesn't necessarily climb with you.

"The health food business doesn't pay very well, but you don't do it for the money. You're in the health food business to be in the health food business."

Advice from Theresa Bulmer

"It's my experience that many health food stores are very open to training new employees. At Cabbages we look for certain qualities in job candidates. We want to see a good attitude, a strong interest, and willingness to learn. It's usually obvious when you interview someone, when you talk to that person.

"When trying to get a job, in addition to scanning help wanted ads, stop by the stores where you would like to work. At Cabbages we don't advertise when we have an opening. We would put a sign in the window or check around through word of mouth."

For More Information

Small Business Administration (SBA)
www.sba.gov

CHAPTER SEVEN

Sharing the Knowledge
Careers in Teaching, Consulting, and Event Planning

P roducts aren't the only way to make a profit in the New
   Age marketplace. Teachers instruct students in a range of
   disciplines, consultants help people with anything from
intuitive business planning or investments to the most beneficial
way to arrange office or home furniture, and event planners
organize New Age and psychic fairs.

Teaching

The activities of sharing and passing on knowledge are almost as
old as time itself. Everything we learned as a child came to us
from our parents or caretakers. Everything they learned was
passed down to them.

The active part we take in teaching and learning is exciting
and stimulating. Speak to any teachers and you're sure to hear
that they learn just as much from their students as as their students do from them.

Those teaching New Age subjects are providing a valuable
service, enriching the lives of their students with new knowledge, personal insight, self-awareness, and growth.

Subjects run the gamut, from vegetarian cooking to astrology
to refining our skills in love and relationships. Many of the topics

one can teach have already been covered in previous chapters: yoga, tarot, hypnotherapy, counseling techniques, reflexology, and so on.

Training

The qualifications you'll need will, of course, depend on the subject and, to some extent, the setting. Teachers of most New Age subjects must be experts in their areas. That old cliché—"those who can, do; those who can't, teach"—doesn't apply here. A degree in education isn't required for many of the subjects and settings, but a certain skill level and an understanding of how people learn are.

For example, if you want to teach future counselors in a university setting, you'll need a Ph.D. in the subject matter as well as experience. But if you want to teach a class in Eastern cuisine or yoga, for example, and your plan is to apply to the local adult education center, being able to demonstrate your expertise and your ability to teach will impress the director more than a string of degrees.

Possible Job Settings

Teachers of New Age subjects have a wider range of possibilities when it comes to job settings than traditional teachers do. Here is just a brief list to help spark some ideas:

• Adult education centers

• Bookstores

• Churches and temples

• Community continuing education centers

• Conferences

- Home offices or classrooms

- Gyms and health clubs

- Hotels and resorts

- Medical centers

- Summer camps

- Outdoors (parks, the beach, the forest, the mountains)

- Parks and recreation departments

- Religious retreats

- YMCA/YWCA

Finding That Job

Job hunting in this field is similar to any field. You check the Internet and the classified ads in the local paper, you send out your resume and make cold calls, and you network. Often word of mouth within the community reveals job openings and provides referrals and references. Who you know will often come in handy.

But in this field, you don't have to rely on getting a job with someone else. Many New Agers are enterprising self-starters—and they create their own jobs. Here's an example.

An experienced workshop leader and speaker worked for other people for many years and developed a following. With a large mailing list of interested clients, she wrote a book and self-published it. To promote her book and earn a living, she decided to set up a series of workshops around the country. She started locally, renting meeting space in a church, making up flyers, mailing them out, and collecting the registration money for the all-day workshop. At the workshop, she provided refreshments and sold many copies of her book. The event was successful, so

she moved further afield. Because her contacts in other cities were limited, though, she utilized the services of an event planner as she traveled.

Her work required a lot of travel and time away from home. But she was able to make enough money to cover her living expenses and more. Even more important, she was able to meet many people and teach her subject matter to a far wider audience than if she had stayed home. Getting the word out and earning a living were the two most important factors to this speaker, and she was successful at both.

An easier way to do something similar would be to contact New Age or metaphysical bookstores, either locally or around the country, and offer to speak. Most bookstores don't have a budget for speakers, but if you have a book or product to promote, your talks will help boost sales.

Those who can't afford to hire you to speak could hire you to teach a class or give psychic readings. (See bookstore owner Joyce Kennett's firsthand account in Chapter 6.)

As a teacher of a New Age subject, you have many options available to you, much more than the teacher of traditional subjects. Use your creativity and imagination and the answer will come to you.

Consulting

Consulting is such a broad term; we hear it used in most every field. In our minds, we probably hold an image of an older person, semiretired from some high-powered career, who now lends expertise to others who seek it. They pay the big bucks, too.

Those consultants obviously do exist, but not all fall into that stereotype. New Age consultants often help clients invest money,

arrange furniture to create the best positive energy, or plan a new business. Some consultants don't use the title *consultant*. They call themselves Feng Shui experts, investment counselors, or even just astrologers, for example. For in addition to explaining personality and behavior, astrologers can also predict the best time to plan an event, change jobs, or move from one part of the country to another. (See Chapter 2.)

Earnings for Teachers and Consultants

Don't be afraid to put a decent price tag on your services. Just because the field is New Age doesn't mean your time isn't as valuable as the engineering or law consultant. In fact, you're probably a valuable commodity. Chances are the area you're in is not flooded with other people competing with you. You have specific knowledge and expertise and should be compensated for providing it. While math teachers might be a dime a dozen, how many Qigong instructors are there?

As a self-employed individual, you also have expenses you're responsible for, such as health insurance or continuing education. Make sure you figure your expenses and build them into your fee so they are covered.

If you're not sure what to charge, decide what kind of an hourly rate you need to earn to live comfortably—$35 an hour? $50? Or maybe $200? Then think about your clients. Are they affluent or struggling students or a bit of both? Can you offer a sliding scale for your services—those who can afford to pay more, will, those who can't, don't? That's the way many teachers and consultants work.

If you've read the various firsthand accounts throughout this book, you'll see the different ways New Agers deal with salary and income. It's not a subject that needs to be whispered about. Even the most selfless volunteer has to eat.

Event Planning

Not only are you a New Age enthusiast, you're an organized one. (You have to be, to be successful at event planning.)

You make to-do lists for all your activities, and you even keep track of them and check off entries as they are completed. You have the knack of being able to pull people together for an event or special occasion. If a party needs to be planned and catered, a seminar orchestrated, a luncheon meeting organized, you're the person at the helm, controlling all the various elements.

You pay attention to details, you can juggle different tasks at the same time, and as the day draws near, you not only watch everything fall into place, you make sure it does.

How can you put these valuable skills to work for you? Many such as yourself channel their abilities into organizing some of the following events:

- Psychic fairs

- New Age conferences and conventions

- Seminars

- Workshops

- Weddings

- Parties

- Associations

- Collectives

- Clubs

- Speakers' bureaus

How to Get Started

The self-employed organizer first needs to see a need or develop one. If you're a writer, you can organize seminars. If you're a plant lover, you can arrange for garden exhibitions. If you're a photographer, you can put on a community photography competition. If you're psychic, you can arrange a psychic fair.

You can also contact existing groups—writers' associations, historical associations, the chamber of commerce, bookstores, to name just a few—and let them know of your services.

Each event or organization has its own particular requirements. Here are some of the details an organizer might have to attend to:

- Raise financing
- Arrange for a venue such as a conference hall, hotel ballroom, or school gym
- Hire speakers, psychics, readers, or musicians
- Cater refreshments
- Design, write, print, and distribute promotional material
- Rent equipment or furnishings
- Keep track of registrations or guest lists
- Send confirmation letters
- Allocate seating
- Arrange for accommodations
- Arrange for transportation

Possible Job Settings

The vast majority of event planners are self-employed. Others work for hotels, the local government body or corporation holding the event, or for businesses that specialize in this particular kind of service.

Training and Becoming ISES Certified

The International Special Events Society (ISES) has chapters all over the world, most of which offer monthly educational meetings. George Washington University now offers a degree in events management. *Special Events Magazine* hosts an annual convention for three thousand event producers, with great education sessions.

Even if you don't go for a specific event planning degree, degrees in public relations, marketing, or hotel/hospitality management can prepare you to some degree. Public relations courses very often include sections on events.

To become certified, you must apply to ISES first to be eligible for certification—you will receive a form outlining the "point system" to determine whether or not you can sit for the exam. You accumulate points from years in the business, attending continuing education classes, and so on. Once you have enough points, you sit for a written exam. The whole process is not that easy, but it pays off in two ways: your respect from your peers and your standing in the event community is raised; and you can use it as a marketing tool for clients. Clients will usually be fairly impressed when you tell them what the CSEP (Certified Special Event Professional) designation means.

For more information on certification, contact the International Special Events Society at the address provided at the end of this chapter. To keep on top of what's happening in the field, you can subscribe to *Special Events Magazine*. The address is provided in the Appendix.

Firsthand Accounts

Elizabeth English, Feng Shui Consultant

Elizabeth English has been an interior designer for twenty years and has been using the techniques of Feng Shui since 1985.

She has traveled to Kyoto for observation of Feng Shui usage and techniques in Japan and has also studied the Japanese arts of haiku and ikebana.

She has consulted in clients' residences, office buildings and home offices, resorts, hotels, restaurants, and surrounding properties—yards, gardens, ponds, roads, and driveways.

She is self-employed and works out of her home office, which faces west toward the mountains in Boulder, Colorado.

A Definition of Feng Shui

"Feng Shui (pronounced fung-schway) is the ancient art of placement to direct energy flow in one's home or business. It has been used by the Chinese for more than four thousand years and is emerging in the West as a tool to create a sense of well-being in any environment.

"Feng Shui, which is based on the flow of energy called *chi*, studies the electromagnetic energy that flows in and around everything. The words *Feng Shui* literally mean 'wind and water.'

"Feng Shui practitioners believe chi mimics the flow of these elements. With knowledge of how these energy patterns work, Feng Shui experts can manipulate environments to benefit nearly every aspect of life. Using understanding of chi as the starting point, Feng Shui consultants, interior designers, and architects work to promote health, wealth, and advantageous relationships within a home or business."

Getting Started

"As an interior designer, I knew there was more to successful design than simply utilizing the standard interior design and architecture methodology, and I was searching for a more human-centered and earth-centered approach to various aspects of my projects. I picked up several books on designing with Feng Shui and knew I'd found what I was looking for. After studying the books, I looked around my own home and realized that I'd inadvertently utilized most of the Feng Shui techniques in the book, before I'd even heard the term *Feng Shui*. Apparently, I'm what's called an 'intuitive' Feng Shui practitioner.

"As an interior designer/architect, I was able to suggest the benefits of Feng Shui applications to my residential and commercial clients. I also write articles on Feng Shui for newspapers and magazines and receive job referrals from them plus, of course, word-of-mouth recommendations from former clients."

What the Work Is Like

"A Feng Shui consultant meets with the clients in their homes or businesses and spends some time getting to know them, learning what problems they're experiencing and what desires they have to improve their lives.

"A special Feng Shui compass is often used to discover problem areas and where to start fixing those areas. Usually, a set of wind chimes can be hung to bring good chi to that area, or a fishbowl, a mirror, or a fluttering red ribbon could do the trick.

"Cracked mirrors, open bathroom doors, dirty windows, doors that lead straight through the house to the back door, a huge tree in the yard obscuring the front door, a ceiling beam over a bed—all of these are chi-blocking elements and can easily be cured, by throwing away the cracked mirror, closing the bathroom door, cleaning the windows, placing a decorative screen or large plant

between the front door and the back door, adding a mirror at the front door, and moving the bed.

"The pathway to the front door should be winding and inviting, there should be a pond in the backyard, there should be no mirror facing the foot of your bed, but there should be a mirror reflecting the dining table, where the family is nourished and where everyone can communicate daily. The children's beds should not be directly above the parents' bed on an upper floor, or they will not respect their parents.

"Have you ever noticed that most Chinese restaurants have large fish tanks in the restaurant, and the cash register is by the door? An uneven number of healthy goldfish in a clean tank or bowl brings wealth to the establishment, as does the cash-register at the door rather than off to the side. A screen or plants in front of the fireplace keep the good chi from going up the chimney. A pair of ducks, side by side and tied together with a red cord, bring love and faithful relationships. Making room in your closet for another's clothes could bring a new relationship. A painting of a snarling tiger at the front door will keep out people with evil intentions. A red, black, and white bowl or basket, placed in your money corner, will bring riches. These are just a very few of the many, many Feng Shui elements that consultants must know. Each case, however, is different for the individuals who live in the home or work in the business.

"I find my information through my library of books on Feng Shui. I also subscribe to magazines on Feng Shui and regularly check in to read the messages at Feng Shui on-line websites.

"I'm a freelance Feng Shui consultant, so the hours vary widely, but usually a job is one to two hours of consultation with the client, then another hour or two of visiting the home or business, then maybe four hours or less of research and design, then another two hours with the clients in the home or business going over the changes needed. Often the client will want you to

make those changes happen for them, so you move furniture, change paint colors, bring in plants and mirrors and wind chimes and goldfish bowls and install them, and remove offending items or cover them.

"Most people want more money and better health and relationships, and sometimes their entire home or business is a disaster of bad chi, so you may need to spend more hours. But often the job can be done in a single day. The fees are generally about $1,000 to $2,500 a day, plus expenses. Occasionally, a client will call in a Feng Shui consultant before they move to a new home or business, and this gives you and the client the chance to set things right from the beginning or to advise them not to move into the new location at all."

Upsides and Downsides

"I love doing Feng Shui because I can help people improve their lives in a simple manner. Being a Feng Shui practitioner and consultant is a wonderful job, and it's very fulfilling and creative, especially when combined with my knowledge of interior design, architecture, and landscape design. When I finish a job, I have the opportunity to know that I've really helped the clients, and the clients can see the results almost immediately. (Clients often call to tell me how their lives have changed for the better after their homes or businesses were set right for the correct flow of good chi.)

"One thing I dislike about the profession is that many people think Feng Shui is a scam, so sometimes one member of a family is reluctant to make the changes and is argumentative or has an insulting attitude toward the ancient art of Feng Shui.

"Also, there are no regular jobs as a Feng Shui practitioner, unless you're very well known and live in an area that is open to what may be considered New Age practices for health, wealth, and well-being. Some areas of the country are open to the field,

such as Los Angeles, New York, Aspen or Boulder, and Santa Fe, for example. Other areas, such as Canada, Detroit, Chicago, St. Louis, and smaller Midwest towns, for example, are closed, generally, to the whole concept."

Salaries

"I earn a minimum of $100 and up to $250 per hour for consultation on Feng Shui. Beginners should not charge as much— maybe $25 an hour for the first several years or until they've learned how to practice the art correctly, have a good feel for it, and have succeeded with truly helping at least ten clients. A full day should be charged at $1,000 to $2,500, depending on your experience, qualifications, and abilities.

"Important note: in reference to being paid for Feng Shui consultations, one should follow the traditional ways and not directly receive cash or checks in hand. The clients should be informed in advance that they are to give you the fee in cash (if possible) in a red envelope or folded into red paper as a gift in exchange for your gift (of consultation) to them; and you should be paid daily."

Advice from Elizabeth English

"I'd highly recommend that people wishing to become Feng Shui practitioners read as many books and magazines on the subject as they can get their hands on, visit the on-line Feng Shui websites, consider taking courses in the art, and practice on their own homes and workplaces and those of their friends and families.

"The qualities one must have is a wish to help others, a desire to learn at the feet of the masters, and an ability to understand human relationships to the earth and its natural chi, and how the invisible but real flow of chi affects our lives—in advantageous ways and in negative ways."

Mary Tribble, Event Planner

Mary Tribble is the president and owner of Mary Tribble Creations, an event planning and production company located in Charlotte, North Carolina. In 1982, she earned her bachelor's degree in art history from Wake Forest University in Winston-Salem, North Carolina. She is one of just a few dozen people in the country to have earned the Certified Special Event Professional (CSEP) designation from the International Special Event Society (ISES). She has attended countless continuing education courses through industry conventions. And she is asked frequently to speak on event planning at regional and national conventions.

Getting Started

"I was working at an advertising agency as an account executive when one of my clients asked the agency to plan a grand opening event for their new offices. As a special project, it ended up being my responsibility. It was a huge event—a black tie gala with a laser light show—and I loved every minute of the planning. I knew I wanted to be involved in events from that time on. At first, we opened a small division at the agency for event planning, but I soon went out on my own. I was twenty-four at the time.

"I started with nothing more than a Rolodex, sitting on my bed in my apartment. No computer, nothing. I received a loan from a friendly investor for $5,000, which tided me over until the checks started coming in. That was more than a decade ago.

"After about two years in business, I rented a small office and hired my first employee, who is still with me. I now have three employees, which is a gracious plenty as far as I'm concerned.

"Now that the industry has gotten so much more sophisticated, I'm not sure I'd be able to get by the way I did back then. Clients want event planners who are educated in the industry,

carry all the proper insurance—and all that takes money. I have very nice offices in downtown Charlotte, and I think that adds credibility to my company.

"Now, because I've been around so long, I get a lot of my business through word of mouth—but I still have to market my services. That's usually through phone calls and sending out my brochure to prospects.

"I don't advertise much—not even in the Yellow Pages. But I'm very active in the chamber of commerce and am a member of our convention and visitors bureau and the International Special Events Society. A lot of business comes through networking with those groups."

What the Work Is Like

"It's crazy, stress filled, but fun. Here's a page torn from my calendar from last year:

7:30 A.M.—meeting with a client about a huge event we're planning for the millennium

9:00 A.M.—back to the office, reworked a budget for a wedding client. (The mother wanted it *all*, but the father had called me into his office—without his wife—to tell me what he was willing to spend.)

10:30 A.M.—meeting with a client about another event

Noon—off to exercise, then lunch at desk

1:00 P.M.—sales calls during the first part of the afternoon

2:30 P.M.—brainstorming meeting with staff interrupted by call from a client to put together an event in a week; reconvened staff to brainstorm

4:00 P.M.—work on writing up a proposal

5:30 P.M.—visit a potential rehearsal-dinner site

6:30 P.M.—home

"My days are rarely, if ever, relaxed. A typical day has three to six meetings, plus phone calls, deadlines for proposals, budgeting, worrying about payroll, dealing with employees' problems, making sales calls, creating diagrams of event layouts, trudging around construction sites, meeting with vendors and clients, fielding phone calls from people who want to pick my brain about the event biz, and so on.

"The work atmosphere is usually what I would describe as 'frantic fun.' I try to run a flexible company with a sense of humor—practical jokes are encouraged—but I expect everyone to roll up their sleeves and get the job done.

"In the busy season, I work sixty to sixty-five hours a week. When it's less busy, about fifty. My employees work about forty-five to fifty hours, since they only work events they are assigned. (I'm usually at them all.)

"Weddings can be especially difficult to plan because there are so many personalities involved. With a corporate client, I'm usually answering to just one person, and that person has usually reached a consensus with his or her staff as to what the event should be. With a wedding, the bride, the MOB (Mother of the Bride), the FOB (Father of the Bride), the in-laws, and the groom all have different expectations.

"In addition to weddings, I plan just about any kind of corporate event—grand openings, client celebrations, incentive events, employee receptions, and so on. This could be anything from an outdoor laser light show for twenty-five thousand people to an elegant cocktail party to a stage-show production. We come up with the ideas, then plan the whole thing from start to finish—invitations, catering, decorating, special effects, entertainment, and so forth. We contract all of that out, though. We don't keep lasers in stock!

"Paying attention to the details is the most important part of event planning. We can come up with all the wonderful themes in the world, but if we don't interpret them with details, they mean nothing. When we plan an event, everything—invitations, decorations, entertainment, place cards, gifts, signage—is selected to enhance the concept of the event.

"Also, the day-to-day planning is very detail oriented. We have to imagine an event from the time someone gets the invitation to how they will get there, where they will park, who will greet them, how the event will begin, and how it will end.

"For every event, we create a schedule for setup, which is a hour-by-hour outline of everything that will happen leading up to the event. Sometimes, if it's a complicated event, that document can be ten to twelve pages long.

"We also create a show schedule that outlines the event itself. Say, for instance, we are producing an awards ceremony. We'll develop a show schedule (a minute-by-minute one) that tells what person goes to the stage at what time, what they'll do or say on stage, how the lights in the house will be set, how the lights on the stage might change, what the audience is seeing on the video screen, and so on. Show schedules have to be incredibly detailed so that there's no down time on stage."

Upsides and Downsides

"What I like most about my work is the satisfaction that I've surpassed the client's dreams and expectations. The gasp factor. Also, I like the diversity—no day is ever the same—and I do get to spend a good deal of my time with creative people, brainstorming new ideas and coming up with new challenges. I also feel a rush from the stress the events create. I like to solve problems on my toes and come up with quick and innovative solutions.

"The long hours are a downside, though. It's not too uncommon for us to work eighteen to twenty hours with no break—and I'm getting too old for that! I work a lot of weekends and

evenings. Other downsides are dealing with all the details of the event—which is why I have employees. I like to conceptualize the event, but the drudgery of all the phone calls and meetings on minute things can be tiresome."

Advice from Mary Tribble

"Education, education, education! Just because you planned your sorority rush parties and dances doesn't mean you can plan events professionally. We take on a great deal of responsibility when we put a thousand people in a hotel ballroom.

"Is the event safe? Does our layout meet fire codes? Are our linens, draping, candles approved by the fire department? Is the event handicapped accessible? Does the caterer meet health-code requirements? Do we have enough liability insurance?

"We have to think about workers' compensation and whether you have permission to record and/or play licensed music. Are we following union regulations? Will the electricity carry the load of the equipment we've brought in?

"Planning events is not all fun and games, and you must make sure you're providing your client with a safe and secure event. You need to stay atop of the cutting-edge trends and make sure your clients are getting the best services possible.

"In addition to education, you need hands-on experience. Volunteer on a committee for a local nonprofit organization's fund-raiser. Intern at an event-production company, hotel, or catering firm. The experience will be a great investment.

"The perfect event-planner personality? You need to be a left brain/right brain person—you need the creative side to come up with new and exciting ideas, but you also need the detail-oriented side to execute them. That's a tough combination.

"You also need to thrive on stress—and learn not to panic in bad situations. You need to be quick on your toes, and you need to be a negotiator, and you need to have a calming influence on people. Our clients need someone calm and relaxed in the face of the controlled chaos."

For More Information

Professional Associations

The Feng Shui Society
377 Edgware Road
London W2 1BT
Great Britain
www.fengshuisociety.org.uk

International Feng Shui Research Centre (IFSRC)
1340 Marshall Street
Boulder, CO 80302
www.fengshui2000.com

International Special Event Society (ISES)
9202 North Meridean Street, Suite 200
Indianapolis, IN 46260

Websites

Chinese Feng Shui
www.chineseculture.about.com/culture/chineseculture/msub53.htm

Feng Shui for Harmony and Relaxation
www.rainbowcrystal.com/atext/fs.html

SpiritWeb: "Feng Shui Giving Us Direction"
www2.eu.spiritweb.org/spirit/feng-shui-liu-01.html

Geomancy/Feng Shui Educational Organization
www.geofengshui.com

CHAPTER EIGHT

Third-Eye Private Eyes
Careers in Paranormal Investigation

D o you believe in ghosts and spirits and haunted houses? What about ESP and psychokinesis? UFOs? The Loch Ness Monster? Big Foot?

Did you see *Ghostbusters* or *Close Encounters of the Third Kind?* Do you watch the "X-Files"? Do books by Isaac Asimov and Arthur Clarke excite and intrigue you?

Or maybe not. When it comes to the realm of the paranormal, there are usually three sides on which people align themselves. There are the believers, those who cannot be shaken from their stands. Then there are the nonbelievers, those who would never be convinced. Finally, there are those in between, the "Show Me" group. They keep an open mind but would need hard evidence to move them off the fence.

The strong beliefs of some, either for or against, have led to some interesting careers. But be forewarned—job opportunities in this area are few and far between. Only a small fraction of dedicated believers or debunkers have been able to carve a niche for themselves in this controversial territory.

What Does It All Mean?

Every discipline has its own jargon. Before we forge ahead, it's a good idea to have two few definitions in our arsenal.

Paranormal—an adjective used to describe activity outside or beyond the realm of "normal."

Parapsychology—the study of psychic phenomena.

A Little History

Interest in psychic phenomena can be traced back to early times. The first modern organizations to investigate such phenomena were the British Society for Psychical Research, founded in 1881, and the American Society for Psychical Research, founded in 1885.

Many of the early investigations conducted by these two groups tended to be unscientific and mostly anecdotal in nature. J. B. Rhine, a psychologist at Duke University in Durham, North Carolina, wanted to change the approach and methods used. He began his work investigating parapsychology in 1927. In the course of his work, Rhine coined the term *extrasensory perception*.

Duke eventually allowed him to split from the psychology department and form the first parapsychological laboratory in the country. That was in 1935. A little more than fifteen years ago, the parapsychology department and Duke University parted ways. But those carrying on Rhine's work did not want to let it die. They soon formed the Institute for Parapsychology, which is also located in Durham, North Carolina. (The address is listed at the end of this chapter.)

The Controversy

The majority of scientists outside the field of parapsychology do not accept the existence of psychic phenomena. As a result, they

do not accept the discipline of parapsychology. In order to study something, there has to be something there to study.

The most weighty criticism launched against parapsychologists is that of fraud. Rhine himself discovered that one of his researchers had been faking results. The man was dismissed.

Parapsychologists counter this charge by saying that they do well in policing their own ranks.

Another charge is that parapsychologists are not trained enough to tell if a subject is committing fraud. Even amateur magicians have been known to fool investigators. Parapsychologists insist that this type of fraud happens only in an insignificant number of cases.

Other charges include shoddy experimental design, incorrect statistical interpretations, and misread data.

A study in 1988 conducted by the National Research Council maintained that no scientific research in the past 130 years had proven the existence of parapsychological phenomena. The council, however, did find anomalies in some experiments that they could not readily explain.

Parapsychologists claim that the study was biased because the members of the research committee were nonbelievers.

Another major criticism is that for extrasensory perception, psychokinesis, and other phenomena to be true, basic physical laws would have to be broken.

To counter that, some parapsychologists believe that breakthroughs in particle physics may one day provide explanations for such phenomena. Others feel that paranormal activity operates outside the realm of science.

Toward the end of his life, Carl Jung also suggested that the deepest layers of the unconscious function independently of the laws of space, time, and causality, allowing for paranormal phenomena.

Firsthand Account

Joe Nickell, Paranormal Investigator

Joe Nickell is one of the very few paid paranormal investigators in the country. He's a staff member of the Committee for Scientific Investigation of Claims of the Paranormal (CSICOP), which is based at the Center for Inquiry, a nonprofit organization in Amherst, New York.

He's had an interesting and colorful career, having worked as a private investigator, a professional stage magician at the Houdini Hall of Fame (as Janus the Magician and Mendell the Mentalist), a blackjack dealer, a riverboat manager, a newspaper stringer, a historical and literary investigator, and a writer of articles and books (see a listing in the Appendix). He has also managed to find time to earn bachelor's, master's and Ph.D. degrees, all in English literature, all from the University of Kentucky in Lexington.

He has appeared on the popular TV program "Unsolved Mysteries," debunking claims of the paranormal, and is a regular consultant for the show. He has also appeared on "Larry King Live," "Sally Jessy Raphael," "Maury," "Jerry Springer," and "Charles Grodin."

Getting Started

"I grew up with magic in the household; my father was an amateur magician. I am largely self-taught, but a retired magician helped me some.

"During my career at Houdini, before I went on to be an investigator, I met James Randi—the Amazing Randi—and he was conducting a lot of paranormal investigations. I thought what he did, exposing psychics, was interesting and exciting. I started my investigative career with surveillance, background checks, and some dicey undercover work. I was even a bodyguard

for a politician. But primarily, I was a part of the cadre of young investigators for a well-known detective agency, doing the more dangerous undercover work.

"We would work in a company's warehouse—as a stock clerk, shipper/receiver, mail clerk, forklift driver—wherever they could slip us in. Our job was really to become aware of and infiltrate theft rings operating there. We'd set them up and bust them. The work was done privately and secretly. We'd assure the owners that we could get rid of the problem without the whole story coming out.

"If the story did come out, it would result in bad morale. The employees would not be happy that the bosses had sent spies in. The police would not be involved. The company would handle it themselves, fire the employees, and hope to keep the thieves out.

"Plus, the detective agency would not want its investigators to have to go to court. Once you did, and you were identified, it would mean the end of your undercover career. The agency would want to be able to use us again and again, not just one time.

"I also did surveillance work, staking out a place where we had undercover investigators. Or at times we'd be on the phone, just checking up on the background and character of different people.

"Unlike some of the guys who hated doing any of the office work, I would look for the general work whenever I was between undercover assignments.

"When you were on an undercover assignment, you were given your paycheck with the other factory or warehouse workers. Then your agency would make up the difference in your pay. You'd also receive additional danger pay on top of that.

"I also worked on insurance fraud cases. I was assigned to conduct surveillance on someone who was claiming he had a back injury. We staked out his house and watched him work on his car, photographing every move. He was bending over, darting up the steps two at a time. We documented it all."

Paranormal Investigations

"Pretty soon thereafter, I think in 1972, I had the opportunity to investigate a haunted house called Mackenzie House, a historic building in Toronto. There were various phenomena happening late at night there. The caretakers would hear footsteps going up and down the stairs—when no one was there. There were other sounds, too, Mackenzie's printing press, for example.

"I found that the sounds were all illusions. They were real sounds, but they were coming from the building next door. The buildings were only forty inches apart, and the other building had a staircase made of iron that ran parallel to the Mackenzie house stairway. Whenever anybody went up and down the stairs next door, it sounded as if it were coming from within Mackenzie House. The interesting thing to me was that no one had figured this out for ten years.

"I was writing a lot at the time and still am, but at the beginning, I discovered that the paranormal was a theme that I kept turning to again and again. There were so many intriguing questions.

"In the early seventies there were all kinds of claims—of psychics, of the ancient astronaut, theories about the Bermuda Triangle. It's a bit passé now, but at the time, I thought of them as burning questions.

"I've always been skeptical, not meaning debunking, just meaning 'prove it to me.' I began to investigate paranormal claims. I was in the Yukon Territory working as a blackjack dealer and would occasionally write a newspaper piece. One day, these guys were all claiming that they could use their dowsing rods to find gold. So I said, 'Talk is cheap. Would you do it under control test conditions?' They agreed.

"I put gold nuggets in some boxes padded with cotton; other boxes had nothing in them, some had fool's gold, some had nuts and bolts. I scrambled them all up, and even I didn't know when I picked a box out of the sack what was in it. The only way they would have known was if there had been any psychic power at

work—and, of course, they failed the test miserably. I ended up writing an article about the experiment.

"I investigated situations all through college. Whenever I heard about something interesting, I'd pursue it myself. The next biggest investigation, where I made a name for myself, was with the Shroud of Turin. On my own, I decided that the image on the shroud—which was supposed to be impossible to duplicate because it's a negative image and no forger in the Middle Ages could duplicate it—could indeed be duplicated. I showed an easy way to duplicate it using a simple process, and I published my findings in several magazines, including one in *Popular Photography* magazine, which put me on every newsstand in America.

"From there and other publications, I attracted the notice of the Committee for Scientific Investigation of Claims of the Paranormal, which was founded in 1976. The committee's founder was Paul Hurtz, who worked closely with James Randi, Isaac Asimov, and Carl Sagan.

"There was a feeling that paranormal activity was being hyped on TV and in the tabloids and there was no voice to speak counter to it. CSICOP was set up to investigate—not to dismiss out of hand, not to start out to debunk, but simply to investigate claims of the paranormal. And if that meant debunking, so be it.

"I volunteered for years for CSICOP, then in 1995 I was hired full-time. The center needed a detective, a magician, a writer, and a researcher, and by hiring me, they found all of them in one.

"I'm sort of a magic detective. Parapsychologists really believe that there is some power of the mind to read people's thoughts or divine the future. In spite of what you might have read, though, there is no scientific evidence for any of this. There have been plenty of claims, but when the claims have been scrutinized, they've been found not to pan out—poor research methodology or tricksters using sleight of hand. And that's where I come in.

"But the phrase 'try to debunk' is very loaded. We go out to investigate. Invariably, we also do end up debunking.

"I was asked to be a consultant on 'Unsolved Mysteries,' for example. Most viewers think of the program as a documentary, but, in fact, it's just entertainment. They don't care whether they tell the truth or not. That's often the case. I've worked with them many times, and often they've left out important details, making it look much more serious, and if you question them on it they say, 'Well, after all, the name of our program is "Unsolved Mysteries."'

"One question 'Unsolved Mysteries' asked me to explain involved some miracle photographs that were taken at a Virgin Mary site in Kentucky. They sent me copies of the photographs, and I was able to duplicate all the effects and explain them. The pictures were made by some girls, Polaroids that showed unusual things, they thought. The girls had attempted to take a picture of the sun—when the picture came out, they had a picture of a doorway with an arched top and straight sides, flooded with light. The doorway to heaven. In fact, that shape was the shape of the camera's lens opening—a light-flooded silhouette of that aperture. At the bottom of a few of the pictures were what they thought were angel wings. In fact, those were due to light leaking into the cartridge.

"The most puzzling was a picture that had a faint image superimposed over the picture of the girls. It was some sort of chart. I kept saying it didn't sound miraculous, it sounded very human. I tried to figure out how it could get on there. CSICOP gave me $50 to buy film. No sooner had I put in a film pack, than it ejected a protector card. On the other side of the card when I turned it over, there was the chart. I had to laugh.

"Another case was a haunted Japanese restaurant in Atlanta. First, Dr. William Roll, a parapsychologist based there, was on 'Unsolved Mysteries' to investigate the phenomenon. One of the things he did was to take in a magnetometer. You ask yourself why is Dr. Roll taking a magnetometer in? Is there a body of scientific evidence that ghosts are influenced by magnetometers? No, there is not. There is not such a reputable body of scientific

knowledge. But often self-styled ghost hunters take in fancy-sounding equipment, and if they get any type of glitches or movement, they assume it must be the ghost doing it.

"They can make fools of themselves. The manager of that very same restaurant told me that he knew that the magnetometer was simply responding to the iron metal in the pipes in the walls. The result of our investigation was that the ghost was mostly a lot of hysteria and hype and some of the employees playing pranks on one another.

"We're often accused of being debunkers as if we start out to do that. But here's the proof that we don't dismiss out of hand. If we did, we would not go to the Georgia restaurant to do an investigation. We'd say that it was just too silly to bother with. In fact, we do the investigations, but we get different results. Why? Because we don't take in silly equipment. We interview people, we look for evidence, we look for causes. One girl privately confessed that the reason the lights went on and off, which is something the bartender told us about, was that, when he wasn't looking, she would reach around and flip the switch. She had great fun doing that for some time.

"CSICOP doesn't just parachute me in whenever there's a rumor of something. We're nonprofit, and most of our money is donated, so we have to be very careful with how we spend it. Some of our funding comes from subscriptions to our journal, the *Skeptical Inquirer.*

"When I do an investigation for a TV show, the show usually pays for us to fly down there. I've been a guest on a lot of different shows, so often I'm the token skeptic. They put on the believers, the UFO abductees and so forth, and I get a minute at the end to say, 'Bah humbug.'

"But once I tested a psychic on the 'Jerry Springer Show.' It was a lot of fun. There were three psychics on, giving all sorts of readings, telling people about themselves. There's a trick to this; it's called cold reading. What you do is fish for info. You start off vague, then if the person gives you a little feedback, maybe he

looks surprised or he nods in agreement, you pursue that. If he shakes his head or says, 'No, I don't have a brother,' then you pursue that. You actually can narrow your choices, and by the time you're through, you've convinced them that you know all about them. And if you've missed a few, you don't back off them. You say, 'Well, I think you will meet someone named Robert, and it's going to happen soon.'

"I was brought on as the skeptic to see if these people were really psychic. I said 'I have three envelopes, containing a simple three-letter word. And I also have a check for $1,000. The check is yours if you can guess or divine all three of the three-letter words.' Two of the psychics refused to cooperate. The third, who called himself Mr. B of ESP, the World's Greatest Psychic, agreed to be tested. Well, he failed the test. I had to tear up the check. There was a mixture of booing and applause from the audience.

"I am most interested in the investigative aspect of my work. I like solving the mysteries. That's the most rewarding part. I've never really been stumped. That doesn't mean that I know the answer to every mystery in the world. I've looked back through history, and sometimes I've been able to find the solution to a long ago puzzle.

"For example, there's the story about the disappearance of Oliver Lerch. As the story went, in South Bend, Indiana, in the 1890s, young Oliver was sent out to the well to get some water on Christmas Eve while everyone was gathered around the hearth and playing the piano. No sooner did he leave on his errand than the family heard him crying for help. Some thought he might even have said, 'They've got me.'

"They picked up the lantern and ran outside, following Oliver's tracks through the snow. Halfway to the well, the tracks ended abruptly. No sign of Oliver. A great mystery. How do you explain it?

"The story has been published in slews of different books and magazines on unsolved mysteries. Well, after further investigation, I found there was no such family as the Lerches. I did a deed

search and found that no family named Lerch had ever owned any property in that area. Some of the stories claimed that the incident was still in the police files. Well, the police say they've never heard of it. No such story. Oliver Lerch never disappeared; Oliver Lerch never even existed. In fact, the story is more or less a plagiarized version of an old Ambrose Bierce horror story called 'Charles Ashmore's Trail.'"

Advice from Joe Nickell

"I think you should read as much of the literature as possible, particularly the skeptical literature. You're going to be misled by a lot of the believers. They'll tell you stories that simply aren't true. Their books are full of the fake Oliver Lerch stories. And they don't expose them, we do. Our journal, the *Skeptical Inquirer*, frequently reviews books and lists articles. That would be a good starting point.

"Then, it would be useful to learn something about magic. Not that everyone has to be a magician, but some of us are. It's useful in understanding how people can be fooled and what the different tricks are.

"In addition to magic, journalism, psychology, and astronomy, depending upon the area you're most interested in, would be useful. One of our people is with NASA, another with *Aviation Science* magazine. Psychology would be very good for investigating people who feel they're possessed or haunted or have been abducted by aliens. There are many different fields. We all count on each other and share. An investigation often doesn't just rely on one person. I often bring in many other experts and collaborate with them.

"As far as making a career of this, I think the best route to go would be investigating phenomena, then turning your material into articles. But I do have to caution: if you are really interested in being a freelance writer and making a buck, you need to be on the other side of the belief coin. You can sell a ghost story far

easier than you can sell one that debunks it. (For more information on writing careers see Chapter 5.)

"But if truth and honesty matter to you, you will not sell out.
You will report fairly and thoroughly."

Training

There are very few university programs in this country now
devoted to training parapsychologists or their counterpart
debunkers. The sixties and seventies saw a surge of popularity in
these areas, but most have now gone by the wayside. Readers will
have to utilize their finely tuned sleuthing skills to track down
existing programs. Three leads have been given to you at the end
of this chapter: the Institute for Parapsychology, American Society for Psychical Research (both mostly for believers), and the
Center for Inquiry (mostly for nonbelievers).

Joe Nickell offers seminars and workshops under the auspices
of the Center for Inquiry. The programs cover investigative techniques, magic used by mind readers and mentalists, and how to
detect them, as well as classes on miracles and other interesting
phenomena.

For More Information

Professional Associations

American Psychological Association
750 First Street NE
Washington, DC 20002

American Society for Psychical Research
5 West Seventy-third Street
New York, NY 10023

Center for Inquiry
P.O. Box 703
Amherst, NY 14226

Institute of Parapsychology
402 North Buchanan Boulevard
Durham, NC 27701

International Security and Detective Alliance
P.O. Box 6303
Corpus Christi, TX 78466

Further Reading

Writing and Editing

The Chicago Manual of Style (University of Chicago Press)
Your Novel Proposal: From Creation to Contract, by Blythe
  Camenson and Marshall J. Cook (Writer's Digest Books)
Guide to Literary Agents (Writer's Digest Books)
*Insider's Guide to Book Editors, Publishers, and Literary
  Agents,* by Jeff Herman (Prima Publishing)
*The International Directory of Little Magazines and Small
  Presses* (Dustbooks)
Magazine Publishing Career Directory (Gale Research, Inc.)
Market Guide for Young Writers (Writer's Digest Books)
Novel and Short Story Writer's Market (Writer's Digest Books)
Poet's Market (Writer's Digest Books)
Writer's Digest Magazine (Writer's Digest Books)
Writer's Market (Writer's Digest Books)
How to Write a Book Proposal, by Michael Larsen (Writer's
  Digest Books)
How to Write Irresistible Query Letters, by Lisa Collier Cool
  (Writer's Digest Books)

Massage

Mosby's Fundamentals of Therapeutic Massage, by Sandy and
  Sandra Fritz (Mosby Year Book)
The Complete Body Massage: A Hands-On Manual, by Fiona
  Harrold, photographs by Sue Atkinson (Sterling Publishing)

Loving Hands: The Traditional Art of Baby Massage, by
   Frederick Leboyer (Newmarket Press)
The Art of Touch: A Massage Manual for Young People, by
   Chia Martin, photographs by Sheila Mitchell (Hohm Press)
*The New Guide to Massage: A Guide to Massage Techniques
   for Health, Relaxation and Vitality,* by Carole McGilvery
   and Jimi Reed (Lorenz Books)
*The Complete Illustrated Guide to Massage: A Step-By-Step
   Approach to the Healing Art of Touch,* by Stewart Mitchell
   (Element Books, Ltd.)

Natural Medicine

The Encyclopedia of Natural Medicine, by Michael Murray,
   N.D., and Joseph Pizzorno, N.D. (Prima Publications)
*Directory of Herbal Training Programs and Recommended
   Reading List* (American Herbalist Guild)

Feng Shui

*The Complete Illustrated Guide to Feng Shui: How to Apply
   the Secrets of Chinese Wisdom for Health, Wealth, and
   Happiness,* by Lillian Too (Element Books, Inc.)
Interior Design with Feng Shui, by Sarah Rossbach (Viking
   Penguin)
Feng Shui for the Home, by Evelyn Lip (Heian International
   Publishing, Inc.
*Feng Shui Handbook: How to Create a Healthier Living &
   Working Environment,* by Master Lam Kam Chuen (Henry
   Holt & Company)
Practical Feng Shui for Business, by Simon Brown (Ward
   Lock)

Special Events

Special Events Magazine
Miramar Communications
23815 Stuart Ranch Road
Malibu, CA 90265

Paranormal Investigation

Extrasensory Deception, by Henry Gordon (Prometheus
    Books)
Pseudoscience and the Paranormal, by Terence Hines
The Skeptical Inquirer (Center for Inquiry, Amherst, New
    York)
Secrets of the Supernatural, by Joe Nickell (Prometheus
    Books)
Looking for a Miracle, by Joe Nickell (Prometheus Books)
Camera Clues, by Joe Nickell (University of Kentucky Press)
Detecting Forgery, by Joe Nickell, (University of Kentucky
    Press)

About the Author

Blythe Camenson is a full-time writer with more than four dozen books to her credit, most on the subject of various careers. Camenson is also the coauthor of *Your Novel Proposal: From Creation to Contract* (Writer's Digest Books) and director of Fiction Writer's Connection, a membership organization for new writers (www.fictionwriters.com). She currently lives in Albuquerque, New Mexico—the Land of Enchantment.